Rachel stret
ing to be mor felt. "They
say Southern California has the sweetest climate in the world," she said brightly. "The light's sharp and the air has a tang like wine."

He put his arm on top of the back of her chair . . . casually. "Texas weather's a mite more . . . interesting," he said.

He was too close. Rachel could feel the warmth of his body, hear the small sounds of his breathing in the dark beside her. "Would you like to go back inside?" she asked. "We could play Scrabble or watch TV . . ."

"Don't you want to sit under the moon?" he asked. "Dammit, Rachel, aren't you in the mood for love?"

"Love? Love is for married people. I believe in marriage, Coe. We're not married."

"You're being stubborn," he said softly. "That's what George Bernard Shaw called 'trade-unionish of the married.' "

"Okay, so it's a union. And you're trying to get me to be a scab."

Coe laughed. "Scab! Now there's a word I haven't heard since the Eisenhower administration."

That got to her. She leaned back against his arm and looked up at the moon, smiling in spite of her resolution to be firm and cool. Then she felt his arm tighten, his lips come closer.

Their first kiss was warm . . . then more than warm . . .

IT'S NEVER TOO LATE FOR LOVE AND ROMANCE

JUST IN TIME (4188, $4.50/$5.50)
by Peggy Roberts

Constantly taking care of everyone around her has earned Remy Dupre the affectionate nickname "Ma." Then, with Remy's husband gone and oil discovered on her Louisiana farm, her sons and their wives decide it's time to take care of her. But Remy knows how to take care of herself. She starts by checking into a beauty spa, buying some classy new clothes and shoes, discovering an antique vase, and moving on to a fine plantation. Next, not one, but two men attempt to sweep her off her well-shod feet. The right man offers her the opportunity to love again.

LOVE AT LAST (4158, $4.50/$5.50)
by Garda Parker

Fifty, slim, and attractive, Gail Bricker still hadn't found the love of her life. Friends convince her to take an Adventure Tour during the summer vacation she enjoyes as an English teacher. At a Cheyenne Indian school in need of teachers, Gail finds her calling. In rancher Slater Kincaid, she finds her match. Gail discovers that it's never too late to fall in love . . . for the very first time.

LOVE LESSONS (3959, $4.50/$5.50)
by Marian Oaks

After almost forty years of marriage, Carolyn Ames certainly hadn't been looking for a divorce. But the ink is barely dry, and here she is already living an exhilarating life as a single woman. First, she lands an exciting and challenging job. Now Jason, the handsome architect, offers her a fairy-tale romance. Carolyn doesn't care that her ultra-conservative neighbors gossip about her and Jason, but she is afraid to give up her independent life-style. She struggles with the balance while she learns to love again.

A KISS TO REMEMBER (4129, $4.50/$5.50)
by Helen Playfair

For the past ten years Lucia Morgan hasn't had time for love or romance. Since her husband's death, she has been raising her two sons, working at a dead-end office job, and designing boutique clothes to make ends meet. Then one night, Mitch Colton comes looking for his daughter, out late with one of her sons. The look in Mitch's eye brings back a host of long-forgotten feelings. When the kids come home and spoil the enchantment, Lucia wonders if she will get the chance to love again.

COME HOME TO LOVE (3930, $4.50/$5.50)
by Jane Bierce

Julia Delaine says good-bye to her skirt-chasing husband Phillip and hello to a whole new life. Julia capably rises to the challenges of her reawakened sexuality, the young man who comes courting, and her new position as the head of her local television station. Her new independence teaches Julia that maybe her time-tested values were right all along and maybe Phillip does belong in her life, with her new terms.

Available wherever paperbacks are sold, or order direct from the Publisher. Send cover price plus 50¢ per copy for mailing and handling to Penguin USA, P.O. Box 999, c/o Dept. 17109, Bergenfield, NJ 07621. Residents of New York and Tennessee must include sales tax. DO NOT SEND CASH.

FLYING HIGH

HELEN PLAYFAIR

ZEBRA BOOKS
KENSINGTON PUBLISHING CORP.

ZEBRA BOOKS are published by

Kensington Publishing Corp.
475 Park Avenue South
New York, NY 10016

First Printing: May, 1994

Printed in the United States of America

One

"You ought to color your hair," said the dressed-for-success young lady behind the imposing desk.

Rachel could almost have laughed, but she managed to limit herself to a small smile. "I don't think I'm prepared to dye, not just yet," she said. "It took me a lot of years of worrying to get this gray!"

She had intended it as a small joke but there was no reaction from behind the desk. The poor girl probably thought she would lose her credibility if she so much as cracked a smile.

Where do people get off, anyway, Rachel wondered, calling themselves "employment counselors" when actually they are only little girls? And full of little-girl ideas. She knew what this one was going to suggest next. A makeover, as if that would suddenly cause her to be employable, when she had been interviewing fruitlessly for nearly a year!

And yet it was the silly child who had a job, a desk, an office, a place to go every morning, and it was Rachel who didn't. Maybe this girl did know something Rachel should hear.

"It makes you look old," her young mentor persisted. "If you did your hair, put on some makeup, got some brighter clothes . . ."

"I'd look like mutton dressed for lamb," Rachel finished for her. "I'm not ashamed of being old."

"There are some things you've got to learn not to do. Don't ever call yourself old. You came right in here and told me how old you are, first thing. You must never do that. Keep prospective employers guessing. You don't look sixty, or anyhow you wouldn't if you fixed yourself up . . ."

Rachel swallowed her resentment and told herself to regard it as a backhanded compliment. The only trouble was, she had thought she *was* "fixed up." She was wearing her Evan Picone suit, the silk Cleo blouse, Capezio shoes. The shoes were flats; she had given up heels years ago, and the suit size was petite, for Rachel was short and slender. Her hair was neatly cut; she probably didn't know it, but what Rachel resembled most was a tidy pixie.

There had been a lot of employment counselors in the last year, so this wasn't the first time she had sat still for a stream of useless advice. It seemed as if every agency she contacted stuck her with yet another counselor who looked (and talked) as if she should still be in high school.

Rachel tried changing the subject. "I worked for Pennine, Ransome for fifteen years and was their materials manager for nearly ten."

"And you've been out of work now for . . ." the girl checked the application before her. "Two years?"

"I quit my job to look after my husband when he was ill. He was sick for a long time, and Pennine, Ransome isn't a big corporation. They couldn't hold the job open for me for so long."

"Materials manager, huh? Well, you're going to have to accept it that you aren't going to get another job like that. Nobody's going to hire a woman who is older if the job can be done by a young man right out of college. You ought to be retrained for something there's a big demand for. Medical transcription, maybe, or tax accounting. Would you be up to learning how to do computer repair?"

"Oh, that would be dandy," said Rachel. "Then I'd have two skills that can be duplicated by a young man right out of school."

The counselor obviously was starting to think that it was her luck to get all the unreasonable ones. She consulted Rachel's application again. "For the really good jobs you need a degree. Would you consider going back to college?"

"It wouldn't be *back*. I never went in the first place. In my day, if you couldn't afford college, you got married."

Rachel crossed her ankles and leaned forward. "Let's take a look at the numbers. It would take me at least four years to get a college degree, at which time I'd be sixty-four and have a year to work before I'd reach retirement age. I think I would still be considered unemployable."

"You could go to night school."

"Why? That would take even longer."

There were several more suggestions, and to Rachel each seemed sillier than the last. She was wasting an afternoon, not that she had anything so important to do, but it was annoying to listen to a veritable child telling her things she already knew, suggesting avenues she had already fruitlessly explored.

But you have to be polite, so Rachel listened to the whole spiel, thanked the young nit nicely, and went home.

She was a bit sorry to reach her own place, to be putting the car into her own garage, for after that there was nothing for her to do but to go inside.

It wasn't the house, of course. She had always loved the house. She had raised her children there. It had always been a comfortable home, spacious enough for her and Pete and all three of the kids, and over the years she had arranged everything in it exactly to her liking. The furniture, the drapes, the carpet, everything was just what she wanted, in just the colors that pleased her eye.

She owned a charming house with nobody in it. The children were grown now, and far away. Just coincidence, but each of the three had had some compelling reason to move to a distant place. And Pete was gone . . .

Would she ever get used to that word? Gone. Irrevocably dead. No wonder people believe in ghosts and communication with spirits . . . anything to soften the finality of it, to chip a few corners off of "gone."

"Snap out of it, Rachel," she scolded herself as she turned her key in the lock. "Get busy doing something. Cook something, sweep, turn out a closet . . ."

The house was clean and shadowed and quiet, all in order. Nothing to be done there; Rachel never left a project uncompleted, or a mess to be cleaned up later. "Another trouble with getting old," she grumbled to herself. "You turn into this big bundle of good habits."

She went upstairs and hung her suit jacket in her bedroom closet because there had to be some reason for going upstairs. She probably ought to change her clothes, too, but she didn't, because she couldn't possibly decide what she wanted to put on.

It had been a hot day and the upper rooms were still uncomfortably warm, although an afternoon breeze was stirring the white curtains in her room. Her pretty little room. She had bought new curtains and linens for it when she first had begun sleeping in it, forced to move because Pete was too sick to share a room and a bed with her any longer as he had for thirty-five years. So Rachel had taken the room vacated by her daughter and slept in the narrow bed the girl had left behind.

Now the big room where Pete had spent his last days stood empty, a guest room with expensive, new, coordinated window treatment, wallpaper, and bed cover. Rachel didn't want to move back in there alone. Her daughter's room felt more welcoming, as if there were still something of Barbara remaining in this small room where she had been an infant. It was only memories, of course. Barbara had her own life. She was married. She had her own children and lived on a ranch in Arizona.

Rachel sat on the edge of the bed, waiting. For what, she could not have said. Maybe she was waiting for the sun to go down. When it was dark she would feel more normal, she would feel like putting on something comfortable and going into the kitchen to make herself some dinner.

But then she'd have to eat it. Could she summon the energy to eat? What difference did it make?

When she heard somebody calling her, she started as if she had been asleep. How long had she been sitting there? She looked around; shadows were gathering behind the furniture. The sky outside the window glowed softly; it was getting late.

"Auntie Rachel, where are you?"

She recognized the voice of her neighbor's daughter, Terry. She called, "I'm coming downstairs," and went.

Terry was in the kitchen. Rachel must have left the back door unlocked; her sons would scold her if they knew that. Terry was a pretty child of fourteen, brown eyes rimmed with dark lashes, just like her mother's; and like her mother, she had a lot of blonde curly hair. It was pulled into a wad on top of her head and streamed down in wild tendrils, as if it were having a temper tantrum. She wore her usual school shorts and carried a backpack full of books.

"Oh, Auntie Rachel!" she exclaimed. Rachel was quite old enough to have been her grandmother, but they both preferred auntie. "I'm so glad you're home! I'm locked out of the house!"

"What happened to your key?" Rachel asked.

"I don't know. I must have forgotten to put it in my backpack this morning. Mom's not home yet and Lonnie will be at baseball practice until six. You will let me in, won't you?"

"Of course, dear, and then we must look for your key. It's really a serious thing to lose it."

She kept household keys on a rack in her kitchen, including a spare for the neighbor's house, in anticipation of just such emergencies as this one. She took down the key, trying to think of something to say to Terry. She should ask about her school activities to show she was interested, but she couldn't remember what any of them were just at the moment. She felt tired. It had been a discouraging day and she felt an uncharacteristic resentment at the necessity for doing this trifling favor.

As they went out her back door, she remembered that it was June and asked, "Is school almost out?"

"Couple weeks yet," Terry replied with an impatient lift of her shoulders. "But I get to go to summer school. Extra credits. Looks good on the college app."

A high school freshman and already worrying about college entrance? Well, perhaps they had to, these days.

They went through the gap that the children had worn in the hedge between the two houses. Rachel thought of all the years that small feet had packed down the earth in that space, children rushing back and forth to cadge cookies or play in the lawn sprinklers on a hot day. She loved that neighborly gap in her hedge.

Rachel was using the key on the front door of the neighboring house when Deena drove up. Terry called, "Mom! There's my mom!" and ran to the car as eagerly as if her parent had just returned from an Arctic expedition.

Rachel stood and waited. Deena deserved an explanation. She felt surprisingly embarrassed at being caught unlocking the door to a house that was not her own, and she tucked the key guiltily into her pocket. Deena got out of the car carrying a sack of groceries, flashing long, silken legs below the fitted skirt of her business suit.

As she came up onto the porch she said, "Thanks for helping Terry, Rachel. Can you come in for a while? I haven't seen you in a week."

She unlocked the door and Terry scampered inside. Rachel called after her, "Don't forget to look for your key! I won't stay, Deena. You're busy . . ."

"All the more reason to have a break.

Come on, I'll make us some tea and we can catch up." She led the way to the kitchen, put down her sack.

Rachel was glad to find her usual seat in the familiar kitchen. She and Deena were friends, despite the gap in their ages. It had to be fourteen years they had been neighbors, because, Rachel remembered, Deena had been pregnant with Terry when she moved in. The pleasures and tragedies they had shared in those years! Christmases and graduations and the weddings of Rachel's children, that awful night when Deena's boy, Lonnie, had broken his leg, and, of course, the long illness and death of Rachel's husband. How grateful she had been for Deena's support during those terrible days!

Deena picked up the teakettle but paused on her way to the sink, looking searchingly at Rachel. "I know, let's have a glass of wine instead. You look like you could use one."

"It has been kind of a tough day," Rachel admitted.

"You were out job hunting? That's no fun." Deena pulled a bottle from the refrigerator and thumbed off the substitute cork. "Anything?"

"I found a couple new agencies to check out, but none of them had what I want. Come and sit down with me a minute. You must be hurting in those high heels."

"No, these are comfortable. Ought to be, the price I paid." Deena came to sit opposite Rachel and regarded her seriously across the table. "I can hardly believe it's taking so long for you to find a job. It was more than a year ago that Pete died."

"I didn't start looking for a job right away, remember? I spent some time fixing up my house. It was so full of the things Pete needed, it was like a hospital. I almost had to redecorate."

"Rachel, you redid one room," Deena reminded her gently.

"And a bathroom. We put down a new floor in one of the bathrooms."

"It's way too long, Rachel."

Rachel shrugged agreement. "I'm sixty years old, Deena. Nobody wants to hire an old fogy like me."

"That's not true, and it shouldn't be true. Everybody knows that older workers are more reliable and experienced."

Rachel smiled grimly. "Everybody knows, but nobody wants actually to *hire* one."

Deena said, "Well, then they're just

short-sighted. I've seen your résumé and it's impressive."

"I guess it'll do for wallpaper."

Deena shook her head disapprovingly, her blonde mane shifting across her shoulder. "Don't talk negatively, Rachel; it's not like you. And you have options. Have you considered taking early retirement? You own your house; there must be some investments. You could probably afford it."

"I guess I could, but why? I've got another five or ten good working years left in me; I'd like to be doing something useful. Just sitting around the house, remembering. . . . Oh, don't ask me to do that."

"Well, you could do something, volunteer work or start your own business . . ."

"Doing what?" Rachel took a sip of her wine. It had been opened too long and tasted of the refrigerator. That was all right. It was good enough for Rachel.

"I don't know. What do you like to do?"

Rachel could not answer. "Oh, I don't know. Just . . . work. I've worked all my life. I don't know how to do anything else."

Deena smiled. "You need a man in your life."

"Me? Oh, my goodness, no. I'm sixty years old!"

"Don't keep saying that. It's never too late to fall in love."

Rachel hooted at that. "Fall in love? A geriatric romance? What a picture! Old bones creaking and banging!"

"What's wrong with a little banging?"

It felt good to laugh. Deena's company never failed to cheer her up. "The arguments. Just think of the arguments you'd have! At the movies—is it polite to demand a senior discount for your date, too? When you're alone together—should he, or should he not, be wearing his teeth?"

Deena laughed with her. "Oh, Rachel, it wouldn't be like that!"

Rachel made a careless shrug. "Anyhow, I've been married. I don't know that I'd go out of my way to do it again."

Deena's smile was a little crooked. "Well, I gotta relate to that."

That made Rachel serious. "You and Ethan haven't been fighting, have you?"

"Oh, no, we never fight. We don't communicate much, either. That's one way to cut down on the fighting, you know."

Rachel smiled determinedly. "What a pair we are! We have our health, our families, and we're crying into our wine about nothing!"

Deena managed a feeble smile of her own. "Yeah, I guess it's nothing. Just an attack of the same-old's, I guess. Or maybe I'm having a mid-life crisis."

"Of course you're not! You're too young for that."

"I'm past forty, darling."

"Anyhow, men have a mid-life crisis. Women don't. They don't because they can't afford the luxury."

"Amen."

They finished their wine and Deena invited her to dinner, but Rachel refused. Deena had a family, a life of her own. There was no reason she had to take Rachel into it just because she was a neighbor—and just because she was lonely.

Two

"That was my piece of bacon!" said Terry.

"No, it wasn't," said Lonnie.

"Shut up and eat your breakfast," said their father.

"There were three strips apiece," said Deena with a patient sigh. "How many have you eaten, Lonnie?"

Her son bit off half the bacon he held in his hand and answered with his mouth full, "I don't know."

"That means he had four!" protested Terry.

Deena sighed again. Terry was a good, sweet little girl and Deena always felt like protecting her from her more aggressive brother, but what could be done with this argument? Lonnie could only share the bacon now by regurgitating it, and Deena knew better than to suggest that.

She was relieved when Ethan growled again, "Shut up and eat your breakfast."

Sometimes an unreasonable solution is the best one for an unreasonable problem.

Then Lonnie got up from the table and Ethan started in on him. "Haven't you got any jeans that aren't torn?"

Lonnie grinned evilly. "Old ones."

"Well, go put on an old pair. You look like a ragamuffin."

"I'm a growing boy, Dad. All my old jeans are too small for me."

Deena picked up Lonnie's dirty dishes and carried them to the dishwasher, turning her back on yet another silly argument. There was no way Lonnie was going to exchange his fashionably torn jeans for something old and intact and square from his closet and no way Ethan was going to make life easier by being a little tolerant.

Somehow she had survived their arguments over Lonnie's haircuts, or rather, his lack thereof, and his earring. . . . How Lonnie had enjoyed his father's distress over that little ring! Ethan would never understand that rebellion is only fun when it encounters resistance.

She busied herself at the sink, hoping Terry would seize the opportunity afforded by the argument to slip away unnoticed. Otherwise Ethan was going to get on her next. "Help your mother!" would be the order, and Deena preferred to finish the cleanup herself. How unfair to insist that Terry do what her brother would not! And what her father never did, for that matter.

The kitchen window overlooked her lawn and a section of Rachel's. The neat flower beds made her think of her neighbor. Poor Rachel! She had seemed so down when they talked the previous evening. She needed something to do. Something interesting to do.

Ah, but then, didn't everybody?

Deena rinsed the last pot and crashed it into the dish drainer. She had to rush; it was almost time for her to go to work. Another day ahead of her on the job, another evening of hurrying home to cook a meal. She would listen to the family bicker while they ate it, and then she would wash some more dishes.

Ah, yes, she had it all.

Deena thought of the years of double work that stretched ahead of her and asked herself, under her breath, "If I've got it all, is this all there is?"

Some day the children would leave home, but it seemed very far in the future and she knew it would not inspire Ethan to help with the dishes anyway. She would still have her job to go to and all the household responsibilities, just as she did now.

Until, like Rachel, she outlived her husband. Probably she would, most women did. A sensible person admitted that. Would she then be like Rachel? A lonely spirit with not enough to do, bored with herself, haunting the house where she had once raised a family?

The kitchen table was clear. Ethan was folding up the newspaper and she startled him with a swift hug. She needed suddenly to feel his warm, living body, needed to know she had not yet reached Rachel's state.

Her guy, right or wrong. She would miss Ethan when he was gone.

The children were in her car, ready to be driven to school, and she hadn't done her makeup yet. Well, it was getting late. She would do it at work, a quick run to the ladies' room before she went to her desk. Deena collected her things—purse, keys, jacket, the bundle she would drop at the dry cleaners on her way home.

Picking up her briefcase turned her mind to office problems and her forehead creased as she walked toward the car. She had brought work home and wasted her time last night making phone calls to try to find somebody for a billing job. Nobody was available; nobody likes to do billing anyway, and it didn't even pay very well. Now it was morning, and the client was expecting somebody to report.

As she walked between the two lawns she suddenly thought of Rachel again. Well, why not Rachel? Rachel was used to an executive position, but this was only temporary. It was only billing.

Deena quickly changed her course and hurried up to Rachel's door, ignoring protests from the children in the car.

Rachel came to the door at once. She was dressed, a simple dress and blazer. Deena asked her, "Are you desperate yet?"

Rachel said, "Huh? Me? Sure, I'm desperate. What do you have in mind?"

"I'm going to make a temp out of you. The money isn't what you're used to and there aren't any benefits, but it's income and it'll give you something to do while you're waiting for the job you really want."

Rachel looked thoughtful. "Well, I've considered it, but who would want an old thing like me for a temp?"

"Nobody cares in my business. And I

need somebody today for a billing job out at the airfield. It's Van Nuys Airport. That's not far away. Think of it as a favor to me."

"Well, in that case, of course I'll do it."

"Come by my office as soon as you can and I'll get you on the books and you can go right out. You know where it is, in Warner Center?"

"I'll be there before you are!"

It didn't take long to make Rachel into a temporary worker. The usual tests were waived; she filled out a few forms and was on her way to the billing job.

Rachel was delighted that the job was at the airport, for she harbored a secret passion for watching airplanes take off and land. For watching them fly. For watching them do anything at all, even just sit on the ground.

She would enjoy the airplanes, she told herself firmly, and refuse to consider the incongruity of wearing her Nordstrom's blazer as she drove her Cadillac to a billing job that paid eight dollars an hour. It was work. She was back in the business world. Maybe temping could even be a toehold, a beginning for her climb back to where she once had been.

She had always enjoyed driving, and this car was a particular pleasure. The handling was quick, the ride smooth, the leather seats luxurious. She flicked a mote of dust from the dashboard and reminded herself, "There's not much mileage on the car, but there's plenty on me!"

She found the street that led into the perimeter of the airfield and, according to the directions she had from Deena, the buildings that housed Burns Air. The road seemed to be a secret, branching off from Hayvenhurst and snaking along beside the runway.

A row of industrial buildings was quickly behind her and then only chain-link separated the road from the airfield proper and a treasure-trove of aircraft parked along the fence. Rachel slowed, the better to admire their astonishing variety. New, shiny planes, old ones, biplanes, handbuilts and antique warbirds all lived together in the narrow space between the fence and the runway. A few seemed abandoned, rotting away under the weight of their history. It was quiet, nobody around, a contrast to the bustle of the streets, to the rest of the airfield. One man lifted his head out of an engine compartment as she went by, but he seemed to be entirely alone.

And surprised to see her. It was obvious she was not headed for a busy service like Burns Air. Rachel found a wide place and turned around. She could have gawked at airplanes all day, but she had a job to report to.

Sure enough, she found Burns Air with a huge sign facing on Sherman Way. She must have missed seeing it because she had been looking instead at a couple of pretty Cessnas, painted blue and white and tied down in front of the building. She made her way onto the parking lot and then into the sprawling complex of buildings that made up Burns.

She reported to the office manager, a grizzled, stout woman named Jewel. Rachel tried to think how many years it might have been since anybody named a little baby girl Jewel, and she couldn't. Jewel must be even older than she was.

"I'll take you over to where you're going to work, or you'll never find it," Jewel offered. "You're going to work for Olsen, and he's hardly ever around."

She led the way down a corridor that

suddenly debouched inside a hangar. Rachel's steps lagged as she looked around. She was inside a real hangar!

It was set up exactly like an auto repair-garage, in bays separated by banks of equipment—only these bays were huge; they were wide enough for wings. Rachel twisted around, trying to see the ship that the men were working on.

Jewel was not the least impressed by hangars and went waddling on, chatting as she went. "Your boss is mostly out in the field, testing stuff, so you have to look after things for him. The department is avionics."

Rachel had not really heard what she'd said but didn't want to ask for a repeat. She followed Jewel through a door, past a couple of closed office doors, and to a wide place in a hallway.

"Well, this is your desk," said Jewel.

"I don't have an office?"

"No, somebody has to be out here because sometimes people get lost and you have to tell them it's a dead end and keep them from going down those stairs over there."

Rachel was about to ask how she was expected to tell strangers from employees, but Jewel was rattling on. "Besides, you'll be glad you're not in a place that has windows because this building is right next to the runway and when the wind is right they take off every three minutes."

"Oh, I wouldn't mind that. I love to hear the engines roar."

Jewel squinted at her suspiciously. "Yeah? Like airplanes, do you? Maybe Olsen can take you when he's testing. He's always trying to get somebody to go with him. Guess it's lonesome up there all the time."

"Sounds like fun. Now, what am I supposed to be doing?"

"Billing. Answer the phone." Jewel gave a heavy sigh. "Janie has been on this job for fifteen years and, besides the billing, nobody knows what she does."

"What happened to Janie?"

"Had an accident, hurt her back. You know how it is with backs. She'd say she was going to come back to work in a week, and then it was a month, and now she doesn't know."

Rachel stared at the clutter before her. "There's a month's work piled up on that desk?"

"Probably," Jewel replied with a careless shrug. Then she began hauling price lists out of the drawers, customer lists, discount schedules, and catalogs, explaining how each influenced the billing.

When finally she had finished and was ready to return to her own office, she turned back to say, "There's something I want you to do for me: Make a job description."

"How can I do that if nobody knows what's going on here?"

"Just write it down. Whenever Olsen tells you to do something, write it down. Every time you do something different, write it down. I really need to know."

Olsen did show up later on that afternoon. A young guy—well, forty or forty-five, but most folks looked young to Rachel these days. His suit was carefully tailored to fit a prosperous belly, his moustache neatly trimmed. Rachel decided he must pull down a good salary if he could afford tailoring.

He was friendly enough, so much so that Rachel got up the courage to ask, "Would you mind telling me what it is you do here?"

Olsen chuckled. "I guess we could tell you that! This department repairs radios and radio navigation equipment for airplanes. That's our shop down there." He pointed down the staircase.

"There's a shop down there? I thought it was the men's room."

"You did?"

"Well, nobody goes down there but guys."

"Those are the technicians you see. It's restricted. Nobody is allowed down there but the techs. And you and me, of course."

"Me?"

"Didn't you know you're supposed to go down there and collect the completed work orders? How can you bill them if you don't go down there and get them? Come on, I'll take you down and introduce you to the techs."

For a taboo area, the shop was not very exciting. Just a long room lined with workbenches. The techs wandered around with that lost, nerdy look they seem to think is necessary to their egghead image.

There was a basket fixed to the end of each bench, and every basket was stuffed with paper. Olsen introduced her to the techs as they walked through and collected the work orders. She didn't know how fast she could process them, but she figured she had at least a week's work ahead of her billing that stack.

She worked at it all day and arrived home bushed, too tired to cook, certainly, and almost too tired to eat. She made herself a sandwich and went to bed almost as soon as she had eaten it. Her shoulders ached from tension and typing, and the thought of her earnings made her groan. At Pennine, Ransome she had bossed a warehouse full of workers who all made more money than she did now.

Rachel rolled impatiently and put a pillow over her head to block the light from a young moon that was saucily glaring in her window. Well, the glory days were over and she was a temp with a clerk's job. It would have to do until she found somebody who believed that a woman of sixty could do a job more important than a clerk's.

At least she was good at it. She thought about the stack of invoices she had completed that day, and it was a satisfaction. She had earned her paltry salary. Rachel relaxed and slept.

It took her a week to catch up on the backlogged billing and then another to organize and streamline all the activities of her workstation. After that, Rachel had to stretch a bit to keep herself busy all the hours of her day. She kept working on the job description that Jewel had asked for, but progressed slowly. Janie apparently had a number of little projects that she toyed with, but so far, none that Rachel had been able to discover were very important.

There was, for instance, Janie's reputation around the offices for knowing where a client could find services not handled by Burns. There was a list, but Rachel found that the only current number on it was for the firm with the peculiar ability to chrome a nose cone. The rest of the references were on scraps of paper scattered through the drawers. Rachel began collecting them and making a Rolodex, but it was obvious Janie had never done this job, so could it honestly be considered part of her job description?

She was putting fresh cards in the Rolodex near quitting time when Olsen drifted up to her desk and asked diffidently, "You want to go for a ride?"

Rachel grinned up at him. "You mean it? You're going to take me for an airplane ride? I'd love it!"

"Okay, you have time to finish what you're doing. The ship will be ready in a little while."

She worked until five-thirty and then she went outside and Olsen was sitting on the porch. Burns boasted a number of splendid, high porches with views of the runway and taxi strips. Olsen was watching a mechanic install the equipment into a plane in the service area in front of the building. Rachel sat down and watched with him.

After a while they both got tired of that and went to the machine for a soft drink and some peanuts, and then they sat on the porch some more. It was a couple hours before the man finished, and finally Rachel and Olsen were able to climb into the ship.

It was the latest model, still smelling of new upholstery. The cabin was cozy and comfortable and the array of instruments on the control panel glittered, gleamed, and blinked. Rachel was delighted with everything.

As they taxied to the runway, the sky was red with the last rays of the setting sun. Olsen got his instructions from the tower and then they were on the runway, heading into a scarlet sky.

When the ship lifted off and climbed, the sky grew lighter and, in seconds, the sun reappeared from its hiding place over the horizon. Delighted, Rachel watched as it set a second time. When it was dark, the Valley appeared as a puddle of lights in a bowl of dark hills. Rachel thought of dollhouses, with tiny lights gleaming from tiny windows.

She never did figure out what Olsen was testing, but it demanded a long leg to the north and then back again, and all the time they were watching a digital display that never changed more than a couple of numbers the whole time. Rachel and her boss passed the time chatting about their children.

Whatever the instrument was, in due time Olsen was satisfied with it and they landed back at Van Nuys. Rachel thanked him for the ride until he offered vaguely to do it again sometime.

Rachel scampered away to her car, pleasantly light-headed from changes in the atmosphere. She had to get to the grocery store; she was out of bread and milk.

Being a billing clerk wasn't so bad, if you could do it around airplanes all the time!

Three

It had been a successful dinner, for a change. With careful calculation, Deena had created a menu that everybody liked, not always easy in the Raymond household. Her options were limited because Ethan wouldn't eat rewarmed meat, Terry didn't like braised dishes, and Lonnie refused anything that had more than two ingredients in it. Deena was pleased to have the whole family peacefully eating everything on their plates.

They were almost finished when Terry dropped her bombshell. She said, "Lonnie's on the baseball team."

It shouldn't have been a bombshell. Most families would have called it good news, in fact, but for some reason it was different in this household. Lonnie leaped up from his chair, furious. "What'd you have to go and tell for?" he demanded of his sister.

"Well, why didn't you tell?" his sister countered. "It's your baseball team!"

Ethan said, "What? You've been trying out for the team and you didn't even tell us?"

Deena said, "I didn't know you liked baseball."

Lonnie was still snarling at Terry. "You've got to tell everything you know, can't keep it to yourself!"

Terry was weeping. "You're a dirty rat and I hate you!" She fled to her room.

"Why are you so mean to your sister?" Deena asked her son and rushed to comfort Terry.

It wasn't until later, when she was cleaning up the remains of the dinner, that she remembered she had not told Lonnie she was proud of his accomplishment.

She was, really, but he definitely was mean to his sister.

She was at the sink, washing, when headlights arced across the lawn. Rachel, turning into her driveway. It was after nine o'clock, and her neighbor was just coming home? What was the old girl up to? Deena dried her hands and went through the hedge to Rachel's back door. It had been several days since they had talked, and she really did need an update on Rachel's job.

Rachel was unloading a sack of groceries in the kitchen. "Deena, how nice to see you! Come in. Can I fix you something? Would you like some tea? I was just about to put the kettle on."

"Nothing, thanks, I just had dinner." Rachel's kitchen was so orderly it would have been suitable for a model home. The counters and appliances gleamed; not the slightest smell of food lingered. Rachel probably lived on salads. Sure enough, she was taking fresh greenery out of the sack.

"I ran a few errands on my way home from work," she explained with a sunny smile.

"Did you work late? You're not authorized for any overtime."

Rachel smiled again, and she looked like a girl. Except for that gray hair, of course. "No, I wasn't working overtime. Mr. Olsen took me with him to test some equipment."

"That's not overtime?"

"No, it was fun! We flew in this marvelous little Cessna. It has upholstered seats just like the inside of a car! There was a beautiful sunset tonight and we got to watch it twice, like an instant replay."

"Rachel . . . flying when it isn't part of your job? Do you think you ought to?"

Rachel laughed and twirled around the kitchen, waving a head of lettuce. "Flying too high with some guy in the sky . . ." she sang and tucked the lettuce into the refrigerator. "What harm could there possibly be in it?"

"I don't know, but . . ."

"I do have a life insurance policy," Rachel admitted. "If I get killed in an airplane that isn't a regular airliner, it won't pay off; but I don't care."

"You don't care about your children's inheritance?"

"The kids are all doing well. They don't need my insurance. Anyhow, I'm not planning to get killed."

"Who is this Olsen? What about him?"

"He's my boss, and he's a young man with a young family, and he's just being nice. He could see how crazy I am about airplanes."

Deena said, "Well, I'm glad to see you so cheerful. I was afraid the job might give you trouble."

"Oh, not at all."

"You said there wasn't any job description . . ."

"I paid a visit to Janie, the one who is laid up at home with a bad back, and asked her about the job. As soon as I figured out that she didn't know what she was doing either, then I knew how to approach the whole thing. No more problem."

Deena's brow creased. "Maybe you shouldn't have done that. Visit her, I mean. It could make people nervous."

"A temp can do anything, because everybody knows she won't be around long. I'm going to the air show on Sunday. Do you want to come with me?"

"Air show?" asked Deena, recoiling. "It's going to be a hundred degrees on Sunday, and you want to go stomping around an airfield? There'll be a million people and no place to park."

Rachel almost looked as if she might pout. "Oh, be a sport. There's going to be a skydiving exhibition, and the CAF is going to do a flyby."

"Who's going to fly by?"

"The Confederate Air Force. You've heard of them. They fly planes from World War II and some of them, the ships, I mean, are going to be sitting around so you can look at them. Bring your family. Wear something cool. I have a sticker to park on the field."

"I have so much to do . . ." Deena broke off. Rachel was positively glowing with excitement over a silly airplane ride and a silly air show. It was good to see her full of enthusiasm again. Why shouldn't they go to an air show? It would be a change, something different to do, something away from her house and her office.

Deena said, "Yes, I'll go with you. Maybe it will be fun."

Deena was sincerely glad to find Rachel cheerful, but she went home with an unsettled feeling that she could not quite identify.

How little it took to make Rachel happy! A little job, a clerk's job, the worst thing of all, a temp job, and she was waltzing in the kitchen. With nothing more than that, her life was suddenly full of possibilities.

And why shouldn't it be? Rachel was free, she had no real financial worries, her health was good. . . . What adventures might she be heading into? She was sixty years old and alone and her children forgot to phone, but at least Deena had identified her own feelings.

She was jealous. She was jealous of Rachel!

* * *

"You ready to knock off for lunch?" Jewel demanded. "Let's go over on Sherman and get a salad bar."

"Sounds good," Rachel agreed. "We can walk; it isn't far."

"You want to cross Sherman Way on foot? You'll get us killed. My car's right outside."

"You want to drive, okay with me." Rachel thought it was silly, but probably Jewel's feet hurt.

The restaurant was crowded as usual. Maybe even more than usual. As they were ushered to a table, Jewel muttered, "Oh, Lord help us, the CAF's already here."

Rachel said, "Huh?"

"Look over there. That table with all the old geezers sitting at it. Confederate Air Force or I'll eat a frozen diet dinner."

Rachel looked. The men at the table did not seem particularly menacing, just a bunch of guys, most of them well past middle age, all casually dressed. They favored windbreaker jackets and old-fashioned slacks with pleats in them.

Rachel said, "That's the CAF? How can you tell?"

"By the uniform," Jewel said smugly.

"Very funny."

Jewel gestured vaguely. "There's just something about them. You can always tell."

Rachel chuckled. "Well, for one thing, they're old."

"They are, all right, but nobody's told them yet." Jewel pursed her mouth and thought fiercely. "They *swagger,*" she managed at last.

"Swagger? They're all sitting down. How can they swagger?"

"Trust me, they swagger."

They slid into their table and ordered iced tea, then Jewel groaned to her feet again. "On to the salad bar. Would you believe salad for lunch? At my age? I've had this weight for forty years; what makes me think I'm ever going to lose it? I'd probably miss it if I did."

"You probably would, if you confuse weight with clout," said Rachel. "You're not too old to change yourself."

Jewel tried to look cross. "What do you know about it? I'll bet you've always been little and cute. I've always been fat and now I'm so old, my face is sliding down my neck."

"Come on, Jewel! Nobody's exempt from getting old. And I guess I was cute when I was a teenager, but that was quite a while ago."

A pretty waitress, her curls tied back with a perky bow, was handing plates out of the chiller at the salad bar. She seemed to be doing it in hopes of moving a pair of the CAF guys who were blocking traffic by the bar. They weren't doing anything, just standing there.

She handed a plate to a tall, rangy fellow, who recoiled. "Ice-cold plates? Brr!"

The second CAF suggested, "You look like a nice girl. Maybe you could bring us some warm ones from the kitchen." His jacket was a crazy quilt of patches and badges, logos of every service and stripes from every battle. He wore a military cap with the wire removed so the sides drooped down and it became what the old-timers had called a "thousand hour cap."

"Don't you want salad?" asked the girl.

"I don't think so," said his taller buddy, squinting venomously at the lettuce. "Ain't you got no cooked greens?"

"We don't cook them," replied the confused girl.

"Look at that!" Jacket broke in. "Somebody made potato salad and forgot to peel the potatoes!"

"Pipe down, Chief. You've seen a salad bar before," the rangy guy said.

Jacket settled back on his heels, and his voice took on a plaintive note. "Sure I have, only it was shaped a little different and the cows was eating out of it."

"You're in California now. Folks in California *like* raw stuff to eat and peelings and things like that."

"Trouble with this place. Nothing's cooked enough."

Rangy looked learned. "I hear in California they even eat raw fish."

"Nah, they're teasing you. Seals eat raw fish."

"Kelp, too."

"Even seals don't eat kelp. Hardly seems worthwhile keeping a guy in the kitchen, he ain't going to cook nothing."

Rangy had hair that was an interesting mix of gray and white, cut rather like President Clinton's. Rachel thought it remarkable that a man that age had enough hair for a Clinton.

He said, "Okay, that's enough of your bellyaching. You're here now, so whyncha do what the locals do? Let the lady give you a plate and you can try the salad bar."

Jacket took the plate, glanced into the

salad bar, and cringed. "What the hell's that?"

"That there's cilantro."

"See what I mean? You fed that to a cow, she'd give sour milk."

"Maybe he don't really want the salad bar." Rangy gave the waitress a fake grin. "What have you got on the menu, honey?"

The waitress finally got them to return to their table and look over the menu, but they never quieted down. None of the CAFs did. There were only about six of them, but they talked mostly all at once. Jacket, especially, had something to say on every subject.

"They are a bunch of rednecks, aren't they?" Jewel muttered as she ladled dressing onto her salad.

Rachel added spinach leaves to her pile of greenery. "Oh, cut them some slack. They're just funning a pretty girl. They must be. Those accents came right out of old 'Torkelsons' reruns."

They returned to their table. "You've been doing a good job with the billing," Jewel allowed, spreading butter on her roll. "After Janie comes back, I'd like to have you do vacation relief for me. I've got some positions that are sort of like Janie's. It's hard to find somebody who can just walk in and do them for two weeks."

"I'm really flattered that you want me back, but you'll have to make the arrangements with the temp agency. I work for them. Talk to Deena."

Jewel squinted wise old eyes. "How'd you get to be a temp, anyway?"

"Must I confess? This is my first assignment. My neighbor knew I was looking for a job and suggested I do this."

"Yeah? What were you doing before?"

"Materials manager. I quit my job when my husband fell ill. It was just a small company and they couldn't give me leave; they had to have somebody managing that department."

"Are you sorry you quit, now?"

"No, of course not. It messed me up; I'll never get another job on that level, but I had to do it."

"He died, didn't he?"

"Yes." Rachel put down her fork, suddenly buffeted by memories that were incongruous in this cheerful place. "I couldn't help him; nobody could. The doctors tried . . ."

"It hasn't been very long, has it?"

"Not long enough. It still hurts. Why

couldn't I have done more for him? I keep thinking of things that might have helped, might have at least made him more comfortable. Why couldn't he tell me what he needed?"

Jewel went on eating her salad. "There's one thing about being old—it's too late for regrets."

Rachel straightened up. "It's always too late for regrets."

Jewel's eyes seemed to have sunk deeper into the pouches around them. "It's an old story, you know. Women sacrificing for the family because nobody else is going to do it. . . . And there's never any payback. My husband's last illness ate up every dime we had. I'm probably going to be working until I'm eighty."

"That's too bad. Do you have children, somebody to help you out?"

"I hope I'm never going to have to ask the kids to support me."

"I was lucky. Pete had good insurance."

"So what are you working for, if you don't have to?"

"I've worked all my life," said Rachel. "I have to be doing something. I'm afraid I'll turn into one of those old women, you know, they're playing Keno, going on cruises, hunting for a man because if you've got man trouble, at least you've got something to think about."

Jewel smiled sarcastically. "Compared to eight-hour days for the next decade or so, it sounds pretty good."

When they left the restaurant, the CAF was still eating and arguing. As she slipped through the door, Rachel caught a glimpse of Rangy-with-the-Clinton-haircut, bent over his plate, frowning. Short, tough nose and craggy chin; a face well-suited to frowning.

A few hours later, she had typed a stack of invoices and decided it was time for a stretch. Walking downstairs to the shop would at least be a change from sitting, so she went to pick up the completed work orders. When she entered the shop, she was startled to find two strangers there.

Well, not exactly strangers; it was Rangy and Jacket, arguing vociferously with one of the techs.

She hastened toward them. "Sir! Excuse me, sir! This is a restricted area! You're not supposed to be here."

Rangy frowned at her. "I know that, but they've got my radio!"

"Well, that's what he does; he works on

radios. Why don't you come upstairs with me, and we'll talk about it?"

Rangy's frown became fiercer than ever. "No, I want him to fix my radio! We're due to go back to Houston on Monday, and that's fifteen hundred miles from here. How are we supposed to do that with no radio?"

Rachel asked the tech, "What's the schedule for his radio?"

"I haven't even started it," the man replied. "I've got four of them waiting on my table."

"Are they all rush orders?"

"Well, one of them isn't."

"Maybe you could shift things around a little?"

"Well, maybe," the tech allowed reluctantly, then shot a defiant glance at Rangy. "If he gets out of my way!"

Rangy crossed his arms over his chest. "I think I'll just stand here and wait."

"You're not allowed to do that," Rachel told him. "You're not supposed to be here at all. This place is like a laboratory. These men are highly trained specialists, and they're very good at their job. It requires high intelligence and a lot of education, and they are all experts."

She had so mollified the tech that he actually picked up his screwdriver again. Rangy observed the act with satisfaction.

Rachel went on, "The work they do is important and they need a quiet, undisturbed atmosphere to work in. You're a pilot; you know better than anybody how important this kind of work is. How would you like to be up in the air with a radio or a transponder that had been worked on by a tech who couldn't concentrate because people kept walking around in his workshop? The air conditioning even blows special air in here, and you're probably getting dust in it just by walking around in your street clothes."

Rangy was actually smiling. Not much, just a slight lift of his straight line of a mouth. "Street clothes?" he repeated. "What about you? You're wearing street clothes. You usually come down here naked? You didn't have to get all dressed up for me. In fact, I kinda wish you hadn't."

She felt a flush of anger washing through her, or was it a schoolgirl confusion to hear a man say "naked" in reference to her? She made herself say evenly, "Let's go upstairs and see what we can do to get priority for your radio job."

To her relief, both men followed her docilely up the stairs. Not without comments, of course. Rangy hung back to watch her from behind and said, a clearly audible aside to his buddy, "For an old gal, she's got great gams."

"Gams!" sputtered Rachel. "I haven't heard that word since the Eisenhower administration!"

Jacket said, "Now, Colonel, why don't you leave that lady alone? She's probably a respectable lady with a nice family. She just looks like a sexpot; she can't help that."

Rangy grumbled, "If she's going to wear those short skirts . . ."

Rachel picked up a pad from her desk. "What hotel are you in? I'll give you a call as soon as I find out when your radio will be ready."

Jacket whistled. "She already wants your phone number, Colonel! You've made a hit!"

"Shut up, Colonel," growled Rangy.

Rachel poised a pencil over the pad. "You're both colonels?"

"Everybody's a colonel in the CAF," Jacket explained. "He's Colonel Flaherty. Colonel Coe Flaherty, and I'm Colonel Chief, because I'm the crew chief."

Only a big ship carries a crew chief. Rachel said, "Oh, yours is the Flying Fortress that got here today? Everybody's talking about it."

"That's our bird. The radio went out over Nevada, and we had to go seventy-six hundred on the transponder."

Flaherty ignored him. "You coming to see it on Sunday?" he asked Rachel.

"I'm coming to the air show," she admitted.

She got the telephone number and showed the two colonels the way out of the building. They never stopped clowning and making sexist comments, but she didn't make objections. You have to be nice to the customers.

And she was looking forward to Sunday at the air show.

Four

Nobody in Deena's family wanted to go with her to the air show. Only Lonnie showed the slightest interest, but he couldn't go because he had reserved time on the school's computer that Sunday.

True to Deena's prediction, the day was hot, so she dressed in a pair of walking shorts and a poet's shirt in cool voile. It was a favorite blouse; she liked the flowing collar and open neckline. The long sleeves would keep her arms from getting sunburned.

Except it looked wrong with the tailored walking shorts. It needed more contrast, something a little startling, like a pair of cutoff jeans. She put on a pair that were raggedy from repeated washings, then got to wondering if a middle-aged Valley matron ought to go running around with that much leg showing.

She was acting like a teenager, Deena accused herself, changing her clothes over and over for a trip to the airport to pick up a hot dog and watch the skydivers. The heck with it. She slipped on a pair of sandals and went to find Rachel.

Rachel wore classic chinos and a T-shirt long and baggy enough to be called a tunic. Perfectly dressed for a Southern California Sunday outing, they set off for the airport.

It felt so good just to be moving, to be leaving behind their homes and responsibilities, that they both got a trifle silly. They laughed at nothing, turned up the radio and bounced in their seats to the beat of a lively song. They giggled as Rachel bypassed all the traffic and turned into Burns parking lot.

The lot was reserved for VIP's and guarded by a Civil Air Patrol cadet, but the kid readily accepted the Burns employee sticker on the Cadillac. Rachel and Deena had only to walk a few yards and they were on the field, recklessly ordering hot dogs. Deena went so far as to drink a cola that wasn't diet.

The north section of the airport had been closed down for the show and planes were lined up along it, baking under a blazing summer sun. Nobody seemed bothered by the heat; crowds swarmed across the tarmac, cheerful and sweating, the children yelling with exuberance. Stands selling iced drinks were doing a brisk business.

The skydivers put on a spectacular show; the Condor Squadron flew by in formation. Rachel and Deena wandered around, looking at the exhibits. The Air Force had sent a giant B-52; enthusiasts displayed their P-51's and AT-6's. Rachel admired some antique Stearmans, pretty biplanes splendidly restored, sitting in a line like a string of blooded horses in a remuda. Most of them were the property of a famous actor.

Deena was not all that interested in airplanes. She ran her fingers through her hair and it felt as hot as if it had been ironed. "Isn't any part of this show indoors?" she demanded.

"Oh, look, isn't that the B-17?" asked Rachel.

"How should I know?"

"It's open, so we can see the inside. Come on, let's go. want to look into the cockpit. I've never seen the cockpit of a big ship."

"Well, it'll be out of the sun," Deena agreed.

They climbed steps and entered the ship

through a door in the waist. The interior was a line of cubicles, divided by steel-framed doorways and lit only by an eerie light that filtered through the gunners' bubbles. The fuselage was narrow and the feeling claustrophobic, in spite of the size of the ship. Deena and Rachel edged their way through the crowd of sightseers and made their way toward the cockpit, where they found Colonel Chief blocking the door, standing there in his patchwork jacket.

"Well, hello!" he said, with a grin that broadened as he took in Deena in her cut-off shorts. "Did you two lovely ladies come to see our airplane?"

"May I look into the cockpit?" asked Rachel.

"Sure you can," said Colonel Coe Flaherty. She had not noticed him standing off to the side, his expression sour as lemons in a drought year. "And you can take special note of the hole where our radio ought to be."

"Your radio will be ready tomorrow, as I told you Friday," said Rachel. "Our men don't work on Sunday; they have families, too."

"That's the cockpit, and this here's the hold," Chief was explaining to Deena.

Rachel remembered her manners. "Deena, this is Colonel Flaherty and Colonel Chief. My friend, Deena Raymond."

"They call me Chief because I'm the crew chief," that Colonel explained to Deena. "Sometimes folks ask me what a crew chief *does;* well, it isn't so much what I *do,* I've just got to *be* there. The pilot and the copilot do all the work, and I just ride along. You're gonna say, that's a pretty soft life. Well, let me put it this way, this ship is fifty years old. How good do you think your car's going to be running when it's fifty years old?"

"It's got a few problems right now," Deena admitted.

Rachel was peering through the narrow door into the crammed cockpit. "Oh, my, look at all those needles and dials! What do they all do?"

"Nothing much," replied Coe Flaherty. "Most of them are just for show."

Rachel gave him a look under lowered brows, and he added, "The only one you gotta watch is the altimeter. Tells you whether you're on the ground or not."

Chief's voice went on behind her. "And

then there was the time we had the electrical fire . . ."

"Could I sit in the seat?" Rachel begged. "I've always wanted to sit where the pilot does."

"Well, I'm not supposed to let you, but I guess it'd be all right," Coe allowed.

She was then faced with the problem of getting into the seat, which was almost level with the floor on which she stood and blocked by a bank of instruments between the seats.

"Put your foot there," Coe instructed. "Watch out you don't step on any of those levers. Just swing in."

She struggled into the right-hand seat and, with practiced ease, he levered himself into the other. He wore a pilot's bright-yellow jumpsuit. "That's the altimeter there," he said, pointing.

Rachel pointed in her turn. "And that's the artificial horizon with the little airplane in it, and that's the airspeed indicator."

"Hey, you've been around more than you've been admitting!" There was even a trace of approval in his voice.

"I know what it is, but I don't know how to read it."

"Just goes in tens. See? A nine's going to be ninety, fifteen is a hundred fifty."

She took hold of the control wheel. "And this is what steers the whole big thing!"

"Well, we like to refer to it as 'flying.'"

Rachel moved the yoke slightly, stared out the plexiglass window, and murmured, "Zoom!"

He chuckled a little at her enthusiasm. "It's not such a big ship. Not compared to some of the things they got these days, 110's and 747's and that Hercules right out there." He waved to indicate an Air National Guard ship so huge its tail was too tall for the hangar. The rest of the ship was inside but the tail remained at the door, towering over the roof and seeming somehow surprised at its awkward position.

"Rachel, what are you doing?" Deena asked, leaning over the back of her seat. "Whew, is it hot in here!"

She was right. The sun was blasting in the windows, two of them almost overhead. The cockpit was hot, and not a breath of air stirred. Rachel had not noticed. She said, "Look, this is the lever that puts the landing gear down."

"This is where the PIC sits to drive the plane," Chief lectured. "PIC, that's the Pilot In Charge. Actually, Rachel is sitting where the old man usually sits. He's sitting where the copilot usually is, that's Whitey, only he ain't here right now . . ."

"Chief, I'll take care of things here in the cockpit," Flaherty told him. "You keep an eye on the rest of the ship. All these civilians running around, you can never tell what one of them's going to do next."

"There's hardly anybody here right now," Chief argued, aggrieved, and went right on talking to Deena. "You know, Coe's a great pilot. You should have seen him the other day, when he had to bring this ship in here with no radio!"

"It wasn't that big of a deal," Coe said. "We could receive all right; we just couldn't send."

Chief raised his eyebrows to Deena. "You wanna be over Los Angeles and you can't tell anybody who you are, or where? And you're flying a bomber? We were lucky they didn't shoot us down with anti-aircraft guns!"

"We never were over L.A.; we came in over the mountains, and they knew where we were from the radar," Coe corrected. Then he chuckled. "But I guess it's been a while since anybody communicated with the tower at this airport by waggling the wings!"

"That's what you did?" Rachel questioned.

"I waggled; they let me come in. It would be nice to have a radio before we go back. I'd rather not have to do that trick at Houston. I wouldn't even be able to listen to their tower, now that you've got our radio."

"You don't change the subject easily, do you?" said Rachel. "I think I'll go find a cool drink."

She scrambled out of the cockpit and found Deena standing with Chief at the only door to the outside. He was talking earnestly, his elbows out so that he blocked the opening.

"That's just the electricity. I gotta know about the hydraulics and the lubricants and the carburetor heat."

"Your car runs really good, does it?" Deena teased, laughing.

"A car's pretty simple, but you gotta have a crew chief on the job in a ship like this, keeping an eye out for all the things that can go wrong."

"Yeah, like the radio," Coe interrupted. Rachel had not noticed he had followed her to the door.

Deena gave Chief a light tap on the chest. "If you'll get out of the doorway, I think I'll be going."

"You don't have to go right now," he coaxed." I've told you all about us and this plane. How about telling me something about you? You live here in Van Nuys?"

"Encino," Deena admitted. "You want my life story? Well, I'm happily married; I have two children, and my business is a temporary employment agency here in the Valley. That's all pretty square, isn't it?"

Chief's smile came with an endearing little squint. "It might be, but you've got style."

"What makes you think that?"

"Just the way you are. Just the way you look."

Deena's mouth pursed prettily. "You haven't been at my house when the morning rush is on."

A group of people came up the steps to the door, and Chief stepped aside to let them enter. Deena also moved aside, and their conversation went on. Rachel seized the opportunity to go down the steps into the open air. Then she sort of poked around, looking at the ship from the outside, waiting for Deena to come out. She wouldn't dare go off and look at something else or she would lose Deena and never find her again in this mob. When she rounded the nose of the ship, Coe waved to her from the cockpit.

When Deena finally came out, they looked at the outside of a couple more ships and then agreed to go home. Both were weary from the heat and both were being reminded that hot dogs are something it takes a young stomach to digest. It was time for home and a cooling shower.

Monday seemed like a very long day. It was a scorcher, as Sunday had been and everybody was getting testy from the prolonged heat. Rachel was wilted when the day was over, glad to get home. She decided to cook something outdoors so the kitchen would stay clean and cool.

No, she couldn't do that, she remembered. She had used up the barbecue charcoal and not yet replaced it. She would have to get back into the car and drive to the supermarket and stand in line, all for one item. Deena came into her drive at just that minute, and Rachel felt desperate enough to borrow.

She called, "Hi, Deena, do you have any charcoal briquets?"

Her neighbor replied, "Sure. Come on over and I'll give them to you." She got out of her car, keys in her hand. "Hey, are you saying you've got a steak? Let's combine our dinners. You bring the steak and I'll supply the rest. My family's all away, so it's just us two."

Rachel moved to the gap in the hedge, where she could see Deena more easily. "Yeah? Where is everybody?"

"Ethan's out of town; Lonnie's got a study date, and Terry's spending the night with a friend. It's kind of nice, for a change. Maybe we could eat something that doesn't have to be cooked at all, like a chef salad."

"Great idea, if you just happen to have a cup of julienned ham and some cooked chicken on hand. A steak will do us good."

Rachel broke off as a car stopped in her drive. Chief and Coe popped out of it. Her head swam for a second, she was so surprised to see in her own drive, not only two guys in suits, but two guys in suits who were supposed to be in Houston. They were real suits, nice ones, with neckties.

The two CAF flyboys looked as dressed and tame as a couple of accountants.

Coe gave her a wave, although he didn't smile. "Hello, Rachel!"

Rachel stepped back through the hedge. "Isn't this a surprise! I thought you had gone home."

"How could we do that?" grumped Coe. "They didn't get that radio installed until three this afternoon, and in a ship that slow, it's fifteen hours to Houston. No point in starting the trip this late."

"And anyhow, we wanted to thank you for getting the radio fixed for us," Chief put in, "and take you to dinner, if you're free."

"Oh, I didn't do anything," Rachel protested. "If you're going to thank somebody, it ought to be Mr. Olsen."

"Is he pretty, too? I think I'd rather go to dinner with you. And Deena, too, of course." Chief raised his voice a little. "You want to go, Deena?"

Deena stepped through the hedge and smiled, but she said, "I don't know. . . . It's such short notice."

"No, it isn't," Coe argued. "It's barely six o'clock. You've got plenty of time to primp; we made the reservations for eight."

Deena had to laugh. "Pretty sure of yourselves, aren't you?"

Coe shrugged. "It's just dinner."

Rachel said, "And I wouldn't dream of turning down a meal. I can't answer for my neighbor, but I'll be ready in fifteen minutes."

"I'll be ready in ten," said Deena and disappeared again through the hedge.

Rachel parked the men in her living room with drinks and rushed to change into a summery dress. She had one that seemed to her perfect for this occasion, a sheer fabric in a print that was mostly subdued shades of brown. The dress had a nice flow to it, and she had never worn it. She couldn't remember what she had been planning when she bought it.

A thought struck her as she dressed, and when she came downstairs she asked Coe, "How did you find my address?"

"Thomas Guide," he replied shortly.

Rachel put a hand on her hip. "That's not what I meant, and you know it."

"You're in the book," Chief explained. "I had your phone number. I just looked you up."

"And then we used the Thomas Guide to find this street, like I told you," Coe added.

Rachel protested, "But I never gave you my home phone number."

"Deena did," Chief explained.

Rachel said, "Oh," and wondered. Deena had given Chief *Rachel's* phone number? When you thought about that, it really was a peculiar thing to do.

Five

She forgot about it as they roared toward the Boulevard. She was trying to get the men to explain why they had picked Pierre's restaurant, and they were both teasingly pretending they could not remember. It was a mystery how they had even heard of it, a trendy, expensive little hideout with hardly any parking. This last alone was enough to kill an average restaurant in the Valley, but Pierre's thrived.

A waitress with perfect manners made no sarcastic comments when both men ordered straight bourbon instead of cocktails. Rachel and Deena each essayed a glass of wine.

Chief behaved himself perfectly until he got his hands on the menu, and then he began to whine. "This is either the menu or a death threat; it's so dark in here, I can't tell which. You got any flares with you, Coe?"

"It's probably in French or something," Coe responded. "You couldn't read it if you *could* see it."

"Don't fret," Deena advised them. "They'll come by soon with the specials, and that's what you want to eat anyway."

"You come here a lot?" Chief asked her.

"Only when I need to impress somebody." The subdued lighting gave Deena a glow and Rachel reflected that it had been a long time since she had looked, really looked, at Deena. Every day she saw her friend, her neighbor, the mother of Lonnie and Terry; but in this setting, she saw a beautiful woman. The light fell gently across perfect cheekbones, her eyes were dark and unfathomable, shaded by thick eyelashes. Maturity had only ripened Deena's beauty.

Rachel asked Coe, "Where did you ever find that amazing ship? A Flying Fortress, after all these years!"

"Utah," he replied. "They'd been using it to make water drops on forest fires. Great big tank in the bomb bay. When they got some helicopters, of course, they were more efficient, so they put the Fort aside and we found it."

"It was covered with fire-retardant gunk," Chief reported. "We cleaned it and then we polished the aluminum skin, all over, with little hand-held buffers. That's how we got that shiny finish on it."

Coe added, "We had a crew working on that thing for months. Rebuilt the engines. Everything in that ship has been put in new. Well, almost everything. We seem to have missed the radio."

That blasted radio again! How could one man be so annoying, all by himself? It was a struggle, but she managed to ask brightly, "A whole crew of CAF colonels? When everybody's a colonel, how do you tell who's in charge?"

"We don't. We just sort of work it out. Everybody does what he wants and what needs doing."

"But you're the PIC," said Rachel. Proud of herself for remembering the phrase, she explained to Deena, "That's the Pilot In Charge."

"Well, in the air, that's different," Coe admitted.

Deena suggested, "You two must have been friends for a long time."

"A long time," Chief confirmed. "When I first knew Coe, Texas was just a little state. All the cows was about as big as poodles; had to be, so's they'd fit in."

"Never mind the Huckleberry Finn act," Rachel scolded. "Why do you do that, anyway?"

He gave her that cocky grin. "Folks expect it." He was a handsome man, a sparkle always in his dark brown eyes. Younger than Coe, he had less hair. Rachel thought the cap he usually wore was not really necessary; his high forehead gave him an open, friendly look that was exceptionally attractive.

She asked, "Why do you think that? Just because you're in the Confederate Air Force?"

"Well, it does have a certain connotation," Coe put in.

"Yeah, like what?"

"Well, what are you going to think a guy would be like who was in an outfit with 'confederate' in the name?"

"Let's see, he's going to be a Southerner . . ." Rachel began.

"Naw, they're not all Southerners," said Chief.

"And he's going to be a pilot."

Coe objected to that. "You'd be surprised. We've got a lot of guys who just work on the ground."

"And he's going to be old," Rachel finished.

Coe actually laughed. "I guess that's true. The way it was, back in The War, the Air Force wouldn't let a guy fly if he wasn't at least eighteen years old. So even if he got his wings the year the war was over, today he'd still be pulling Social Security."

"We weren't all in WW II!" Chief protested.

"That's right; we've got some babies in the organization. This one, now, he flew in a couple other wars, I forget what they called them."

"Well, Korea for one," grumped Chief.

"Were you eighteen when you learned to fly?" Rachel asked Coe.

He leaned back in his chair, comfortable. He might even have been smiling, but it was too dark to tell. "Round about. They had this program during the war, called it 'acceleration.' A kid could graduate from high school early if he joined the service. I thought getting out of school a year early sounded just fine; what they didn't tell us was we were going to have to fly those airplanes."

Rachel laughed, as she was expected to. "Oh, come on. I'll bet you were thrilled. I remember when I was eighteen, I wanted to fly more than anything else in the world."

His grumpy look returned in an instant. "Not anything, or you'd of done it."

"That's not so! There just wasn't any place in aviation for a woman in those days."

"You think there is now?"

"It's not like it was then. There are lots of women flying now. There are even women astronauts!"

He lifted quizzical gray eyebrows at her. "You want to fly, why don't you?"

"What, you mean now?"

The grumpy look was almost fierce. "What's wrong with now? It's the only time you've got. It's the only time any of us have got. All you gotta do is go over to Sonny Whales' school and sign up for lessons, and you'll just fly away."

"Oh, I couldn't do that, Coe! I'm sixty years old!"

"See good, don't you? Never had a stroke? What's to stop you?"

"I never had a stroke, but I'm a little far-sighted lately."

"Happens to all of us. For a pilot, it's an advantage."

What was stopping her, Rachel realized,

was more than forty years of believing that it couldn't be done, of making herself forget about it. The idea glimmered in the back of her mind. This old man stirred something in her.

Well, she'd think about it sometime when things were quieter. For now, she laughed and said, "You know what you'd be good at? You ought to be one of those gurus who sits on a mountain top and bawls out everybody who comes to see him. You can be very insightful," she grinned up at him, "and you're certainly grouchy enough."

She had made everybody laugh, even Coe. The waitress came back and recited the specials. Chief complained that none of the dishes were dressed with pineapple chili, but the waitress was a pretty young woman and everybody knew he was only doing it to make her laugh.

Coe ordered bouillabaisse. He pronounced it correctly, but then the waitress had just done so and Rachel worried that Coe might not know what he was getting into. He fooled her, however, forking the crab legs neatly from their shells and knowing exactly when to toss in the bread. Rangy the redneck had other facets to his personality.

They had a lovely dinner, relaxed and friendly. They ate well and laughed a lot. How very long it had been, Rachel thought, since she had enjoyed an evening like this with friends! She must think up some excuses to do it more often.

When they got back to Rachel's house it was getting late. The lights were on at Deena's; Lonnie must have come home.

Rachel, who had an excellent memory, remembered what to do to avoid awkward farewells at the front door. As soon as the car stopped she was out of it, leaving Coe behind the wheel. Then she spoke to him through the window, thanking him for the evening.

Deena followed her lead, got out of the back seat and shut the door before Chief could follow her. He rolled down the window quickly and said, "I want to thank you ladies for making this such a pleasant evening for us."

Deena stood looking at him, something sad in the droop of her shoulders. She said, "Have a nice trip back to Houston."

Suddenly she bent, put her head into the car window and kissed him on the mouth. She broke away quickly and left him sitting there, staring out the window, as she ran up the walkway and onto Rachel's porch.

Rachel followed more sedately and unlocked the front door.

Deena said in a muffled tone, "Let me come in with you, Rachel."

"Of course, dear. What's wrong?"

"Nothing, nothing at all. Just give me a minute to get myself back together."

They moved into the lighted entry hall. "Deena, you're crying!"

"Lonnie's home, I can't let him see me cry . . ." Deena broke off, and Rachel put her arms around her.

"There, there, dear. It can't be as bad as all that!"

"Oh, yes, it can!" Deena straightened up and glared at her. "They're married, you know."

"Huh? Who?"

"Chief and Coe. Both of them. You know it, too, Rachel. Don't pretend you don't."

"Well, I thought . . ."

"Yeah, what did you think? At our ages, did you expect we were going to meet a couple of carefree bachelors and double date? Get real! They're all married. Anybody our age is. Once you get out of your twenties you've got one choice. Either you're going to mess around with married men or you're not going to mess at all."

Rachel flapped her arms distractedly. "Well, of course I do not mess; but cool it, Deena! All we did was eat a dinner with some people we know from work! Why are you making such a big deal out of it?"

"Because it is a big deal! Don't tell me you don't feel it, too! I saw the way you looked at Coe, and I don't blame you. He's impressive. He makes younger guys look juveniles—even older younger guys, like Chief. But Chief . . ." Deena began again to sniffle.

"He has a lot of charm," Rachel admitted.

"He makes me feel young. He makes me feel pretty. He makes me feel like somebody a man would want, somebody who isn't just a mother, a cook, a bottle-washer, and a second paycheck."

Rachel said soothingly, "Well, you probably shouldn't have flirted with him, but that's all it was. Nothing happened; we're safe at home now, and tomorrow they'll fly back to wherever they came from and it's over."

"What the hell do you suppose I'm crying about? Nothing happened, and now it's over!"

It was some time before she would stop crying. Rachel made a pot of herb tea and a cup of that soothed Deena sufficiently to go home. She remarked that it was lucky the only family member at home was her son. He would seldom look her in the eye anyway.

Rachel worried about Deena for a while, but she had something else to think about and it kept intruding until she gave in and let it take over.

Sonny Whales' school, he had said. Just go over to Sonny Whales and sign up. She could walk across the street from her office to Whales'; she saw his advertising every day as she turned into the Burns parking lot. All she had to do was sign up and learn to fly.

Why not? She was healthy and strong, and she had money in the bank. The costs that had kept her from taking lessons when she was eighteen could easily be covered now. So what if she were supposed to be a grandma type, knitting in a rocking chair? Who said she had to do it? Tomorrow she was going to see Sonny Whales!

Rachel used her lunch hour to go to the office of the flight school and make the arrangements; and when she returned to her desk, she found Coe standing next to it.

"Well, you went ahead and did it, didn't you?" he demanded.

Why was she so ridiculously glad to see him? She couldn't wait to tell him that she was going to fly. But she said, "Coe, what are you doing here? You were supposed to leave for Houston at first light this morning."

"Well, I'm stuck here again, and it's all your fault," he snapped. "I got to thinking about what you said—you were going to take flying lessons; and I woke up this morning and realized you might have meant it, and you did, didn't you?"

"Yes, I did mean it."

"And so you went right out and signed up! It's written right here on your desk calendar. It says, 'Sonny Whales, noon.' You can't deny it; that's what you did!"

"What is this—you go around reading people's private desk calendars? Of course I did it. What's wrong, Coe? You're the one who told me to!"

"Yeah, but I didn't mean just go learn how to steer an airplane around like you were driving a bumper car at the amusement park. It's different, you know! The world's full of pilots like you're going to be. They know which buttons to push, and that's all they know. Can't navigate. Can't figure load factors. They just go ahead and guess how much runway they need to take off! All they know how to do is punch buttons on a calculator, and then they do whatever the calculator says—because they don't know any better. You have to understand the principles or you're an accident waiting to happen, and airplane accidents are usually fatal!"

Rachel sat down in her desk chair and looked up at him reprovingly. "You stayed in Van Nuys just to tell me that? Isn't it a little inconvenient? Didn't your crew expect to go today? Isn't your family expecting you home?"

"Crew's a little antsy, that's so," he admitted. "But I had to keep you from doing this."

"Well, you wasted your time, because I'm going to do it."

He smiled a tight, reluctant smile. "Good. I think you ought to. But you got to promise me you're going to go to ground school first."

"All this was to get me to go to ground

school? Actually, I was rather planning on it. Mr. Whales said the same thing you did, just about. Only he was nicer about it."

"Ground school?"

"He suggested the local community college. They have a course that starts in a couple of days."

"Are you signed up? Let's get over there and make sure you get into the class."

"I've used up my lunch hour, and now I must get back to work. I'll stop on my way home and take care of it."

"If the class starts soon, it's liable to get filled up. Maybe I better go over there and sign up for you."

She smothered a smile. "That would be a lot of trouble for you. I can take care of it."

"Well, what time do you get off? I'll meet you and we'll go to the school together. It'll give me a chance to check out the course, see if it's going to be what you need."

"Okay, five o'clock. Now clear out of my work area. I've got to get some billing to do."

"Have you had lunch yet?"

Just the sound of Chief's voice on the phone and Deena's heart leaped like a trout in her chest. Why had she given him her office number? Her assistant's desk was right outside the door; she ran a friendly office where people kept track of one another, and just at the moment, she was wishing she didn't.

Deena swiveled her chair around until her back was to the rest of the office and murmured, "You shouldn't have called."

"I want to see you. Where can we meet?"

"Meet? Aren't you in Houston?"

He chuckled. "No, when we got to the field this morning, the old man had all the plugs pulled out of one of the engines and now we can't fly until somebody puts them back. I think there wasn't anything wrong with them; he just wants to stay in town. He's not the only one, you know. There's somebody else who knows a beautiful woman in this town, who wants to see her."

"Well, now, Chief . . ."

"Come on, you've got to eat. It's only lunch."

"By the fountain," she said hastily. "There's a fountain in front of the building." She added the address and quickly hung up.

Then she got to wondering why she had chosen the fountain, of all public, exposed spots. Anyone might see her there with Chief, anyone from the building or from her office. She paused only to touch up her lipstick and fluff up her hair, and then she rushed downstairs to wait at the fountain.

She had been there only a few minutes when he arrived; he must have been nearby when he called. He was wearing that patchwork jacket; anyone would notice him. Deena hustled him into the parking garage.

That wasn't much better. People from her office might be there, getting out their cars to drive some place for lunch. She all but pushed Chief into her car, jumped behind the wheel, and drove out of the garage.

He settled comfortably into the seat, somehow very masculine, accepting a place in her car as if he were part of her life. "Where are we going?" he asked. "Some place you like to eat?"

"No, I'm looking for a place where I don't like to eat," she explained. "Some place I've never been."

She turned onto Oxnard, a hilly street broken up with stops. Nobody ever used it. "Some place in Chatsworth, maybe." She thought about that, briefly. "Only there isn't any place to eat in Chatsworth."

"That's okay," said Chief. His smile understood her and sympathized.

She turned onto a bucolic side street and braked the car under a tree. "Chief, what are we doing? We haven't got any right. . . . We've both got families."

"Yeah, I know, but I can't help it." He reached for her. "Looks like you can't, either."

Just a kiss. It didn't matter a lot if they shared just a kiss. She nestled into his arms, startled by the scope of that kiss. She was aware of his arms, his breath, the taste and feel of him, the different scent, different from Ethan . . .

She broke away from him and shoved herself under the wheel. "We mustn't do this."

He folded his arms and settled back, almost as comfortable as before. "Hey, look, I didn't come out here to pressure you. I just need to be with you. There's nothing wrong with our being friends, is there?"

"Yes, there probably is. You're far too attractive to me."

"That's a problem we've both got, but there's no reason we can't handle it. We're both grown-ups. What's the harm in it? It's only lunch."

Deena started the motor. "Well, okay. Just one thing, though."

"What's that?"

"Why do I keep calling you Chief? You do have a name, don't you?"

"Harry. Harry Saunders."

She echoed, "Colonel Harry Saunders."

"Well, I guess you can see why I'm not so crazy about being known as Colonel Saunders. Chief's okay."

That made her laugh and they felt so good, they both laughed as she headed for Ventura Boulevard.

They were almost to Calabasas before she found a place she wanted to eat in, one she never had seen before and felt sure nobody from her office was likely to drop into. The food was superb.

Six

It was a little before five and Rachel was working away at the billing when she looked up to discover Coe and Chief standing by her desk. They were Jacket and Rangy again, dressed in comfortable clothes, lounging against the edge of her desk, talking, talking, talking. She was getting used to it. When they started egging one another along, their banter could be endless.

"Why do you suppose she works so hard when there's nobody here to check up on her?" Chief asked.

"Beats me," growled Coe. "None of my employees ever did."

"Well, if you ever decide to go back in business again, you'll know where to find somebody to do the billing."

Coe rubbed his head thoughtfully. "I have thought of opening a hamburger stand on the field at Harlingen. That'd be a good business, and profitable, because I'd be feeding the whole CAF. They eat a lot, and most of them are too dumb to count their change. You know how to cook hamburgers, Rachel?"

"Sounds like the perfect career for me," said Rachel, covering her machines. You can't do any work anyway with two chattering guys infesting your office.

"Why don't we go in your car?" Coe suggested. "I don't know where this college is, anyhow."

"Sure, I'll drive," Rachel agreed. "You'd never find it. It's way up the Valley in Winnetka. That's the other side of Encino. You have a car here, don't you?"

"We both rented cars," Chief explained, "but they're over at the hotel. We just walked here."

"Well, it's out of my way, but I don't mind. I'll drive you back here when we finish at the school, Coe," Rachel offered. "If you like, Chief, I can drop you off at the hotel right now."

"I'll ride along with you," said Chief. "I don't have anything else to do."

They got into the Cadillac and Rachel followed a route she knew, slipping down the 405 to miss the always-heavy traffic where the two freeways joined, and then along the 101 to Winnetka. After that fine performance she was lost on the college campus and they wandered around until almost dark, searching for the building where she was supposed to sign up.

Chief didn't mind. "A real college campus!" he rhapsodized. "Doesn't that take you back, though? Stately buildings, well, maybe they're not so stately, but buildings, trees, grass, coeds . . ."

"Wouldn't know anything about it," growled his buddy.

"You didn't go to college, Coe?" asked Rachel.

"Naw, I was in business for myself. Nobody asks you to show a sheepskin if you're doing that. I hired and fired guys with degrees." He paused to give Chief a swat on the arm. "Cut it out, Chief. Your eyes are rolling around like they were on swivels."

"Oh, those California girls!" sighed Chief.

Rachel ignored him. "Are you retired now?"

"Yeah." Coe tucked his hands comfortably into his pockets as they strolled along a tree-bordered path. "There were all these bright guys I trained to be executives; and the next thing I knew, they turned into young Turks. All full of big ideas about new, different things the company ought to do. I got tired of fighting with them and, the hell with it, I retired. Get out of the way and let them do what they want. Let 'em run the company into the ground if they want to; it'd be no skin off my nose."

"Are you sorry you did that?"

"Hell, no. I get to do what I want now, fly all I want, and besides, the company is making more money now than it ever used to when I was running it."

"Flying is all you want to do, now?"

"Pretty much. That old Fort, it's sort of my baby; I put up most of the money for it. About all I do is fly it around to air shows."

That surprised Rachel. "Air shows? I didn't know you liked them. On Sunday you didn't seem happy at all."

"Sure I was."

"You kept complaining because civilians were walking around inside your ship."

"Well, there's some little disadvantages, but mostly I enjoy it."

When they finally found the building for the extension division, Rachel signed up for her course, received her "Golden Years" card, and paid for a parking pass. They went back to her car again and climbed in.

As she started the engine, Chief asked, "Is anybody else hungry? What do you say we find some dinner?"

"I'm starving," Rachel admitted. "I skipped lunch."

"I know what let's do," said Chief. "Let's pick up some steaks, take 'em over to your place, and have a barbecue."

"Now, that's not polite, Chief," Coe reproved. "It would be nicer if you asked the lady out for dinner. How about that, Rachel? Did you like it at Pierre's?"

"Very much, but French food two nights in a row is a little too much for my lipids," Rachel demurred. "Let's go someplace where you don't have to wait very long for the food. She twisted around to look at Chief, in the back seat. "There's no point in going to my house, all of Deena's family will be home and she wouldn't be able to join us. There will be steaks at the Sizzler."

They didn't argue, so she drove to a Sizzler and turned into the parking lot without consulting them further. The guys didn't complain. They didn't even go into their act when they found the place had a salad bar.

They had a nice meal and a good time together, but Rachel was rather glad when the meal was finished and she could drive the guys back to their hotel. It had been a tiring day and she was weary with the driving.

At Airtel Plaza, Chief got out of the car, thanked her nicely, and went into the hotel. Coe didn't move.

" 'Bout time he left," he grumbled. "Some guys just don't know when they aren't needed."

"Oh, I didn't mind his coming along. He has such a cheerful disposition."

Coe ignored the barb. "What I think I better do is, I better give you the first lesson myself. It's the most important one, in a lot of ways. If you don't start right, you're never going to get it right."

"You're talking about my flying lesson? You don't trust Sonny Whales' man to do it right?"

"He's going to be a good instructor, all Whales' men are, but I'm better."

"I believe that."

He gave her a suspicious glance. "You don't have to, but it's true."

Rachel said sincerely, "I know. I meant it; I do believe you."

He didn't smile at the compliment, but it may have been an effort for him. "Okay. You have to work tomorrow, so we'll do it on your lunch hour. I'll have the plane ready and we'll just go right out."

Rachel sat silently behind the wheel for a moment, her arms folded across her chest. "Coe, I would like very much to have my first lesson from you, but I think instead you ought to go back to Houston tomorrow as you originally planned."

"You seem awfully anxious for me to go away."

"It's not that. I really will be sorry to see you go. It's Chief that I want in some other town. Houston will do nicely."

"Aw, what are you worrying about? Him and Deena? It's nothing. He does this kind of thing all the time."

"Deena doesn't. For that matter, let me give you notice right now, neither do I."

"Neither do you what?"

Her resolve firm, Rachel said, "I do not mess around with married men."

"Whoa! When did I say anything about messing around? Have I said one word . . ."

"Just in case you were thinking of it."

"All I did was offer you a flying lesson.

You could do that with a married man, couldn't you?"

"Well, yes, of course, but . . ."

"Tell you what. Whitey, that's my copilot, he's getting pretty peeved because he wants to go home, so I'm going to be putting him on a commercial flight tomorrow morning. If it'll make you happy, I'll put Chief on it with him. Then will you take your flying lesson?"

"Oh, yes! Thank you, Coe! But why are you sending your copilot away? Who will help you fly the plane?"

"I'm not sending him away, he's going. He's got things to do in Houston. The next thing the ship's scheduled for is a show at Brown Field, down in San Diego, so it doesn't matter if I keep it here in California for a while. Fact is, there's no particular point in flying it all the way to Wing Headquarters at Harlingen just so I can bring it back to San Diego in a week. If Whitey isn't back by the time I need him, I'll get somebody else, that's all. Now, about tomorrow, I like the Piper Tomahawk for training, so that's what we'll use."

"Where will you get it?"

"I'm renting it from Whales."

"Oh, Coe . . ." She broke off because

she didn't know what she had been going to say. There was a real airplane out there someplace, and tomorrow she would get to fly it!

He turned up in her office just before noon, wearing the yellow jumpsuit. There was a large CAF insignia painted on the back, and it stretched a little between broad shoulders. He looked taller in that suit, straighter, a man in his own element.

And grouchy as ever. "Just what I figured," he snarled, glaring down at her as she sat behind her desk. "Stockings, a skirt, tight little jacket. You think you're going to fly in that outfit? Here." He thrust a package at her.

Actually, she had a pair of chinos tucked away in her desk and had planned to change into them before she went to her lesson, but she let it ride and peeked into the package.

It was another of the yellow suits and she yanked it out, delighted. "A jumpsuit! Just like a real pilot! Really, is it for me?"

"You're going to be a real pilot, you might as well dress like one."

Rachel shook out the folds. "Do all pilots

have to wear these things? If they do, it explains why most of them are men."

"What do you mean?"

"A jumpsuit is very practical for a man, but a different story entirely for a woman."

"Don't you like it?"

"I love it, and I don't care that it's not practical. It is a thoughtful gift, Coe. Thank you very much. I'll go to the ladies and put it on; it will only take a minute, I promise."

"Don't stop to primp," he yelled after her. "You don't have to be pretty to fly, just smart!"

"No primping, I promise." But she did. After she had combed her hair and refreshed her lipstick, she transferred the essentials from her purse to her pockets. The jumpsuit had at least a dozen pockets, ample room for everything. There were even pockets on the knees, but she couldn't figure out what one might put into them.

They went onto the field but did not get into the plane right away. First he took her on a walk around it, observing and naming every part until she was wild with impatience. He pointed out the pitot tube and went on and on about its function and the difference between it and the static port.

They looked over the ailerons, the rudder, the stabilizers, the flaps. He lifted the cowl and discussed the engine.

When he finally let her get into the little ship, he spent another ten minutes going over the controls and the instruments, with explanations for each one. Then at last she had her hands on the control wheel and the engine turned over and they were speeding down the runway for takeoff.

Smoothly they lifted over the golf course and then the buildings beyond. She had flown before, of course, even flown from this airport in a small plane with Olsen, but this was different. She had her hands on the yoke; she was wearing a pilot's jumpsuit, and Coe was beside her, talking about rate of climb. She could feel the subtle movements of the wheel as he controlled the ship.

They were over Simi, almost to the desert, before he actually let her take control. He had her make gentle S-turns while he lectured on the coordination of rudder and ailerons and why she had to keep the "ball" in the turn-and-bank indicator centered. It took so much concentration, it almost wasn't fun.

Then it was time to return, and he delivered another lecture on how to figure her course so they would enter the flight pattern on the downwind leg and at the proper altitude of eight hundred feet.

"What's that going to be on the altimeter?" he demanded. Van Nuys is a thousand feet; what are you going to see on the altimeter?"

"Eighteen hundred," she replied. "The long hand on eight, the short one on one, and that squiggly thing on zero."

"It's a pointer," he growled. "And it's not squiggly."

Two gliding turns, and the runway was before them. They were too high; she knew they were coming in too high, and then the runway was in their faces, too close, and then Coe set the ship down perfectly and they were rolling to a stop.

She knew she could never get it right, all by herself; but it was all such fun, she didn't care. She could take lessons; she could take them forever if she wanted, flying around with an instructor at her side. That would be safe enough. It would even be legal.

She was late, of course. She should have been back at her desk twenty minutes ago. They walked toward the Burns building, hurrying but not too fast. He moved smoothly, long legs swinging out, his shoulders moving with them; and she imitated him. She had always wondered why pilots swaggered, and now she knew. It was the only way you could walk in a yellow jumpsuit on a bright hot day, across the tarmac of a field from which you had just made a successful flight.

He said, "I don't suppose you've got a logbook."

"Oh, no! I didn't get around to buying one yet."

"That's all right. You couldn't log this hour anyway. You don't have your student pilot license yet."

"I know, but it was a lesson . . ."

"Doesn't count. That's all right. When you go up with your regular instructor, he won't know it's not your first time and he'll think you're pretty smart." He smiled, smugly pleased to be putting something over on the unknown instructor.

"Always worthwhile to impress somebody," Rachel muttered.

"Don't forget to get over to the FAA and get the license! That's one thing I can't do for you."

Rachel smiled sarcastically. "I guess there

are a few things I'll have to do for myself. After all, you can't fly for me."

"That's true, you know." He mused for a moment and then said, "Flying is the most honest thing you'll ever do. There're no lies in the air, and no covering up your mistakes, either. You might bury a few, but you'll never cover them up."

They bounded up the steps to the porch and stood facing each other, each feeling a slight awkwardness at parting. She said vaguely, "Jewel's going to be mad because she had to answer my phone for so long."

His smile looked somehow a little fake. "Well, I sent Chief back home like you wanted, and now I don't have anybody to eat dinner with."

"I do believe that's a hint! Well, okay. Thank you for the flying lesson, Coe. If you would like to come to my house for dinner, I will cook you a steak."

His smile turned downward in satisfaction. "That sounds okay."

She stopped at Larry's on the way home and picked up some big steaks. An anachronism, Larry's, where the butchers were real human beings who stood behind a real counter and wrapped your purchase in thick butcher paper. There was always a barrel of big, baking-size potatoes at hand and another of brown onions. The people who shopped at Larry's were feeding men.

Coe liked the steak and the potato and even ate some of the salad she served with it. By the time they had stacked the dishes in the dishwasher and straightened the kitchen, the barbecue smoke had cleared from the patio and they could sit there. Rachel turned off the outside lights, so as not to encourage flying insects.

"Some folks have a light that kills them," Coe reported. "Sort of a blue thing. Bugs fly into it and zap!"

"I've seen those. They attract insects from miles around. I think they are best if you don't have one, but your neighbor does."

"I've got a little place in Harlingen and sometimes I sit outside there, but it isn't always nice in the evenings. You've got the Gulf on one side and the desert on the other."

Rachel stretched her legs comfortably. "They say that Southern California has the sweetest climate in the world. I haven't been everywhere, so I can't say; but I love this valley. We came here more than twenty years ago, but it still surprises and delights me to wake up on one of those mornings when it's going to be hot and the sky's clear. The light's sharp and the air has a tang like wine."

"Texas weather's a mite more . . . interesting." He put his arm on top of the back of her chair.

It made Rachel uneasy. He was too close. She could feel the warmth of his body, hear the small sounds of his breathing in the dark beside her. It was almost as if he might make a pass at her. She got up from the chair and suggested brightly, "Would you like to go back inside? We could play Scrabble or watch TV."

And sure enough, it was a pass. He was out of his chair and blocking her way to the patio door. "Stay here a while. The moon must be coming up; we should be able to see it soon."

There she was with her nose right up against his chest and he had an arm around her, strong and hard as a log.

"Don't you want to sit under the moon?" he continued. "See your favorite valley by moonlight and we could . . ." He bent his head and Rachel broke away from him.

"You will please stop this nonsense!" she demanded. "Sit out under the moon, indeed! Aren't we old enough to know better? Look at me! I'm sixty years old! I have gray hair and sensible shoes!"

He stood staring at her, obviously startled. "Yeah, I know. That's what I like about you."

"Really, Coe! Don't you think we're old enough to have outgrown sex?"

He put his arms down at his sides and managed a rueful chuckle. "As a matter of fact, I thought I had gotten over it years ago. I'm really surprised to find out it isn't so. You do something to me."

"Me?"

"Yeah. I never thought gray hair was sexy until I met you."

Rachel folded her arms defensively. "Well, if I gave you a wrong impression by feeding you, I apologize. It was just a friendly steak. I'm not sexy. If I ever was, that part of my life is in the past."

"In other words, I don't appeal to you?"

"Why do you have to put things like that? Nobody appeals to me. Sex doesn't appeal to me."

He rocked back on his heels and folded his arms. "I don't believe that, Rachel.

You've got passion in you. I've watched your passion to fly. You just haven't got the right situation."

"And you're just leaving. Good night, Coe."

"You've got it all wrong, Rachel. People don't outgrow sex. Right now we've just reached the ideal age for it."

"The what?"

"Exactly right. There're no financial worries; you already have a house and a car. No family pressures—you can't get pregnant; you're free. You can do whatever you want, now. Nothing to stop you. You could sleep with everybody in town if you wanted to."

"Well, I certainly do not want to, and you might give some thought to the danger of germs."

"Hell, we probably won't last long enough to develop any venereal diseases. Why not enjoy the time we have left?"

"You are totally irresponsible!"

"Nah, just horny. Come on, Rachel, this is about the only erection I've had in the last decade. Aren't you going to help me out with it?"

"That's a shocking thing for you to tell me, and somehow familiar. Back in junior high the little boys had a line that was something similar. But you're a grown man—and married, besides."

"Oh, don't worry about that. We're separated."

Rachel regarded him with sarcastically wide eyes. "And your friend Chief and his wife, are they separated, too?"

When he didn't answer, she said again, "Good night, Coe," and he left.

Seven

"Yoo-hoo! Rachel! Are you home?"

"Yes, Deena, I'm in the kitchen. Come in." Rachel suppressed a sigh, for of course she knew what Deena was going to want: news of Chief.

"I haven't seen you since Monday, and here it is Thursday already!" Deena said. "How are you?"

"Just fine. What are the children doing?" Rachel added that last mischievously. She always said it to Deena, but she knew that, this time, Deena had not come to complain about the kids.

"Oh, the usual. Lonnie's on the baseball team."

"Lonnie? That's wonderful! Just what he needs, to be part of a team, to be successful at getting onto a team. Aren't you thrilled?"

"Yeah, sure, only it would have been nice if they had given it to him earlier in the semester. There're only a couple of games left to play. He has so much practicing to do, he's even practicing on Saturday. Ethan will be away. You want to do something together? Go shopping or something?"

"I'll be tied up Saturday; that's when I scheduled my flight lessons. Why don't you take Terry shopping with you?"

Instead of answering, Deena asked, "Have you seen Coe and Chief lately?"

Rachel idly fingered the controls of the dishwasher. "Chief has gone back to Texas. He left yesterday. That's what you wanted to know, isn't it?"

"Yeah." Deena continued gamely, "Did Coe go, too?"

"Not yesterday, but he may have left since. I haven't heard from him today."

"It's better that way, I guess."

"Yes, it probably is." Rachel sat down on a kitchen stool. "Of course, I'm not in any danger; I'm too old for boyfriends and dating and sex, but you, Deena. . . . You have to be careful. Let yourself be too interested in a man, and you could find yourself involved in an affair."

"Would that be the end of the world?" Deena tossed her blonde mane. "Anyhow, it already is an affair. If you're emotionally involved with somebody, it doesn't matter what you've actually done; it's an affair. And I don't know but what it might even do my marriage some good. Lord knows that's gotten boring enough."

"That's not a reason, Deena."

"Doesn't everybody have an affair or two?" Deena demanded hotly. "Marriages are supposed to last fifty years . . . more! In all that time, couldn't there be just one little incident? One little bit of fun?"

"Absolutely not!" Rachel was definite. "Marriage means loyalty and truth. You can't have partial loyalty, partial truth, partial love."

"Easy for you to say, if you're too old to be interested in sex!"

Rachel thought a minute. "Maybe it's easy for me to say because I never was pretty like you. Men never pursued me. Maybe if I'd ever been in the situation you are . . ."

Deena grinned at her. "Aw, come on! You're saying nobody but your husband ever came on to you? Your whole life?"

Rachel thought hard. "Well . . . there was . . . maybe there was. . . . Maybe there was one or two, but I never paid them any attention."

Deena couldn't help laughing. "Oh, Rachel, I'll bet that's just exactly what you did! You didn't pay any attention. You'd be a master at that. I wish I had done it—not paid attention, I mean; but I didn't, and now it's too late. I keep wondering what it would be like, another man, somebody besides Ethan; and this could be my last chance to find out. In a couple of years I'll lose my looks—and maybe I'll lose interest, too, since you say that's what happens—and then I'll never know."

"We're of different generations. I was raised to believe that one love, one man, is all a person gets in a lifetime; but you were brought up in a different world. Deena, didn't you . . . before you were married . . ."

"Nope, never. I fell in love with Ethan and I thought that was it. Same as you. He was my man and that was the end of it. And now I'm kind of wishing I'd done more experimenting back in the days when I didn't have responsibilities. Or stretch marks."

Rachel smiled gamely. "Well, I don't know where those two bad boys are, but with any luck they are safely gone away and we won't have to deal with them ever again."

"Yeah," agreed Deena. "That would be really lucky."

On Saturday Rachel put on her yellow flight suit and reported to flight school. Her instructor was Randy, a handsome, charming boy younger than either of her sons, and he treated her like a child.

Together they went over all the same things that she had studied with Coe: The inspection of the ship, the instruments, the takeoff, the gentle S-turns. It was even the same ship that Coe had rented from Whales.

Somehow this was different from being in the comfortable company of a friend; Randy was an official instructor. Rachel was nervous and the ball of the inclinometer slipped several times on her.

"Step on the ball," he kept repeating. "Step on the ball! That means a little more rudder on the side where you see the ball, dear."

And she exploded, "Don't call me dear!"

He shaped up a little after that and gave a lucid explanation of the method for losing altitude and speed at the same time while preparing for landing. Then he brought the ship in for a perfect three-point. Showing off.

As they walked toward Whales' office, Rachel was a little ashamed of her outburst in the plane. She was opening her mouth to apologize when she spotted Coe. There he sat, slumped on a bench, wearing a ratty old leather jacket, grumpy as a hungry, skinny bear who had just wakened in his cave to find it was still snowing.

"Coe, what a surprise! I didn't expect to see you here; I thought you had gone back to Texas."

"Well, did you take your lesson?" he demanded in a tone usually reserved for a child who is trying to get out of piano practice.

Rachel didn't mind; she was getting used to his grumps. She responded sunnily, "Yes! Now I have a whole hour of flight time that Randy is going to enter in my logbook. This is Randy. He's my instructor."

"Yeah, we know each other. What's the matter, you can't write? You're supposed to make your log entries yourself; all he does is sign it."

"I'll show you how," Randy offered and

added, "Hello, Coe. Did you find that guy I suggested you call?"

"Yeah, he's going to copilot for me when I go down to Brown if he can get away for the weekend. Either way, he's going to help me with some test flights I want to make. One of the engines been acting up."

"But he's not definite for the weekend?" Rachel questioned. "What will you do if he turns out not to be available?"

"There's another CAF guy with the group up in Camarillo has the rating, and he'll drive down here and do it for me if I can't get anybody else. I'm covered."

"The logbook's no big deal," Randy was explaining. "You just fill in the little boxes—date, aircraft type, aircraft identification . . ."

He guided her through the line and put his signature at the end of it. After he was gone, Rachel still stood with the logbook open in her hand, grinning at the single entry. Her first. Her very own first logbook entry!

Coe demanded, "Well, what was it like?"

"The lesson?" She looked up at him. "Randy's okay, but he tells me everything at least twice. He must think I'm an idiot."

"He doesn't think you're an idiot. He thinks you're a woman."

Rachel laughed. "You didn't phrase that very well, but I hear what you're saying. With some of these macho types, it's the same thing. As for the lesson, it was just like the one you gave me. We went over all the same material. Maybe it isn't a good idea to take the same lesson twice. It gets a little boring!"

"Bored, huh? You're such a hotshot pilot you know all about it, you can't profit from going over the same stuff twice?"

"You told me once and he told me twice; that's three times. However, he did miss a few things you told me. The static tube, for one."

"Static port!" he corrected. "Get it right! You want some lunch?"

Rachel's forehead creased. "Coe, don't you ever get tired of being the biggest grouch in town?"

"I am? At least I'm the champion of something. What town? Here, or Houston?"

"You're grumpy enough for both. Can't you ever say anything nice?"

His tone became aggrieved. "I did say something nice. I invited you to lunch."

He had. She did remember that he had. She conceded, "Well, okay, but you have to promise to be cheerful."

"I'll grin my head off. Let's go over to Airtel. It's close by and they've got an over-priced buffet. There's big silver covers on the dishes and a bunch of dudes standing around wearing puffy white hats. You'll love it."

She said okay, but even as she did she wondered why he had picked Airtel. It was the only hotel on the airfield and therefore much used by the CAF. Lunching with a woman not his wife, it could easily happen that Coe would be spotted by someone from Texas who knew him.

Well, that was Coe. He didn't care about gossip.

After lunch they strolled toward the parking lot where they had left their cars. He stopped in the middle of a lecture on aircraft safety to ask, "When am I going to see you again?"

Rachel protested, "Coe, we're not dating!"

"Yeah, I know, but when? I've supplied a lunch, how about inviting me over to your place for a dinner?"

"After your performance last time? Not likely."

"I'll be good."

"I expect you probably are, but that's beside the point. From now on, we meet in public places. I'm not taking any more chances."

"Aw, Rachel!"

Rachel relented a little. "Well, at least, places where there's somebody else around. That might work. It's been ages since I had Deena and Ethan for dinner. If they'll come, I'll invite you to dinner. You like Deena, don't you?"

"Sure. She is a looker."

"You and your old-fashioned expressions! The word today is foxy, I think."

"Okay, foxy," he said agreeably.

"I'd love to do a dinner," was Deena's prompt reply to Rachel's suggestion. "Can we have it at my house?"

"I'm inviting you to dinner," Rachel insisted.

"Any time I go out to dinner, I still have to cook a meal for my kids," Deena explained. "It's easier to be the host."

"Well, okay, but let's share the cooking."

"Great! Bring a big green salad and something for dessert."

"You got it."

"Why are we doing this, anyway? Is there some special reason?"

Rachel smiled. "I guess you might say that. You two are my favorite dinner guests, and I need a little help with Coe."

"How's that?"

"He's been awfully nice, helping me with the flying, and I don't mind feeding him, but I don't want to be alone with him, either."

Deena gave her a searching look. "That's an interesting thing for you to say, Rachel. Veeery interesting."

"What else do we need for this dinner? Maybe some rolls? Bottle of wine?"

Coe turned up at her house just in time to carry the salad bowl through the hedge to Deena's patio, where Ethan was already fussing with the charcoal briquets.

She introduced the two men while Deena and Terry trotted in and out of the house, bearing dishes, napkins, snacks, and drinks to the outside table. Deena's patio was shaded by a spectacular Chinese elm that dropped tiny annoying leaves all over everything but made the area shady and cool. It felt good to sit back among the green shadows with a cold beer at the end of a hot day.

Coe was asking, "You lived here long?"

"Fourteen years," Ethan answered. "You live out of town, don't you?"

"Houston, mostly. I got a little place down in Harlingen, too."

"Yeah? Where's that?"

"Way down on the southern tip of Texas, almost to Mexico."

"It's easy to keep track of the years we've lived here," Deena put in, "because we moved in the year Terry was born. This is Terry. Say hello to Mr. Flaherty, dear."

Terry said, "Hi."

"That's her mama's girl, all right," said Coe with approval.

Terry's expression went sour and Rachel said to her, "That's a compliment, dear. Not very well phrased, but a compliment."

Coe growled, "Rachel don't like the way I talk."

"I didn't say that," said Rachel. "But on the other hand, I don't think you're in any danger of being drafted into the diplomatic corps."

"I've got a boy, too, Lonnie, but he isn't here right now," Ethan said. "Probably at baseball practice."

Deena corrected him. "As a matter of fact, when I told him he had to put on some clean clothes for dinner, he suddenly remembered that he was eating at a friend's house. I guess Gordon's mom doesn't care what they wear to the table."

"Plays baseball, does he?" said Coe. "Maybe you're raising a Dodger. They sure could use somebody knows how to hit."

They fell to talking baseball, somewhat to Rachel's relief. The marinated roast was put on the coals and smoked abominably. The women went into the kitchen and busied themselves with the side dishes.

Terry asked, "Auntie Rachel, are you really taking lessons to fly an airplane?"

Rachel said, "Sure. Coe Flaherty's helping me with it."

Deena asked a little impatiently, "But what are you going to *do* with it?"

Rachel shrugged, only a little guiltily. "Probably nothing. You have to understand. . . . It isn't a goal; it's a process. Knowing how to do something that exacting and important makes me feel important. I'm somebody. I'm a pilot!"

"I can see it," Deena admitted. "I can see the change in you, but that doesn't mean I understand it."

"Well, I think it's boss," opined Terry. "Auntie Rachel is really bad now!"

Rachel laughed and gave her a hug. "I hear what you're saying, but that doesn't mean I understand it!"

Terry returned the hug but grumbled, almost under her breath, "Yeah, it's bad, but does a person have to be a hundred years old to cut loose?"

With an exaggerated frown Rachel replied, "Uh-huh."

Ethan called from the patio, "Deena! Bring the platter!"

The roast was carved and the meal served. They sat around the table until it grew dark and Deena brought candles.

Coe asked her, "How's your business been? You feeling the tough times here?"

"Some," she admitted, "but the temp business is practically immune to economic swings. When times are good, the companies need more people, so they hire temps. When times are bad, they cut staff and hire temps. I'll ride out the recession."

"My business is way down," said Ethan. "I've had to expand my territory. I'll take a job anywhere, now. Lately I've had more business in Nevada than I can get in my own town."

"What is it you do?"

"I'm a contractor for commercial installations. I guess you'd say I'm basically a plumber. What's your business?"

"I'm retired from an airplane factory," answered Coe.

"And you live in Houston now?"

"Pretty much always have. I like it there."

Deena laughed a little. "How does that song go? It's barbaric but, what the hell, it's home?"

Coe laughed, too. "Come on, it isn't that bad. We've got a symphony, a university, even theatre. Not like here, of course, but all the shows go to Houston when they're on tour."

"Are you into classical music?" Rachel inquired.

"Not much, but I like to see a show."

"It would be a shame if you didn't get to see one before you left town," said Rachel.

He raised an eyebrow at her but didn't offer her a show.

They made the guys help with the dishes, and everybody laughed a lot. In all, it was a successful evening.

* * *

"Mother, you're going to *what?*" Her daughter's telephoned voice was fraught.

Rachel answered calmly, "Fly, dear. F.L.Y. I'm taking flying lessons."

"What do you mean? Is it some kind of a computer simulation? Like a Nintendo game?"

"No, dear, it's a real airplane and I'm really going to fly it. I've already had two lessons, only one doesn't count."

"What?"

"Never mind. I've always wanted to take flying lessons; and it just came to me one day that all I had to do was sign up and write a check, so I did."

"But it's dangerous!" Barbara protested. "Airplanes are falling out of the sky all the time! I'm going to worry about you!"

"Barbara, darling, do you remember the motorcycle you used to ride when you were in high school? The karate class you signed up for? I worried about you then, but I tried not to nag you about it. I hope you will have the same courtesy, now that things are reversed."

"But flying. . . . Mom, what do you need it for?"

"I'm having a glorious time, Barbara."

She had calmed her daughter down by the time they hung up the phone, although she couldn't get her to be happy about the flying. Nor could Rachel explain what was so glorious. Why it mattered so much to her to learn to guide a plane into a perfect flight.

And why it was so important to prove to a certain stubborn old man that she could do it.

But she was proud of herself because, even in the heat of argument, she had remembered not to throw it up to her daughter that she, Barbara, was doing the most dangerous thing of all, insisting on having a third child when the doctors had all warned her against it. Barbara's second delivery had been difficult and yet she was doing it all over again, the new child growing in her belly even as she and Rachel talked.

This time Coe was waiting by her car, leaning, in a proprietary sort of way, on the front fender. Well, the Burns parking lot wasn't all that big and never had a lot of cars in it. Her Cadillac wouldn't have been very hard to find.

Rachel exclaimed, "Coe! What are you doing here?"

He asked, "Isn't tonight when you have your first class of ground school? Well, I want to see this guy who's going to teach it and what he plans to teach. There's no point in your learning a bunch of stuff that won't do you any good. Is he even a flyer?"

Rachel pursed her lips to smother a smile. "It's kind of you to be concerned, but I should think the college knows what it is doing."

"That's what doesn't sound right to me. What do they know about flying in a college? I'll ride along with you. Won't hurt anything for me to sit in."

Rachel continued to purse. "It's possible they won't let you do that. If you must come along, why don't you drive your own car, so you won't have to wait around for me if you can't get into the class? It's going to last three hours."

"They're going to let me. Come on, open the door."

Rachel unlocked the car door; they got in and turned on the air conditioner. "It's an hour and a half until the class begins,"

Rachel said. "I was planning to pick up a sandwich."

"The hamburger stand will do fine. I want to get there a little early."

"Hamburgers?" said Rachel. "Maybe we could find a nice salad or something."

"This is faster, and it's right there. That red place on the right."

Rachel turned into the parking area for the hamburger stand. They had their hamburgers and went to the college.

The ground school class was held in a bungalow on the outskirts of the campus. The building was a casualty of endless budget cuts—paint peeling, blinds broken, the air conditioner inoperative. This last was probably fortunate, for when they worked, the machines were so noisy nobody could talk over them.

Providing the legally-mandated handicap access had made it necessary to build a ramp and a long cement porch along the side of the building, a far more pleasant spot than the steaming interior of the bungalow, and that was where Rachel found the group of students, hanging around out there as long as possible before it was time to begin the class.

She noted at once that she was not the

only older person taking the class. Most of the students were young, of course; and this particular bunch could have come from Central Casting—slender, model-lovely young girls; lifeguard-handsome boys. But there were three or four older men, all looking prosperous enough to afford the price of a recreational airplane. The youngsters, Rachel surmised, might be their children or the children of men just like them.

Everybody was already clustered around the instructor, demanding his assessment of the newest models in the air. Coe joined the discussion and before the class began he not only had permission to audit it, he and the instructor were fast friends.

The instructor was named O'Hara, and he kept deferring to Coe throughout the class that followed. "What's your opinion on that, Colonel?" he would inquire. "Do you want to answer that question, Colonel?"

Some of the questions were so technical only a working pilot could have answered them, and a few were just plain dumb. Coe fielded everything with the air of an elder statesman. Rachel even got to wondering if he had made it clear that his title of Colonel was not from the Air Force.

O'Hara passed out a package of books. He

had brought them in on a wheeled dolly, and Rachel wished she had one for carrying hers out. There was a workbook, a text, a practice map, and a big thick tome that held all the Federal Aviation Regulations. FAR's. Rachel was already learning to talk like a pilot, that is, in monograms and acronyms. FAR's, VFR's, ARSA, NOTAM's . . .

When the class broke up, Coe tucked her books under his arm and they strolled toward the parking lot. Rachel remarked, "It's been a while since a boy carried my books. I'm glad you're here for that load!"

"You don't have to carry this FAR book around," he explained. "You don't even have to read it, except the part that pertains to private pilots. It's just a reference book."

"That's a comfort."

"I'll carry them for you anyway, next week, if you want."

"You're coming to the class again next week?"

A smug grin lightened his craggy face. "Have to. I'm going to teach it."

"What?"

"Why do you suppose that O'Hara was so friendly to me? It wasn't my personal charm; he's in a bind. Something about Greek dancing."

"What?"

"They sent him the wrong schedule. I told you these college people don't know what they're doing. He set up his appointments and so forth according to the calendar they sent him, and when he got here, he found out they'd given him all the dates and the place for a class in Greek dancing and the ones for the course he's really supposed to teach were different. He's got a commitment he can't get out of next Monday and needs somebody to teach that class for him."

He intended to make her laugh, and she did. "And you walked right into it! You've been suckered!"

"Uh-huh."

"Are you experienced as a teacher?"

"The subject's navigation and you don't have to be a teacher to teach that; you just have to know navigation, and I do. I'm hungry. That hamburger we ate was about big enough for an appetizer. Let's go someplace and get some food."

"It's after ten o'clock. There won't be any restaurants open this late."

"Sure there will. Any place that's got a bar. Just drive along the Boulevard. There's sure to be something."

He not only found a bar, it was a country-western bar with barbecue sauce on all the food and a band playing noisily. They ate ribs and danced until after midnight.

Eight

Deena did knock, but the door was unlocked, so she came right in. It was like a sitcom, where the neighbors always walk in. Why shouldn't they? It's only a door in a set.

Well, she wasn't in a TV sitcom, but Rachel was grateful that she did not need to get up from her seat at the breakfast table and the cup of black coffee before her. She was still in her robe, and her gray hair stood up in tufts above a gray face.

She glanced up briefly and muttered, "Hello, Deena."

Deena was dressed for the office, the shoulders of her suit padded square, her hair combed into a smooth blonde fall. "Rachel, I've been trying and trying to get you. Did you get the message I left on your answering machine?"

"Answering machine," mumbled Rachel.

"I don't think I checked it. I got in a little late last night."

"A little late! I stopped trying to phone you at eleven!"

Rachel dropped her head into her hands. "I can't believe it! I closed a bar! At my age! Do you think, if I should get up the courage to drink that cup of coffee, it would help the headache or would it only upset my stomach more?"

Deena smothered a giggle. "Rachel, you? You and Coe? Drinking at a bar until closing?"

"I had one glass of wine. I don't think it was the drink so much as the dancing and the barbecue sauce. I'm too old for hot foods and the boot-scooting boogie." She shuddered. "And the electric slide."

Deena slipped into the chair opposite her. "So! You two are dating!"

"No, no, it's not that, really. He's going to be teaching part of the ground-school course I'm taking, and we just drove over there together."

"Teacher's pet, teacher's pet!" chortled Deena. "Ground school doesn't seem to be the only thing he's teaching you!"

"Cut it out, Deena. I'm very fragile this morning. There's nothing between us; I just can't digest that much barbecue sauce anymore. Coe is a good friend to me and I do like him, even if he is a charter member of the Grouch Club."

"Is that a branch of the CAF?"

"Not that I know of. It was a radio show, back in the forties. Mel Blanc."

"Well, the good news is, you don't have to go to work today. Your job's over."

Rachel started. "What? What happened? Did I do something wrong?"

"No, no, no. The woman you were replacing came back from sick leave, that's all."

"I didn't know she was going to do that! Why didn't somebody warn me? I'll have to get over there and show her where things are. There's a new price schedule for some of the services that she won't know about."

"Easy, easy! She'll figure it out. This is the way it's always done."

"It is? Why? It's so. . . . It's inhumane!"

"It has to be like this. There are people who would slough off if they knew the job was about to end. They've even been known to set traps for whoever follows them. I had one punch a virus into the computer and when the regular employee came back and booted up, it erased all its own memory!"

Rachel dropped her head again, leaning over the coffee. "You know I wouldn't do anything like that. I don't even know any virii."

"Look, Rachel, now don't get down and depressed again. I'll find you another job right away. I can send you out today." Deena broke off, regarding the dark circles under Rachel's eyes. "Well, maybe today wouldn't be so good. Tomorrow."

Rachel straightened up. The surge of adrenaline caused by Deena's news had done her good and the headache was subsiding. "No, don't do that. I'm going to be busy."

"Rachel . . ."

"I'm going to step up my flight lessons. I'll take one every day if I can arrange it, or two! I'll get my hours in and if I really work at it, I can solo in a couple of weeks!"

"You ought to keep working. You were so down the last time, I was worried about you. You can still do your fun things, like the flying. You were fitting it all in before."

"I was down because I didn't have anything to do. I've learned something already, Deena. You can't wait for somebody to come along and give you an occupation; you have to go get it for yourself. I'm not dependent on a paying job for my living, and I'm not dependent on it for my sense of worth, not anymore. Getting depressed isn't going to happen to me again."

"Well, that's okay, but do you think it's right for you to use up the savings you and Pete worked all your lives for? What about your children's inheritance?"

"It's in no danger; and if it were, so what? They're all doing well. The rest of us all got along without inheriting anything; they can, too."

Deena smiled, but with a question mark in her expression. "You're sure about all this?"

"Sure I'm sure. Don't get me any more jobs. When I'm ready, I'll tell you. And for right now, I'm sure I'm going back to bed."

Later on in the day she telephoned Sonny Whales' office to set up her new schedule. Randy was not available to teach her every day, a development that did not entirely displease Rachel. She would have another instructor, and the first lesson was arranged for the following morning.

As she was leaving her house for the lesson, Coe drove up. Rachel went down the driveway to meet him at the curb. There he sat, the grump behind the wheel, chin thrust out and mouth turned down. She longed to make him smile. She knew she could: A few words, a pointless joke, and the frown would clear away; he would chuckle and be the Coe she wanted to be with.

But why did she always have to be the one who was sunny and sweet? She said coolly, "Hello, Coe. Was there something you wanted? I'm just about to leave for the airport. I have a flight lesson."

"I know," he replied. "I didn't want you to forget your appointment, so I came to drive you over."

"I can drive myself," she began, but he was already there and he was stubborn. She knew that if she drove off in her own car he would only follow. Rachel trotted around the car and got into the passenger seat.

"This is really nice of you, but how did you know about my lesson time? Does my new instructor report to you, like Randy did?"

"Nah, they don't report to me. I just called the office and asked them."

It wasn't funny but it made her laugh, and suddenly they were laughing together and it was a beautiful morning and it was a splendid thing just to be.

And just to be with Coe.

The new instructor was Eleanor, and she was much stiffer and tougher than Randy had ever been. Rachel approved of that. You don't fly any planes by being nice to them. It was a grueling two hours aloft, but she did well and came down exhilarated, thrilled with her own progress.

Coe was waiting patiently to drive her home again. Over the lunch that somehow followed, she admitted to difficulty with her assignment for ground school and he volunteered to help her with it. He spent the afternoon in her living room, lecturing on the venturi effect.

He explained, "A venturi is a tube that is narrower in the center than it is at the ends. A liquid flowing through the tube flows faster in the narrow part, and that's the principle of the airfoil. An aircraft is not pushed up by the air under it, but pulled up by the vacuum created by the venturi effect over the top of the wing."

"Why does the liquid flow faster in the narrow part of the tube?" Rachel demanded.

"Because it's the same volume in a smaller space."

"No, it's not. A liquid can't compress, so there is a smaller volume in the narrow part. Why doesn't it just flow the same?"

"It's being pushed by the liquid around it."

"But air isn't in a tube, so nothing's pushing it until the airfoil comes along."

He glowered at her, shaggy eyebrows almost covering his eyes. "You see all those airplanes up there, flying around, don't you? It works. Take my word for it, woman, it works!"

Rachel sighed. "I guess it's like geometry. Some things you just have to believe. Maybe we ought to drop this one and get to the navigation. That's what you're going to be teaching on Monday, and it's a whole new world to me."

"Maybe we had better," he agreed. "Everybody knows you're my special student, so you gotta look good. I'm going to be out of town the next couple of days, so I'll only be able to help you today."

"Let's get to it, then."

They studied until well into the evening. So they would not have to interrupt their work, Rachel cooked dinner.

She didn't put barbecue sauce on anything.

* * *

"Okay," said Eleanor, "today you're going to do it all. Is the ship ready for takeoff?"

"It must be; you only landed it ten minutes ago."

"Check it anyway."

Rachel checked the gas, checked the oil, made a visual inspection of the ship.

"What about the load?" Eleanor asked.

"No problem. Neither of us weighs much more than a hundred pounds."

"Suppose I weighed two-fifty?"

"Well, I'd make sure you sat in a front seat."

"Suppose I weighed two-fifty and had a fifty-pound suitcase?"

"I'd load it on one side and you on the other. On a really hot day like this, I might make you leave it behind."

Eleanor nodded, a compliment from her. She could not have been much more than thirty, but she cultivated a schoolteacher's no-nonsense attitude. She was a pretty girl, or would have been without her perpetual sunburn and a disreputable hat she always wore pulled down over unruly reddish hair.

Rachel got into the left-hand seat. Eleanor always put her students there, theorizing that it was the position from which they would eventually fly and, besides, most folks are used to sitting in that position while driving a car. Eleanor settled herself on the right, saying, "Now, I'm not the CFI, I'm only a passenger and this is the first flight of the day. Check the NWS and see if it's VFR before you call the ATC."

Rachel did. Following the instructions of her Certified Flight Instructor, she checked the National Weather Service, who said that the area was clear enough for visual flight rules. She started the engine and was ready to taxi before she contacted Air Traffic Control.

And she was really too busy to ask herself if she were ever again going to be able to make herself understood to ordinary people.

They flew over Simi and Santa Clarita, practicing climbs and glides, then returned to Van Nuys and shot landings. It all went so smoothly that Eleanor actually complimented her.

"You stick to the path," she said in her growly voice. "A lot of people see all that sky up there and think they can just fly anywhere.

"That's what's so interesting about it,"

said Rachel. "The logic of flight. Every flight has one correct flight path and it's the most direct route at the correct height in the designated air space. It's as definite as a superhighway and it's up to the pilot to know where it is and stay on it."

"You've got the right attitude and with these daily sessions you're progressing. A couple more, and you're going to solo."

Rachel felt good as she drove herself home again, strong and tall. And a little pleased to have an evening to herself, to be alone. She would get a lot of studying done. She would cook a favorite meal, lamb stew with artichokes. It was one of those things that improves with rewarming and so she would have a meal the next day, too.

When the stew was bubbling on the stove, she settled down with her book. Categories of aircraft certification . . .

She had been working an hour or so when the bell rang and she opened the door to find Chief on her doorstep, wearing his suit, cleaned up as if for a date.

He cried, "Rachel! Lovely as ever!"

The only thing she could think of to say was, "I thought you were in Houston."

"I couldn't stay away!"

"Er, ah. . . . Come in, Chief." Rachel

held open the door. What was she expected to do now? Silly question; she knew what he wanted from her.

What she would like to do, she reflected, was fire him out of a cannon, preferably one powerful enough to send him all the way back to Texas. But even while she was thinking it, hostess habits were taking over and she was showing him to a chair, offering him a drink.

Luckily, she had thought to pick up a bottle of Jack Daniels at the supermarket. It was not something she would usually have on hand. She didn't drink it, and her sons preferred beer or an occasional Scotch. Barbara, the perfect mother, never drank at all.

Well, what the heck. She had paid for it; she might as well sample it. She poured two drinks, put ice into hers, and returned to the living room.

"You missed Coe," she said as she handed Chief his drink. "He was here last night, but he's out of town today."

"Yeah, I know. Every Thursday and Friday. It's his air ambulance thing."

"His what?"

He twinkled at her and took a sip from his glass. "You didn't know about that?

There's this bunch of doctors who go down to Mexico and take care of folks there, and sometimes they bring somebody back to Houston for special treatment. Coe flies them all in this ship he has. He's been doing it for years."

"He's been flying all the way to Houston every week so he can jump into an airplane and fly to Mexico and then fly back the next day to Houston?"

"That's Coe for you."

Rachel thought it over. "But then, when he's in Houston, he can be with his family."

Chief raised an eyebrow and sipped again. "Oh ho, going to pump me for all of his info, are you? You want to know about his wife? He doesn't see her. They really are separated."

"I didn't mean . . ." Rachel stopped herself. She *had* meant to find out about Coe's wife, and it was dishonest to say she had not. She finished lamely, "I didn't know that."

"They have been for years. Something sure smells good in here."

"I had almost forgotten. I made a lamb stew and left it simmering while I was studying. I hope it didn't get overcooked."

He smiled that charming smile. "It smells just right."

Rachel raised an eyebrow at him. "For dinner I'm planning to serve very well-cooked lamb stew accompanied by supermarket bread and lettuce wedges. Would you care to join me in my frugal meal?"

"Thank you, Rachel, I would like that very much."

"Would you really? Most men don't like lamb."

"You know me. I'm different."

"Yeah, I know." She took a sip of her drink and found it remarkably smooth. "Don't think you're fooling me; you're here because you thought Deena might be here."

"Of course you're right, Rachel, but this is very pleasant–nice drink and a good dinner . . ."

She served wine with the meal, but he returned to the whiskey as soon as he had polished off the stew. He was turning on the charm the whole time, telling her stories that made her laugh and carefully not mentioning Deena; but she knew it was Deena he wanted to talk about.

She poured herself an extra wine to fortify her resolve and began. "You know, Deena and I are not Siamese twins. We're only neighbors. She isn't here all the time. Sometimes weeks go by that I don't see her."

He leaned forward eagerly. "You could ask her to come over."

"No, I couldn't."

"Aw, come on, Rachel, I need to talk to her. Just call her up; ask her over for a while. You could do that for me, couldn't you?"

"No, I couldn't, and there's a name for a person who would. Please understand me, Chief. I believe in marriage. I believe in fidelity. You're a danger to Deena, to her marriage, to her family. A danger to her children. I don't want to see you around her, and there's no way I'm going to help you two get together."

"But you're our only link!"

"Then you just lost your only link."

He squirmed guiltily in his chair. "Rachel, I know how this must seem to you. I probably look like nothing but a tomcat sniffing around, but it isn't like that. Deena is special. This whole situation is very painful to me. Not to be able to approach her in any honest way. . . . Well, it hurts."

Rachel went right on glowering. "You

must be used to it. I get the impression this isn't the first time you've been hurt that way."

"Well, maybe that's so. I have a hard time resisting the ladies—I guess that's common knowledge—but Deena's different. She's got something. . . . I don't know. The way I feel about her . . ."

Rachel nodded sagely. "Yeah, I've got the picture. They're all special."

He gave her a feeble smile. "You know something? That's right. They really are special, all of them, probably a lot more special to me than I am to them."

"Don't go putting yourself down."

He shifted forward, resting strong arms on his knees, an earnest expression on his face. "They've got their own agenda; don't you think they don't. Pretty ones are the easiest—do you know why that is? They figure life owes them something, they deserve some fun. You take a homely girl; now she's likely to be loyal, trustworthy, true, and honest—all those character things. A pretty girl uses her looks; she doesn't have to develop character. She'll do it. She'll do it because just one guy loving and appreciating her isn't enough, not for a whole lifetime."

He was close to analyzing Deena's restlessness, close enough to make her uneasy, and so she denied it. "You're not talking about Deena. Deena isn't just some pretty girl, and she doesn't deserve to be another notch on your bedpost."

"I don't want that either. I just want to love her. I can't help loving her."

"If you really do love her, you'll do what's best for her and that is you'll leave her alone."

Chief rose, feeling about for the jacket he had taken off before dinner. "I'd better go."

Thank God, thought Rachel. At last she was going to be able to stop arguing and go to bed. Her eyes were blurry. Next time she would know better than to drink hard liquor before dinner.

She was, she knew, a trifle drunk. She looked at Chief; and he was more than a trifle drunk, standing there with his wrinkled white shirt drooping over his belt while he tried, with repeated failures, to ascertain which end of his jacket was up. His eyes, too, were barely open. He had taken two drinks before dinner, wine with the meal, and how many after? She should have paid more attention.

"Hold it!" It was almost a shout. "You're not going out there and drive a car! Do you know how much we've drunk?"

He bowed mockingly and a little unsteadily. "My dear lady, I am far too much of a gentleman to count your drinks."

"I don't need to count yours; you've had too much. You're going to sleep here tonight."

"Why Rachel, are you coming on to me at last?"

"Drunk as you are, it wouldn't do me a bit of good if I were," she growled. "The guest room is to the right at the head of the stairs, and that's where you're sleeping if you can manage to stagger that far. Now get yourself up there before you fall down!"

"Who could refuse such gracious hospitality?"

He did get himself into the guest room, and she never heard another sound from him. She could only hope he had found the bed before he passed out.

When she woke the next morning, he was gone. She was startled at first and then glad. How strange, at her age, to be grateful to a man for having the consideration, and the skills, to make certain his car would not be seen parked in front of her house all night.

Nine

"I'm in Cudahy," Ethan explained, and she knew right away he was going to ask a favor. Deena's husband was not in the habit of phoning her from outlying areas just to say hello. She rapped manicured nails on the desk top. Drat the man. Right in the middle of a typically hectic day, the demands of his business were going to take precedence over the needs of hers.

"I've written a check for some equipment," he went on, "and it cost more than I thought it was going to. Will you see to it I'm covered in my business account?"

"Yeah, okay, what's the amount?" She scribbled on a pad by the phone. "It's all right; I'm probably going to have to send somebody to the bank today anyway."

"Deena, this can't wait. They're going to be phoning the bank for verification, so the transfer has to be made right away. Do it yourself and be sure to tell the bank manager to expect the call."

"You mean right now? Ethan, I've got a business to run here, too!"

"It'll only take you a few minutes, and otherwise I'll have to drive all the way to Canoga Park to do it and that'll eat up the rest of the day for me."

Of course he was right. She was a couple of blocks from the bank; he was forty miles away. But why hadn't he taken care of this before he left home? Or why hadn't he made prior arrangements with the bank, like any other business would do?

No point in asking him now. It was like those questions you ask the kids: Why didn't you take your lunch box with you this morning? Why didn't you tell me before about the teacher conference? There could be no answer, certainly none that was satisfactory.

She wrote down the details and, as soon as she had hung up, rose from her desk and collected her purse. It was almost noon; if she delayed until the gotta-do-this-on-the-lunch-hour-or-else crowd hit the bank she would lose a half hour.

She deliberately kept brief her instructions to the assistant who would mind the office while she was gone. If she tried to tell everything, she would never get out the door at all. Deena wafted a few generalities at the poor girl and rushed downstairs to her car.

As she turned into the bank's parking lot, she noticed a stretch limousine following her. She watched it creep carefully up the ramp and sniffed to herself. How rich can you get, to need a chauffeur to take you to the bank? Deena parked her own car and hurried inside to do her business. Or, more accurately, Ethan's business.

When she came out the door again, she was thinking about things that needed her attention at her office, her forehead creased with concentration, and she was somewhat annoyed to find the same limousine blocking her path, parked athwart all three of the handicapped spaces. It was one of those elongated, slick limos with dark, impenetrable windows. She was about to walk around it when the back door opened and Chief stepped out. With a bow, he handed her a single, long-stemmed red rose.

Deena was jolted right out of her concentration. About the last thing she had expected in the middle of a busy business day was a rose and a smouldering smile from anybody, especially that handsome rascal Chief, whom she had thought to be in Houston.

But there he was, in his best suit, and that smile. . . . She just stood there, beginning slowly to smile back, losing her way in those dark brown eyes. He took her elbow and said, "Get in," and she did.

She didn't know exactly why she was getting into the limo; she was leaving her own car in the bank's lot, leaving her work undone at the office, her people expecting her return; but it all seemed far away and unimportant as she sank into the cushions of the back seat.

Chief slammed the door and the limo moved smoothly away. The seats were soft, the floor deep with carpet, the driver nothing but a cap and the back of a robotic neck. On a shelf strewn with more red roses sat an ice bucket with a champagne bottle in it, half-wrapped in a napkin.

He said, "Hello, Deena."

"Chief, what are we doing?"

"I'm taking you to lunch. It's almost noon. You have to eat lunch, don't you?"

"In a limo? Usually I have a hot dog sent up to the office from the stand on the corner."

"You deserve a break for once. Sit back and let somebody else take over."

"But I should go right back to the office. They'll miss me! They'll think I've been mugged!"

He grinned and shook his head. "This isn't a mugging; it's a kidnapping. You've got no choice, so just enjoy yourself. We're going to a perfect, peaceful spot where nobody can bother us; or anyhow, that's what this guy tells me."

"Just for lunch," Deena said. "Well, okay, why not?"

He lifted the napkin from the bottle. "Champagne?"

"In the middle of a work day?" Deena protested, but Chief was pushing the cork out of the bottle. It popped and foamed a little, making him jump to save his pants; and she laughed and said, "Well, okay, one glass."

He poured the wine into tulip-shaped glasses, and they sat back to watch the Valley move past their one-way windows. The tulip shape of the champagne glass had obviously been invented for convenience in the backseat of a limo; as long as you held it in your hand, there was no way it could spill.

"This is a hoot!" Deena exclaimed. "Look at all those poor slobs out there in the heat, rushing back to work! We're in here and nobody can see us or catch us drinking champagne, on account of those one-way windows! Chief, what are you doing in L.A.? I thought you'd gone home."

He was still grinning. "I came back to see you."

"In a limo?"

"Well, I can't go to your home; I can't even call you there, and I couldn't get your neighbor to cooperate. You don't like me to call you at your office; about the only thing left was to ambush you around lunch time."

"With a limo?"

"I thought you might like it. Anyhow, this guy knows the town and he says he knows a good place for a picnic."

Deena stirred restlessly. "I don't have time for a picnic. I should be back in the office."

"Come on, enjoy yourself for a few minutes. The office will wait."

"A magic carpet with driver," sighed Deena. "I've left everything behind—office, family. . . . You shouldn't do these things."

"I know. I just like to see you smiling

and not worried about anything. You're sure pretty when you're smiling. You're always pretty, but I like it best when you're smiling."

"And you're a rascal." They were turning onto Mulholland Drive, a famous make-out place at night; but daytime was for families, for tourist sightseers. She felt secure, as safe as if she were showing the sights to a visiting auntie.

Chief sat beside her, warm and friendly. He was so close she could feel the warmth of his body, sense the masculine smell of him, but he had his hands in his lap and never touched her.

It was considerate, she thought, but she could feel that touch he had not given her, feel where he might have put his hands. Her breathing was constricted, her breasts heavy, crowding a bra that had never been uncomfortable before.

She murmured, "Don't you have a job to go to?"

He replied, "Yeah, but they can get along without me for a couple of days. I told them I had a fever. It wasn't much of a lie. What I've got is sort of like a fever." He grinned down at the object of his heat.

"Fever." She giggled; and even while she

laughed, she knew she should have been asking instead about his family. But she didn't. She refused to think about any of it, about Chief's wife and children, about her own family. She was lost in the moment. Blissfully lost.

It was, after all, just a moment. A half hour snatched from her work day, from her real life, traveling up Mulholland with a champagne glass in her hand, laughing over nothing and enjoying the heady knowledge that she shouldn't be doing it but she was.

The place the driver had chosen for the picnic was only a turnout, a wide place for a view of the Valley, but he found a spot shaded by trees and there was a gentle breeze blowing at this altitude that was not felt in the sheltered Valley. He spread a cloth and put down a basket and the ice bucket that held the champagne bottle, and then he modestly disappeared.

Chief opened the basket, and it was full of dainty little treats: crackers and pate, morsels of cheese with olives, thin slices of smoked chicken, fruit, and tiny cookies dipped in chocolate.

Of course you can't eat that sort of thing without washing it down with more champagne. Deena enjoyed the meal until the sun was slanting down over the Valley. The bottle lay dead on the cloth and she was leaning on Chief's shoulder while they sang a song they both remembered from childhood summer camps. Late-afternoon traffic roared and honked on Mulholland. The air magically cleared, as it sometimes does late in the day, and the city below sparkled in the sun's long rays.

He asked, "Did you ever go on picnics when you were a kid?"

"Only at the beach. Did you?"

"Well, we lived kind of far from the beach."

"I mean, did you have picnics?"

He shifted a little, folding his legs. "Oh, sure, folks are always having picnics and barbecues where I grew up. Mostly because in Texas everybody's got so many relatives that you pretty much have to feed them outside; there wouldn't be room in the house."

"What did you eat?"

"Well, barbecue, if we could get it, or fried chicken and potato salad. What did you eat?"

"It sounds like the menu is pretty universal. We always got ice cream. Mother had a cooler that was cold enough for ice cream, and she always took it on picnics. Ice cream is great at the beach. It's the only thing you can eat fast enough so no sand gets in it."

"Sometimes we used to have ice cream in the freezer locker . . ."

Deena lifted her head and moved a little away from him. "We have to go back. I have to get back to the office."

"Okay," he agreed readily and stood up. "I'll whistle up our driver and he can pack these things back in the basket."

"You know, Chief, I have to tell you how much I appreciate the way you are. . . . Well, you are such a gentleman."

"It isn't because I want to be, you know." His eyes were dark and earnest, looking into hers. They stood staring, the packing up forgotten, the office, the whole world—just the two of them on a hilltop.

She whispered, "What we want, and what we can have, aren't always the same thing."

"Yeah, I know. I know I'm wanting something that's not mine, something beautiful and rare and warm. When I'm trying to go to sleep at night I see your face, dream about seeing that blonde hair spread out on the pillow beside me . . ." He broke off, turned, and suddenly let loose an ear-splitting whistle.

Sure enough, the driver appeared at once and started gathering up the picnic basket and cloth. Chief ushered her to the limo and handed her in.

"Here comes trouble," Deena told herself. All the way back to Warner Center in the backseat behind those opaque windows. . . . She was in for a fight.

The driver got into the car, started it up, and worked his way back onto Mulholland. And there Chief sat, saying nothing, watching her with an expression that seemed almighty pleased—and maybe amused.

She asked, a little desperately, "What's your favorite kind of ice cream?"

"Any kind you've got," he replied and hitched a few inches closer to her. "Now, you, Deena, you're sweeter than cream and you've got the most beautiful skin. Just looking at it gets me hot; just *thinking* about it gets me hot. I can be thousands of miles away from you and I think about. . . . do you know what I think about?"

"Please don't, Chief. Please don't tell me."

"I think about seeing you naked, about taking off your clothes and feeling that skin, all your beautiful skin. Or maybe you're taking off your clothes. You're taking them off for me, one by one, slowly, to tease me. You're taking off your bra, unhooking it, leaning forward a little. Your breasts are beautiful. The lights are on; you'd let me have the lights on so I can see you, wouldn't you, Deena? Deena, my beautiful darling, you'd let me see you, let me watch you. You're taking off your panties, pulling them down your legs . . ."

"Chief . . ." She could feel his eyes on her, touching her like a beam of light, knowing her body although his hands were nowhere near her; his fingers were curled over the edge of the limo's plush seat, clutching it as if to provide an anchor. But how could she ask him not to look at her? It sounded so silly.

His voice was low and deep; it rumbled through her. "I dream we're together. We're both naked; I'm caressing you, gently, softly. You're beautiful and hot and moist under my fingers because you want me, Deena; you would want me, wouldn't you? You'd open your legs, spread those beautiful legs for me . . ."

She was pinned down, pressed against the car seat by his voice, by the heaviness of her body. Her breath came in gasps; she thought if he did not touch her, if he didn't stroke her breasts, she was going to scream.

She managed to whisper, "You mustn't, Chief . . ."

"Mustn't think you're beautiful? I can't help that, anymore than I can help dreaming about you, wanting that beautiful body." He showed her his empty hands. "I want to have it in my hands, to feel you respond to me. I don't even care about my own satisfaction, I'd make you come first. I'd make you come in my hands so I could watch the expression on your beautiful face when you did. You would—I know you would, Deena—you're a passionate woman; you'd respond."

Would? She already was responding, her body heavy and hot. He made her want to rip off her own clothes, to pull him to her, to make him do the things he was describing.

The limo was turning onto DeSoto, the familiar wall of oleander on the river bank warning her she was almost back to her workplace. "You clever bastard," she muttered. "You know what you're doing to me."

"You're doing it to me," he defended quaintly.

"Well, cut it out. We're almost back in Warner Center. I've got to go to the office and I don't even know if I can walk."

"I know I can't." He closed the tiny space between them, and his clothes brushed lightly against hers. No closer, but so close she could feel his warmth, hear his ragged breath as he spoke. "Give me a night, Deena. Just a night. One night I'll remember all my life, one night for everything we might have had together; it's as close as we'll ever come."

"I can't! How could I? I have to be at home at night. The family. . . . The only time I'm not with my family is when I'm at work."

"An afternoon; you could make an afternoon. Just a few hours . . . tomorrow."

"I can't, I can't! I've already messed up the whole office schedule, and we're shorthanded anyway. I can't tomorrow."

"I'm at the Pines Motel in Van Nuys. Noon tomorrow. I'll be waiting for you. Number seven."

"Tomorrow is Saturday. Saturday isn't even a work day!"

"Lots of people work on Saturday. Park

your car in the lot behind the building. Nobody will ever know."

The limo had stopped; she recognized the familiar parking lot of her bank. Desperately she threw open the door and jumped out.

"Goodbye, Chief. I won't come tomorrow. Don't be in town tomorrow. Go back to Texas, please; don't wait for me. Please don't call me." She raced to her own car, fumbling in her purse for the keys. Her hand shook as she forced the key into the lock, opened the door, climbed in behind the wheel.

She started the engine, put the car in gear. When she dared sneak a look, the limo had not moved but sat exactly as she had left it, the black windows revealing nothing. He was behind one of them; was he looking out at her? Of course he was, only she couldn't see him.

The thought made her shudder and she burned rubber as she pealed out of the parking lot and pushed on toward her office.

Ten

When Deena got back to her office she found everything in order. Her assistant had taken over and done all the work perfectly, with only a few minor exceptions. Deena ferreted out the exceptions at once and was delivering a good tongue-lashing about them when she remembered that what the poor woman deserved was praise for her smooth handling of a totally unexpected situation. And she, Deena, was reacting to her own disappointment at finding out she was not, after all, indispensable.

That, and a very large lump of physical frustration. She retreated to her office and shut the door.

There was a pile of work on her desk. Obviously. There had been a pile of work there when she left, and she had been gone more than three hours. Deena grabbed the phone and started returning calls.

She worked until late and worked furiously. She worked so fast she couldn't think of anything else but the work, and she didn't stop until her desk was clear. Then she went rooting through the files and, when she didn't find anything, realized that the only thing she was looking for was an excuse to telephone somebody. It was late, and everybody had gone home; there was nobody who would be in the office to answer if she did phone.

Deena got her purse and went home.

She played the car radio full blast all the way to Encino, letting it shout the news and silly commercials at her because it covered up the noise in her head.

Covered up the little voice that kept repeating, "You'll be forty-four years old this year, Deena."

And, "Crow's feet! Crow's feet! Take a look in the mirror, Deena; you've got crow's feet! Some of those blonde streaks in your hair are suspiciously white, too.

"He isn't going to wait forever. Probably he's already tired of hearing you say no."

And, loudest of all, it screamed, *"Chicken!"*

Deena turned onto the ramp that would lead her to her home. The act of driving was automatic, already she could not remember getting onto the freeway.

The little voice talked on surface streets, too. On and on it went. "He's exactly what you wanted, a charming, sexy man who's crazy about you. You think that kind grows on trees? And he's safe, perfectly safe, because he's married and when it's over he'll go back home to another state and nobody you know will ever see him again. When do you think it's going to be better? Safer? It's probably your last chance, and you're blowing it. The parking lot is in back; nobody will ever know."

That last was a lie. She knew it was. Well, the parking lot might have been where he said, but it wasn't true that nobody would ever know. For every movement there is a countermovement, for every action a reaction.

And besides, *she* would know.

When she got home, the kids were in the kitchen. She could hear them bickering, a familiar sort of background noise, like the music in a movie. She found them setting the table, quarreling over the placement of the napkins. A stew bubbled on the stove; bread thawed on the counter.

"We decided to surprise you and fix dinner," Lonnie explained.

"Yeah, since you and Dad were both working late," his sister finished for him.

"I don't know how late your dad will be," Deena managed to say. "He was in Cudahy on a job and there wouldn't be any point to his coming all the way back here before it's finished."

"Well, I guess he can eat his dinner when he gets here," said Lonnie. "Everything's ready and I'm hungry."

"This is so sweet of you," said Deena, sitting down and unfolding her cloth napkin. Her children. Her beautiful children, working together, thinking with consideration of their hard-working parents! She could have wept to see their fresh, sweet faces, the napkins from her best dinner set, the mushy vegetables in her bowl.

Deena was inspired. "Tomorrow's Saturday," she pointed out. "What do you say we forget all the junk we're all supposed to be doing and just get in the car and go someplace all together?"

"Magic Mountain?" said Lonnie.

"Yay!" agreed Terry.

They *would* pick some place expensive. Deena shrugged off the thought. "Sure, Magic Mountain."

"Can I bring a friend?" asked Lonnie.

"If he gets to have a friend, I get one, too!" yelled Terry.

"You may each bring a friend," Deena decreed, "but only one each."

"Even if it's Gordon?" Lonnie pursued.

Gordon, the instigator of at least half the trouble Lonnie had been in since the third grade! Deena steeled herself and said gamely, "You may bring Gordon if you like."

"All riiight!" said Lonnie.

"Yay!" agreed Terry.

"If your dad wants to go, that's great; but even if he doesn't, we're going to do it. First thing in the morning, and we'll stay all day."

All day, yes, yes, all day. Magic Mountain was a good fifteen miles away from where she now sat, even farther than that from the Pines Motel in Van Nuys. At noon there could be no tryst; she would be trying to elbow her way into some overcrowded cafeteria to buy lunch for the kids. Four kids, and they would already be on a sugar high from the ice cream and candy they had been eating all morning.

She could hardly wait.

She was saved. Saved by the family.

Maybe that's what they are for.

* * *

Rachel did not study late for she had a flight lesson in the morning. She was, in fact, getting ready for bed when Coe phoned.

She said, "Oh, you're back!"

It really was a bit surprising. The time was barely ten o'clock, and he would have been in Mexico that morning. Somehow, in less than twelve hours, he had returned his ship to Houston, caught a commercial flight to LAX, and then arranged his ground transportation to Van Nuys.

The weariness in his voice was obvious. "Yeah, I had to get back here; I'm taking the Fort to San Diego tomorrow. I'm about to turn in, but I thought I'd check and make sure you studied that navigation chapter. I want you to look sharp on Monday."

"I've studied every night." Rachel remembered last evening and amended, "Well, almost every night. Do you have a copilot for tomorrow's flight? Is the Van Nuys man going to do it?"

"Yeah, he's okay."

"How nice," said devious Rachel. "Then you'll have a full crew."

A little puzzled, he said, "Well, I guess two guys is a crew. We hardly ever have any need for gunners these days."

"I wasn't expecting you to shoot down any Focke-Wulfs, but won't you have a crew chief? I thought, since he was in town . . ."

"What are you talking about? Who's in town?"

"Chief."

Coe sounded seriously annoyed. "Chief? You mean Harry?"

"Is that his square name? I never heard him called anything but Chief."

"Is he bothering Deena again?"

"I don't know, but he's trying. He was here last night, trying to get me to ask her over. I wouldn't, of course."

Coe put his hand over the phone, but it didn't completely muffle his expletive. "He's probably right here in the hotel. Okay, don't worry, I'll take care of it."

"Oh, that's great! Thank you, Coe!"

"I guess this is good night, then. I'd better start looking for Chief right away; it might take me a while to find him."

Rachel was grateful to say good night and head for bed. It had been a difficult day, but the ending wasn't bad. She snuggled into her pillow smiling. Not bad at all.

* * *

Coe returned from San Diego on Sunday, early in the evening. She found him on her doorstep, still in his yellow jumpsuit, looking weary and grubby.

"Why, Coe, come in. I'm surprised to see you. I thought you would still be at Brown Field with the air show."

"It was finished at sundown," he growled, "and that Van Nuys copilot of mine couldn't wait a minute. He had to get right back here."

"How thoughtful of you to return him so promptly to his family," murmured Rachel. "Have you had dinner?"

"No, that guy wouldn't stop for anything. He kept yakking about going to work tomorrow morning."

"It happens to some people. Let me see what I have in the freezer. I believe there's Jack Daniels in the cupboard, if you'd care for a drink."

He had already learned his way around her kitchen, and he went at once for a glass and some ice. "I sure could use one. It was almost as hot at Brown as it was at the Van Nuys show."

Rachel poured herself a soda. "Was Chief at the hotel the other night?"

"No, he was staying someplace else, but I guess it wasn't very lively there because he came up to the Airtel bar to have a beer with his buddies. That happened to be the first place I looked for him and there he was, so I took him with me to Brown."

"And where is he eating dinner tonight?"

"Damn if I know. I sent him back to Houston."

"Oh, Coe, that's wonderful! How did you manage it?"

"There were a bunch of CAF ships at that show. I just picked one that was going to Houston and persuaded the guy he needed a crew chief for the flight."

"Oh, I am relieved. Tell me something. Why is it Chief does everything you tell him to? It isn't like you outrank him."

Coe pushed back in his kitchen chair, relaxed. "I don't know. He just does. I guess he knows right from wrong, only he slops over the edge now and then."

Rachel chopped vegetables on a board. "When is Whitey going to come, so you can take the ship back to Harlingen?"

"Probably not until next weekend. He's got a family wedding or something going on. He didn't want to go to Brown in the first place, so he was glad to get out of it. And I've got that class to teach tomorrow."

Pleasant smells were beginning to rise from the stove as Rachel prepared the meal. The kitchen seemed an oasis of light in the darkened world, a nest warmed with glimmers from chrome and polished copper. She knew she ought to ask Coe why he was not going home to his wife. He knew right from wrong; he had just finished saying so. But it was such a pleasant moment, and she was busy with the cooking; she put it off. Another time, she'd ask.

They rode together to the college for the class. On the stroke of seven, Coe had the students assemble in groups around a couple of big tables and open up their practice maps.

"All right," he ordered, "everybody draw a line from Holdenville to Arrowhead."

Pointing out a hapless youngster, he demanded, "What's your average true course?"

"Three hundred twenty degrees?" hazarded the young man.

"Where'd you get a dumb idea like that? True course is a straight line between your takeoff point and your destination. Use your ruler! Anybody got it?"

Somebody came up with the right number, and then they all corrected for magnetic variation.

"We'll forget compass deviation for the purposes of this exercise," Coe offered generously. "Now figure in the wind direction, and you've got your heading. Okay, what's the heading?"

When the first young man had at last found a heading for his theoretical ship, Coe started in on the next student.

"Okay, now you want to go back. What's the true course? You ought to be able to figure that. Obviously, it's going to be a hundred-eighty degrees from the true course going! And what about the wind? Wind direction is the direction it's coming from, not the one it's going to!"

The sweating students plotted course after course. No detail escaped Coe's attention; every potential pilot had to produce a set of numbers that satisfied him before he would go on to the next problem. He was especially hard on the couple of students who had brought in their electronic calculators, snapping numbers at them until he confused them and they goofed.

"Watch those decimal points!" he snarled at them. "If you don't know where the decimal point is, it's for damn sure that machine doesn't either!"

It was a grueling session, and everybody was glad when the time came to depart.

As they strolled through the darkened campus back to the parking lot, Rachel remarked, "Well, maybe it's just that teaching isn't your thing."

"What do you mean?" Coe said. "I thought it went pretty well."

"Oh, sure it did. You treated those adults like inattentive schoolchildren, called them dolts, ridiculed their answers . . ."

He only grinned. "They all finally got their course figured right, didn't they?"

"I guess they did. I was too busy figuring my own to take a head count."

"I teach the way the Air Force does: Yell at them until they get it right. And they'd better get it right. You don't know how to use your compass and the whiz wheel, you could fly around lost for a hundred years. Sure, they've got all those calculators and computers to do it for you these days, but you'd better know the principles, 'cause all you have to do is punch one of those itty-bitty keys wrong and the computer will take you to Timbucktu. Besides, what are you going to do if you're at fifty thousand feet and your batteries run out?"

Rachel admitted reluctantly, "Well, maybe the Air Force has something. I do feel, now, that I can figure any course."

"Not every course. You've just got the basics. And remember, those were just short trips. On a long one, you have to figure your course all over again every time the wind changes."

Rachel smiled secretly. "I think I've got enough information for tomorrow, anyhow. If everything goes right, Eleanor said she might solo me."

"Yeah? You're going to solo tomorrow? That's great. That's important. First solo calls for a celebration. Let's have a party. We'll invite your friends."

"You're the only friend I have who would understand what this means to me."

His smile was broad. "So, okay, we'll celebrate, just the two of us."

"I'd like that, but no drinking and dancing this time."

"What other kind of celebration is there?"

"Oh, a nice dinner someplace. . . . Pierre's?"

He grinned his acceptance. "Sure, if that's what you want."

It happened almost exactly the way she had dreamed it, way back when she was a skinny child with scabby knees, peering through the Lockheed fence at the airplanes. Eleanor had her do some takeoffs and landings, and then they pulled onto the taxi strip and Eleanor got out of the plane.

Her expression was sad, almost grim, and she said, "All right, shoot a couple more landings." She shut the door and rapped once on the roof of the ship for luck, and Rachel was on her own.

Well, she had practiced pretending the CFI wasn't there; now she would just pretend that Eleanor was still at her side. She asked permission from Air Traffic Control and got it. ATC apparently recognized her voice and knew what she was doing, for he added, "Go for it, Moreland!"

Maybe he could see Eleanor from his tower. Eleanor on the ground, waiting, hands deep in her pockets and her head thrust tensely forward.

The throttle was open, Rachel was picking up speed. The Piper was light in her hands, so eager to fly it almost took off by itself. She knew the right moment to "rotate." She felt it. She was in the air. She was soloing.

Once around the pattern and then the landing. It went well. She continued into a new takeoff and did it all over again.

Three landings later, her hour of instruction was over and she taxied to Whales' tie-down area. Eleanor and Coe and a couple of airfield acquaintances were waiting and they hugged and pounded her, whooping congratulations.

To her disgust, they also poured beer on her; but Coe said it was traditional so she forced herself to smile, accepted, and drank the remainder of the beer from the can while they lifted their own cans in a sort of rough-hewn toast to her.

She had to go home and wash her hair before Coe could take her out to dinner.

He always insisted on driving and always insisted on taking his car. She had become so accustomed to it she hardly ever bothered to protest any more. So, after she had washed and dressed, Coe picked her up and took her to Pierre's. The dinner was lovely, as always.

When he brought her back to the house, she unlocked the front door and the telephone was ringing. There was something about that ring in the night that told her that there was something wrong. She knew even before she picked up the receiver that it was not going to be good news. The voice was that of her son-in-law, Marc.

Coe had followed her into the house and when she hung up the phone he was dancing with impatience. "What is it? What's wrong? You're as white as beer foam!"

"Oh, Coe, it's my daughter. She's in the hospital. They think she might be losing the baby!"

Eleven

Rachel fumbled a phone book from the shelf. "I have to go to Barbara, right away. I'll get a plane . . ."

"I'll drive you to the airport," Coe offered. "Where does she live?"

Rachel was pawing at the pages of the book. "Airlines, airlines . . . Arizona. It's a ranch in Arizona. I'll have to go to Phoenix and rent a car. Air West goes to Phoenix, doesn't it?"

"Can't somebody pick you up in Phoenix?"

"It's nearly a hundred miles to the ranch. They live near this little town called Alcalde, but it has no airport. I expect Marc's too busy for any long drives; there are two little kids at home for him to look after."

"Trip like that's going to take you all day. All that driving, and the roads are dangerous! Hold on a minute; don't call the airline yet. Let me see if I can figure something out."

He went to his car and came back with the map case he carried on flights. He pulled out an Arizona map and spread it on the dining room table. It was the same type as the map they had used for the navigation lesson at school, only it covered territory that was more familiar to Rachel; she leaned over it and pointed out Alcalde to him.

"There is too an airport there!" he said.

"Circle with an R in it," Rachel pointed out. "That means it's a private airport. You told us that in school yourself."

"I'll find out who owns it and get permission to land. The strip's long enough for the B-17 and it'll be daylight, so it won't matter that there aren't any lights."

"Do you think the owner will allow it?"

"Of course he will. It's just a courtesy, one pilot to another; and he's got to be a pilot or why does he need an airstrip? We'll take off at sunup and be there by the middle of the morning."

"Did you say B-17? You're going to fire up a four-engine bomber to take two people to Arizona?"

He glowered at her. "You got a better

idea? It's here; I'm here, and I don't have a smaller ship with me."

"Well, of course it will be better to fly; but couldn't we rent something that's a reasonable size, maybe from Whales, like you did before?"

"Whales rents his ships by the hour. You're going to want to be away a couple weeks, maybe. You can't keep one of his planes that long; he needs them every day."

"But you can't fly the B-17 without a copilot and you don't have one; Whitey's still in Houston."

"Sure I do. You're it."

Rachel gasped at the very outrageousness of the idea. "Don't be ridiculous! We can't do that! I don't know the first thing about flying a B-17!"

"There you go again! Just because you've got a few gray hairs, you think you can't do anything! It's easy! The instrumentation is simpler than it is on the ship you've been flying. I can teach you everything you need to know while we're in the air."

She stared at him, tasting conviction on the tip of her tongue. "You're not kidding, are you? I'm going to fly a B-17?" Her tone strengthened and she repeated, "I'm going to fly a B-17. To Arizona. Oh, that's exciting! Can I use it to satisfy my requirement for a cross-country? For my license?"

He gave a small chuckle. "No, but it'll make a hell of an impressive entry in your logbook!"

There was not a lot of packing to do; Rachel had left clothes at Barbara's house the last time she had visited. She put a nightgown and underwear into a bag, then shifted things in her refrigerator to ready it for her absence. She went to bed as soon as she had finished, but then she couldn't sleep. She needed to, she would be up long before dawn; but all she could do was think of Barbara.

Her precious child, her baby! Was she alone? Was she in pain? It was late at night, so of course Rachel couldn't phone. She could only send a message, a psychic telegram across the miles. "Hang in there, darling! Your mother's coming!"

In the morning Coe picked her up in his rental car, drove it to the airport, and turned it in. Inordinately pleased because he had avoided paying parking fees, he led the way to the tiedown area where the B-17 waited.

Rachel muttered to herself as they approached it, "Well, maybe a 747 is bigger, but this old warbird certainly is big enough." The wings stretched a hundred and five feet, holding up four massive engines, each with a long, three-bladed propeller.

And far, far down below was tiny Rachel, wearing her yellow jumpsuit and carrying her little overnight bag of lingerie. "I'm going to fly that," said Rachel. It was a statement for her own ears, and she didn't believe it for a minute.

Coe, not the least impressed, took a walk around his ship, checking. With a special rod he tested the level in the gas tanks. He loosened a tiny petcock at the bottom of each tank and drained off the water that had condensed there during the night.

He opened the little door to the pilot's escape hatch and tossed his mapcase and the flight bags inside. Then he looked at Rachel and said, "Oh. You probably can't do this. I'll open the waist door for you."

"You're going to get into the ship through that hatch?" said Rachel. "Okay, I'll do it, too."

"You're probably . . . uh . . ." He looked her up and down. "Too short."

"Show me how you do it."

He put his hands on the sides of the hatch, jumped up, swung his legs inside, and rolled onto the floor. Then he poked his head out to see what she was doing.

She was putting her hands on the side of the hatch, a determined frown on her face. Thought she was too old and feeble for acrobatics, did he? She'd show him.

But she was shorter than most pilots, and her first couple of jumps didn't get her high enough to straighten her elbows so she could swing her legs up. Coe offered, "Here, take my hand and I'll pull you up."

"Out of the way," she replied and made the biggest jump she could. Her arms straightened, and her legs were inside. Coe grabbed her and rolled her into the ship before she fully realized that she had not anticipated the roll and was about to drop right back out of the hatch again.

Inside the cockpit she took her seat in the right-hand chair. Coe hauled out the checklist, a page of closely-spaced type. They proceeded slowly since most of the controls were unfamiliar to Rachel and he had to read each item, then check it himself.

"Fuel transfer, valves and switches," he read, and then his hand flicked across the instrument panel. "Right, all of them. Intercoolers, okay. Gyros . . ."

An orange crescent of sun was showing over Mount Wilson by the time Coe started the engines. One by one, the massive propellers sprang into life; the engines coughed and roared. The big ship shook with their racket. When he was sure all four engines were running smoothly, he shut down the two inboards for the taxi.

At the end of the runway he started them again, received clearance from the tower, and they turned into the takeoff. Coe pushed forward all four throttles at once and they were thundering down the strip, probably shaking the good folks of Van Nuys right out of their warm morning slumber. She had her hands on the control wheel, but he was in charge and he knew exactly when the needles pointed to the right time to rotate. The ship lifted smoothly off and they were flying.

He called out, "Wheels up!" and Rachel threw the lever. With mighty thumps, the big wheels folded into their wells.

Then Van Nuys filled the window as they made their mandatory turn and climbed for altitude. They would fly at six thousand, five hundred feet, he explained, for the next east-west altitude was eight thousand, five hundred feet and at that height they would have to go on oxygen in the unpressurized cabin.

"Back in the War we held off until eleven thousand," he remembered, "but we were young and cocky and we didn't know any better. Even at eight thousand the air's thin and it starts to get cold."

He was busy throughout the climb to altitude, checking and re-checking the instruments, fine-tuning their settings. By the time they leveled off he was satisfied, and he sat back, relaxed and cheerful.

"Ought to make our ETA, no problem," was all he said.

"That's good. Marc's going to pick us up," she said, but of course he already knew that.

They were droning along over the desert when Coe suddenly lifted his hands from the yoke and said, "You can take over now." And then he unbuckled himself from his seat and went aft to the relief station.

And there she was with fifty thousand pounds of airplane roaring under her hands. Stiff with tension, Rachel went on scanning the empty desert sky in ten-degree increments. She snatched a look at the instruments; course correct, airspeed, altitude, all the engines at the proper settings, then back to the scan.

After a while Coe returned and he said, "Did you notice? We've got a contrail."

The ship was angled against the wind and when she looked back she could see the contrail, a stream of gleaming cloud that flowed, still churning from the prop wash, from behind them all the way to the horizon.

"It's mine!" cried Rachel. "All mine! I'm making my very own contrail!"

Even after he took back the controls she kept scanning and checking. There was so much to learn, and she did have to concentrate. She didn't feel tired. The adrenaline generated in her body by the sheer excitement of flying kept her alert, and the concentration kept her from thinking about Barbara.

Alcalde was almost in the mountains, set in a confusing jumble of foothills and mesas. She would not have recognized it, things looked so different from the air, but Coe said, "That's got to be the airfield," and they were into the landing procedure.

Sure enough, there was the field, stretched out on an eroded mesa. It was the only level ground for miles around, and the runway looked short and narrow to eyes used to big-city airfields.

Half flaps, wheels down, Coe was fiddling with the trim tabs, leveling the ship against a wind that refused to blow exactly parallel with the single runway. Coe's steady hand was steering it down; the wheels touched; the landing was perfect.

Marc was waiting, and he had the two children with him. Also waiting, to Rachel's surprise, was a little knot of onlookers. Somehow the word had gotten around and townspeople of Alcalde had gathered for a look at the legendary Flying Fortress, a warbird out of the past landing at their tiny town. It seemed to them cause for celebration, and they broke into a cheer as Rachel and Coe swung out of the cockpit.

Coe was apparently used to it. He grinned and flashed a genuine WW II "Victory" sign. What a good memory he had! Rachel managed a feeble wave before she caught sight of her grandchildren and rushed to pull them into her arms.

Susie returned her hug; but little Peter, who was nearly five, regarded her with blue eyes as round as grapes and demanded, "Grandma, did you fly that plane?"

"Yes, I did, darling, with a little help

from my friend." She introduced Marc to Coe and pointed out the children. Three-year-old Susie had already lost interest in the adults, and Peter hung back, apparently awed by the pair of yellow jumpsuits before him.

Marc regarded it all with the young person's veneer of never being surprised by anything. He was tall and blue-eyed, a working cowboy from his wide-brimmed hat to his dusty boots. With equanimity he accepted Coe, the airplane, and grandma in a yellow jumpsuit and loaded everyone into his car.

Rachel sat in the back seat all the way to the house, playing finger games with Peter and Susie. If Marc and Coe had any conversation, she did not overhear it; nor could it have been very informative, for when they were unloading the luggage Marc said to her, "I've put you in the guest room as usual, Mother Moreland. There's a double bed in there; I guess you'll both be comfortable."

"Marc!" Rachel stopped on the porch steps, shocked. "What in the world makes you think . . ." She broke off, for Coe was watching her, an evil grin on his face.

Rachel said firmly, "Colonel Flaherty is

an aviation instructor and kindly has provided a ship so I could get here as fast as possible. I certainly hope you will offer him your hospitality—but not in my bed!"

"Well . . ." Was Marc actually blushing? "Well, there's only the one guest room. He'll have to sleep on the couch."

"That's okay," said Coe.

"It unfolds into a bed," Marc explained. "Will you be staying long?"

"Gotta stay as long as she does," Coe growled. "I can't fly that ship without a copilot, and she's the only one I've got."

The information hit Rachel like a second shock. Of course he couldn't fly back without her. How silly that she had never before considered that!

But first things first. Rachel asked, "When can I see Barbara?"

Marc said, "She's doing fine, and the hospital lets her have all the visitors she wants. You can go any time. Take my car, if you want. Do you know how to get there? I'll write you some instructions."

"Why don't you take her yourself?" Coe asked. "I can stay here with the kids."

"That'd be great," said Marc. "I haven't seen Barbara today; There's no place for the kids in the hospital, and they won't let them go where Barbara is. You don't mind? They can be a handful sometimes."

"Don't let them play outside unless someone's with them," Rachel added. "There's a culvert west of the house."

"We put up a fence," Marc assured her. "It's okay now."

"Watch them anyway," said Rachel.

"I'll tie leashes on them," Coe promised. "Go along and make your visit."

Barbara opened her eyes wide when they walked into her hospital room. "Mama! How did you get here so fast!"

"Special airplane." Rachel rushed to hug her. Barbara looked pale and frightened. Her dark hair was pulled back into a careless braid, her belly huge with the expected child, but still she was beautiful. Conversation ceased while she and Marc kissed and exchanged endearments.

"What is the doctor telling you?" Rachel asked. "Is the baby all right?"

"Just fine. They thought I was going into labor, but they were able to stop it and now I'm just fine. But Mama, they're going to keep me in bed until the baby's full term, and that's six weeks off!"

"Otherwise you're okay? You can come home and stay in bed there?"

"I suppose so, but somebody will have to take care of me—and the kids, of course. Are you going to be able to do it, Mom? Please say you can stay; otherwise I'll have to stay here in the hospital. There isn't anybody who can come and keep house for us, except you."

"Of course I'll stay, dear. What every grandmother longs for is the chance to take care of the children."

"They're good kids, aren't they?"

"They're our kids."

Barbara turned to Marc. "Did the vet come to see that horse with the bad hoof?"

"Yeah, it's getting better now," her husband replied. "I'm going to put all that bunch into a higher pasture. The trouble was it's kind of boggy in the bottom part of that meadow and I guess he was standing around in the water. You'd better get your ma to tell you about that airplane she flew here."

"*She* flew here?" Barbara asked.

"Big airplane!" said Marc, grinning and spreading his arms like wings. "You ever seen a B-17? I never did before."

"Oh, don't listen to him, dear," said Rachel, somewhat embarrassed. "I needed to get here right away, and it was available."

"You flew it?" Barbara questioned. "You were talking about learning to fly, I remember you said that, but you really flew?"

"In a B-17," Marc affirmed.

"Oh, I wasn't alone," protested Rachel. "I was only the copilot. Colonel Flaherty flew it; it's his ship, after all."

"Why doesn't anybody ever tell me anything?" demanded Barbara. "Who is Colonel Flaherty?"

"He's an instructor and he's been a very good friend to me."

"Not that good a friend," Marc interrupted. "She makes him sleep on the couch."

Rachel hoped she wasn't blushing. "I am just shocked at you two! Haven't you ever heard of somebody who will put himself out for a friend?

"He's definitely doing that," said Barbara.

They spent an hour talking with her; and when they returned to the ranch house, Coe had already given the children their supper. He had scrambled eggs together with green chilies and bacon, and they had eaten every bite. Green chilies, they declared, kept it from being breakfast. Rachel made a dinner for the adults, and everybody turned in early.

She had expected to be wakened by the usual chaos of two small children fresh from sleep, but she even overslept a little and when she woke she heard not a sound. No thunder of little bare feet; no cries of joy, hunger, or pain; no shrieks of surprise or frustration.

Was something wrong? Hastily she slipped into jeans and a shirt and rushed down the stairs.

The sofa-sleeper on which Coe had spent the night had its back to her. It was still open; she could see the disordered blankets and a tuft of gray-white hair that showed above the sofa back.

And she could hear Coe's voice. "Okay, what's that one?"

Peter's triumphant reply, "Hen in a hat tooray, hooray!"

She moved around to the kitchen door and she could see Coe, still in his pajamas, both children nestled against him. Susie was sucking her thumb, Peter reciting from a long-since memorized Dr. Seuss. But it was the expression on Coe's face that held her in the doorway, stiff with astonishment. He was beaming, actually beaming, eyes dancing, lines smoothed from his face, all his grouchiness gone as he patiently worked his way through the alphabet with Peter.

Rachel slipped into the kitchen. An empty coffee cup on the counter demonstrated that Marc was already outside, like any good husbandman, doing the chores before breakfast. She prepared the children's breakfast, then called to them, "Come and eat, Susie, Peter. Let Grandpa Coe get dressed."

The title pleased Susie, who chanted, "Grandpa Coe, Grandpa Coe," as she slid out of his lap and raced into the kitchen.

They were finishing off their oatmeal when Coe returned, washed and shaved, again wearing the jumpsuit. And still smiling. He poured himself a cup of coffee.

It was an imitation of his old growl as he asked, "What's with the 'Grandpa Coe' stuff?"

Rachel filed bread slices into the toaster. "You would prefer they call you Colonel?"

He actually laughed. "Aw, Rachel! I don't mind. Guess the kiddies are short one grandfather."

"They don't have any. Marc's father was killed in an accident a long time ago. His mother took the insurance money and moved to Florida. That's why Marc has this big ranch to run."

He gave a grunt of understanding as he sat at the table.

Rachel reported, "Barbara can come home any time if there is somebody here to take care of her. She will have to stay in bed until the baby is born, and it isn't due for six weeks."

"And the other grandmother's in Florida? You'll have to stay, then."

"Yes, and I'll have to stay the whole time. There aren't any neighbors or even anybody around here she could hire. She has friends, of course, but they have their own families. None of them could come here and live."

She sat down at the table so she could see his face. "If you want, I'll help you take the plane back to Van Nuys, or Houston, if that's better for you. Then I'll catch a commercial flight to Phoenix. It will take me a couple of days to get back here, but Marc can handle things as long as Barbara stays in the hospital."

"Houston? You want to fly all the way to Houston? You're not that good, not yet."

"I could do it."

He chuckled, but his eyes approved of

her confidence. "I'm not sure I could. It doesn't matter. The ship can stay here until you're ready to leave. It doesn't have any appointments or air shows or anything right away."

"But can you stay? Don't you have any appointments? Don't you want to go home to your wife?"

He jumped as if he had been stung. "My wife? What are you worrying about that for?"

"Well, you haven't seen her in a while."

"I haven't seen her in years. We're separated, didn't I tell you that?"

"Oh, that's too bad," she murmured; and to cover up that she didn't think it was too bad at all, she asked, "And what about your air ambulance to Mexico?"

He raised one shaggy gray eyebrow. "You heard about that, too, huh? The last trip was such a bitch, I hired a charter service to do it for me next time. Go get Barbara. Bring her home. I'll help you with the kids."

"You're sure? You could get stuck here."

"I'm not stuck. I could send for Whitey, and there's always ground transportation. Give me some credit. I'm old enough to know what I'm doing."

She gave him a smile, but still there was a worry line between her brows. "Sometimes I wonder if I am."

Twelve

Rachel phoned the doctor and he agreed that Barbara might as well be at home as long as her mother was there to take care of her. When Marc was finished with his morning chores, they drove into town and picked her up.

While they were gone, Coe looked after the children and kept them playing clean indoor games so they would look neat for the homecoming. Susie and Peter looked ready to be runway models, faces washed and hair combed, when their mother arrived. They squealed with joy as Marc carried Barbara up the steps and into the house. He laid her gently on the couch, which had been closed up and piled with cushions for her comfort.

Rachel squeezed back sentimental tears as she watched the children greet their mother. They squalled and elbowed one another in their impatience to hug her.

Rachel separated them. "All right, kiddies, that's enough. You may sit here with your mother, but only if you don't fight. That's right, Peter. Sit down quietly." She laid a light cover over Barbara's knees.

When she introduced Coe, Barbara turned up her huge brown eyes to him. "Thank you, Colonel, for bringing my mother to me! I don't know how I would get through this without her."

"It wasn't any trouble. She does whatever she wants to with me, anyway," he responded. "I hope you're going to call me Coe."

"If you like, and I'm Barbara."

Marc looked at Coe and perhaps remembered that he had been shut up in the house with the little children for two days running. He said, "I've got to go check the herds that are up in the canyon. You want to ride along?"

Coe said, "Sure," and had followed Marc out the door before Rachel could get in a word to warn him that when Marc said "ride," he was talking about horses.

Rachel rushed to the door, but they were already halfway to the barn and it was too late to chase them. She went back to her kitchen chores but kept going anxiously to the door to peer out. In due time, the two men reappeared on horseback—Marc in his boots and jeans and ten-gallon hat, Coe with his yellow jumpsuit and baseball cap. Away they trotted, giving not a glance backward to the house and the women.

"The pilot on horseback," muttered Rachel, closing the door against the heat. A well-rounded man? Or an old fool about to humiliate himself trying to play John Wayne? Well, worrying wasn't going to help any and she probably shouldn't worry about Coe anyway. He had been taking care of himself for sixty-eight years. She reminded herself that he looked like a good rider should on a horse—that is, comfortable.

But she couldn't help fretting. She complained, "He's going to sunburn the back of his neck."

"That's a very charming man," said Barbara.

Rachel smiled dryly. "Well maybe he would seem that way, to somebody who hasn't seen one of his grouchy moods yet.

"What did you say he does?"

"He's retired. He teaches a little, flies an ambulance, plays with bombers."

Barbara said, "Well, he's obviously in love with you, so what's going on there?"

Rachel was startled but answered smoothly, "Why, nothing at all, dear. I'm sure you're mistaken. He's only helping me get my pilot's license. I told you about that."

"Uh-huh. When I write a book, I'm going to call it *Things My Mother Never Told Me.*" Barbara teased.

"I'm going to get you some cold fruit juice."

"I want some, too!" yelled Peter.

"Me, too!" echoed his sister.

By the time they had sipped their juice, the children had become used to the idea that their mother was home again and they drifted to another corner to play. Rachel sat down with Barbara, satisfied. This was what she had traveled to Arizona for, to create for Barbara an orderly house with contented children in it. To see to it Barbara was comfortable and resting as she should, waiting serenely for her baby.

Rachel asked her, "Do you feel like taking a nap?"

Barbara reached out and took her hand. "Not quite yet. I just want to *be* here for a little bit. I need to take it in that I am here, I'm at home. I've had a pretty good scare, you know."

"Yes, I expect you have." Rachel patted the hand.

"I'm so lucky!" Barbara was blinking away tears. "I have so much! The family, Marc, my children. And I could have lost it all, by just being careless!"

"But you didn't, dear. Everything's going just fine."

"It was all my own doing. I love my children so much! I was warned that I shouldn't have another; but it's such a wonderful thing, to be a mother! I couldn't bear the thought that it would never happen to me again, that I'd never be pregnant again, never again experience the miracle and hold a tiny baby who was my own! I wanted it so much! So I said the hell with the doctors. I told myself they don't know everything."

"Well, they don't," said Rachel.

"They were right about this. I shouldn't have gotten pregnant. I just did what I wanted, took what I wanted. It was plain greed. Now, if this baby dies, I've killed it. If I become toxemic again, like I did before, we could both die! The baby, and me, too! I didn't have the right to risk my own life and maybe leave Susie and Peter without a mother. You have to promise me that if I die, you'll take care of my kids. I want them to have a mother."

"Of course I will, but you're nowhere near dying. You only went into labor prematurely, but they've stopped it. It happens all the time. And there's no sign of toxemia. The doctor said so."

"I was so sure that nothing bad could happen to me. I almost died with Susie, but they knocked me out with drugs and I don't remember much of it. I should have remembered."

Rachel sprang up briskly. "You've been lying around for three days now; it's enough to get anybody depressed. Let's do something that's fun and get your mind off things."

"I'm not allowed to do anything that's fun," pouted Barbara.

"Sure you are. We're all going to . . ." Almost too late, Rachel had her inspiration. ". . . Eat ice cream!"

At least the children thought it would be fun. They heard the word from across the room and came running, shouting with enthusiasm.

After the ice cream, Barbara and the kids settled down to watch TV while Rachel started dinner. It was going to take a lot of TV to get Barbara through six weeks of bed rest, she reflected, and it was likely to teach the children bad habits.

Well, once she had things started in the kitchen, she would take them outside for a bit. Perhaps to the vegetable garden, to pull some carrots for dinner. Susie loved pulling carrots.

They had made the trip to the garden and the kids were back in front of the TV when Coe and Marc returned from their ride up the canyon. They came in laughing and making jokes; Coe had obviously enjoyed himself. Rachel examined him closely for evidences of sunburn and also to see if she could detect any signs of the love Barbara had observed.

Was there an extra twinkle in his eyes when he looked at her? Now that it had been pointed out to her, she rather thought there was. How very sad if there were! Sad for a man to be in love when he was too old for it.

And the woman of his choice was too old also.

* * *

Susie and Peter each had a playgroup, an informal weekly meeting with other children who also lived in isolated areas. It was up to Rachel to get them to their appointments, and she spent hours driving Marc's car to farmhouses far out on unmarked roads. She learned to rely on Peter, who knew his way around the countryside pretty well. The only trouble was that if he made a mistake, he didn't know how to correct it and he would cry with frustration and then sulk for hours, even after Rachel had searched out a friendly neighbor to set them right.

In Susie's group there was one family who lived in town and everybody looked forward to the day it was the "town lady's turn" and they had an opportunity to drop the toddlers off and go run errands. Rachel had a long grocery list ready. She also had Peter and Coe in the car, both having expressed a desire to go to town.

Coe agreed to entertain Peter while Rachel shopped for groceries. When she returned to the car, they were waiting for her to come with the keys and she was astonished to see that Coe had been to the clothing store and outfitted himself head to toe. He wore jeans, plaid shirt, shiny new boots, and a stiff new Stetson. The toy store had not been neglected; Peter was fiddling with an electronic game.

She chided, "Coe, you're spoiling him!"

"Oh, I got a trinket for Susie, too, so she won't feel bad."

"Good thinking," grumbled Rachel.

As he climbed into the car, the new hat bumped its brim on the doorframe and he grabbed it with a touch of irritation. "Dang hat! Stiff as a dry cowpat!" He squeezed the crown punishingly. "It takes at least five years to break one of these things in and make it fit right."

She smiled a little. "Do you have a broken-in one back home?"

"Everybody in Houston does, and some broken-in boots, too."

She started the car, trying not to look at Coe in the seat beside her. He might have been an urban manufacturer, but he looked perfect as a cowboy. The hat suited his craggy features and the jeans were right on his long, lean frame. He was relaxed in the seat, legs thrust out before him. New fabric stretched over his thighs, and Rachel blushed to find herself remembering what he had said to her the night after her first flight lesson. If it happened again, she was wondering, would it be obvious in those tight jeans?

Well, of course "it" wasn't going to happen again and of course she didn't remember things like that. It was her thing, to not pay attention, that's how she had always handled it. And yet she couldn't resist sneaking a glance to see if the new jeans were giving away any secrets . . .

The morning chores were finished and Coe came into the kitchen, hanging his dusty hat on the peg by the door. "Something sure smells good in here!"

"Cinnamon rolls," Rachel said. "I have to spend all my time in the kitchen anyway; I might as well make something that's fun to do. Do you want one now? Get yourself some coffee."

He went willingly for the coffee, and as he passed close behind her, Rachel sniffed. "You smell like a horse!"

He sat down with his cup. "I guess I should have bought more than one outfit, but I didn't think of it. Farm women don't generally complain about horse smell."

"This is a civilized farm," she said, putting a couple of hot rolls in front of him. "Your jumpsuit is clean; I put it through the washer yesterday. Wear it tomorrow, and I'll wash what you're wearing now. I guess in the meantime I can keep on the other side of the table from you."

She got herself a coffee and sat down. It would be nice to get off her feet and just talk for a bit.

He sampled the roll and said, "Hey, that's good! You got a lot of this stuff? Recipes and things?"

"Recipes? What do you mean?"

"I knew you were a good cook. I'm just surprised that you're this good."

"Well, you're full of surprises, too. You're so good with the children. It's not what I thought you were like."

"I never had any kids," he explained.

"Maybe that would add to their charm," Rachel admitted.

"I always wanted kids, but Addie and I. . . . Well, we just never had any. I guess she didn't want them."

"You guess? You don't know?"

The question seemed to surprise him. "No, I never knew what she wanted. Oh, I guess I know she likes society teas and fancy duds and charity balls and fishing—

yeah, she's crazy about fishing—but that doesn't mean I could ever figure her out."

"Did you ever tell her what you wanted?"

He gave her a twisted look, as if reacting to a sudden pain. "Do you really want to hear about this?"

"Yes, Coe, if you want to tell me."

He pushed crumbs around his plate, watching them with an expression that dared them to escape him. "When Addie and I got married, it was during the war. I'd just finished training, and we got what everybody knew was going to be our last furlough before we went overseas. We knew what we were heading into; the Eighth Air Force was bombing Germany every day and casualties were running about fifty percent."

"I didn't know they had such heavy losses."

"They didn't, not all the time. Once they started getting cover from the faster fighters with longer ranges, like the P-51 and the P-38, things got a lot better; but that's how it was in '43. Was I scared? You bet I was scared. I was eighteen, a second lieutenant, as green as grass. I'd never had a legal drink; I'd never been any place, seen anything, been in love or been married or had a kid, and there was a fifty percent chance that before another couple of months was up, I'd be dead. You want to know the truth in plain language, a man in that position will do practically anything to get laid. So, I got married."

"Had you known her a long time?"

"For years, I guess; we were all in school together. When I got back to Houston for my leave, just about all the girls I knew were going steady with somebody; but Addie happened to be at loose ends, so we had a couple dates. I wanted to get married. I thought maybe I'd get lucky and be able to start a kid while I was still alive. We decided we were in love and had the wedding a couple of days before I had to get back to my base. I figured I'd done the best I could."

"And then you went overseas?"

"Until the end of the war. There wasn't any baby, but I didn't get killed either, so I figured we had time after all. After the war I went back to Houston and started my business. It turned out Addie and I didn't know each other very well, and when we got better acquainted we didn't like each other much; but we were married, and in those days you made the best of it."

"It's an old-fashioned idea, but there's a lot to be said for it."

"With us, it was probably a mistake. We got to fighting; we fought a lot. It got so we didn't do anything but fight, and I decided I'd had it. I moved out, rented an apartment over near the plant. When I changed my address everybody knew we were fighting; and that made Addie really mad, so she had an abortion."

The telling was obviously hard for him; he gripped the edge of the table, looking down at his plate. "I didn't even know she was pregnant. It was the first time it had ever happened, and we'd been married ten years. It never crossed my mind, and she didn't tell me until it was all over. She killed my kid, Rachel, just because she was mad at me! I still miss that kid, wish I could have known him, wish I'd even known about him when he was still alive. After that, well, there just wasn't any way we were going to get back together. She's got the house and I pay her bills, but I haven't talked to her about anything in years."

"You never got a divorce?"

"There wasn't any reason to. She didn't want one as long as I kept supporting her, and I got so it was kind of comfortable that way; it kept the women from bothering me."

He was serious, and Rachel smothered a smile. "They bother you a lot, do they?"

"There was a time. Right after the split-up got to be common knowledge, it was like a stampede. Everywhere I turned were these women who knew I had some money. Seemed to me like they were all alike. Hard bodies, hard minds, hard hearts. Young. Fancy clothes, piles of makeup, perfume . . . whew!" He fanned his face with his hand, grimacing.

"You have never been in love?"

"Before this time? I'm even going to admit that I was, a couple of times. In those days I used to spend time at the plant." He wrinkled his brow, striving for truth. "I used to spend *all* my time at the plant. The only woman I really was serious about, she figured it out: Even if I broke down and married her, I'd still spend all my time with the business, and that wasn't what she wanted and she dumped me. That was a long time ago. Before I retired."

"What did you make at your plant?"

"I build airplanes." He reconsidered. "I used to build airplanes. I built small, slick, fast airplanes and now the young Turks that have the company are putting them in a kit! A kit! There's going to be pea-brains all over the country putting those kits together wrong and killing themselves in ships with my logo on them!"

"It won't be your fault."

"Yeah, I guess not. You got any more of those cinnamon rolls? I spilled my guts; now tell me about your marriage."

Startled, she replied at once, "It was a good marriage." Then she amended, "Well, it was satisfactory, of course it was, most of the time."

What an odd, weak thing to say! And it had come right out of her own mouth! Rachel hopped up and put another couple of rolls on his plate. "Pete was a fine man."

He didn't say anything, just started eating his roll.

She said, "Somehow, we were never really in communication. It wasn't the style back then. Well, you know how it was. We never told anybody what we really felt, especially if it was negative. We were always uptempo. Donna Reed always was, so I guess we figured we had to be, too, but the way that comes out. . . . Well, pretty soon you've had a whole marriage and it was all small talk. I don't know. Maybe it would have been better if we had been able to talk to each other."

Coe said, "I don't know if it was the times. There must be people who talk to each other, must have been even back in the olden days."

"Maybe you're right. Maybe I've just never had the knack."

"We can talk to each other, you and I," he pointed out.

"We just started this morning, though."

"Aw, come on. We've always understood each other. You understand that I'm likely to overstate myself when I'm mad, and I understand that you . . ."

Rachel prodded impatiently, "That I what?"

He gave her a hard, piercing look. "That you think it's easier to be old."

What did that mean? She demanded, "Easier than what?"

"Easier than to keep trying, keep reaching out, struggling for the things you want. Easier to just say you're too old."

Rachel sat back and regarded him with an old and experienced eye. "Is there some specific thing you think I ought to be struggling toward?"

"You know."

"Do I, now?"

"Dammit, Rachel, you know what I mean. You keep saying you're too old for love."

"I don't think I said that. Nobody's ever too old for love."

"I mean for loving a man."

"There's all kinds of love."

He was firm. "When it's between a man and a woman, love and sex are the same thing."

"I'm not sure about that, either; but if you're talking about you and me, of course there can't be anything, couldn't be even if we were youngsters, because you have a wife."

"I just got through explaining all that! Yeah, I'm married, but only technically. We haven't lived together for thirty years. I love you, Rachel. I want to spend the rest of my life with you, and you're not even listening to me!"

She got up from the table. "I can't. It's not right."

"What's wrong with it? I told you why . . ."

"I believe in marriage, Coe. I believe in keeping the vows."

"You're just being stubborn. This is what George Bernard Shaw called 'trade-unionism of the married.' "

She was startled. "I didn't know you read Shaw."

"Everybody does."

"Okay, so it's a union, and you're trying to get me to be a scab."

At that, he laughed in spite of himself. "Scab! Now there's a word I haven't heard since the Eisenhower administration."

"If you will excuse me, I am going to try to discourage Susie from beating her brother with a plastic toy; she's been at it far too long already." Rachel exited from the kitchen and went to scoop up Susie and distract her to some more positive activity.

Thirteen

Somehow, in the tiny town of Alcalde, Coe found a car to rent, and every Wednesday he would drive it to Phoenix. From there he caught a flight to Houston and on Thursday took care of his obligation with the air ambulance. He would arrive back at the ranch late Friday night, weary and hollow-eyed.

"Why do you push yourself like that?" Rachel demanded of him as he was watching her cook. "You've got an apartment in Houston; why don't you spend a couple days there, or even just a night, and get a good rest?"

The grumpy lines formed next to his nose. "What's that? I'm so old I've got to go spend my time resting?"

"A schedule like you've set for yourself would wear anybody out."

"I've got to get back here and help out with the chores," he argued. "You and

Marc can't handle everything yourselves, you know that."

He came back to be with her; Rachel knew in her heart it was so. She said, "If you're going to help with the chores, come here and peel the potatoes for me. Why do you have to fly the Mexico trip at all? What happened to the charter service that was going to do it for you?"

"Oh, well, about that Mexico thing . . ." Coe picked up a knife and a potato. "I guess I oughta explain about that—how it got started. There's this friend of mine, he's an orthopedic surgeon, and somebody told him about a little boy in Mexico who needed an operation and the doc talked me into flying down there and getting the kid and bringing him back to Houston so Doc could operate on him. So we did all that and it came out fine, but the kid had to stay in Houston for physical therapy and he was lonesome, so I went back to Mexico and got his mama and brought her up, and a couple more of the family. How do you want these potatoes cut up?"

"Big chunks. I'm going to roast them with the meat. Marc likes them that way."

"So do I. About that time, the doc and I got to thinking. We had spent a lot of money and time on that kid, and now he was all fixed up and so healthy he could go do stoop labor in the fields. It didn't hardly seem worthwhile, somehow, so we made arrangements for the kid to go to school, get an education. Well, that was fine, but nobody's going to stick to his books if his family's back home starving in a hovel. So we started fixing houses and doc got to vaccinating folks; and by that time there was a couple of other doctors wanted to help out, so we had to scrounge around and find somebody who was sick with whatever matched up to each doc's specialty and then I would ride them all around in the plane. I helped some small local manufacturers get started, so there'd be jobs and, well, you can see the whole thing just snowballed on us and now we've got to have the plane going there every week and I've got to be there looking after the businesses and you can see it isn't something a charter outfit can handle for me."

Rachel gathered the potato chunks in a pot. "I guess I do see."

After that she took to packing snacks and a thermos of coffee for him to take with him on the long, dark drive to Phoenix every Wednesday night.

Marc usually came in from the morning chores about the time Rachel was serving breakfast. Since he had gone out with only a cup of coffee in his stomach he would be ready to eat, and Rachel would give him a farmer's breakfast with potatoes, eggs, ham, and pancakes. Even Coe wouldn't eat all of that.

As soon as his father was at the table, Peter said, "Daddy, I want to ride my pony today."

Marc thought it over. "Well, I'm only going up to the west pasture. I guess you could ride that far."

"Me, too!" hollered Susie. "Me, too, go pony!"

"Don't yell, Susie," Rachel chided. "You're too young to go riding."

"Oh, she can ride," said Marc. "She has her own pony."

"Tunder," affirmed Susie. "My pony Tunder."

Rachel eyed the child apprehensively. "She's three years old and her pony is named Thunder?"

"Well, it's only a name," said Marc. "She's a gentle pony. Hey, you want to go riding, Mother Moreland? I'll take Peter and you can take Susie; and then if Susie gets tired, you can bring her back home."

"She'd probably outlast me," admitted Rachel. "I'm not much of a rider."

"Let's all go," said Coe. "Come on, Rachel. It'll do you good to get out of the house."

"We'd be leaving Barbara all alone."

"That ought to be okay," said Marc. "I'll ask her."

Barbara allowed that she could watch TV alone as well as with company, so in due time all the family was dressed and booted and Marc and Coe brought around the saddled horses.

It seemed to Rachel that Thunder was a lot bigger than a pony ought to be. "That's a cow pony," she protested. "I thought it was going to be a pony pony!"

Marc said, "Sure it is. It's a lot smaller than the other horses."

It was shorter in the legs, but that was not much comfort to Rachel. Susie was too small for a saddle and rode sitting on a little blanket, clinging to the cinch strap that held it. Peter's arrangement was similar, but he handled his own reins. As soon as he was on the horse, he and his father dashed off. Rachel was stunned to see Peter galloping, without a saddle or stirrups, gripping the horse with his little short legs. He looked no bigger than that mythical elf that is said to gallop horses in the night, making them unfit for work in the morning.

The other horses wanted a gallop, too, and Rachel's took off at a brisk trot. They were well out on the path to the mountain before Rachel could convince the pony that today's pace would be a walk. After a while Coe caught up with her. He moved at a sedate walk, holding the reins of Susie's pony.

He smiled at her. "Got a frisky one there, have you?"

"Sometimes it takes a few minutes to convince them that you're the boss," she explained. "I'm glad you were able to do it so fast with your horse."

"Well, we've been acquainted before, me and this horse. How you doing, Susie? You want to go back home yet?"

"Giddap!" was Susie's reply.

With all the horses resigned to walking, they plodded up a narrow canyon and when they came out of it they were in the higher pastures. The land opened up in front of them, rolling hills with the grass already turning golden, the land rising toward mountains green with pines.

The sun was warm on their backs, but cool air rolled down from the higher hills, as clean and clear as spring water. In a hollow, Marc's horses had gathered to munch green grass. Most of them were buckskins, tawny animals with black manes and tails. Occasionally one would break from the group and run for no reason, just to feel the breeze flow over his glossy body, just to be beautiful on the hillside.

Marc and Peter had ridden all the way to the other side of the herd and could be seen loping away over a hill. No point in trying to catch up with them.

"Grandpa Coe, I want down!" complained Susie. "Down, Grandpa Coe!"

Coe got off his horse and lifted the child down. Walking around seemed like a good idea, and Rachel also climbed down. She dropped her reins so they touched the ground in front of the horse, and the well-trained beast stood quietly.

She said, "This is beautiful country up here. I can see why Marc loves it so much."

Coe looked around appreciatively. "It's a good kind of a life. And he's going to have a cowboy in that son of his before the kid's old enough to go to school!"

"Yeah, it's a good life."

"You don't sound very enthusiastic."

"I'm not," Rachel admitted. "I guess I'm a city person, at heart. Horses strike me as an anachronism. Who needs 'em? We've got lots of better things to ride on. My dream for Barbara was to see her with the kind of career where she would wear designer suits and go to an office every day with her hair done. Susie would wear dresses with big lace collars and go to dancing school with little legwarmers on."

"I guess kids sometimes turn out in ways that surprise us."

Rachel laughed, just a little, at herself. "I guess the real point of my dream is that they would be living in the same city I was."

"I wanna go home," said Susie.

Coe picked her up. "Okay, let's get you back on Thunder."

Susie screamed, "No! No! Don't wanna!" and kicked. Coe swung her away before she could connect with the horse and put her back on the ground.

He smiled down at the tiny tot in the grass. "Well, Susie, what have you got in mind, here? Going to walk back to the ranch?"

Susie began to cry. "I wanna go home! I want my mommy!"

Coe's expression was nonplused, and Rachel couldn't help laughing. "So, here we are, miles from anywhere with a three-year-old having a tantrum!"

"I guess we are," said Coe.

She picked up the weeping child and stroked her, talking in a soothing tone. "Poor baby, are you tired? I bet you want to be carried."

After a while Susie stopped crying and put her thumb in her mouth.

"You want Grandpa Coe to carry you?"

A nod around the thumb.

Coe climbed back onto his horse, and Rachel handed him the baby. He sat her in front of him, where she could grasp the saddle horn, and held her around her waist. She was instantly cheered. "I'm going to drive Grandpa Coe's horse!" she proclaimed.

Rachel took up Thunder's reins and got back onto her own horse, and they turned toward home. The horses perked up immediately. They stepped lightly and quickly, glad to be heading back to their own troughs of oats and hay.

By the time they reached the ranch house, Susie was asleep in Coe's arms, the thumb firmly in place. He handed her down to Rachel, who carried her, still stubbornly sleeping, into the house for a nap in her own crib.

Coe took care of the horses and Rachel started catching up with her neglected kitchen chores. After a while she went into the living room, where Coe was sitting beside Barbara.

"I'm trying to get him to tell me about his plane," she explained. "Everybody's gotten to see it except me. Marc says it's historical."

"It's a Flying Fortress," said Rachel.

Coe told her, "You gotta remember, to kids like Barbara, a thing like that's only history. It's like the Punic Wars or the conquests of Alexander the Great. Old stuff, dead stuff."

"Tell me about the Flying Fortress," Barbara begged.

Coe said, "In a lot of ways, the Fortress was the plane of The War. The Fort did most of the bombing that knocked Germany out. Yeah, I know, it's not politically correct these days to admit you're glad we won the war or to talk about the things we had to do to win it. The losses we took, the things we did. . . . Yeah, there were some terrible things that had to be done. We made a giant parking lot out of Berlin and a pile of ashes out of Dresden, but what nobody seems to remember is that the Nazis started it. Real early in The War, before we even got into it, they flattened Coventry and Rotterdam. They terror-bombed London for three years running. We had to beat the Germans and the Japanese, too, and our casualties were terrible. Thousands died at Bataan, at Iwo Jima, on D-Day, in the air war over Germany."

"And that's where you were," said Barbara.

"Yeah. In the Eighth, you had to fly twenty-five missions. You know how they got that figure? The losses were four percent per mission. After twenty-five missions, they didn't figure you were going to need your rations anymore and they stopped providing them. If you chanced to be still alive, you had beat one hundred percent odds and they sent you home. But you didn't have any friends, not anymore. You made sure never to make any friends, because you got so tired of having them die. You wanted the guys you flew with to be strangers."

He shook his head and smiled feebly. "That was all a long time ago. You asked about the Fort, well, what it was famous for was being able to take punishment and still fly. The Liberator was a good ship, but it had a narrow wing. Take a hit on the wing and it went down. Not the Fort. Chew it up, knock out a couple of engines, it still flew. I forget how many times I brought one in on ground effect."

"On what?" asked Rachel.

"Ground effect. Didn't they teach you that in school? That's okay; they never taught it to me, either. I had to find out by accident."

He made airplanes with his hands. "When an airfoil, a wing, goes through the air, the air flows over it and under it. There's got to be a point where the two flows come back together, and it's called the burble point because that's what the air does there, it burbles. Causes drag. Now, if you're so low the burble is hitting the ground, you lose that drag. Burble occurs at a point below the ship equal to half the wingspan, so on a Fort it's fifty feet. There I am—two engines out, a wing that looks like Swiss cheese, tail shot to hell, and wounded aboard. It was maybe my second or third mission; I barely knew where the controls were. I kept losing altitude until I was right on the deck, and then, she just started to fly. Ground effect. Carried us clear across the Channel and we landed in the first field we came to. It wasn't our field, but the ground crew dragged that Fort back to our base, stuck patches all over it, and put it back in the air."

"Hey, you guys back already?" yelled Marc as he came in, Peter riding gleefully on his shoulders. "Couldn't keep up, huh? What have we got here, a bunch of wimps?"

Fourteen

The following Friday Coe called from Phoenix and asked, "Did you like that Piper you were flying with Whales?"

"What? The plane I was learning in? Of course I liked it."

"I've found a guy here will rent me one for a couple of days. I'm going to bring it there tomorrow morning. Ask Marc to let you use his car, and come pick me up."

Rachel said, "Well, sure. You're leaving your car in Phoenix?"

"For now. I want you to put some air time in. You shouldn't stay away from it so long; you'll lose your edge."

"You're bringing a ship here all the way from Phoenix so I can put in some air time?"

"Don't you want to?"

"Of course I do. It's . . ." She paused, touched by his generosity. "It's extremely thoughtful of you, Coe."

She felt very lonely that evening. She was accustomed to sitting up late Friday nights to share a warm snack with Coe when he got in. Marc went to bed early as he always did, worn out from the physical labor he did all day. Barbara was always in bed, and Rachel sat alone.

She wished she had thought to bring along her aviation books; she could have brushed up on some of the things she would need to know for tomorrow's lesson. She had her logbook, but none of the texts. So she just sat and thought, and mostly she was thinking about Coe.

She must have been, because when she finally went to bed, she dreamed about him.

It was Coe as she had never seen him, naked and panting and on top of her. He was deep inside her, thrusting; she felt his skin against hers, his heavy breath. Her whole body was coiled toward a center, a center that was Coe.

She was the center. She was a hidden flame of pleasure. She pulled it to herself . . .

And woke in her lonely bed, with Coe still miles away in Phoenix.

Well, heavens to Betsy, Rachel muttered

as she separated herself from her tangled bedcovers and went to the bathroom for a drink of water. It had been a long time since she had had a sexual dream like that. Fancy these steamy fancies still coming along in the autumn of her life!

And there was no use thinking about Coe. Simple arithmetic told her that he had been separated, but firmly married, for thirty years. It would take a foolish woman to dream that he would change.

Marc left early the next morning. He planned a long trip through the upper meadows and would not be back until evening. Rachel packed sandwiches for him while he filled a canteen.

Well, he had his work to do, but Rachel had hoped he would be around to look after the children while she went to the airfield. How could she take a flying lesson with two children in tow?

She didn't mention the problem to Barbara. Barbara wasn't supposed to worry, and what would be the point of increasing the frustration she already felt that she was not able to get up from the couch and take care of her own children?

Nothing for it but to dress the kids, promise them games, put them into the car, and take them with her. They were agreeable; they loved the airfield.

To her surprise, they remembered the B-17 and demanded a closer look at it. So Rachel carried Susie across the field to the tiedown area where the big ship waited and let them touch the tires while she told them tales of the long-ago exploits of the Flying Fortress.

They had not waited long when Coe came in. Peter jumped up and down and cheered to see the little Piper land. Susie squirmed in Rachel's arms and kicked her with hard little shoe soles. She didn't mind. She was excited, too, just to see Coe, big and vital and real—this time.

He made his usual fuss over the kids, whirling Peter around in a hug, kissing little Susie. "Didn't know you were going to bring the kids," he said. "It's still early; you could have put some air time in."

"I had to bring them," Rachel explained. Marc's going to be gone all day, and I can't leave them with Barbara. They can't understand that she isn't allowed to get up, and they pull tricks to try to make her. You know, go into the next room and start screaming, just to see what she will do about it."

"I guess they're used to a more active mama. We can't take them up with us. They'd be a distraction and anyhow, it's illegal."

"I don't think Susie's car seat would fit in there, anyway. When do you have to take the Piper back? Maybe you can give me a lesson tomorrow."

"I'm planning to keep it until Wednesday, but let's do something now. Tell you what, I'll watch the kids and you can put in an hour shooting landings. You don't have to be checked out in that ship; you already know how to fly it."

"You're going to keep those two amused for a whole hour?"

"Sure. We'll have a good time; and when you come down, we'll all go home to lunch."

The plan had its ridiculous side; but Rachel was eager to fly, so she kissed the children, ran across the field to the ship, and got in.

There was no radio at this unnamed field, which simplified the takeoff procedure. She looked at the windsock and then she went. The little ship lifted briskly. She was in the air, and free.

She made a left turn and could see the town, nestled in a valley. The mesa that held the airfield and the ranch of its owner was south of town and also of Marc's ranch to the west. Rachel suddenly wanted to see the ranch from the air, and she turned west. It was all right, she was at five hundred feet, too high to scare the horses.

The ranch came in sight, looking like a miniature of itself, toy fences and the toy house where her daughter was.

And Rachel buzzed it.

She couldn't help herself. Well, she could have, if she had tried, but it was an instinct, probably the same one that makes dogs run after rabbits. The pilot who sees a familiar place wants to get closer, wants to have some effect on it.

It was a conservative buzz; she was fifty feet above the roof and made only one long, giddy pass. She knew Barbara would hear her, might even see the plane from the window.

Then she regained her altitude and flew back to the field.

On the downwind leg she checked the windsock and noted the wind had veered.

It was now blowing straight down the runway, fresher than it had been before. That should make the landings easier, she reflected. A good, strong wind down the runway is the pilot's dream. She could have the wheels on the ground right at the white line that marked the beginning of the pavement.

She was lined up with the runway, speed low, losing altitude, when suddenly the altimeter needle dropped and she was looking, no longer at the runway, but at the cliff below it. Her windscreen was full of mesa and the landing field was now above her head.

She was almost at stall speed. Nose up and she would surely stall and maybe spin. This close to the ground, there would be no hope of recovery. If she kept straight on, she would plow right into the side of the mesa. Rachel did three things simultaneously: She poured on the power, turned into a sharp bank, and let the nose go a little down.

The high wall of the mesa went by, it seemed, right under her feet; but there was blue sky ahead, and she was pulling away from the rocks into the safety of the uncluttered air to the south. Her heart was beating so fast it made her slightly dizzy. Maybe it was only from that steep bank.

She picked up altitude. Of course, she should have thought. The wind was blowing across the mesa and it went over the edge like water over a waterfall. She had approached too low, let the downdraft catch her with her nose high, vulnerable at that slow speed.

Well, never again at that airfield! She would go in high, and the heck with those flashy three-points that Randy used to make!

She turned the ship and again lined it up with the airstrip. This time she was careful to have altitude when she went over the edge of the mesa. The downdraft lowered her almost to the ground and her landing was not bad at all. She touched down a bit before the center of the runway.

She didn't have enough runway left to "shoot" the landing—that is, to take off again on the same pass—so she rolled to the end of the runway and would have turned, to go back to the beginning for her next takeoff, but Coe came running toward her.

He was carrying Susie, and Peter trailed after him, wailing because he couldn't keep up. Rachel was shocked. "My goodness, he shouldn't be running in this heat. And carrying the baby! He's as red as a beet!"

She threw open the door and said sharply, "Watch Peter! Don't let him get near the propeller!"

He was panting from his run, his hair on end and something wild in his eye. He reached for her. "Rachel, my God, Rachel . . ."

She took Susie from him, and he collected himself sufficiently to take Peter's hand. "I should have told you. Low ground in front of an airstrip, I should have told you to expect a sink."

"Is that what that was?"

"Downdraft caused by air flowing downhill. You pulled it off, Rachel! You did everything exactly right!"

"That's good to hear. Now, if you will please clear the field, I am going to shoot some landings."

He stared at her, loosening the grip he had on her shoulder. "Aren't you shaken up?"

"A little, but I have another half hour of flight time coming and I intend to use it. Would you take Susie, please?"

He accepted the child and backed away

from the door. "By God, you're a cool one! I wish I'd had you with me over Germany in '43!"

Rachel said, "What good would that have done? I was only ten years old."

As she turned the ship to go back to the foot of the runway, she saw him walking away, Susie under his arm, Peter holding his other hand.

Rachel did four landings without a mistake, none of them flashy, all conservative; and when she felt she had done enough, she taxied the plane to the tiedown area, put chocks under its wheels and looped ropes through the hooks on the wings.

Coe was subdued on the way back to the house, but the children weren't. They sensed that Grandpa Coe was upset, and it made them wild. Peter poked at Susie until she cried; both shouted for no reason and complained when they had to wear their seat belts.

Rachel was glad to get them home and inside the cool house. She gave them cold drinks and settled them in front of the TV with Barbara so she could start the lunch. For some reason, Coe objected.

"You're going to start *cooking* lunch?" he demanded.

Rachel continued hauling vegetables from the refrigerator. "What were you expecting? Breakfast?"

"You're taking this all so calmly," he complained.

"What other way is there to take it? Nothing happened; everybody's fine. You're like the kids; you want to jump up and down and scream for no reason."

"That's sort of how I feel. Rachel, I could have lost you! For a few seconds there, when you dropped out of sight over the edge of the mesa, I thought I had. I'm going to take that ship back to Phoenix. It was a bum idea to bring it here. Maybe it wasn't the right thing. . . . Maybe I shouldn't have encouraged you to start flying in the first place."

Rachel put down the bunch of carrots she held, and her hands went to her hips. "You brought that thing here so I could use it and now you want to take it back? Just because I learned something new today?"

"Suppose you had tried to climb instead of turning, like you did? At that speed you would have stalled, no matter how much power you turned on."

"Suppose pigs had feathers," she interrupted. "There'd be a good job for somebody, plucking at the slaughterhouse."

"Just seems like it would be better if you left the flying to somebody else."

"Somebody else like whom? You, I suppose! Let me remind you that you can't get your Fort off that airfield down there without me. You'd better want me to learn as much as I can and as fast as I can, and you'd better trust me to know what I'm doing."

"I wasn't saying you don't know what you're doing. I didn't mean it like that."

"And I suppose you think you've got a monopoly on worrying? Don't you think anybody else worries when you're flying? Don't you think I worry about you every Wednesday, driving all night and then flying to Mexico the next day?"

"It's different for you," he argued. "Women are used to worrying."

Rachel gave him a very sour look, but she couldn't keep it up. She shook her head and laughed. "Coe Flaherty, you are a piece of work!"

He ducked his head apologetically. "Well, I guess that isn't fair; but Rachel, I love you and I'm afraid of losing you."

"You do?"

"I'm crazy about you. I've been following you around like a puppy for the past month. What did you think I was doing it for?"

"Well, I thought it was because Whitey had to go to a wedding . . ." She broke off because she had never thought that, not really, so why was she pretending she had?

She said, "I'm afraid of losing you, too. I guess I love you that much. You'll just have to get used to the worrying; it's something that goes with aviation."

"You do love me, Rachel?"

"Enough to worry about you. That may not be very much, so don't try to make anything out of it."

But he was smiling, pensively. "You think it might grow into something?"

"It's late and everybody's hungry, so I'm going to make a skillet meal because it's fast. I could do with a couple of ripe tomatoes. Would you please see if we have some in the garden?"

"You didn't answer my question," he said softly.

"That's because I don't have an answer," she replied, and he went to look for the tomatoes.

Fifteen

The skillet lunch came out a little sloppy, which made it unpopular. The children would not eat it; after a couple of tastes they began to play and squabble.

As usual, Rachel had served the meal on a folding table in the living room so Barbara would not be eating alone. Barbara, propped up with many pillows, ate from a lap tray that was not, of course, in her lap. She had it by her side and awkwardly spooned the meal up to her mouth.

Susie sat in her high chair. She was still a sloppy eater, and Rachel always put a cloth down to protect the carpet. It was a lot of trouble to set up the meals in this way, but Rachel felt that it demonstrated that the family was still together.

This occasion, however, was not one of the happy ones. Coe was sullen. Marc was too polite to say so, but he obviously did not like his meal. The children were still acting up from earlier upsets. Peter pushed his food around the plate, shoving bits deliberately off the edge onto the tablecloth. Susie tried to get out of her chair and, when she could not, set up a non-stop whine.

"Eat your lunch," Barbara begged her. "It's really very good. Look, Mommie's eating it! Yum, yum!"

"She's probably tired," said Rachel. "I'll put her down for her nap as soon as I'm finished eating."

Peter slipped out of his chair and went to Susie's. Whatever he did there made Susie howl and Barbara said sharply, "Peter, come here please!"

Peter went to his mother, climbed onto the couch, and upset the tray with her lunch on it. Silverware and the tray clattered to the floor; the plate turned over and spread the skillet supper—tomatoes, meat sauce and vegetables—down the side of the couch. Barbara exclaimed; Susie bawled.

Rachel jumped out of her chair, retrieved the plate and a knife, and began scraping vegetables off the couch. Marc gave Peter a swat, and his howls joined Susie's. Barbara went into the kitchen and returned with a wet cloth, with which she began mopping at the spots on the couch.

Rachel said, "Barbara, what are you doing? You're not supposed to get out of bed! Get back in; I'll clean this up."

"Look at this couch!" Barbara replied. "It isn't even a year old, and look at the condition it's in!"

Rachel gently took the cloth from her hand. "Well, you can't say you're not getting a lot of use out of it. Get back in bed, dear."

Instead, Barbara went to Susie's chair, released the strap, and lifted the howling child down. Susie was so surprised she stopped crying. Peter had already sobbed into another room, and there was a tense silence.

Marc said, "Barbara, don't do that! You're not supposed to lift things!"

"I've had it!" Barbara said angrily. "This is it; I'm not getting back in that bed! I'm not allowed to do anything. I can't even take care of my kids! I just have to lie there as if I were already dead!"

"It's only for a little while longer," Rachel argued.

"Maybe it seems like a little while to you, but do you know what it's like for me? The hours go by and there've never been so many of them in a day before. Nothing to look forward to but the next meal! I look at my watch, and it's always about two hours earlier than I thought it was. Everybody gets to do things, except me. My own mother is flying over the house, and I didn't even get to look at it! I want to go look at the airplanes! I want to ride my horse over to the airstrip and look at the Flying Fortress!"

Coe stuck a chair behind her knees and said, "Sit down, Barbara," and she did. "You're being sort of silly. Nobody rides horses when they're as pregnant as you are, not even if everything is normal."

"I am normal!" Barbara insisted. "I feel a little dizzy, but it's just because I've been lying down for so long. There's nothing wrong with me. I'm going to rejoin the world."

She reached out and drew Susie against her, and the child nestled contentedly against her mother.

Rachel went back to scrubbing the couch, talking as she worked. "I can understand that you feel imprisoned, Barbara. What you have to do is difficult for you. But let me remind you that the whole thing was your idea. You went against the doctor's orders to start this pregnancy; now they are telling you that only bedrest will save it. It's about time you started to listen to them."

Barbara argued, "Can't I do what they say, only just not have it be so extreme? Look at me, I'm sitting in a chair! God, but it feels good just to sit in a chair! Why can't I do a few things if I take it easy? Play with the children, take a walk outside. Can't I take a walk, Marc?"

Marc was still sitting at the table, and he folded his arms sullenly. "Don't ask me to make your decisions for you. You make them yourself when it suits you; now you're going to ask me so you'll have somebody to blame later on."

Barbara's eyes filled with tears at his harsh tone. "All I want to do is take care of my family and my own house. I want to see the sky and the land, go somewhere, visit somebody."

"You're going to," Coe assured her. "Only later on. As you keep saying, you're a normal person. The thing is, right now, you've got a job to do. It's a very important job; that's why you started it, and only you can do it. Only you can finish it. It'll be finished soon, and then you can do the things you want to do. You can last out until then, can't you?"

The tears rolled out of those big brown eyes and streaked down her cheeks. "Can't there be a compromise? Can't I sit in a chair once in a while, take a shower? That's what I'd like the best! I want to wash my hair!"

"Okay, here's the deal," said Marc. "I'll carry you upstairs to the shower so you can wash your hair, and after that you're going to stop giving everybody a hard time." Marc carried her upstairs every night at bedtime. He continued, "Your mother's practically giving up her own life to help you out, and Coe, too. This isn't easy for any of us, and you've got to do your part."

"Easy for you to say. You don't have to do this."

"I guess you've got the hardest part, but the only way it's going to get done is if we all pull together."

Barbara knuckled the tears on her cheeks. "I'm sorry, Marc." She added dutifully, "I'm sorry, Mom. I'm sorry, Coe."

"Come on, let's go get the shampoo." Marc hoisted her up in his arms and walked up the stairs as easily as if she had been one of the children. He remained up there, supervising, while Rachel rounded up the children and put them down for naps.

"Barbara's getting stir-crazy," she confided to Coe. "We've got to think up some ways to amuse her."

"We're all going to put on paper hats and do the buck-and-wing?"

"I was thinking more in terms of getting her friends to visit more often. I'll just call them up and invite them."

Coe groaned. "Do we have to have that one with the laugh?"

"I'm afraid that's one of her best friends."

"It's like being inside the house with a donkey. Well, I guess I can find something to do in the barn when she's here."

"I'll invite her on a Thursday," Rachel promised.

After that Barbara came to the table for meals. Rachel suspected that she had felt a couple of cramps during the hair-washing incident; but if she had, she never admitted it. She never complained again, either.

Rachel invited the friends over, singly or in very small groups, and served them cake and goodies to encourage repeat visits. Somehow, in spite of cake-baking and all the other chores, she managed to put in some flight time every day that the Piper remained at Alcalde. Twice they even got Marc to watch the children so Coe could give Rachel a lesson.

She loved those afternoons. The sky was always clear; they flew in an immense dome of hot, still air, the ground green below them and, in the distance, the mountains blue with sharp white peaks.

Every day that the birth of Barbara's baby was delayed was a little victory, every hour improved the child's chances of being born healthy. All the family was glad to see the weeks go by, to mark them off on a mental calendar, only five weeks until the baby will be full term, four, three . . .

Then one afternoon Barbara woke from a nap crying, "Mom! Mom! The water broke! I felt it!"

Sure enough, the couch was wet under her, and even as Rachel provided a towel, a new gush joined the puddle.

"A contraction! The baby's coming!"

Rachel tried to sound soothing. "Maybe it was just a Braxton-Hicks contraction, honey."

Barbara raised those huge dark eyes.

"No, it wasn't. This one meant business. I felt the sting in its tail."

"I'm going to call the hospital and alert them that we're coming. The guys are both out chasing horses someplace and we can't wait for them; you've got to go now. Can you walk to the car?"

"I think so, but we can't leave the children here."

"They'll go with us."

"But what will we do with them when we get to the hospital? You know they aren't allowed inside."

"I'll worry about that when we get there."

Rachel wrote the word "hospital" on a paper and stuck it to the refrigerator door. That's where Coe and Marc always went first, anyway. She shooed Susie and Peter into the car and helped Barbara in and they were away, laying a long dust cloud as they headed for the hospital.

Barbara had had no further contractions and she was encouraged by that. She fastened the children into their seat belts and sang songs to them while Rachel concentrated on covering the miles.

At the hospital, Rachel took the children into the lobby and parked them there while Barbara was admitted. It didn't take long, fortunately, for the contractions had resumed. By the time Barbara was wheeled away she was weeping, clutching her belly as if she could hold the baby inside with her hands.

Rachel had to stay with the children. Peter was already investigating the aquarium, and Susie was trying to climb up to see what he was doing. She couldn't follow Barbara. She had not a toy or a book with her, and the kids were stimulated by the change in their routine and ran all over the lobby. The only thing that was going right, she reflected, was that they were not upset. They had become quite accustomed to rushing their mother to this hospital.

Rather desperately, she collected them and did finger games, but they had scarcely begun when Coe and Marc arrived. It hadn't taken them long to find her note. As usual, Coe took charge of the kiddies while Marc and Rachel rushed upstairs to find out about Barbara.

She was in the birthing room and crying wildly. Rachel rushed to hold her, repeating witlessly, "It's going to be all right, darling; it's going to be all right!"

Another contraction hit Barbara, and she writhed away with a shriek. Then Marc took both her hands and said firmly, "You've got to stop fighting it, Barbara. You learned better than that in your first Lamaze class, way back when it was Peter. Now come on, relax and get ready to take a deep breath."

"It's too soon," wept Barbara. "I can't have the baby yet; it's too soon!"

"The doc says it's all right," Marc assured her. "The baby's going to be fine."

The doctor had actually said it was too late to stop the labor, but Barbara believed Marc and began to get herself under control.

She cried a lot. Between pants, she asked piteously about her children; and a few minutes after being assured they were in good hands, she would ask again. But Marc was a good coach. He made her focus, and she was breathing and panting correctly. Rachel felt superfluous, and after a while she went downstairs to report to Coe.

He had somehow acquired coloring books, and the two kids were scribbling away. Rachel reported, "She's having the baby. It's going well; she isn't in any danger this time. I only hope it isn't too early."

He didn't say anything, but took her hand and they sat together, watching Susie and Peter work on their books. It was a good feeling to have a strong hand wrapped around hers, Rachel thought. It wasn't the kind of strength that Barbara needed right now, but it was doing Rachel a lot of good.

Periodically, one or the other of them would get up and go inquire about Barbara; and the answer was always the same, everything was proceeding normally. Around lunch time, they took the kids to the cafeteria and the complications of finding out what the children wanted and getting it onto trays occupied everybody for a space. Susie regarded every article of food she saw as alien, except for one item. Like all hospitals, this one was very large on Jello.

Rachel ate scarcely more than Susie did, picking at the over-boiled chicken on her plate.

"Come on, eat something," Coe urged her.

"How can you say that?" she whined. "When something is so bad the patients won't eat it, they send it to the cafeteria; everybody knows that."

"Peter and I thought the hot dogs were pretty good." Coe smiled, sympathetic and encouraging. "Don't worry, Rachel."

"I just can't bear the thought that she's

in pain right now, my little girl!" Rachel mumbled so the kids would not hear.

"This is worse than being with the expectant father," Coe complained. "Him, I could at least take to a bar for a couple of stiff ones."

"I'd love a stiff drink," Rachel admitted. "But let's face it, if this cafeteria had one, it would probably taste as bad as this chicken."

"How many grandchildren do you have?"

"Five. Almost six."

"If you take it this hard every time, I don't know how you've survived."

"You don't understand. A mother suffers when her daughter is in labor; but when it's a daughter-in-law, that's different. Let *her* mother do it."

"I sure don't feel like going back to that lobby. Hey, would you kids like another Jello?"

The children were eager to try a color different from the one they had just consumed, and another half hour was passed. Then boredom set in, and they began running around the cafeteria and had to be collected and taken back to the boring old lobby.

Around dusk, the baby was born. A little

girl, a few ounces short of five pounds, but perfect in every way. Her name was Nancy.

Everybody jumped up and down with joy. Rachel sat with Barbara for a short time while Marc grabbed a bite to eat, for he was spending the night on a cot in the room with his wife and new daughter.

As they were gathering up the coloring books and getting the children ready to go, Rachel overheard a fragment of conversation from one of the lobby workers. ". . . those children. The grandparents are going to take them home now, thank heavens."

Grandparents, Rachel was thinking as they herded Susie and Peter to the car. She and Coe must look exactly like a matched set of grandparents. It was a nice thought, even if it were only an appearance. The children had grandparents. They had family.

When the children had been fed and the bedtime stories read and all was quiet, it was lovely to sit alone with Coe and just enjoy the evening. They both felt tired and glad and grateful that Barbara and the baby were both all right. And there was something more, a deep contentment in just being where they were and who they were. They didn't even talk much, but sat under the lamp together. The grandparents.

After a couple days of observation, Barbara and Nancy were pronounced ready to come home, even though Nancy's weight was still not ideal. Marc and Rachel strung paper streamers and balloons through the house to celebrate this homecoming.

It had been a splendid visit and Rachel had gloried in the chance to participate in her daughter's life, but there comes a point when a mother-in-law in the house changes from a necessity to an irritant and it is time for the young family to be on their own again.

Rachel recognized the time when it arrived, even though she did not welcome it. She had thought to stay until the baby was sleeping through the night, but so small a morsel of humanity could not easily manage that and Nancy still woke up hungry. Rachel ached to think of the hardships Barbara was going to face without her, but it was time to go.

And as for herself, she felt like a kid out of school. Coe had been readying the B-17 for days—oiling things, tuning, fussing. He had returned his rental car, packed his expanded wardrobe into a new bag. The whole family went along to drop them off at the airfield and stayed to watch the take-off.

Rachel had kissed her daughter, wept to kiss the children; but it was astonishing how they dropped from her mind as soon as she was scampering across the tarmac toward the plane, toting her overnight bag, wearing her yellow suit again.

Inside the plane she waved to them through the plexiglass, and four hands waved back. Nancy was too small to wave, of course.

Coe paused over the checklist. "You sorry to be leaving?"

"I'll miss the children so," Rachel began and then laughed at herself. "My God, but I'm glad to get out of this place! I want to see my own home again and my own garden and my friends and put on civilized clothes and eat a meal I didn't cook myself!"

He laughed with her. "Pierre's?"

"You are an understanding man."

"I'm kind of glad to be going, myself. Little kids are great, but I'm sure glad I don't have to have any around all the time! How do those young people do it?"

"They're young," she explained.

Sixteen

Deena knew it was Chief's voice the instant he said her name. She was up to her elbows in paper work and phone calls kept coming in, and suddenly there was a halt in the whole progress of her day because she heard that voice.

He said, "Deena? Is that you? You're answering your own phone now?"

"The switchboard girl's on her break. Hello, Chief. How are you?"

"Hoping you'll talk to me. Is this a bad time? Should I call back later?"

"No, this is fine," said Deena and genuinely thought so. She was alone; the office was empty. Not even the switchboard girl would know Chief had called. Nobody could ever know what they said to each other. "I'm glad you called."

And then the stupid buzzing began and she had to say, "I have an incoming call. Do you mind if I put you on hold?"

"That's okay."

She took care of the call and then pressed the button that would get her back to Chief. She even had rehearsed in her mind what she would say. "I am glad you called because I feel like I owe you an apology."

"You don't have to apologize."

"I know, but I'm sorry about that Saturday. I told you I wouldn't come; but still, I know you waited for me and. . . . Well, I'm sorry."

"You didn't . . . didn't come," he fumbled, but for only a second. "It's okay, Deena, I understand. I really do." Did his voice change, just there? Somehow it seemed brighter, more confident, quite as if he had moved closer to the phone. "I miss you so much, I had to call. I just miss everybody out there on the Coast. How's your friend, Rachel, these days?"

"I haven't seen her in a while; she's out of town. Her daughter is ill, and she's at her place looking after the children."

"That's too bad. Deena, I need to talk to you, see you, touch you."

A little alarmed, she asked, "You are in Houston, aren't you?"

"Yes, but I'll come there if you'll let me.

Do you miss me? Deena, darling, do you want me to come?"

"No, don't."

"I need to be with you. All I can think about is you. All these weeks, and it doesn't get any better."

"I think about you, too, Chief."

His voice broke, and he stammered, "Deena, I love you! This never happened to me before, not like this! I can't get you out of my mind. Don't you love me? I have to talk to you. That's all I want to do, just talk to you."

"Don't start that," she interrupted. Another incoming call buzzed for her attention, and she deliberately disconnected it.

He was still talking. "Please let me see you. Please let me come."

"Lunch only," she decreed. "In a public place, understand? No limos."

"Public place. I promise. Anything you say. I'll be there tomorrow."

They met at the restaurant in Calabasas and her heart turned over at the sight of him waiting for her outside on a bench that must have been put there especially for impatient swains. He stood up and smiled, and suddenly she was freed. Her workaday world had faded away like something of no importance. Nothing mattered but to be with Chief, to be in paradisiacal Calabasas on a sunny afternoon with nothing to keep them from being together.

It was just for an hour. Only a lunch.

They chatted about themselves, briefly discussed the current political situation. They ate the mahi-mahi and drank a glass of wine, and it didn't take long enough so they ordered coffee and a dessert that neither particularly wanted. Then they poked at it with forks and mostly just smiled at each other.

Until Chief suddenly grabbed the flowers from the vase on the table, threw himself onto his knees beside her chair, and cried, "Deena, I can't keep this up any longer! I don't want to live without you! Say you'll be mine! Marry me, Deena; I love you!"

Everybody in the place was staring at them, and Deena recoiled in horror. "Chief, get up!" she hissed at him.

"Not until you promise! Love me! Marry me!"

She took the flowers he was offering, stuck them back into the vase, and muttered, "If you don't get up, I'm walking right out and leaving you down there. You'll have to pretend you're picking up cigarette butts!"

"If you won't promise, I'll stay here on my knees until you do!"

"Get up," Deena begged desperately. "I'll promise."

He leaped up and kissed her. The other diners applauded. Chief sat down with a smile of satisfaction. "You meant that, didn't you, Deena? You'll promise?"

Of course she would. She'd already said it, so she had to, didn't she? She whispered between clenched teeth, "We are both married; how can you say something like that?"

"We are going to be married to each other. I'm getting a divorce. You'll do it, too, won't you, Deena?"

"How can I answer that? Do you really expect to rearrange our whole lives, both of us, over a chocolate brownie, right here, right now?"

He took both her hands across the table. "It's all going to take time, but tell me it's going to happen. Tell me you love me."

"I guess I must. I keep meeting you . . . The chances I'm taking . . ."

"I can stay here in L.A. another day. You'll meet me, won't you, darling? Tomorrow noon at The Pines. It's going to happen for us. It's going to happen this time."

And Deena said, "Yes."

When Deena pulled into her own driveway that evening, there was a car in Rachel's drive. So, Rachel was back. She knew she should go over and give Rachel a report on the houseplants Deena had been watering for her, but she didn't. At this point, she didn't want to talk to Rachel.

On the other hand, it wasn't Rachel's car. Suppose robbers had driven right into the driveway? Sneakily, she waited in her own car, shielded from sight by the hedge, until she spotted movement next door. Through the kitchen window she saw a man; and sure enough, it was Coe.

Deena got out of the car and bustled into her own home. Coe! He certainly spent enough time at Rachel's! She could not have been home more than a few hours, and yet Coe was already there. It could make a person think.

It could make Deena feel a whole lot better.

So much better, she was humming as she went upstairs. A little song about love, love,

love. She pushed open the door to Lonnie's room to say hello to him, but it was empty. More baseball practice, probably. She pushed open the door to Terry's. "Hello, dear!"

Terry was flopped on the bed, a book close to her nose. Papers were scattered about, the usual signs of a study session. But Terry's study buddy was a boy, and he was sitting on the bed with her.

Just sitting, just pointing something out in the book she held, but a boy! And one Deena had never seen before. Was his face familiar? How could she know? They all looked alike to her, every one of them—gangly, pimpled, unkempt, their noses and lips too big for their faces.

She said, "We'll have the door open, please," and continued on to her own room.

Behind her own closed door she stripped off her work clothes and hung them up, reached for a pair of jeans. Still holding them in her hand she paused, seeing herself in a full-length mirror.

The face changes over the years, the hands, even the arms; but those parts of the body that are covered by clothing remain the same, like something packed away in the closet for use later. Her skin was as fresh and smooth as it had been twenty years ago, her curves better. Full, heavy breasts, narrow waist with the flare of hips just below it. Chief would be excited; he would say extravagant things . . .

If she went to him tomorrow. She hadn't done it yet. She was going to. She had promised. It was all set up, but she still could back out. She still could let it go, this adventure, this gambler's game where the stakes grew higher with every move.

She wasn't the type to take foolish chances, but even as she reminded herself of that fact, she was checking the drawer to be sure she had available a set of her favorite silk underthings.

It was still early in the day when they landed at Van Nuys, so after Coe rented a car, he and Rachel stopped on the way to her home and picked up groceries.

It wasn't until she was unloading the bags in her kitchen that Rachel realized the significance of what she had bought. Her grocery order included all the things Coe liked best to eat, including his favorite breakfast.

She stood staring at the eggs and the

chilies, things she had given up eating years before, and she burst out laughing. "Look at that! I'm so used to having you around, I've just assumed you're going to be eating here!"

Coe laughed, too. "Can I call this an invitation?"

Rachel only had to think about it for a second. "If you want to use my guest room, I would be delighted to have your company; but I do understand if you have some other place to go. You know, Coe, I've said this before, but you have been so kind and considerate to me and my family and I do appreciate it. You've given us four weeks right out of your life, and I know it wasn't convenient for you. I am grateful; and if there is anything I can do for you, I'll be glad to."

"I've got some suggestions," he said with a lecherous smile.

"You know what kind of things I mean. In fact, you've got to promise not to pressure me about sex. I don't want to have a fight with you."

"I'd like to stay," he said. "I'm not real fond of spending my evenings all alone in a hotel. And I guess I'll promise not to have any sex with you." He made his fake smile. "Unless you beg me, of course."

Rachel did not laugh. "I'd appreciate a moratorium on the sexual innuendo and jokes, too. If you want to clean up before we go to Pierre's, the guest room is on the right at the top of the stairs. You can put your things in there."

"I'd better call the hotel and tell them where I'm going to be. Whitey's coming, and he'll expect to find me at Airtel."

He ambled off, and Rachel fell to scrubbing the vegetables so she could package them for the refrigerator. It felt wonderful to be in her own home again. Comfortable, her own things around her, her own closet full of her own clothes to choose from, and Coe for company.

Yes, the real wonder was having Coe to talk to, to cook for, just to be there. That he wanted to intensify the relationship she knew; and she was getting so the idea came to her own mind more and more often, but now she was afraid of it.

What if they tried it and it didn't work? Chief had once called her a "sexpot" but he had been teasing; she knew she was not sexy and never had been. She wouldn't know how to approach a sexual relationship with Coe . . . with anybody.

It was so satisfactory, just being with him, just talking to him; why did he have to want to change anything? As far as she was concerned, it could take Whitey forever to make the trip to Los Angeles. Coe could stay forever in her guest room; she wanted nothing but continuation of everything she had now, just the way it was.

Deena was in the kitchen and had dinner well under way when Terry's friend left. She heard their footsteps on the stairs and then the front door slammed. Terry stalked into the kitchen, the picture of adolescent outrage.

"Mother, how could you *do* that to me? Of all the insensitive things!" Terry sputtered, too angry for speech.

"I never thought to lay down rules on this subject," Deena admitted. "I didn't because I thought your natural good taste would keep you from doing things that are questionable, like that one."

"I didn't do anything!"

"I know you didn't. Well, yes, you did do something, and I'll tell you what. You set yourself up. Having study dates is fine, even having study dates with boys. But a study date with one boy, in your room, on the bed, with the door closed and neither of your parents at home? That's plain dumb!"

"Kevin is a nice boy!"

"So are they all, all honorable men, and all nice boys. Listen to me, Terry; you are a special person. You've got brains, you've got looks, you have the opportunity to go to college, to make something out of yourself; and you're not only going to do it, I know you, you're going to do it all with class and with style. Nobody's going to take advantage of you. Nobody's going to push you around, and don't you ever let them. Especially don't let a man get the upper hand with you. Don't ever let him get power over you."

Terry found this tirade puzzling, but at least it was making her forget her grievance. She murmured, "I wasn't planning on *empowering* anybody."

"You probably are too young for this, but you might as well hear it anyhow. Sit down."

They faced each other across the kitchen table. "I'm going to tell you about men, and boys, too. They itch. You've got to feel sorry for them, because they itch all the time. It's as if they were constantly buried to the neck in anthills and you've got the only thing that can scratch them. The world is full of guys who want you to scratch them, who want to use you; and the better-looking you are, the more the guys are going to try. You're probably meeting them already, young as you are. The itch makes them do funny things. It can make them do violent things, some of them, and there's no way to tell which guys are violent or when one might go over the edge. That's why all those rules exist, all those rules you find so stupid. You don't go places alone with them. You don't dance in the dark; you don't trust blindly. You don't set yourself up."

Terry was staring at her, overwhelmed, her mouth slightly open but nothing coming out of it.

Deena went on, "They're not all into rape, but sometimes the ones that aren't can be the most dangerous. They'll tell you anything, make promises, say anything; but they're all crashing lies. The minute they've been satisfied, they don't know you any more. The act is important to them, the consequences are important to you."

Terry crossed her arms impatiently. "Yeah, yeah, you keep telling me. I can get pregnant."

"And you are the only party to the transaction who can. Besides that, there is a whole list of diseases that are transmitted that way, several of which can kill you and one that will for sure. AIDS is surer than hanging. And I'll tell you a nasty consequence that isn't on the disease list: you could fall in love. You could fall in love with a guy who doesn't care, who has gone off some place and doesn't even remember your name. You're only going to be young once; don't throw yourself away trying to please a boy who doesn't care about you."

"I'm not going to do anything like that."

"Probably Susie Wong didn't think she was going to, either. Sex can be beautiful, but only when it's an interaction between two people who care about each other—when there's love and sharing and consideration on both sides, when it's truly a partnership."

Terry tossed her artfully-disordered hair. "Yeah, yeah, I understand. Why shouldn't

I when I'm surrounded by such great role models?"

"What do you mean? Your father and I are always considerate of one another."

"And you and Chief, too?" A smile twisted across Terry's face at her mother's reaction. "You didn't expect that from me, did you? Mousy little Terry—keep her in the dark, don't tell her anything, don't pay any attention to her and she won't give any trouble! Well, I see more than you think I do, and I saw you kissing him that night I was supposed to be at Marilyn's!"

"You did? Well, it wasn't anything, just a friendly peck," protested Deena.

Terry jumped up from her chair, too full of resentment to sit. "You never even asked me why I was home and not at Marilyn's slumber party. You never even asked how I got home. Well, I had to walk. Marilyn and some of the other kids were smoking dope, and I had to walk all the way home in the dark because nobody was home at my house to come and get me. My mother and even Auntie Rachel were out on a date with some guys from work!"

Deena sat back with a puff of surprise. "Wow! This is a whole new can of worms!

You and Marilyn have been friends since elementary school!"

"Not any more. I'm still trying to get her to understand she's being a sucker to get into that stuff, but I guess that's what she wants."

Deena asked, "Do you think it would be the right thing to report her?"

"To whom? It's not likely to be news to her parents that she's smoking."

Deena slumped in her chair, her eyes wide from the pressure of thoughts behind them. "Don't ever tell anybody I admitted this, but you're a lot smarter than I am. Just one disclaimer. It's true that I kissed Chief and it's also true that I find him very attractive. I even had lunch with him a couple of times. But nothing has happened, I promise you truly, nothing has happened and nothing will. You are far too important to me. I'm not going to put my home, my family, in jeopardy."

And she wouldn't.

Seventeen

They had a delightful dinner at Pierre's, where no babies cried or whined, nothing smelled of horses, and there were no dishes to wash. It wasn't until they got home again that Rachel thought of the children and missed them, their noise, their demands, their precious faces. She walked into her house and it seemed cavernous, dark, and lonely.

"It's so quiet," she complained, turning on every light. "It's so quiet, MTV would be an improvement. Well, almost."

Coe smiled wisely. "Missing the kiddies, are you?"

"Yes, I miss Susie and Peter and Nancy. But you know who I'm really missing? Kenny and Dan and Barbara."

"You just saw Barbara."

"Not now-Barbara. Then-Barbara. Barbara the chubby baby with big brown eyes and a mop of brown curls. Kenny and Dan with their sturdy little short legs and their cute tricks and their smart mouths and their mobs of voracious friends stripping my refrigerator bare, hogging the living room, getting the furniture dirty, spilling on the rug . . ."

Coe laughed indulgently. "Those were the days, eh?"

"If I could have it all back again," dreamed Rachel, "I'd . . ." She paused to consider and finished, " . . . probably die from the stress. Let's go watch the late news before we turn in."

After Coe had gone to the guest room and closed the door, Rachel checked the locks, put out the lights, and climbed to her own room. The lonely feeling remained, and she regretted having packed up Barbara's toys and artifacts when she had moved into this room. The presence of a teddy bear or two would be comforting right now.

Or would it? She tossed on her narrow bed, weary but sleepless. No point in pretending she was a child who could be satisfied with teddy bears. Perhaps it had been a mistake to invite Coe to the house. Having him so close was ruinous to her sleep. She reached up and touched the wall by her bed. He was just on the other side, warm and strong and so very dear to her. She had only to call him . . .

And then what? She wouldn't have the least idea how to proceed. A seduction scene? As if she had ever known how to do that! And suppose she got him into the bed, what then? Pete had never complained of her performance in bed, but then he had never praised it, either. She could have been doing it all wrong for thirty-five years and never have known.

Coe was sixty-eight years old—suppose he could not perform? That would be her fault, too. Better just to leave well-enough alone. Why open up a whole new area for misunderstandings, quarrels, and disappointments? Better not to risk losing a friendship she had come to value.

Better to be too old.

She might have known, Deena reflected, that The Pines was going to have closed-circuit TV. She drove slowly under the sign and into the parking lot behind the building. She was rather surprised to analyze her own feelings and find the one that was uppermost was hunger, along with a bit of annoyance because she was going to miss her lunch.

She knocked on the door of number seven and Chief had her in his arms before she could say a word, giving her a burning kiss while he kicked the door shut. He even managed to shoot the brass bolt above the doorknob without loosening his grip on her, and she wondered how long he had needed to practice to learn a skill like that.

When she could break the kiss she began, "Chief, we have to talk . . ."

"Deena, you came! You do love me, you're here!"

"I'm here because it didn't feel right, standing you up a second time. Now, listen to me . . ."

"Just let me look at you. You're so beautiful, do you know what you do to me?"

He had his hand inside her shirt—where had the buttons gotten to?—and the fire was burning between them. She couldn't get her breath to protest more. All that came out was a feeble, "Chieeeef!"

His fingers touched her bare skin and felt the curve of her breast. Between kisses he mumbled, "I want you so. I want you forever. We'll be together. I'll marry you, Deena."

"Now that did it!" She broke away from his hands, pulled her shirt together. She was suddenly angry, really angry—not, as she generally was, just irked by his lies. Her daughter could fall into the hands of a guy like this; she was as angry as if she were protecting Terry instead of herself.

"Stop that!" she ordered, brushing away his attempts to embrace her again. "I came here to talk, and you're going to shut up and listen!"

"Aw, Deena, don't start playing hard to get at this late stage!"

"I'm not playing! I have kids; I have a marriage; and I'm not putting it all on the line for a roll in the hay with you, no matter how much I'd like to!"

He rolled back on his heels and prepared for debate. "Now that's it right there. You want to. You even admit you want to. When are you going to do something just because you want to? Do you really want to spend the rest of your life sacrificing yourself for the sake of your family?"

Deena buttoned her shirt, ignoring the disarray of her underwear beneath it. "This is seeming like less of a sacrifice all the time."

"You're not happy with your husband.

Do you know how I can tell? You never say his name; he's your 'marriage,' an abstract. You're giving up your self for an abstract."

"Lucky me," grumbled Deena. "I get my choice between an abstract and a scam."

"Deena, Deena, do you really think that? Can you really think that about me? Can't you see I love you? I'll do anything for you. I'll break up my marriage for you. We'll break up both marriages, and then we can be together forever."

"Boy, is that a great plan! If you really mean to do it, and I doubt that, it's a little complicated, Chief! Two divorces: You and—what's her name? Tricia; me, and Ethan. Four people involved, not to mention the kids. As a friend of mine always says, let's look at the numbers."

He spread out his arms. "Deena, what's the matter? You love me. You know you do."

"Probably. Fool that I am. How old are you, Chief?"

He mumbled, "Fifty-five."

"Ten years from retirement. How long have you been married? Thirty years or so? Do you know what a divorce is going to cost you? Only everything! She'll get the house and half of everything you've earned for the last thirty years. Are both your daughters married? No? You still have a *wedding* to pay for? And maybe a little something to help the young couple get started?"

"Oh, come on, Deena. It won't be that bad."

"The hell it won't! And don't count on me to help you! This is a community-property state, and my business is worth a lot more than Ethan's is. I'd be lucky if I didn't lose the business; he'd clean me out. I'd have to get a job. I'd be doing data entry somewhere for coolie wages, and I've got two kids who are both headed for college. My baby's only fourteen. Are you ready for stepchildren, Chief? And oh, yes, incidentally, I'm not uprooting my kids from their home and their high school and moving them to another state. If we're going to be together, you'll have to give up your job in Houston and move here. You'll be job-hunting at your age in an economy that's not exactly booming right now. If you lose your job and I lose my business, we're going to be scratching to survive; forget retirement. We'll both be working forever!"

"You're exaggerating. Tricia wouldn't do that to me; she's not the kind to skin a man alive." He sat down on the edge of the bed, loosening his necktie impatiently. "We've got something beautiful between us, Deena. Beautiful and rare and fragile. If you're going to come in here talking like a tax accountant, you're going to spoil it all."

"There are a few things I'm sure of, and one of them is taxes. The other is that this love is already spoiled. It is over. It was nothing but a little blip in the sameness of our lives. Forget it."

He sprang up. "Forget? I'll never forget. All the days of my life I'm going to remember you . . . Deena."

Dear Chief. The sheer desolation of his stance reminded her of her teenagers, and she said, "It's a shame the Air Force got you in your youth; you'd have been a fine actor. A method actor. You take a pose and as soon as you have taken it, you believe in it. You believe I've broken your heart. I'll bet the feeling lasts about as long as it's going to take you to drive back to the Airtel bar."

He turned his face away, so she couldn't see his eyes. "Go ahead. Be cynical. Make fun of me. I must look pretty silly, a bald old man longing for a beautiful young woman."

"You may be a little short on hair," she interrupted, "but God knows you can talk, and I'm not giving you the chance to start. Goodbye, Chief. I'm outta here."

Coe had spent the day running errands of his own. Rachel had cleaned her dusty, neglected house. She had a service that did the windows, a gardener for the outside, she really needed only to dust and vacuum. There was time to create a dinner menu. She had a chicken marinating, some strawberries for dessert.

Her kitchen, like Deena's, overlooked the front lawns of both houses. She could see Ethan outside, examining a flower bed, poking at the primroses that had bloomed their season and were drying to crisp brown stalks in the August heat.

She was shredding things for the salad when Coe returned. When Coe came home. How pleasant it was to think of her home as his, to be ending the day with this meeting, to share shelter and food with . . . all right, with whom? A friend? A companion, a mentor, an associate. . . . She didn't really have to fish for words; she knew exactly the right ones. She was sharing her home and her meal with someone she loved.

The moment lacked only the hugs and kisses of a real family, but of course they couldn't have that. He wasn't her husband, after all.

He was somebody else's.

Her greeting was a little too bright, too loud. She waved vivaciously with a wet lettuce leaf and called, "Hello, Coe! Come in! Did you have a good day?"

His scowl did not lighten; he was finding the moment as awkward as she was. "Yeah, sure. Got everything done okay."

"Dinner will be ready soon. Would you like a drink while you wait?"

"Something light. You got any more of that fruit stuff?"

"You mean that cranberry drink? In the refrigerator. Do you want a . . ." She broke off, looking out the window. "Deena just got home. I haven't talked to her since I got back. Maybe I can catch her before she goes in the house."

She watched as Deena got out of her car and walked over to the flower bed and stood beside her husband. Probably they were discussing what they would plant next.

They talked for a while and moved to the border that ran beside the walkway.

Rachel had about six more strawberries to stem, and then she would put the bowl into the refrigerator and go outside for a chat with the neighbors. For the moment she left Ethan and Deena to their discussion of pansies and petunias.

And then another car drove up and parked in front of Deena's house. Rachel dropped the bowl to the counter with a thump. "That's Chief out there! He's getting out of a car in front of Deena's house! Coe! Do something!"

She didn't have to tell him; he was already thundering out the front door. Rachel followed, wiping her wet hands on the back of her jeans.

Coe was sticking out a hand, grinning just a little too widely. "Hello, Chief! Long time, no see!"

"Outa my way, Coe," his buddy replied grandly. "I've got important business."

Coe responded by blocking his path. "Hey, look. I've got the Fort over at Van Nuys now . . ."

"Out of my way," Chief repeated. "I have to see Deena, right now. I'm in love with that woman. I've got to have her; she's got to know it."

Rachel begged, "Chief, please shut up and go away. Ethan's at home."

He was not only at home but right at hand, and he came over to see what the disturbance was. Deena followed him anxiously.

Chief was on him at once. "Are you Ethan? I'm sorry to have to tell you this, but Deena and I are in love. You've got to step aside . . ."

"Oh, Chief, shut up!" Deena begged.

Ethan seemed to grow in size. He stepped forward belligerently. "What the hell is this?" he demanded. "Who is this guy, Coe?"

"He's in my crew," Coe admitted. "He has hallucinations sometimes. Old war injury. Come on, Chief, let's get out of here."

He pushed at Chief, who only brushed him aside. "Nothing's going to stop me now. I've been waiting for her to come home. I've been sitting down the block all afternoon waiting so I could tell her. It's got to be; we've got to . . ." Chief broke off, momentarily distracted as a car drove up and parked behind his own.

Coe, too, seemed rooted to the ground.

He stared as two well-dressed, elderly women got out of the car.

He said, "My God! It's Tricia and Addie!"

Eighteen

"How bad could it be?" Rachel was asking herself as the two women approached. Two nice old ladies; they didn't look a bit dangerous. Somehow Rachel knew that Tricia was the one with too much weight on her and Addie was the overdressed one.

Addie wore a high-fashion designer outfit in shades of peach. There was a long, flowing jacket, a flowing skirt well below the knees, and a long, flowing peach scarf that blew about as she walked. Her bright makeup made her look older than she possibly could be.

Coe recovered himself first and greeted them. "Tricia, Addie. What an unexpected surprise!"

"Most surprises are unexpected," Addie pointed out.

Chief sputtered, "Tricia, what are you doing here?"

Tricia looked like everybody's idealized

grandmother—sweet-faced, comfortably plump, a lap with a woman attached. She glanced around and answered uncertainly, "Well, Addie said . . . you and Coe . . . some Hollywood playgirls . . ."

Addie took up the frayed end of Tricia's sentence. "Since it looked like we both had the same problem, we decided to come together and find out about it. So, Roscoe, are you and your friend ready to quit your playing around and come home?"

That held Rachel for a second. Roscoe? Of course. Roscoe, Coe.

Coe said, "Addie, you're making yourself ridiculous. I haven't gone home with you since 1965."

Deena said, "Hollywood playgirls?"

Chief said to his wife, "This isn't like you, Tricia."

"Well, Addie said . . ." Tricia began, but Coe interrupted her.

"How did you find us, anyway?"

Addie answered. "We expected you to be at the hotel, but you were not and they gave us this address."

Coe said with an ease that seemed remarkable under the circumstances, "I left the information for Whitey; I wasn't expecting you."

"Obviously," said Addie.

"Who are all these people?" asked Ethan of nobody in particular.

"Well, there's been a mix-up . . ." Rachel began but could not continue because there wasn't anything, actually, that was mixed up. In plenty of trouble, maybe, but not mixed up.

Chief took his wife's arm and urged her toward the car she had come in. "Honey, there's no reason you have to stand out here in the hot sun. Why don't you go back to the hotel, and I'll meet you there when I've finished my business."

Addie was glaring at Deena. "Is this your latest floozie, Roscoe?"

"Hey, where do you get off calling me . . ." Deena began.

"You look like the type," Addie confided. "It isn't the first time I've had this trouble with him, you know."

"Who are you calling a floozie?" Deena demanded. "You superannuated old bat, you didn't need to come all the way from Texas just to call me names."

Chief paused in his efforts to get Tricia into the car. "No, Addie, leave her alone! She's not Coe's girl, Rachel is."

Coe muttered, "Thanks, Chief."

Addie turned. "And you're Rachel?" Her surprised look went from the worn jeans to the gray hair. "You're as old as I am!"

"I didn't know it went by numbers," said Rachel. "Look, Addie, let's not talk out here in the street . . ."

Addie jerked a thumb at Deena. "Then who's she?"

"She's my neighbor. You happen to be standing on her lawn."

Addie narrowed her eyes at Deena. "Neighbor, huh? Then how did she know I'm from Texas?"

"Oh, I don't know," Deena replied airily. "You just have that tacky, Texas look."

Chief returned, apparently not aware that Tricia was stubbornly following him. "Deena, we have to talk . . ."

"Oh, now I'm getting the picture!" cried Addie, pointing at Rachel. "You're the one after Roscoe, and this cat is after Tricia's man! Strange neighborhood! The local industry seems to be adultery!"

"You probably know more about that subject than I do," Deena snapped. "Colonel Chief Harry Saunders has nothing to do with me and the sooner he gets out of here, the better."

"It's time he did," Coe agreed. "Chief,

why don't you and Tricia get in your car and go back to the hotel? You're not doing anything here but damage."

Deena turned her blazing gaze on Tricia. "You came all the way from Houston just to find out about me and Chief? Well, there's nothing to find out and he's all yours. . . . Although why you want that philandering, lying, manipulative creep is more than I can understand. Why didn't you dump him years ago? You've certainly been married to him long enough to have figured out what he's like."

Tricia spoke quietly but quite firmly. "Yes, I know."

"Where's your spirit?" Deena demanded. "Haven't you got any pride?"

"Deena! I never lied to you!" Chief protested.

"You just leave my wife alone," Ethan growled at him.

Addie threw out her arms in mock surprise. "Oh! A married Hollywood playgirl!"

"And you shut up before I pull out some of that dyed hair of yours!" yelled Deena.

Chief thrust himself toward Ethan. "You want to get mad, you came to the right place!"

The sight of upraised fists sobered Deena

suddenly. "Oh, guys, don't!" she wailed. "What are we playing here?"

"Schoolyard games," Rachel sniffed, stepping between the two men. "All right, children, knock it off. Cool it! Mama's here now, so chill!"

Chief lowered his fists but went right on babbling. "I love her, Rachel! He has to see that! He has to step out of the way, because I love her!"

"We all do, Chief. Let's go over to my place." Rachel took one arm, Coe grabbed the other, and they urged him down the sidewalk and up the walkway that led to Rachel's home.

Tricia and Addie followed. As they went up the steps to her porch, Rachel caught a glimpse of Deena and Ethan, going into their own house. They were arguing vociferously, Deena shaking her hair as she always did when she was angry.

Rachel dropped her hold on Chief's arm and let Coe finish getting him into the house. She turned to Tricia and Addie and said politely, "This is my home. Please come in and we will talk. There must be some way we can all come to an agreement."

They came in—Tricia quietly, Addie remarking, "You certainly do have some odd friends, Roscoe."

"Addie, that's just about enough!" thundered Coe. "Mrs. Moreland is a lady, a fine lady, a mother and a grandmother. What in the world makes you think you have any business coming here to her house, I don't know. We're going to have a talk. Rachel, would you be so kind to let us use your living room for a few minutes?"

"Of course," said Rachel. "We'll sit in the breakfast room. I'll fix you a nice cup of coffee, Chief, Tricia. Come on."

She had spoken rather grandly of a breakfast room, but of course it was only part of her big kitchen. Chief sat down at the table and Rachel began making the coffee, but Tricia lingered in the doorway rather obviously trying to hear what Coe and Addie were saying to one another.

When Rachel put an empty cup in front of Chief, he got up, went to her cupboard, and filled it with whiskey. She went on filling the coffee maker. For all she knew, it was a good idea. He did look totally devastated—his hair standing straight up, pouches under his eyes as if he were a hundred years old. He sat down silently and addressed himself to his drink.

From the living room raised voices could be heard. In the kitchen, the coffee maker grumbled softly.

Chief took a couple of gulps of whiskey, then raised his haggard eyes and asked, "What am I going to do, Rachel?"

"You're going to leave Deena alone," she told him. "You've done her enough damage."

"I didn't mean to. I love her. I love her so much, I don't think I can go on living without her."

"This isn't like you, Chief. Usually you can take these things in your stride."

"Not this one. I thought it was. I thought she was just going to be another thrill, but it's different! She's Deena! So beautiful, so wise, so good! Like a dream princess come to life. And I never got to hold her, never even once! I can never see her again, never, ever! That's why I came over here. That's why I came to California in the first place, just to see her, one more time, just to look at her! I didn't expect this mob scene we've got here. Whitey told me he couldn't find Coe, so I figured he was out of town. I didn't want to hurt Deena!" His head drooped, leaning over his cup. "But I did, and she hates me now!"

"Damn straight she does." The coffee was ready, and Rachel picked up the pot. "Do you want some coffee in your coffee?"

He held out the cup. "Sure." There was room for her to pour in some of the hot brew.

Rachel said, "So all right, you saw her, and now it's time to get on with your life. Your wife is here, Chief. Tricia is here. . . . Where is Tricia, anyway?"

"Gone to the can or something," he replied carelessly, slurping coffee.

"You've hurt her badly, you know. We may have kept Ethan from figuring out what you meant out there, but you'd better believe Tricia knows. You completely ignored her while you made a fool of yourself over Deena. You are going to have to beg her forgiveness."

"Beg? I don't like to beg."

From the living room the voices were becoming louder. Coe was shouting, "Well, you can't do it!"

Addie, only a little lower, "It's your choice, Roscoe. I'm going back to Houston tomorrow. If you change your mind, I will be at the Airport Hilton tonight."

Addie must have gone out the front door, for Coe called after her, "Hey, Tricia's right here! Don't you remember she came with you?"

Addie's voice came back from outside, "I don't care." Seconds later there was the sound of her car starting, driving away.

Coe and Tricia appeared in the kitchen doorway. She must have carried her eavesdropping all the way into the living room.

Rachel said, "Would you like a cup of coffee?"

Coe slumped into a chair, grunting assent, and Tricia sat down daintily. Rachel poured. She couldn't add anything to Chief's cup; he had the bottle in his hand again.

The soothing routine of adding sugar and cream occupied them for a space. Chief sipped at his cup and then he put his hand over Tricia's and said, "I can explain everything."

She said, "Yes, I know."

Rachel said cheerily, "There certainly have been some mix-ups!"

Coe patted her hand, a little warning, and Rachel was still.

Chief began, "What I was going to say was . . ." Then his cup clashed into the saucer, his eyes rolled wildly, and he demanded, "Where's the bathroom?"

Rachel pointed it out, and he glared at her. "Woman, don't you know better than to mix coffee in a man's whiskey?" he demanded and rushed from the room.

Rachel said, "I didn't do it on purpose!"

"Don't worry about it," said Tricia cozily, stirring extra cream into her coffee. "He gets over-excited sometimes."

Rachel sat down and picked up her own cup. "It seems to be his regular state of mind."

Coe asked Tricia, "Are you checked in at the Hilton, too? I'm sorry Addie went off without you."

"No problem," said Tricia. "Harry has a car here."

"He's pretty drunk," Rachel warned.

"I won't let him drive."

Rachel smiled at her. "I must say I admire your steady nerves. In all this mishmash, you're the only one who is calm and quiet."

"I never learned anything yet with my mouth open," said Tricia, and somehow it seemed to put a damper on the conversation, which hadn't exactly been flowing before.

Tricia took a few sips of her coffee and then confided, "My mother always told me, find a man who brings home a paycheck and stick with him. She went through the Depression, you know. Harry has his faults, but he always comes home again . . . after."

"He's been pestering Deena," Coe said. "She was pretty mad when she called him those names out there . . ."

"Oh, she had to do that," interrupted Tricia. "Her man was right there. She has to look out for her paycheck, too."

Coe flicked impatiently at the spoon beside his cup. "I guess you heard most of what was said in there; this isn't going to be news to you. Rachel, I don't know what to tell you. Addie wants everything. All of my interests in the company. If I have to give that away, I have no way to build it back. I'm retired and not part of the company anymore."

"So don't give it to her," said Rachel.

Chief appeared briefly in the hallway, then lurched out of sight again. Tricia called, "Harry? Where are you going?"

"Get some air. Back yard," he replied and went out onto the patio. Tricia promptly got up and went after him.

Coe continued, "It's her price for a divorce. If I don't give it to her, I can't ask you to marry me."

"So, don't ask," shrugged Rachel. "At our age, promising 'until death us do part' doesn't mean much. How much time can we have?"

"We could live another twenty years or twenty minutes; but whatever it is, I want to spend it with you."

"And I want to spend it with you, Coe."

She took his hand and slipped into his arms and he held her for a precious minute, whispering into her ear, "Do you mean that? We'll get married, I promise, I'll give her anything."

A cheery voice interrupted him as Tricia returned to the kitchen. "Harry's about ready to go back to Houston, but he needs a little more air first. Okay if I pour myself another cup of coffee?"

"Help yourself," Rachel invited. "Would you like some cookies or a cracker or something?"

Tricia plopped herself down in a chair. "Sounds great. I've been on the run all day. Addie never stops, and boy, is she ever a pain to travel with! All she does is bitch about the service everywhere she goes."

She smiled crookedly and added, "It

works, you know. She gets treated like a queen."

"Oh, I believe you," said Coe.

"I'm kind of sorry I ever even told her that Harry was making one of his business trips here. I don't usually follow him around like this, you know."

Tricia made the crooked smile again. "I'd get frequent flyer miles if I did. But Whitey talks to her and he calls Harry every couple of days, so he knew and I guess he told her because then Addie was ragging on me to come here. She talks like we're bosom buddies but we're not really, you know. We've known each other a long time, but that doesn't mean she invites me to her dinner parties. I'm nobody except the one she calls up when she needs a fourth for bridge."

"Are you sure Chief's all right?" Coe asked her. "Maybe I ought to check up on him. Usually he can hold his liquor."

Tricia only shrugged. Coe got up and went to the patio.

Tricia watched him go as she munched a handful of cookies from the plate Rachel had put before her. "He doesn't listen, does he?"

Rachel was surprised. "Coe? He's a good listener."

"Well, he ought to listen to some things about Addie. They've been married since I was a little girl, and he doesn't know anything that goes on. Everybody in Houston knows about Addie, everybody but him."

She was going to tell or burst, Rachel could see, and she made encouraging noises. "Um, uh-huh."

"When he married her, he was the only one who would even date her on account of he'd been away with the army so he didn't know she'd screwed about every guy in the high school. She had an abortion, you know."

"I guess I did hear that."

"Well, they weren't very safe in those days, you know, and she got messed up good. She's had nothing but female troubles since." Tricia giggled around another cookie. "Maybe that's why she's so crabby. Imagine, having female troubles since you were seventeen!"

"Wait a minute! She had this abortion when she was seventeen? Not later, when she was married to Coe?"

"Why would she do that if she were married? Nah, she was always messing around and she hasn't changed a bit. If Coe would only pay attention, somebody would tell him about the tennis pro that lives in her house. Teaching her tennis, she says! She sure must know a lot about tennis; he's been there seven years!"

"And all this is common knowledge, you say? In Houston? Obviously, I live in the wrong town."

"And I could tell you some things about Coe, too . . ."

"Don't do it now. The guys are coming back."

Coe and Chief came slowly through the living room. Chief looked more tattered even than before, his face pale, necktie dangling. He said in a hollow tone, "Well, I guess I've caused enough trouble for one day. I'm ready to go."

Tricia held out her hand. "Car keys."

He fished them out of his pocket and pressed them into her palm. He said, "Tricia, I'm an old fool."

She said, "Yes, I know."

When they were gone, Coe locked the front door. "Well, it certainly has been a day."

"I've got a coupon," said Rachel.

"What?"

"A coupon. Good for a discount at a bed-and-breakfast in Coronado. I got the coupons in a promotion and never had a chance to use them. What do you say we drive down there and spend the weekend?"

Coe said stupidly, "It's Tuesday."

"Well, it may not be a weekend, but we can fake it, can't we?"

A light was growing in Coe's eye. "Do you mean it, Rachel? A weekend? Just you and me?"

"Just you and me for good, Coe. We may not have a lot of time left, so let's not let that witch ruin things between us. I don't care if you never get a divorce. I'd like for us to be married, but it's not that big a deal as long as we're together."

"Rachel, I've waited so long. I thought you were never going to give in."

"It shouldn't have been so long. I should have listened to my heart. I should have trusted you to know what's right."

"Well, now we're together."

"Yeah. Kind of scary, isn't it?"

He smiled indulgently. "You've got no reason to be afraid of it."

"You're as bad as I am. You can't even call it sex; you say 'it.' Don't tell me you aren't a little afraid, too."

"Well, it's different for a man. If he finds out he can't perform . . ."

"A woman has to worry whether or not she still can please with her clothes off."

"Well, if we're both sort of flexible and considerate . . ."

"Generous and open . . ."

"Do you love me?"

"You bet I do!"

Their kiss was warm and quickly more than warm. Suddenly joy had melted into heat and they settled into kissing, their bodies pressed together, arms ever tighter. He rubbed his hands down her back, and she felt him throbbing against her. She was so much shorter than he, his hardness was pressed into her belly; and she moved, a clumsy caress. He pulled her even tighter.

She whispered, "Now, Coe?"

He echoed, "Now, Rachel?"

"Yes, yes, yes."

He pulled down the zipper in the front of her shirt. A sudden thought struck her, and she put her hand on his to stay it. "Maybe we'd better find out before we go any further . . . do you have. . . . We sure don't want to stop in the middle of this while somebody runs to the drug store."

"Two healthy people in a monogamous relationship don't need it."

"But are we? Have you had a physical since the last time you were in a relationship?"

"Several of them. My insurance company checks up on me more often than the Department of Water and Power. How about you? You had your meter read lately?"

"Yes, I guess that makes us monogamous."

He pushed the shirt down to her waist, running his hand over her breasts as he did so, and the heat that rose inside her at his touch so startled her that she laughed and pushed him away. "I said now, not here!"

He pulled her against him. "Why not here? I don't know if I can get up the stairs."

"You had better! I'm not doing it on the floor at my time of life."

He laughed. "Well, if I only make it halfway up the stairs, it'll be worse."

The doorbell rang.

Coe cursed. Rachel said through gritted teeth, "If it's that kinky Chief, I'm not opening the door."

"Why do you have to have a door with a window in it? We can't get away with not opening the door."

"Oh, my God! Whoever is out there can look right in!" Quickly, she pulled up her shirt and zipped it.

"Well, it's your door. Hasn't this problem ever come up before?"

"Certainly not!" She walked toward the door and Coe followed her. The sky was still light, and she could see the man's shock of white or white-blond hair.

Coe said, "It's not Chief. It's Whitey!"

Nineteen

Deena and Ethan entered their home already arguing.

"What's wrong with that guy?" Ethan had demanded. "What's all this crap about loving you?"

"You *would* think it was crap!" Deena was crying. "Something you wouldn't understand! And I hurt him. I never meant to hurt him; I never intended that."

"It sounds like a lot's been going on behind my back! What have you been doing that I don't know about?"

Deena mopped her eyes with a tissue. "I don't want to talk about it now. I'm too upset to talk now."

"Well, we're going to talk about it!" His face dark with anger, he took her arm and shoved her into a chair. "Some guy I never saw before stands on my lawn yelling about how he loves my wife and she loves him for all the neighbors to hear and we're not going to talk about it?"

The look in Deena's eye was dangerous. "Don't you push me around! Don't you ever push me around!"

"That wasn't much of a push," he mumbled.

"It doesn't take much, Ethan. I'm not putting up with abuse. Not ever. Not even in teensy-weensy amounts."

"All right, I'm sorry. I didn't mean to get so rough, but do you think you're the only one who's upset?"

"I could walk out right now, Ethan. I'm close to doing it. Don't push me; you might regret it."

"You'd walk out because I lost my temper one time?"

"I'd walk out because we've got a marriage that's stale, boring, and exploitive. The rough stuff's just a little icing on the cake."

"And maybe I'll just let you walk. You've been messing around; that guy said so. You've got no respect for me, no respect for our marriage."

"You don't even know what you're talking about. You haven't even asked me what happened. Do you call that showing respect for me? Twenty years we've been married, and you jump to the first rotten conclusion you can think of. I should think you'd know how to trust me by now."

Ethan paced a circle around the room, opened his mouth to say something, thought better of it, and paced another circle.

At last he said, "I'm angry. You're angry. Maybe it's not such a good idea to talk when we're angry."

Deena leaned back in her chair. "So, we're angry. At least something's happening. At least we're talking about something more important than crabgrass. Do you know how boring we are?"

"So boring you've got to go and cheat on me?"

"I didn't. Nothing happened between Chief and me. Oh, he gave me a big rush; there were a couple of lunches. I was attracted to him. I was . . . tempted."

Deena rose from her chair and paced a little herself. "But when it came to the nitty-gritty, I turned him down. I cared too much about my family, about you, about what we've built together in all these years. I just didn't know he was going to take it so hard."

Ethan's forehead wrinkled with distaste.

"That bald old guy? How could you be tempted by him? You called him all those names . . ."

"And I meant every one of them. He's a funny kind of guy. Completely superficial, but I guess when a superficial person is in pain, he hurts the same as anybody. I'm not mad at him, not really. He can't help being what he is. Even while I was giving him what-for, it was me I was mad at. I almost swallowed that line of his. How dumb could I be? You want to know why I acted so stupid? It was because he was paying attention to me, and nobody has done that for a long, long time."

Ethan's mouth was tight. "I think I see where this is going to lead. You're going to say I never take you anywhere anymore."

"Pretty much."

"It's the way we're both working these days, Deena. I don't have time for anything except trying to build my business."

"Chief flew here from Houston, twice, just to see me. Just to talk to me."

"Maybe he inherited money. I didn't. You're making him out to be pretty stiff competition! Flowers and candy, too?"

"Red roses and champagne." Deena tossed her hair. "What's so strange about that? Is it so unbelievable that a man might find me attractive? Might try to make love to me? Might even offer to break up his home for me? He might even have done it, just now; that was his wife out there on the sidewalk."

"It sounds like he's had more of your time lately than I have. Do you have any idea what it takes for me to get your attention? You bring work home every night; I hate the sight of that briefcase of yours! You're always rushing around . . ."

"And that's another thing," she interrupted. "I'm sick of being the one that does the dishes, the one that does the cleaning, the one that does the shopping. The one, the only one."

"Let's stick to the important points."

She interrupted again. "This is an important point! You're complaining because I'm always busy; well, I'm busy doing stuff that shouldn't be my sole responsibility. Everything gets shared around here except the housework. I'm exhausted, and you get pissed because I'm too tired for sex!"

"I don't know what you expect of me!"

"It sounds pretty silly for us to break up because you won't do the dishes, but that's about what it's coming to. We can't afford a divorce—I've looked into the figures—but if we separated, I could do pretty much what I please."

Ethan's long face grew longer, the color pale. "Is that what you want, a separation?"

"No, that isn't what I want. But it's preferable to the way things have been. What I want are changes."

The mouth was still tight, but he nodded, just a little, almost subliminally. "Well, what are we going to change?"

"That's what I needed to hear you say! That's all I want, is for you to agree we need changes, that you're going to work with me to make them!"

"Well, there're a few things I want to change, too."

She was smiling. "All right, we'll negotiate."

He put his arms around her. "Deena, you know I love you. I want to do what's going to make you happy. I don't want to lose you."

She nestled into his familiar embrace. "There's a little hotel in Coronado that Rachel got coupons for and she gave me some. What do you say we take a weekend there, just the two of us? We'll be alone; we can talk. We can negotiate."

He nuzzled her ear. "What'll we do when we run out of things to say?"

"We'll think of something."

"It can't be this weekend, I've got a . . ."

She interrupted, "Ethan!"

"Don't you have a meeting? It seems to me you said . . ."

"My assistant will handle it. It'll be a surprise for her, but she'll handle it."

Coe cried heartily, "Whitey! Long time no see! Come in, come in! I didn't figure you were going to be here until Saturday!"

Whitey stepped inside and, by way of greeting, growled, "Where's the Fort?"

Coe's smile was fake, and so was his chuckle. "Well, it ain't in my pocket! It's at the airfield, where else would a B-17 be?"

"It's been more'n a month, Coe, you haven't brought that thing back. You were supposed to bring it back to Harlingen."

"I took it to Brown like I was supposed to, didn't I? I'll have it to Harlingen in a couple of days." He sidled a glance at Rachel and amended, "Week or so, maybe. Rachel, I guess you haven't met Colonel Gruber; we call him Whitey. Mrs. Moreland."

Whitey shook hands in a perfunctory way and went on scolding. "Coe, I know you put up most of the money for that ship, but all the same it belongs to the CAF and it just ain't right your flying it around to wherever you feel like going to. You could have at least told us where you had it."

The lines were deep beside Coe's nose. "Well, I didn't because I knew if I did some officious colonel would come around and start telling me what I can do and what I can't. I know where that ship belongs, of course I do, but they weren't going to miss it for a couple of weeks."

Coe's voice suddenly sounded weary and he added, "You came here to take it back, didn't you?"

"Well, that was the idea, if I could find it," grouched Whitey. "Where the hell have you been, and how did you fly it by yourself? You could have wrecked the thing trying that!"

"Oh, I had a copilot."

"It wasn't anybody from the CAF. I checked that out, called up about everybody when I was trying to figure out where you might be. Even your crew chief didn't know where you had gone! Then I got your call yesterday. That was pretty sneaky, leaving it with my secretary!"

"Well, you weren't in your office."

"You didn't let some *civilian* fly our plane, did you?"

Mischief flashed briefly across Coe's sullen face. "Sure I did, and not only that, it was a lady civilian. That's her right there."

He was staring at her, horrified, so Rachel said sweetly, "It's rather late, Colonel Gruber. Perhaps you would like to join us for dinner?"

"No, we can't stop for dinner. If we get over to the airport right now, we can still make a daylight takeoff. This time of year, the sun will be well up by the time we get to Houston."

"Is it really necessary to fly all night?" asked Rachel.

"I've got to get back to Houston," said Whitey. "I've already put a lot of my business on hold to come here; I can't afford another day. We'll leave the ship at Houston airport and run it down to Harlingen over the weekend, or maybe next week."

"Tomorrow's Wednesday and I'm due to make my Mexico flight Thursday. It's going to be Saturday before I can get back here!" Coe protested.

"Reckon so," Whitey agreed.

Rachel shrugged, resigned. "Saturday's a good time to start a weekend."

Coe grinned at his copilot and confided, "She's one in a million."

"People my age don't fall apart over a disappointment," Rachel explained.

"Listen, buddy," Coe went on. "Give me a chance to say goodbye to my girl, will you? Go sit in the car. I'll be out in a few minutes."

"Don't you have a car with you?" Whitey asked.

"Of course I do."

"Then I got no reason to wait for you. You're not a kid and I'm not a Federal Marshal. I'll be waiting for you at the field. Nice meeting you, ma'am." And Whitey was out the door.

Coe said, "Rachel, I've got to go. I'm obligated."

Rachel gave a small chuckle. "Yes, I know. You have been a very naughty boy with that plane. Why did you take it to Arizona? You know you could have found a rental plane."

"Yeah, but I was hoping the bomber would impress you."

This chuckle was larger. "It did."

"Rachel, I don't want to go. How am I

going to wait until Saturday to be with you?"

"The same way we have both learned, in sixty years or so of living, to wait for what we want."

"I love you."

"I love you, too."

He said suddenly, "Come with me."

"Huh?"

"Come with me to Houston, then I won't have to wait until Saturday to see you. You can ride in the crew chief's seat."

"You want me to fly to Houston right now? I just got home yesterday; the sink's full of vegetables, and I . . ." She stopped her own rush of words and said, "I'd love to go with you."

"Grab your bag. Have you got any kind of a thermos? Put some coffee in it. It's going to be a long, cold night up there."

"The coffee's gone, but I can make some more."

"Never mind. Just bring the thermos, and we'll go to the drive-through at some fast-food place and have it filled up. We can grab a sandwich, too."

"I have to put those vegetables away. We'll only be gone a couple of days, won't we?" She shoved the vegetables any which way into the refrigerator, stuck the chicken in the freezer, found the thermos. "We do have time to get the coffee, don't we?"

"Sure. Whitey will be doing the checklist. On the airlines, now, the copilot does the whole thing, and the captain doesn't even show up until the passengers are boarded, if he wants. I'll just pretend it's the airline, and we can take time to eat the sandwiches."

She checked that the windows were closed and everything was turned off, dropped a note into Deena's mailbox, and they were on their way to the airport.

It was, indeed, a long, cold night. They flew at a dizzying nine thousand, five hundred feet in order to clear the Rockies, and Rachel discovered why pilots treasured those scuffed, worn, old leather jackets. Nothing else could keep out the cold drafts that howled through the cockpit. They passed around the thermos until every drop was gone and droned on through a night that seemed as if it would never end.

Rachel watched Whitey's every move; after all, he was a *real* copilot and not just winging it as she had been. She learned a few things she had not known before, but they were minor. She thought that, all in all, her performance had been pretty good. It seemed even better when Whitey fell asleep several times during the flight.

At long last the sun rose over the Texas plains, and they went down to a lower, warmer altitude. Whitey woke up so cheerful he sang a half-dozen choruses of "I've Got Sixpence."

He wasn't much of a singer, so Rachel encouraged him to talk and he told her about his family and his work as a quality control engineer.

And when they had landed in Houston, he put his necktie on again and went off to work. Rachel watched him go, impressed.

"What a remarkable man! Will he really do a day's work now?"

"Why not?" Coe replied. "He got his sleep last night. You hungry?"

"Starved."

Of course he had a car at hand and of course he knew a place where the breakfasts were huge, and they both ate everything. The coffee tasted wonderful, but there wasn't enough of it in the world to make Rachel stop feeling tired. Her eyes were grainy; she wondered that she could go on eating and her digestion keep on working. Everything else was too tired to function.

"We'll go over to my place and get some sleep," Coe decreed. "A couple of hours nap will fix us up."

"Oh, Lord, yes, sleep," said Rachel.

His apartment was military-neat. The floors were polished, chairs lined up, sharp corners tucked into the bed covers. And books. She was surprised at the number of his books, all standing at attention in rows in the bookcases.

"I'll let you have the guest room," he offered.

"Oh, but . . . well, okay."

"But what?"

She smiled shyly. "It's the sensible thing, of course, but I'll miss you."

"We've got to be sensible," he agreed. "I'm too tired even to think about sex, and you must be just as tired. I'm past the age where I could pull these all-nighters and still function."

"I don't care if you function or not, I want to be with you."

He smiled, pleased. "Well, if that's what you want, Rachel, come in my bed and we'll just sort of cuddle."

"That's what I'd like."

They got into their nightclothes and kissed tenderly and got into the bed. Tired bones at last horizontal! She felt as if she were sinking into down; it was so good, so comfortable. Coe pulled her close to him and they matched their bodies together, nestling. Sleep . . .

But she wasn't asleep. For a space, she thought she was, but she was aware of Coe even as she thought it. He was asleep, she could tell, his body relaxed. One knobby hand, curled into a loose fist, rested lightly against her shoulder. Of course he was tired, poor man, and should be asleep; but how could he be when she was not? When she was feeling his body with hers, matching his warmth with hers, and she was remembering his caresses the night before in the entry hall of her home?

He said, "You asleep?"

"Of course not. How can I be asleep when you keep doing that?"

"Doing what?"

"It's your breathing."

"Breathing? I can't help breathing."

"It's the way you do it. How can you be asleep and not be breathing evenly?"

"I'm not asleep. I'm talking to you."

"This isn't going to work, Coe."

"I know. Having you this close, I'm never going to sleep. My hands keep twitching."

Rachel said tartly, "I think you had better do something about that."

The hand moved immediately and began to stroke her breast. "Ah, Rachel, I want you. You're sure you're not too tired?"

She squirmed around to face him. "We're both too tired, but obviously it isn't going to make any difference. Make love to me, Coe."

He moved quickly to lean over her for a kiss, this one long and luxurious. At last, there was nothing that could interrupt. They were safely together.

His hand stroked down her body and found the hem of the nightgown. Her pleasure escalated as he touched bare skin. She shuddered as he ran his hand the length of her thigh.

"Rachel," he mumbled against her neck. "God, what you do to me, Rachel! I'm so hot." He pressed against her thigh, proving his heat. "I don't know how long I can wait."

She pulled him closer. "So don't wait."

"You're not ready."

"The hell I'm not! Don't argue with nature; do it now!"

Afire with impatience he straddled her, his hot hands holding her buttocks. He was pushing into her, gently at first; but finding her receptive, he thrust heavily, again and again until, with a shout of triumph, he climaxed.

He flopped down and lay on her, panting, "Aw, Rachel! Aw, Rachel!"

"Coe."

He kissed her face, pushing back her hair with careful fingers. "What do you want? Do you want me to . . ."

"Go to sleep, Coe."

"But you're not satisfied, are you?"

"Of course. At this age, it happens very rapidly."

"It does, huh?" He snuggled wearily down at her side. "I don't know about that, but I think I am going to enjoy exploring the theory with you."

Twenty

When she woke she was alone and she felt, for a fleeting instant, the same sense of loss that had devastated her when Pete was gone. But of course Coe wasn't gone. Coe was well and alive and somewhere in the apartment; she had only to find him.

She needed to find him. She was so impatient she jumped out of bed and padded through the living room barefoot, wearing nothing but her nightgown—her innocent little white voile nightgown with the fussy lace insert and the neckline as high as her collarbone. What kind of nightgown was that for a living, active woman with a virile lover?

She would get another immediately.

She found Coe sitting at the kitchen table reading a newspaper. He looked up and smiled. "Oh, you're awake?"

And there she stood in her white voile without the least idea what a person is supposed to say to the man who has just become her lover. What do lovers say, the morning after? Or the afternoon after? It was still light, so if it were still the same day, it must be afternoon.

She tried, "Uh, what time is it?"

" 'Bout four. Getting hungry? I made us a reservation at Tony's. Do you like Italian food?"

He had obviously been up a while. He was clean and shaved and wearing a white shirt. Probably he was all ready for Tony's.

She mumbled, "Well, Italian food is fine, but the place better not be very fancy because all I have to wear is some beat-up jeans."

"I thought you brought a bag with you."

"I did, but it's the one I take to Barbara's and I've got a whole closet full of clothes at her house. All that's in that bag is nighties and such."

"Well, then, get dressed and we'll go buy something. We'll go to the Pavilion."

"Can I buy a nightgown there?"

"You can buy anything in the world you want at the Pavilion."

You could, too. Rachel ended in Saks where she bought a silk suit. Instead of a blouse, there was a camisole; Houston was as hot as Encino had been and much more humid.

A squabble developed when she discovered that while she was in the dressing room, Coe had quietly slipped his credit card to the saleswoman and she was busily writing up the sale.

Rachel said, "Don't do that!" so suddenly that the poor woman dropped her pen.

"You don't want the dress?" she asked.

"Yes, but I'm paying for it. Here's my card."

Coe captured Rachel's hand with the card in it. "You don't have to do that."

"Oh, yes, I do," Rachel said fiercely. "I'll ride around in your airplane, but you don't pay for my clothes. I'm not a kept woman!"

"Don't be silly, Rachel. That isn't what this is about. I'm paying because I can afford it."

"That's not what this is about, either, and this lady wants to finish writing up her sale. Let go of my hand, please."

"I don't understand," he protested. "You didn't fuss like this when I gave you the yellow jumpsuit. You were pleased as punch."

"That was different."

"What's so different?"

"We weren't sleeping together then."

She fervently hoped that, if she ever got the suit paid for and left, she would never see this place again or the patient lady waiting to be allowed to use some card or other and finish the sale. Coe may have felt somewhat the same, for he released her hand and accepted the return of his card, the expression on his face folding itself into accustomed grouchy lines.

Rachel signed the slip, and the saleswoman carefully folded her jeans and shirt and put them into a bag. As they walked away, Coe muttered, "I wish you hadn't done that."

"I wish you hadn't forced me to do it," she countered. "I may never be able to come back to Saks the rest of my life."

He didn't laugh, but his expression lightened a little. "What did you do it for, then?"

"It's because you have more money than I do."

"Huh?"

"You don't see that? If you pay for my clothes, I'm no better than one of the hardbodies taking your gifts, taking your money in exchange for the body. When you gave me the jumpsuit, it was a gift from a friend; but now things are different."

"That's a pretty fine line. How do you figure out where you're going to draw it?"

"I'm not at all sure myself."

That cheered him a little and he shrugged. "Well, I guess we're going to have to work it out as we go along."

Tony's was crowded, trendy, noisy, and the food was good. They laughed and had a little wine with the meal and Coe looked happy across the table from her, making jokes and talking about flying, sometimes both at once. They shared an unspoken appreciation, the knowledge of what an astonishing day it had been and that there were things ahead that might yet astonish them more.

He leaned toward her and said softly, "I like that dress. And I like what's under it even more."

He did know what was under it, and the memories stimulated by that thought so unnerved her that a blob of linguini dropped from her fork onto her new suit.

"Oh, look at that!" she wailed, mopping vainly at the spot with her napkin. "It'll have to go to the cleaner's and I'll have nothing to wear again!"

"You can go shopping again tomorrow. It'll give you something to do while I'm gone to Mexico."

And indeed she could. She would have to. Only a cleaner could remove food spots from silk; and if Coe were going to take her to places like Tony's, she would have to have something nice to wear.

The only trouble was, the outfit she had already bought was beyond her means. Another one like it, and she would be withdrawing money from her mutual funds to pay for it.

She had regarded herself as comfortably off, but now she felt like the little match girl. Or at least like a social climber who had outclimbed her ladder. Drat the man, why did he have to be so rich?

And they really were going to have to have a talk.

It was just as well she had planned to send the new suit to the cleaners. By the time he finished taking it off her a little later that night, it was ready.

She got only as far as to hang the coat in the bedroom closet when he put his arms around her from behind, stroking her through the soft charmeuse of the camisole.

"I do like you in silk," he whispered, nuzzling her neck.

She said, "All right, Coe, go get in bed. I'll be there in a minute."

"This is more fun. I'll help you get ready for bed; you're not half fast enough. Where're the fasteners on this thing?"

"It doesn't have any; it just pulls off." She turned slowly until she faced him and lifted her arms so he could take off the camisole.

It ended up on the floor, but she didn't notice because he was running his thumbs along the edge of her bra. He found the hook. In that raspy whisper, he said, "You have a beautiful figure, Rachel. Let me look at you."

The bra joined the camisole on the floor and she whispered, "Put your hands on me."

He kissed her and gave her the caresses she desired, and she began unbuttoning his shirt. "I'm undressed; why are you wearing all those clothes?"

He let her take off the shirt and unbutton his pants. As soon as he had stepped out of them, he pressed her against the closet door with his body, with his kisses. Her bare breasts were pressed against his chest, skin against skin. The contact was exciting; she wanted more. He had his hand at her hemline again, repeating that sensual stroking up her leg. He was pulling the skirt all the way to her waist. Since it was cut rather narrow, he had to tussle with it and she protested.

"What are you doing to my new dress? Let me go, and I'll take it off and we can get in the bed."

"Don't you want to do it standing up against the door?"

"Standing up? There's a trick I never mastered."

But his hands were on her bare legs and she was getting so hot even standing up sounded like a good idea.

"Okay, on the bed," he agreed, picking her up and carrying her the few steps to the bed. He was on her at once—caressing, kissing, teasing—until she pulled him to her and wrapped her legs around him.

"Now, Coe, now!"

Almost as soon as he touched her, she came. It was something about feeling him, hard and warm, soft and warm, against her. They rocked together, murmuring words of love.

She went to sleep still in his arms and

woke in the middle of the night to realize she was still wearing nothing but a skirt that was wrapped around her waist.

Well, maybe she could find an understanding cleaner.

They got up early the next morning, had breakfast together, and Coe left for the airport. Rachel planned to explore Houston while he was gone and, of course, shop.

But first she was going to have to clean up the remains of the breakfast. She had actually cooked in that pristine white kitchen; she felt as guilty as if she had rumpled the pillows in a model home. She was working away, scrubbing counters, when the doorbell rang.

And there stood Addie in another of those fashionable outfits, this one in shades of blue and gray. She started at the sight of Rachel and said, "I didn't expect to find you here!"

The reply that leapt to Rachel's lips was, "If I'd known you get visits from witches around here, I would have hung a sprig of garlic over the door," but she managed to bite it back before it was actually said. She mumbled a reluctant, "Hullo, Addie."

She suppressed the insults because she was curious about Addie. What was this woman like? Could the things Tricia had said about her really be true? Was it her disposition always to be angry and combative or did she just happen to be that way the single time Rachel had seen her before?

So, curious, she opened the door wider and said, "Why don't you come in?"

"I suppose it would be the best thing," said Addie, stepping across the threshold in her beautiful steel-gray, high-heeled shoes. "Around here we don't air our quarrels out in public the way you seem to do in Encino."

"Come on, Addie. We haven't got any reason to quarrel. Even if we did, we're old enough to know better than to pull each other's hair over a man. Let's sit down and talk. I'll put on some coffee."

Addie looked around, surprised. "Is Roscoe not here?"

"No, he had a flight to make."

"The CAF, I suppose. I'm so weary of that organization! The money he has poured into it! And for what?"

Rachel let it ride. Obviously Addie didn't know about the Mexico trips or she would not have expected to find Coe at home on a Thursday.

Why explain? Rachel only shrugged. "Well, it keeps him out of bars."

While Rachel made the coffee, Addie sat regally in the living room. That was okay with Rachel; she needed some time to organize her thoughts.

When Rachel came with the tray, Addie began at once with her own agenda. "How long have you and Coe been dating?"

Rachel smiled to hear that word. "Dating? Well, I guess that's what we're doing. He's helping me to get my pilot's license."

"A pilot's license? At your age?"

"Why not? I've already had my first solo and some other really interesting experiences."

Addie stared at her. "What an odd thing to do."

"Cream? Sugar?"

"Milk, please, and just a bit of sugar. And your husband? Where is he?"

"He passed away a little over a year ago."

"How lucky for you!"

That was enough to jolt Rachel. "What?"

"Being a widow is the best thing of all. You get everything; you don't have to put up with him, and he can't turn up later and make trouble."

Rachel said stiffly, "Pete was a fine man, and I miss him."

"Did he leave you well off?"

"Enough to get by. Tricia tells me you have a very active social life in Houston."

"Tricia!" It was a snort. "She's got nothing else to do but gossip about other people. I tell her all sorts of things that aren't true because the only pleasure she gets out of life is giving away other people's secrets. It's her empowerment."

"You've probably got her pegged. She would need empowerment more than the average. Having a husband like Chief would give a person self-esteem of about zero."

"She should stop catering to him and get a life. You make rotten coffee."

"Sorry about that." Rachel went right on sipping hers. It tasted okay to her.

"You think he's going to marry you, but he won't."

Rachel sipped serenely. "Well, he can't, can he? Unless you two were to divorce."

Addie snorted. "Fat chance! What I know about him . . ."

Her voice trailed off and Rachel asked alertly, "Yeah? What?"

"Hanky-panky in that plant and that floozie that worked for him for so long . . ." Addie trailed off again and shrugged, as if everybody was bound to know what she meant.

Rachel asked, "Why do you want to be married to him? You talk as if you hate him."

"Of course I do; but darling, he's rich! And do you think I want my name followed by 'former wife of . . .' every time it's mentioned in the papers? Damn him! Why does he always have to be stirring things up? I am perfectly content with our marriage as long as he leaves me alone."

"He'd be sure to if you were divorced."

Addie eyed her suspiciously. "He's such a bore; what do you see in him?"

"I really enjoy his company, and he seems happy when we're together."

"I don't think that man knows how to be happy. He was always complaining about something; all he ever seemed to want was the impossible."

Rachel said, "He has accomplished some remarkable things. Some of them probably seemed impossible before he did them."

"Children! He was forever nattering on about children!"

"Another coffee?" Rachel asked. "Yes, he likes children. Did you talk to him about what you wanted?"

Addie held out her cup. "What good would that have done? I can't have any children, but I wasn't about to tell him that. A little milk, please. He was yakking about kids even before we were married; but it wasn't any big deal to me so I didn't figure it was to him, either, but he's obsessed with the subject."

"I think he would have been a good father. He's very good with little children."

"I couldn't; I told you. I had an abortion." She put down her coffee cup with a small clatter, suddenly agitated. "It wasn't so easy in those days, not like now! No nice, clean clinics, no anesthetic. It was a horror, a nightmare! They held me down and scraped the inside of my uterus with a tool like a nutmeg grater. I still suffer from the aftereffects."

"After such an appalling experience, I'm surprised that you would do it all over again."

"Do what?"

"Have a second abortion."

Addie laughed briefly and picked up the cup again, apparently in quite a good humor. "Oh, Roscoe told you about that, did he? I really pushed his buttons with that one! I'll bet he believes it to this day!"

"It wasn't true?"

"I told you! I had an abortion when I

was seventeen. They messed me up inside; I was lucky to live through it. I could never have any kids, but I was damned if I was going to tell Roscoe that. He used to ask me when my period was due, and I'd make something up. He never caught on."

"There never was any baby? The child he still mourns for never existed?"

"Of course not. I don't mind telling you because I know you'll never tell anybody. I've got you pegged."

"I guess you do," Rachel admitted. "To tell him wouldn't make him any less sad; it would only make him feel foolish for mourning."

"I told him I'd saved him the price of a college education and a new Corvette, but he didn't think that was funny."

"You do have a different sort of a sense of humor. Would you. . . . What was that?"

Addie said, "I'd say it was Roscoe, coming home." Sure enough, the sound was a key in the lock and Coe came in.

Addie smiled, bright lipstick outlining her teeth. "Good morning, Roscoe. I was hoping to see you today."

He growled, "What the hell are you doing here?"

Rachel explained, "I invited her in, Coe. I'm surprised to see you; I thought you had a flight."

"Mechanical trouble; the plane won't go today."

"Would you care for a cup of coffee?"

"What I'd like is her out of my house. This is my home, Addie. I took this apartment thirty years ago just so I'd have a place to keep you out of. You've got no business here."

Addie was still smiling, if not as broadly as before. "Yes, I do. We didn't finish making our agreement last time we talked."

"We've got too much old business between us ever to agree about anything. Why don't you let our lawyers argue it out with each other? That's what they're for."

"Let them handle things and they'll schmooze all afternoon and charge us for the time. I can give him his instructions if I know what you are going to give me."

Coe sat down, picked up the coffee server, and—seeing no cups—appropriated Rachel's. He poured with a steady hand and said, "You've already told me what you want, all my stock in the company."

Rachel broke in, "You don't have to give

it to her, Coe. Ask her about her tennis instructor."

He demurred. "We're not going to go into that. It'd be like one outhouse calling the other stinky."

"Oh, very true!" chortled Addie. "Even if we forget about that other floozie, there's this one, here."

"Never mind that!" said Coe sharply. "Let's get to the question I want to ask. How did you pay for that boat of yours?"

Addie sat back with a little wave of satisfaction. "You paid for it, Roscoe, and very generous of you it was."

"You conned my controller out of that check, and then you forged my signature on it."

She widened her eyes theatrically. "If there was a forgery, it must have been your controller who did it."

"He didn't forge, but he did goof up. He should never have cut that check in the first place or given it to you in the second. You convinced him that we had reconciled and that I wanted a boat. . . . Hell, I hate boats."

Addie asked, "If he did something wrong, why is he still working for you?"

Coe smiled grimly. "I know how to get

loyalty from my employees. And you can bet your boots he's never going to make the mistake of listening to you again! He came to me with it as soon as he figured out what you had done, and I've got that check locked away in a really safe place. Forgery is a felony, Addie."

"Between husband and wife? A Texas jury would never convict."

"In large amounts, those checks require two signatures. You didn't just forge my signature; you did the treasurer's, too. You must have really wanted that yacht!"

"It's only a little yacht! Just a fishing boat, really."

"I'm going to be making you an allowance," Coe went on. "I guess alimony is the right word. It's enough so you can run the house and even support that boat, but it's all you get, forever. You don't need to come running to me with any of your emergencies or to get money for some pretty thing you've set your eye on."

Addie stood up abruptly and picked up her purse. "You've spoiled it," she accused him. "You've spoiled my pleasure in that boat. It will never be the same now that I see what it's going to cost me."

"Don't worry about it," Coe said reassuringly. "If it hadn't been the boat, it would have been something else; there's plenty more. Think back a little, you'll probably remember some incidents yourself."

As soon as she was gone, Coe picked up the phone. "I'd better call my lawyer now and get a property agreement signed with her before she thinks of some new angle to try. You got to give Addie this: She's a fighter."

While he talked on the phone, Rachel cleaned up the coffee things. She didn't hear his conversation finish; but when she returned to the living room, he was sitting with his hand on the silent instrument, staring into space.

"Are you all right, Coe?"

"I'm closing a door," he replied slowly. "One I should have closed years ago, I guess, but still. . . . It's a sorry ending for something that could have been . . . could have been a lot more than it ever was."

"You tried. Nobody can say you didn't try."

"She's cold, selfish, and dishonest; but it seems like—if things had been just a little different and if she'd been a different kind of person . . ."

"And if pigs had wings, they'd be robins.

You don't have to be beating up on yourself."

"I'm not. I'm only seeing one thing end so another can begin." He looked up at her and smiled. "What a beginning, Rachel! We can get married and you'll stop making fine distinctions about where I can buy you clothes. I can't do it at Saks, but The Supply Sergeant is okay!"

"I don't remember ever saying I'd marry you."

"Well, of course you will! Nobody turns down a man with my money."

"Exactly why I will do it. How would it look for me to marry a man sixty-eight years old who has no children? Do you even have nieces and nephews?"

"Sure, and a demanding little group they are. You're going to turn me down on account of the money? Now, there's a switch."

"You know, you still could father children. You're not too old. If you married a young woman, you could have a family."

"What? Marry one of the hardbodies just to get a kid? Be a damn fool thing for me to do." He thought briefly and added, "Be a damn fool thing for her to do, too."

"You're the one always saying age is just a number."

"It is, but I'm past the point where I want to live with little kids in the house all the time. I like them, but not every day. Grandkids are what I need, and the only way I can get those is to marry somebody who already has some."

"Oh, so that's the basis of my charm for you?"

"Well, it's not quite all of it—you do have certain other assets—but I covet your grandchildren. Come on, promise you'll make me a grandfather."

"What a charmingly romantic proposal! Suppose I check it out with Susie and if she still likes you, then okay, it's a deal?"

"I'm pretty sure I can bank on Susie."

"Their attention span is pretty short at three. She may not remember you."

"Ah, but you do, don't you?" He wrapped his arms around her and nuzzled her hair.

She nestled against him, glad for the return of his good spirits and already feeling a stir in her own body. "I think I remember. You're the guy who's always telling me about the static tube and the pitot port."

"Pitot tube and static port!" he roared, but he knew she was teasing. He pulled her shirt out from her belt and ran his hand under it. Satisfied that the front door of the apartment was solid and locked, she let him caress her.

"It's going to be a lousy day tomorrow," he grumbled. "We'll have to make the whole round trip in one day. It sure would help if I had a copilot."

"Now, wait a minute. You want me to learn another ship while we're in the air? A whole new thing all over again?"

"This one's easy! Everything's automatic; most of the time I fly it by myself. But if you were there, I could take a break once in a while; and besides, then I wouldn't be so lonesome."

"Well, okay." He had his hands deep inside her jeans by then, and she would have agreed to just about anything. "You'll have to promise not to boink me in the cockpit, though."

"Aw, Rachel! Never?"

"Well . . ." She paused, pretending to consider, but really just to enjoy his stroking fingers. "Well, okay, but not when we're in the air."

Twenty-one

Coe's air ambulance was not an ambulance at all but only a six-passenger Cessna 340. He explained that they only occasionally needed to carry a patient on a stretcher and when they did, they "just crammed it in."

Rachel was delighted with the ship. After the B-17, it seemed compact and easy—only two engines, pressurized cabin, upholstered seats, and a short checklist. She was delighted with the comfort, the quiet, and the convenience of banks of helpful gadgets.

Coe was amused by her enthusiasm and laughed as he started up the engines. "Better'n we used to have it in The War, huh, Rachel!"

"Pretty cool ship," she said.

Today's doctor was a surgeon and his name slipped right by Rachel because she was already in her seat and studying the instrument panel when he got aboard. He was so young, she almost asked him if he really had finished his internship.

Then she scolded herself for even thinking it. Most doctors play golf on their days off. This one flew for hours just to dispense pills in a remote village.

Also aboard were two little girls, one four years old, the other six. Poor victims, they lived so far in the mountains that they had not received their immunizations for polio and had contracted the disease. Now they made the trip to Houston regularly for physical therapy. Seasoned travelers, they solemnly fastened their seat belts and sat quietly. They would be met by relatives at the end of their journey, but for the flight, they were traveling alone.

Minutes after takeoff they were flying over the Gulf; and when they had reached altitude, Coe put the ship on automatic pilot. He never left his seat but sat at his ease, endlessly scanning the sky, ten degrees at a time.

The engines snored away, so peacefully that Rachel could clearly hear the children behind her. They had made the trip many times and knew there would be nothing to look at but water most of the way. They were bored and pinching one another, and the four-year-old set up a steady, nerve-wracking whine.

The doctor was immersed in his newspaper and heard nothing. After a while Rachel got up and separated the two kids, buckling them into different seats and dividing the toys they had squabbled over.

Coe twisted around in his chair and shouted, so loudly the doctor was startled and dropped his newspaper, "Hey, where did you go? Come back here; I need a fuel report."

Rachel checked the six-year-old's seat belt one more time and slipped back into the right-hand chair.

Coe went on scolding. "Don't go roaming around the cabin without saying anything! I'll tell you when you can do that. We've been in the air an hour; we need to check the fuel."

Rachel calculated the fuel in the tanks and gave him the figures. Her scowl was almost as good as his.

Two hours out they made landfall and headed straight into the mountains. They could look up at mountain peaks as Coe glided toward the airfield, a narrow asphalt strip in a lush green valley.

There was a crowd waiting for them, all

chattering in Spanish and squealing with joyous welcome for the children. Coe stopped the doctor in the doorway to ask, "Is your watch still on Houston time? We're taking off at three sharp, so be here. *Tiempo Americano,* you got me? I don't wait for anybody; I won't fly these mountains in the dark. You want somebody to help carry those toolboxes of yours?"

The doctor assented, so Coe cut a couple of young men out of the herd around them and told them to carry the luggage. Coe's Spanish was confident; Rachel's was not good enough to allow her to form an opinion of whether it was fluent or not.

Coe locked up the ship, chatted with the people around him, exchanged *abrazos* with his friends. One of them, an older man, was detailed to guard the plane.

Coe took Rachel's arm. "Come on, I'll show you the town."

She asked, "Do you think we ought to help the doctor?"

"If he needs any help, he'd better bring it with him. I've got enough to do."

He strode off toward the village and Rachel scampered behind him, puffing in the thin air. The altimeter had read 5600 feet when they landed; this place was higher than Denver.

They went through an open-air market laid out in the square in front of the church. The women sat on blankets, shawls wrapped tightly around their heads and shoulders. No tourist trifles here; the offerings were vegetables, grain, eggs . . . a village grocery. Coe stopped several times to exchange greetings with the market women.

"Buenos días, cómo está?" he would say to each. Rachel's Spanish was up to that, anyway. To the smiling women who tried to press their goods on him, it was. *"No, gracias, muy amable."*

"You're so gracious and charming," Rachel grumbled, "in Spanish."

"This is the place," said Coe, charging into a building. "I've got to check up on these guys."

It was a pottery factory, and the heat from the ovens hit Rachel like a blow. A row of painters seemed not at all bothered but brushed away, putting designs on plates and tiles.

Coe paid them no attention but went straight to the office, where he demanded to look at the books. Several managerial types had appeared by that time and they created delays with greetings and conversation, but nothing stopped Coe for long. The books were produced; he examined the figures, and then he bawled everybody out. Then he and Rachel left.

The scene was repeated in three separate factories. Coe came; he saw the books; he yelled. In only slightly crippled Spanish he made his suggestions, which sounded more like orders. By the time he had finished, it was three o'clock and they went back to the plane.

When they got there, the doc had not arrived and it was already several minutes after three. Coe began the checklist.

He paused, however, just before starting the engines. "There's a cooler in the baggage compartment," he told Rachel. "Why don't you fetch it, and we'll have a sandwich before we take off."

Rachel found the cooler. "Here it is. Did you pack it? I didn't see it before."

"Standing order with Airport Services," he explained.

She was glad to find soft drinks nestled among the sandwiches. "These look good to me! We moved so fast, I haven't had a drink of water all day."

He stopped unwrapping his sandwich and gave her a sharp look. "Good thing you didn't. Don't ever eat or drink anything in one of these villages. You'll be running for a week if you do."

They had taken only a few bites of sandwich when the doc appeared. As he came hurrying across the strip, toting his bags of medical supplies, Coe put his sandwich into his lap and started the starboard engine.

That got Doc's attention and he sprinted to the ship. He tossed the bags through the open door and climbed in, spouting apologies. Coe made no response except to secure the door and start the port engine. He began the taxi at once, while Rachel babbled her way through the last part of the checklist.

They took off with a mountain dead ahead of them, made a turn, and climbed out of the valley the way they had come in. As they rose to altitude, there was silence in the cabin. The pilots munched at their sandwiches. After a while, Rachel passed the cooler back to Doc, and he took it and selected a sandwich, but he never said a word. Perhaps he was contemplating the possibility of having been left behind in a mountain village where you couldn't drink the water to wait for Coe's return, six days away if the weather were right.

It wouldn't be the first time, Coe confided. He had several times left behind docs who couldn't keep to the schedule.

During the long flight back to Houston, Rachel watched Coe covertly. She could tell that he was tired, but he would not relinquish the controls to her for any length of time, certainly not long enough for a nap; and of course he was going to have to handle the landing himself.

She would study this ship, Rachel vowed to herself. She would learn it, master the skills needed to fly it so she could really share the flying with Coe, help him with this brutal trip. No wonder he had always returned so weary those Friday nights in Arizona!

But he was smiling when they finally landed and had taxied the ship to its tie-down spot. The engines were turned off. The doctor scrambled out of his seat, and Coe said to her, "It was really nice to have an extra pair of hands for that flight. Thanks, Rachel, that was swell."

"No it wasn't," grumped Rachel. "You

still had to do all the flying; I was about as much use as another passenger. I've got to get some instructions, learn to fly this ship."

"Well, you can study the POH."

"Pilot's Operating Handbook," she translated automatically. "I said *fly* it. Sure, I need to study that book, but I want some air time, too."

"You'll get it," he promised, climbing out of his seat. "For now, let's go find a cold shower and a stiff drink."

As they trudged across the tarmac toward the car, he put an arm around her. "I'm sure glad you want to help me with those Mexico trips. There's four different villages and about a dozen doctors and only one of me. It seems like somebody's always wanting something."

"I'm glad to help you, but we need some ground rules. Not ground ground rules, I mean air ground rules."

That made him laugh. "You got yourself really tangled up in that one, didn't you?"

"I can't seem to edge around the subject, so I'll just spit it out. You yelled at me up there today!"

"I wasn't yelling at you. I was just trying to keep the navigation on track."

"Well, it sounded to me like yelling."

"Okay, I'll try to keep the volume down when it's you."

"Thank you. You know, Coe, we are both of us coming from marriages where the communication was not satisfactory. I don't think either one of us wants that again. I want to be able to talk to you and to know that you will listen."

"I didn't think we were so far off the track, but we'll do something about it if you think we should. What do you want? A therapist or something?"

You couldn't say he wasn't agreeable. She said, "I don't think we need professional help yet. Besides, all a therapist would do is give us exercises to do at home."

"Yeah? Like what?"

"There's one I always thought sounded useful. Each partner talks for ten minutes."

He scratched his hair. "What's so special about that?"

"The other has to promise to listen and not to interrupt. He has to wait his turn."

"Sounds like the only thing lacking is a podium and a mike; but okay, if that's what you want, I'll try it."

They ordered Chinese food to the apartment and were glad to be cocooned there, doors locked against the world. When they had cleaned up and tucked the leftovers into the refrigerator, they sprawled on the couch and he asked, "Do you want to watch television? Or not? You said you wanted to talk."

"Well, I didn't mean I had anything specific to say," Rachel protested. "Is there something on TV you wanted to see?"

"Nah, go ahead and talk." He put his head in her lap and looked up expectantly.

"Oh, gee, I don't know. Maybe I shouldn't have started this. I don't think I have any ten-minute subjects."

He smiled encouragingly. "Just say whatever you're thinking about."

"What I'm thinking about right now? Well, that's kind of silly. What I'm thinking, I'm worrying about Deena. I wish I'd had the chance to talk to her before we left town; but we were in such a hurry and it didn't look like a good time since it was really obvious that Ethan was angry. I wish I'd been able to keep him and Chief apart."

Coe didn't say anything, but then, he had agreed not to. She went on. "I hope Deena hasn't done anything foolish. She was feeling so restless and Chief. . . . Well, you can't help liking Chief. I hope he was able to work things out with Tricia. I suppose he was; he always does.

"I wonder how Barbara's getting along. I just hate to think of her, way out there on the ranch, coping with three little children and all those ranch chores. Well, it's her life. She chose it. She knew when she married Marc that he was dedicated to his ranch. He's just like Kenny. Kenny's my own son, but I don't understand why he has to always do jobs that keep him traveling. He leaves his wife alone for months at a time. No wonder she thinks one child is enough. She probably doesn't have the chance to get any more, he's so seldom at home. Do you think I worry too much?"

Coe's answer was a gentle snore. He was relaxed, his head heavy in her lap, the weary lines smoothed from his face. What a day he had had—what a week, for that matter. All that flying . . .

She touched his hair, felt his warm ear under her palm, and she murmured, "You're an old grouch, but I think you're wonderful. I love the way you go at everything, full speed ahead, no matter what. And the life you've had would make anybody grumpy. The War and those terrible, bloody missions, and then you came home and had to live with Addie. I think you might even mellow out some if you were to get treated well and fed regularly. I'm going to try it, anyhow."

Her legs were going to sleep, and she nudged Coe lightly. "Hey, pal, why don't you go sleep in a bed? You're snoring."

His eyes sprang open and he said, "No, I'm not. I heard every word you said."

"Oh, if I'd known that, I wouldn't have called you all those nasty names."

He pulled her head down and kissed her, but since it was a severe bend of her spine, it lasted only seconds. She squawked, "Don't do that! Get off my lap; my leg is asleep."

"Which one? I'll rub it for you." He sat up and grasped her thigh with both hands. His massage didn't last long; very soon he was kissing her again, and his hand had found more interesting places to caress. It still surprised her how quickly he could make her respond. Her whole body was warming, drawing her closer to him.

She protested feebly, "Coe, what are you up to?"

"These jeans are a pain," he complained, tugging at the zipper. "Why'd you leave your jumpsuit in Encino?"

"You're supposed to be tired."

"I'm supposed to be old, too," he answered, pushing the jeans down her thighs, "but it doesn't seem to matter. I can't get enough of this."

Rachel kicked the jeans to the floor. "When there's enough, I'll let you know."

He pounced on her, pushing her down on the couch. "I like this idea of yours, the talking for ten minutes. It's a real turn-on."

She cocked a sarcastic eye. "If we practice, maybe we can eliminate the talk entirely."

"Nah, we'll keep talking, we just won't time it anymore."

"All right, we'll just talk."

Twenty-two

Saturday morning and a whole weekend ahead. . . . Rachel stretched happily in Coe's bed. He was already awake, sitting against the headboard and watching her, a little smile touching his lips. Then she remembered.

"We have to get up right now! You have to go to Harlingen today! Whitey wants you to take the Fort there today!"

"No he doesn't. I got rid of him."

"You got rid of Whitey? The most persistent man since Inspector Javert? What did you do to him?"

"I just told him he didn't have to give up his weekend, we'd take the ship down to Harlingen next week."

Rachel sat up, startled. "We? Meaning you and me? We're going to fly to Harlingen? Wing Headquarters? They'll have a fit!"

"I guess they can if they want. It won't hurt them."

"All right, but I need some time to learn the Fort. I don't want to be a passenger riding in the copilot's seat anymore."

"Aw, what do you want to bother for? It isn't as if you're going to be flying that ship regularly."

"If I'm going to do it at all, I want to do it right."

He agreed, sounding indulgent as he did, but there was no indulgence in the hours they put in together studying the ship. It was all ground work. They climbed into the ship and sweltered in the cockpit while the sun beat down on the tarmac and Rachel struggled to learn the name and function of every control.

"It isn't as if there're so many of them," Coe insisted. "It's just that there're four engines, so there're four of everything."

"Not to mention the fuel system, the hydraulic system, the rudder, the ailerons, the flaps," grumbled Rachel. "The radio, the transponder, the trim tabs . . ."

"Hey, you want to fly, this is how we do it. We don't issue angel wings."

"Angel wings? Are they any simpler? I'll bet they're not. When I get mine, they're probably going to have a turn-and-bank indicator on them."

That made Coe laugh. "Flying them looks easy, but how do you control them when there's no rudder?"

"Do they have a control stick, like old planes used to?"

"Sure they do! That explains why there aren't any girl angels!"

They made the flight to Harlingen the next day; and the colonels at Wing Headquarters didn't have a fit, after all. In fact, they took Rachel's presence in the cockpit of the Fort with an entirely reasonable calm. They even talked about making her a colonel, but nothing came of it.

Rachel and Coe caught a commercial flight back to Houston, and she discovered that Coe was absolutely impossible in the passenger seat of an airliner. Up in the air with nothing to do, he amused himself with nuzzling and tickling Rachel.

"Wouldn't you like to read something?" she asked him. "Look, the airline has generously provided a magazine, you could work the crossword puzzle."

"I don't want a magazine."

"Or look out the window or something."

"You get the greatest views in the world

from an airplane, but only if you're in front. I don't like watching them go by sideways."

"You're as bad as one of the children. When are you going to grow up?"

He leaned over her, breathing into her hair. "Did anybody ever tell you you're a very sexy woman?"

"As a matter of fact, no. And I don't think I am."

"Oh, yes you are, and that's why I can't keep my hands off you."

"Does it make any difference that you're driving me up the wall?"

"No. Well, yes, that's part of it. You always respond. That's one of the things that's so sexy about you."

"At the risk of repeating myself, grow up, Coe."

He asked in a suggestive whisper, "Ever hear of the Mile High Club?"

"Everybody has."

"Well?"

Rachel confessed, "In my youth . . . my extreme youth. . . . I thought it was a real club and everybody got together later and compared notes; but now that I know it's just another male scam, I am no longer interested in membership."

"I'll have the stewardess bring us a blanket. Nobody will notice."

"Nobody will notice? Both of us under a blanket? In August?"

"Suppose the plane crashes? Suppose we never get to Houston, never get another chance to do it? Don't you want to do it one last time?"

"If this ship is going to crash, maybe you ought to go up there in the cockpit and tell the captain what to do."

"I didn't say it was going to, but there's always the possibility and we should hedge our bets."

"Somehow, I am not in the least concerned," said Rachel.

To nobody's surprise, they got to Houston in good order.

Then they had three whole days to see the town. She made him give her a couple of instruction flights in the 340, but he kept them short and they had all the rest of their time just to be together.

They visited NASA and saw the spectacular film there. Rachel insisted on standing in the long line to touch a moon rock. It had to be meaningful, that touch. To have her hand actually in contact with something that had lain for unthinkable eons on the surface of an alien world, a dead satellite. . . . Her fingers tingled afterwards when she thought about it.

They went shopping, ate in restaurants, and lolled in bed until late almost every morning. Rachel didn't even phone her children. They probably would not notice, she thought, but if they did, let them wonder where she was for a few days.

This time when they were on the Mexico flight, Coe turned the ship over to her for more than an hour while he sat in back and chatted with the pair of doctors who were their passengers. It was wonderful; it was what she had dreamed of since she was a child. The ship was in her hands and she was alone with the sea and the vast sky.

Well, there were three men in the back of the plane, but the responsibility was all hers. Coe didn't return to his chair until the peaks of the Sierra Madres were showing on the horizon.

This time they would be overnighting in the village, and Coe took her to the home where he and the docs were accustomed to spend the night. It was the biggest house in the village, set on top of a hill, and built in the Spanish style—low, tile-roofed rooms clustered around a courtyard. They were greeted warmly by their hosts, the Aravenas, an elderly couple, white-haired and handsome in their robust health and strength.

Coe introduced Rachel as *"La Señora,"* so they would be given a room together and also, he explained later, to give the Aravenas something to call her. Both "Rachel" and "Flaherty" were impossible for a Latin tongue to pronounce.

They were shown to a pleasant, if simply-furnished room, where they put down their bags and Coe's cooler.

"There's the usual stuff in the cooler," Coe explained. "Sandwiches and soft drinks and bottled water. They're careful with the food here, and you can eat what they give you in this house if it's been cooked and it's hot when you get it. They even boil the water for us, but they probably don't boil it long enough so maybe you better stick to what's in the cooler. You might as well stay here for now; I'm going to go take a look at the factories."

"I don't want to stay here by myself," said Rachel. "Why can't I go with you? I did last week."

"We were in a hurry that time; and anyway, I'm going to go look at the pottery mine, see what the trouble is there."

"What kind of trouble?"

"Damned if I know. They keep talking about *aflojarse* and I thought that meant temporary work, so I've got to go see."

"I don't think I want to go hiking at this altitude," said Rachel. "You take it easy. You can overexert yourself when you're not used to this thin air."

"I am used to altitude. I'm a pilot."

"You're too macho for your own good, that's what you are."

When he was gone Rachel felt the afternoon like a weight. What was she to do all day? Conversation with her hosts was limited to pleasant greetings. If she took a nap, she would only wake and be bored in the middle of the night.

She remembered how forlorn last week's doc had looked, trekking off all alone with his medical bags. Maybe this week's men could use some help. What were their names? Larry and Moe? No, that wasn't right. She inquired directions and set off for the clinic.

The layout of the town was complex, but it was so small she easily found the clinic and offered her assistance to the two doctors. Their names turned out to be Jack and Sam; she had been close. They were both affable, middle-aged guys, and very ready to put her to work.

They were examining and vaccinating children, and Rachel made a chart for each one and took the tot's temperature for the first entry. How many children there were! They had to be coming from all over the surrounding mountains. Many of the tired, dusty children she handled had trudged for miles with their parents to reach this, the only medical care they ever saw. They were adorable, every one of them, brown-skinned children with eyes as black as espresso. They were wrapped in hand-woven blankets and wore colorful hats of the same fabric.

There was an interpreter, and he taught Rachel a few words of comfort and reassurance in Spanish. She became skilled at murmuring, *"Ai, pobrecito,"* while hugging a baby that had just felt the needle.

"We're not going to finish by dark," Doctor Sam said to his colleague, eying the line that stretched out the door.

"We can't turn anybody away," argued Doctor Jack. "They've come so far."

"We can't work in the dark, either. You

can't tell anything about a patient you examine by lantern-light."

"We can have them come back tomorrow, but how . . ." Doctor Jack broke off, listening. "What's all that racket?"

"Just people yelling," said Doctor Sam.

"Emergencia," corrected the interpreter. "It's an emergency."

A couple of men burst into the room, waving their arms, shouting their news between pants. Rachel picked out the words. They had run all the way from the mine. There was an accident. At the mine.

She shrank back against the wall, frozen with horror, while the interpreter bustled around, breaking up the line, and shooing people out of the tiny clinic building.

A group of people was hurrying toward the clinic. They were clustered around a crude stretcher, four men carrying it, a crumpled figure lying there. They squeezed themselves into the room, hoisted the injured man to a table.

It wasn't Coe, thank the gracious saints, it wasn't Coe, but she recognized the man. He was one of the managers they had talked with the previous week at the pottery factory.

One side of his face was skinned and

bleeding; he held an obviously injured arm with the other hand. He seemed to be conscious but confused. Rachel asked him, "Where is Coe?"

He was looking at something over her left shoulder, maybe it was Doctor Jack, and he did not answer.

She repeated, "Coe? Was Coe with you?"

He focused blearily on her and answered, "*Señor* Coe? *Sí.*"

Rachel started for the door, but Doctor Jack said firmly, "Rachel, come here."

"I have to find Coe."

"They've got a crew down there taking care of things. Anyhow, if I know Coe, he's there telling everybody what to do. You said you wanted to help us; now don't run off when we need you. Bring me that tray over there."

He was right, of course. She would be less than useless in a mine, and she had work here. She picked up the tray of medical supplies and, moving as if in a dream, held it where the doctor could select what he needed.

But what of Coe? She had to know, had to find out. She tried to pick out something from the babble of Spanish around her, but they were all talking fast, in loud, excited voices, and she couldn't understand a thing. Doctor Jack was examining the victim's arm, Doctor Sam taking his vital signs.

Where was Coe? At the mine, ordering people around, as Doctor Jack had suggested? Or had he been involved in whatever had gone wrong down there? Was he hurt and helpless? If he were hurt, surely they would have brought him here. Was he less hurt than this man and so had remained behind? So badly hurt they couldn't move him? Or out of reach, buried alive in the mine? She closed her eyes, unable to bear the horror of that thought. She and Coe had found each other such a short time ago; had she lost him already?

A second man hobbled through the door, supported by a friend. He was bleeding from a cut on his head, and Doctor Sam went to him. Doctor Jack didn't even look up from his careful examination of the arm.

"Clean break," he opined at last. "We'll put a cast on, make him comfortable. Bump on the head doesn't look like much. I'll take another look at it tomorrow."

"Shall I wash his face?" asked Rachel.

"Good, Lord, don't wash anything with

water around here! Clean him up with alcohol and put bandages on those scratches. Then he'll look better."

Rachel took the things she needed from the tray and began to clean. Once she got all the blood and dirt off the man's face, he had only a few bad scratches. She created bandages and was sticking them on when they came in with Coe.

She had not noticed that the men had taken away their stretcher; now they returned with it, carrying Coe. Doctor Jack hurried to his side, directed the crew to put Coe down on a cot. She could not see a mark on Coe anywhere, but he was unconscious. Rachel quickly finished her bandage and went to his side.

"What is it, Doctor Jack?"

Doctor Jack fingered Coe's hair next to an insignificant-looking bloody spot. "Blow to the head; hard to say how bad it is. Check his pulse and respiration; I'm going to get that cast put on the other man."

Rachel pulled up a stool and sat. Coe was so quiet, frowning, quite as if he were asleep; but he didn't move. She took up his hand and it was heavy and limp, but warm, just like Coe's hand always was. She felt for the pulse.

It was a task she had never been good at. All nurses can take the pulse and count the respirations at the same time, but Rachel had trouble just counting pulse and checking her watch simultaneously.

She counted everything four times, until she was getting consistent figures. Both pulse and respiration were a little fast, but only a little.

By the time she had finished her counting, Coe was beginning to stir. His hands twitched; he groaned and then began to blink.

A couple of blinks, and the eyes opened. Rachel cried, "Coe, can you hear me? Do you know me?"

And he smiled. He smiled a big white smile in that dirty face and said, "Rachel. I have a new word for you, Rachel. *Aflojarse.* It means loose, like shale in a mine."

Twenty-three

"Oh, Coe, you're all right!" She covered his face with kisses, weeping with joy.

He didn't respond except to smile at her. "Rincon and the other guy, are they all right?"

"There's two guys in here, neither hurt very bad; I don't know what their names are. You lie still. I'm going to get the doctor."

Both doctors were working on the messy job of casting the broken arm, wetting long white strips that dribbled plaster onto the floor, but Sam wiped his hands and came over to look at Coe.

"Hey, you look pretty good!" he said cheerily. "Don't try to sit up yet. Can you move your hands and feet okay?"

Coe lifted both his hands, then waggled his feet and said, "Ow!"

"Oh, look at that!" said Doctor Sam, as he stepped to the foot of the cot. With skillful hands he removed one of Coe's shoes and then cut the pant leg, revealing an ankle swollen to basketball size.

Sam explored the swelling, gently, with his long, supple fingers. "It could be a break, but it looks like just a bad sprain. Get it elevated and put some ice on it."

"There's no ice in this town!" protested Rachel, staring at the swelling and the poor man's foot with a blue stain already forming across the instep.

"Do the best you can," advised Sam. "He's okay. You can take him up to the house if you want. He'll be a little more comfortable there."

Addressing Coe, he added, "Come see me when we get to Houston and I'll X-ray it." He returned to assisting Doctor Jack with the cast.

Coe cursed under his breath, frowning at his foot. "If we ever get back to Houston!"

There was no transportation to be had in all the town. Rachel dickered for a while with a man who owned a donkey and cart; but while he was still considering if carrying a passenger in his cart was the right thing for him to do, the young men who had carried Coe from the mine appeared. Willing, even enthusiastic, they reassembled their stretcher (it was made of tree branches and a blanket) and carried Coe to the house of the Aravenas.

They carried him to bed where Rachel, being Rachel, washed him. She piled pillows under his swollen ankle, laid wet cloths over it, and sat fanning it with a palm-leaf fan. It must have made him comfortable for he slept most of the afternoon.

When Sam and Jack finally came back to the house for dinner, they dropped in to examine Coe and pronounced him doing fine.

"You're a lucky bunch," was Jack's opinion. "Only three people hurt and none of you bad; that's a pretty nice mine accident!"

"Well, it isn't much of a mine," Coe explained. "It's a clay mine, for God's sake! It's open, maybe twenty feet at its deepest point, and nobody was down there but us three. The rest of the guys were standing around at the top, watching."

He shifted on his cushions and ordered, "Stop fanning, Rachel. You're making a draft. Rincon didn't have anybody working in the mine because of the loose stuff; and as soon as we started moving around down there, it just went. It was shale and it broke up in pieces as it slid, so there weren't too many big rocks to bonk us, I guess. I don't know what happened, really. I can't remember anything after it started to slide."

"You took a pretty good knock on the head," Jack said easily. "Get a good sleep tonight and you'll be fit to fly tomorrow."

"The head's okay," growled Coe, "but what makes you think I can fly with that foot?"

Jack was surprised. "Oh, you need to use your feet?"

"I couldn't even drive an automatic-shift Buick with that foot!"

Jack was shocked. "A thing like that can take six weeks to heal! I have to get back to Houston! I have appointments on Saturday!"

Having broken Doctor Jack's composure, Coe grinned with satisfaction. "Don't worry. I brought along my copilot. She'll do the flying tomorrow."

Rachel didn't even gasp this time. She was getting used to Coe's outrageous demands on her.

Jack didn't gasp, either, but took it as a matter of course. He said, "Okay, that's good. Be sure and get that thing X-rayed. It is a pretty spectacular swelling."

She waited until the doctors were gone

to protest. "Coe, I'm not supposed to fly that ship! It will have passengers in it and I don't have a license to fly passengers! It's illegal!"

He shook his head, irritated. "I'm going to have to see to it you get your license. You're always complaining about being illegal. You were flying the ship yesterday; you didn't complain then!"

"That was different. You were right there, and you're a CFI."

"It was illegal, and tomorrow it'll still be illegal and I'll still be a CFI. Or would you rather stay here until I get better? You heard what he said, six weeks!"

Rachel picked up the fan and waved it at his damp cloths. "I'll do it, of course I will. Please go over the takeoff with me. I've only watched it once, and I may have had my eyes closed when you went into that bank."

"Nothing to it. You've just got to rotate at exactly three-quarters down the runway and go into the bank with full power."

"Isn't that hard on the engines?"

"Going to be harder on them if you don't turn before you hit that mountain!"

As a special treat, their hosts served a *menudo* at dinner. Neither Rachel nor Coe was fond of the dish, and the tripe had been cut in large, awkward pieces that made it especially difficult for Coe to eat while propped up in bed.

After a few spoonfuls of the soup, Coe gave her a conspiratorial glance and said, "I feel sorry for those poor docs. They've got to sit out there at the table and look like they're enjoying this. All you have to do is shut that door and nobody will be able to tell what we're up to."

Rachel closed the door, quietly disposed of the *menudo*, and they ate up the sandwiches that had been packed by the airport people.

In the cool evening, the townspeople strolled in the square or sat on the churchyard wall to chat and strum their guitars. That was about the sum of entertainment in the town, and Rachel, stuck inside the house with Coe, could not even join the *paseo*. She lit a lantern for a while, but it only attracted bugs so she blew it out and they arranged themselves for sleep very early.

Too early to actually sleep. They lay there for a long time, talking some, mostly just nestling together. She had her head on his shoulder and she caressed his chest, feeling his warmth, his living pulse under her fingers.

She murmured, "I could have lost you."

He made a wry chuckle in the darkness. "For a little bit there, I thought you had, my own self. What a way for a pilot to go, down in a hole buried with rocks!"

"Promise me you're going to stay out of rocky holes!"

"Well, I'll try. I guess you can promise me you'll stay out of sinks."

"Sinks like low ground in front of the airstrip? I'll try."

A small laugh rumbled in his chest. "I guess we've each had a chance to scare the other."

"I was more scared than you were."

"No, I was more scared than you."

"Mine lasted longer."

He chuckled again. "I guess you were right—we just have to get used to the worrying. It's just something that goes with loving somebody."

"I love you."

"You going to prove it?" He was already fumbling for the hem of her nightgown.

"Coe, what are you thinking of! The trauma you've had today, your leg, you could have been killed . . ." He had his hands on her bare skin and she was already having trouble completing a sentence.

"That's just what's making me feel so sexy. I'm alive! I didn't get killed; I'm alive! Every cell in my body wants to holler, *I'm alive!*"

"But this place is a cracker box. There's no lock on the door, no glass in the window, and the house is full of people!"

"Sneaky sex, then. Let's see how quietly we can do it."

She ran her hand down his body. "All right, no shouting."

"No laughing, no giggling." He rolled toward her and pulled her close. "It's not allowed to have a good time."

"Anybody caught enjoying it will be shot." She gripped him firmly as he found her lips with his.

They were very quiet after that.

In the morning Doctor Sam came to examine Coe and pronounced him sound. The swelling was down a little in his ankle, and Sam bound it up with an elastic bandage and presented Coe with a pair of crutches. They were extremely well-used and a bit too short for Coe, but he practiced on them until he could hop along nimbly.

He was glad to be vertical again and wanted to sit in the main room so Rachel helped him to dress. The doc had ruined his jumpsuit anyway, so Rachel trimmed off the split leg to about knee length and he was then able to get his bandaged foot through it. He sat in a big chair with the foot propped up, and Rachel put hot compresses on it.

The hot compresses were more trouble than the cold ones had been since she could only get hot water by heating it on the cookstove. She was rather glad when Coe declared that the heat was making him uncomfortable and ordered her to quit.

After lunch he crutched his way, very slowly and cautiously, with Rachel hovering anxiously, down the hill to visit his friends from the factory. Rincon was back at his desk, the arm in a sling, the other man was still resting. It was decided that Rincon would explore for a new mine and close the old one. Threatened by unstable shale, it would always be dangerous.

Rincon even procured a donkey for Coe to ride to the airstrip. Coe trotted through the town sidesaddle, crutches cradled in his arm, waving and calling to his friends in a voice that vibrated with the jouncing of the donkey. Rachel scrambled after them, carrying the flight bags and the cooler.

In the plane she elected to sit in the right-hand seat since she was more accustomed to it in this ship. They went through the checklist exactly as they always did.

The doctors arrived on time, loaded their gear into the proper places, and Rachel started the engines. Coe sat at his ease—he even had a cushion under his foot—and he was smiling. Smiling with a smug confidence. Once the checklist was finished, he said not another single word. The ship was all hers.

Full power for the takeoff and the first turn, rotate at the final quarter of the runway. . . . She was ready. The throttles went forward; the ship sped along the asphalt; she had only seconds, and she had to be right. No second chances to make this takeoff!

They were in the air, climbing, and then the turn. Green cliffs flashed by the windows and the mountain was behind her, the ocean ahead. She reduced the engine speed slightly and continued to climb into the vibrating blue of the sky.

Coe said, "Okay."

The doctors never even noticed. They

were discussing golf, and to them the take-off was routine. It happened every time they came here.

Coe radioed Houston to let them know that they were coming in with a "passenger needing assistance."

"I do that every chance I get," he confided. "It's fun."

It was, too. She made the landing at Houston and was directed to taxi to a designated spot. She turned off the engines and waited, and along came three automobiles and an ambulance. It was the Customs and Immigration people, who came aboard to check the passports and luggage. Then Coe and Doctor Sam were loaded into the ambulance and it took off, the siren wide open. Doc Sam directed the ambulance into the parking lot, where they dropped him off at his car, siren howling the whole way. Sam would follow the ambulance to his hospital, and Coe would get his X-ray.

Rachel unloaded Doctor Jack, took the plane to its tiedown area, returned that doggone cooler to Airport Services, and then she collected Coe's car and drove to the hospital.

She found him in the waiting room, his foot bound up in a bigger, more official-looking elastic bandage, a new pair of crutches at his side. She said, "Well, the first part of it was fun, anyhow."

"I enjoyed the whole thing," he said. "Even this part wasn't bad. Doc Sam looked at the X-ray, and there's nothing broken."

She glared at the foot. "Are you sure he knows what he's doing? Even your toes are blue!"

"Perfectly normal. All I have to do now is sit around and be pampered for a couple of weeks. Are you going to do the pampering? Or do you have to go home right away?"

"There're all those vegetables in my refrigerator . . ." Rachel thought briefly. "It's okay. I'll think of something. Are you ready to go home? Let's get going; I'm parked in the loading zone."

She managed to make him sit still for most of the first twenty-four hours. She rented videos with airplanes in them for him to watch, and he put his foot on a heating pad and was quiet for most of the day.

Rachel phoned Deena and gave her a brief resume of events. Deena didn't say much; obviously her whole family was in the room with her. She agreed to clean out

Rachel's refrigerator and water the house-plants.

First thing the next morning, Coe was bobbing around the apartment on his crutches and decreeing, "What we have to do this week is get your license! There isn't anything left to do but the written; we'll work on that."

"Not true," said Rachel. "I haven't done a solo cross-country yet, and I don't have enough time in my logbook—unless you count all those illegal hours with passengers in the ship."

"Well, of course they count! Just because it's illegal doesn't mean you're not learning anything!"

Rachel calculated, "If I did a solo cross-country that gave me three or four hours air time, I'd have my forty-five hours; but of course, I have no hope of passing the written test. I dropped out of ground school after the first two classes, remember."

"College courses!" he sniffed. "No substitute for hands-on experience. Tell you what. Go to that pilot's store near the airport and buy the Red Book. It's got all the questions in it. Study that and you'll pass in a breeze. And while you're down at the airport, take my 340 and make a flight to Waco or Corpus Christi and back and you'll have your time in and you can do the test and get your license Tuesday or Wednesday."

Rachel eyed him doubtfully. "Is there some special reason you want me to do it this week?"

"Well, sure. Then you'll be ready for next week's Mexico trip."

"You are going, too, aren't you? You're not going to send me out there to deal with those mad medics all by myself, are you?"

"Don't worry, I'll go along. But I'll be a passenger, and it'll be legal!"

Rachel said, "Okay, sure."

The next day she purchased a Red Book and took the 340 to Waco and back. She returned to the apartment carrying the Red Book and the mapcase that held the records for the 340.

Coe hobbled into the kitchen to find her with papers spread over the table, punching away at a pocket calculator.

"Studying?" he asked.

"Looking at the numbers," said Rachel. "When I went to Waco, I calculated the gas as we always do; but the difference was, I had to pay for it—and it was a shock. Running a plane makes owning an automobile look like a kid's game. Do you know what it costs you to make that flight to Mexico every week?"

"Of course I know what it costs!"

"Gasoline, maintenance, and depreciation on the ship—it's thousands, even if you consider your own time as worth nothing. Every time you go, you take along a couple of high-priced medical specialists and all they do is vaccinate people and hand out tummy-ache pills."

"Vaccinating is important. Look what happened to those two poor little girls that didn't get their polio immunization."

"It's important, but any paramedic can do it."

He sat down in a kitchen chair and leaned his crutches against the wall. "What are you trying to do? Make me admit that I enjoy making that trip and the docs do, too? Those people down there are my friends."

"I'm trying to tell you it's inefficient. For the same money, your friends could have a clinic seven days a week. They could have gold-plated thermometers and designer blood-pressure cuffs. You don't need to fly a neurosurgeon five hundred miles out and five hundred back to dispense some Mylanta."

Coe grinned feebly and quoted, "It keeps him out of bars."

"Someday one of your engines could cough as you go into that climbing turn and wipe out your ship, you, and a bunch of upscale medical talent; and then your Mexican friends aren't going to have anybody at all to look after them."

"It isn't all just for fun. We've fixed some people who were really sick. You just didn't happen to see anybody who needed a lot of help because we've got things sort of under control now."

"There ought to be somebody there all the time, a real clinic. Suppose you had some of the locals trained as medical assistants? Or sent a couple to medical school? Nursing school? Or maybe the School of Mines."

"I know where there's a job for that graduate! Trouble is, a kid gets an education, sees the rest of the world, and he doesn't want to go back to a sleepy little place in the mountains."

"I'm not saying this is something we can get done tomorrow; I'm trying to get you to look at the long picture. What's going to happen in the future? Who's going to look after them when you're gone? Who's going to be there a hundred years from now?"

"You're trying to get me to phase myself out!"

"I'm trying to get you to look at the whole thing from another angle. There's a lot more that has to be done. You've got to keep looking after those factories. They don't know the first thing about business. There should be a permanent place for the clinic. Maybe you should build a hospital . . ."

"I don't know about building stuff," he interrupted. "People need help from people. A building's just stones on top of each other with somebody's name chiseled over the door."

"If there were a hospital they could train people there. Then maybe they wouldn't leave. Or how about schoolhouses? Would you build a schoolhouse or would your edifice complex get in the way of that, too?"

"You've got an exam tomorrow; why aren't you studying?"

"Oh, I am!" Rachel grinned at him. "I'm studying the most important question in aviation today: How many air miles can you put on your gasoline credit card?"

"Come on. You get through this Red Book and you'll pass for sure."

Rachel picked up the book. "You're going to think about it?"

"Yeah, I'll think about it."

As Coe had promised, most of the material she needed to know for her exam was already part of her practical experience. And Coe was right there to explain anything that puzzled her. She studied the book, took the test, and passed; and they gave her a slip of paper to show that she was now officially a pilot.

Coe took her out for a celebration. He was getting so skillful with the crutches he could go just about anywhere he wished, if Rachel did the driving or, of course, the flying. His swelling had subsided; for comfort he still wore the elastic bandage. Rachel wound it on for him every morning, and then slipped a clean sock over it to hide the wild colors his foot had turned. Besides the angry blues and purples, he was now getting faded spots—red, brown, and yellow.

They went to Tony's where he ordered champagne and toasted her new status, but then he added sadly, "I reckon you're going to be wanting to go back home pretty soon."

"Not until you can drive. I wouldn't run off and leave you without any way to get around."

"That's no real problem. I could always get a driver or something, but what about the Mexico trip? Could you come back for that?"

Rachel widened her eyes at him. "You mean, I'd be the one doing that Thursday-Friday routine every week? No way! I guess I'm staying until you're fit to fly."

He grinned secretively. "Doc says a man my age is going to be very slow to heal."

That made Rachel laugh. "You're not slow at anything else. I think your doc's a liar."

"I wish you didn't have to go away."

She smiled her secret smile. "I have business to take care of. As soon as I can make the arrangements, I'm putting my house up for sale."

Twenty-four

"Sell your house? What for? You love that house," Coe protested.

"I do, but it's only a house. I can learn to love another." She smiled again, only a little sadly. "It's an empty house without my children in it."

He eyed her doubtfully. "What are you going to do when you've got it sold?"

"I just don't think I'm up to a long-distance romance, Coe, so I'm going to rent an apartment in Houston."

"You'll move to Houston? Aw, Rachel, that's great, but you don't have to rent anything. You can move in with me. You like my apartment okay, don't you?"

"As a matter of fact, I'm not fond of it."

He was not fazed. "Okay, I'll build you a house."

"No, of course not, don't build a house for me."

"You sound like you don't want to move in with me."

Rachel toyed with the stem of her champagne glass. "I'd like to, but I can't do it, Coe. I need to preserve my independence and what's left of my reputation. I have children, after all. I want to be with you, but we can't move in together on a permanent basis."

"Why not? Nobody pays any attention to things like that anymore. Besides, we're going to be married."

"Maybe. I'd like that to be optional, too. On both our parts. If I can sell my house, at California prices, I'll have money enough for an apartment and maybe even for the clothes I need to keep up with you."

He pushed back in his chair, exasperated. "I don't know what this is all about. I can pay your rent and buy your clothes."

"That's exactly what it's about. You don't pay for my rent or my clothes, and you don't control where I live and you don't control me."

His face was cold, the creases deep beside his nose. "In other words, we won't be living together because you don't trust me."

"It's not a matter of trust. Well, maybe it is. I trust you, but burning all the bridges is for kids with stars in their eyes. Somebody my age has to leave herself with options."

"I don't understand that. I'm ready to commit myself to you, but you can't do the same?"

"It might be unfair to remind you, but you're the one who is married."

"Oh, ho!" He nodded wisely. "After all, this is about marrying, isn't it?"

She tossed her head and acquiesced. "I guess it is. I'm going to love you no matter what happens; but unless we're married, I want my own apartment."

He thought a while and then said, "Tell you what. I'll build the house. It takes a while to build something, so by the time it's finished maybe I'll have the divorce and we can get married—and then will you move in?"

Rachel smiled. "Oh, yes! A house that's ours! Not yours and not mine, but ours together. I'd love that, Coe! Something small, easy to care for, a little rose-covered cottage . . ."

"It's too damp for roses here; they mildew. I've always wanted to build a house." Suddenly, his face was lit with dreams. "It'll be white. There'll be pillars in front, fat ones, and a veranda. I want a fish pond with those flowers floating in it. Lots of space to entertain and for your family when they visit. We'll put in a swimming pool for the kiddies."

"I didn't know you were planning on building a Tara! A place like that takes a whole staff of servants, and I have no experience dealing with servants."

"We'll find you some who won't bully you, too much. There'll be plenty of furniture, anyway, what with your stuff and mine."

"What there'll be is two of everything. The right way to furnish our new place is with everything new. Like the house, everything will be ours, not yours and not mine."

"Okay, you've got it. New house, new furniture."

"Well, except for a few things we'll both want to keep. We'll both want to keep our books, for instance. I've got some pictures and area rugs . . ."

"We don't have to decide everything at once. We'll work it out as we go along."

It only took a couple of weeks for the swelling to go down in Coe's ankle. After that he wore a pair of heavy boots that laced up well above the ankle and claimed he felt no more pain. Rachel still did the flying and became so skillful at flying that climbing turn out of the Mexican valley that she began to enjoy doing it.

It was September before she got back to Encino. The house looked dusty and neglected and somehow faded. She was already separating herself from it in her mind, and the very colors she used to love did not look as bright to her as they had before.

Anything has to be clean to sell, so she set to work scrubbing and was well into it when Deena started banging on the back door.

Rachel opened it and hugged her friend. "I'm so glad to see you! Come in! We have to talk!"

"What have you done to your kitchen?" was Deena's response.

"Just a little reorganizing and cleaning."

"You've got the stove all taken apart. Why don't you come over to my place and I'll make the tea? My stove's okay. It's all in one piece, anyway."

Rachel followed her willingly through the hedge. Deena was dressed in weekend garb:

A short T-shirt and tight jeans. On Deena, it was a sexy outfit. She looked good and, best of all, she looked happy. The stress Rachel so often had seen in her was missing.

In Deena's kitchen they both started talking at once, but Rachel was the more determined. "I've been concerned about you. I thought perhaps you and Ethan were quarreling around the time I left town."

Deena smiled that gleaming smile of hers. "Remember those coupons you got for the bed-and-breakfast in Coronado? I used the one you gave me and we went there for a weekend. The kids stayed with Gordon's family."

"Both of them?"

"I made Gordon's mother do it. I've done a whole lot more than that for her and she owed me big time."

"So, what about the weekend?"

"It was wonderful. We fought the whole time. We'd fight; then we'd make love and then we'd fight some more. It was wonderful."

"Fighting all weekend? That's something a little beyond my experience."

"We both had so many resentments we needed to air. I didn't even realize how many I had! And fighting can be a positive thing, if you do it right. You have to fight fair though—no put-downs, no dredging up old stuff that's over with."

"And now things are better?"

"We still fight a lot, but we're getting someplace when we do it. We're making compromises and changes." Suddenly she sat down close to Rachel and whispered, "When you were in Houston, did you see Chief?"

"I didn't, but Coe talked to him a couple of times. I can't tell you anything about him; guys never talk to each other about anything important."

"I wish I knew he was all right. I certainly didn't set out to ruin his life."

"I doubt if you did."

"What kind of tea do you want?"

"Whatever that is you have in your hand will be fine."

Deena looked, bemused, at the box she held. "Herbs and spices, yeah, this one's good."

Ethan came in from the back yard, said hello, and went to the sink to wash his hands.

Deena asked him, "Do you want some herb tea?"

"A beer would be better," he replied and

reached for a towel. "I'll get it. Good to see you, Rachel. What have you been up to?"

"I'm putting my house up for sale," she answered and sat back for their expressions of surprise. "I'm selling everything—all the furniture and everything—and moving to Houston, so you get first crack at anything you want to buy."

"The piano?" said Deena at once. "You're selling the piano?"

"Why not? No point in shipping that to Houston. I never played it; and my kids didn't either, not voluntarily."

Deena spotted a head going past the back door and stuck her head out to call, "Lonnie, will you put away the gardening tools, please?"

"Yeah, later," Lonnie's voice came back.

Ethan stood behind Deena and said, "Lonnie, put the tools away now."

Lonnie turned, muttering under his breath, and a few seconds later there was a crash, as of tools thrown into the garage. Ethan went outside without a word.

"That's new, isn't it?" said Rachel.

Deena beamed. "Yes, we are backing each other up on everything now. It really tears the kids up. It's not what they are *used* to and they can't handle it."

When Rachel checked the mail that had piled up in her mailbox while she was gone, she was surprised to find a note from Jewel, the office manager at Burns, where she had briefly worked. It was an invitation for a housewarming, and the address was in Laguna Niguel, fifty miles down the coast from where she had last seen Jewel. It was also a week out-of-date.

She called Jewel, who was delighted to hear from her. "I'm sorry you missed the party; we had a great time. I'd love to show you my new place. Why don't you come down for lunch tomorrow and we'll talk? It's a nice drive, and it's always pretty here."

It sounded reasonable to Rachel, so the next morning she got into her car and started driving to Laguna Niguel. It was not the best of days on the 405: Traffic was heavy, and she encountered a couple of slowdowns caused by minor fender-benders. The Los Angeles County line fell behind her, then the Orange. Well, of course she had known that Laguna and its satellites were in San Diego County, but this was taking forever, and she had so much to do! Could Jewel actually be making this trip every day, commuting to Burns?

Jewel came to the door smiling, her round body comfortable in a loose caftan, her feet in open sandals. Proudly she showed off her house, which was small but airy and bright, decorated in primary colors as if she lived in the midst of a modern painting.

They sat over cold drinks and Rachel said, "It's an adorable place, Jewel, and I'm so pleased for you! But the commute! How do you do it?"

Jewel laughed happily. "I'm not commuting, honey. I retired!"

"I'm glad you were able to swing it. I remember that you were worried that it might not happen for you."

"Well, it did after all. I inherited from my nephew!"

"Nephew?"

"Backwards, isn't it? Nephews are supposed to inherit from their old aunts, but it just came out that way. Of course I knew my nephew was sick, and of course I knew he had never married and his parents had been gone for a long time; but I didn't expect him to die, and I didn't know he had made a living trust years ago. I was the only person named in the trust who is still alive, so I got everything! It's not a fortune, but he was quite successful—he was in the film business—and I got enough so I could buy this place. So I quit my job and moved here."

"Are you glad you did that?"

"You bet! I always wanted to be in a place like this where I didn't have to find my own plumber or pay the gardener or any of that junk anymore. They even wash the outside of the windows for you here; I only need to do the inside. Everybody's so friendly. I've made lots of new friends. They *like* fat old women around here. Well, of course, everybody's pretty much in the same boat. We're all retired, all older. It's wonderful not to have to deal with young people any more!"

"I'm so happy for you."

"I invited one of the neighbors to lunch. I hope you don't mind."

"Of course not."

"His name is Sully. He's had a stroke and it's hard for him to do things for himself, especially cook. That's probably him now."

She was referring to a racket that turned

out to be Sully, coming up the walkway in a wheelchair and yelling, "Hey, Jewel, hey Jewel, hey Jewel! I'm here, I'm here, here's Sully!"

Rachel had been afraid he would be old and wizened and drooling; but he was robust and lively, filling his chair to the armrests. He wheeled right in since the front door, like all of them in this community, had been constructed for wheelchairs.

Jewel introduced them and served the lunch. They talked about the politics of the community, about TV movies, about the neighbors.

Jewel was carrying the dishes back to the kitchen when she suddenly exclaimed, "Oh, my God! The sandwiches for the Mah-Jongg game!"

Rachel said, "What?"

"I made finger sandwiches for the Mah-Jongg game this afternoon and froze them so they would slice evenly and forgot all about them!"

"Well, let's slice," said Rachel. "I'll help you."

"Oh, thank you! First, would you wheel Sully home? He only lives next door, but it's sort of uphill and hard for him to do by himself."

Rachel said, "Sure," and grasped the handles of the chair. She pushed Sully out onto the walkway; he waved his arms, yelling happily, "Goodbye, Jewel, goodbye Jewel, goodbye Jewel! Thank you for the lunch, thank you, thank you!"

Rachel had never pushed a wheelchair before and she was surprised how much effort it took, especially with a heavy man on the seat jerking it back and forth with his happy waving.

And the situation turned really sticky when she got to the sidewalk and, sure enough, there was a rise to the next house. It might have been easy for a big woman like Jewel; but Rachel's feet slipped and she struggled to keep the chair moving, lest it stall and fall backwards, running over her and sending Sully and his chair schussing to the bottom of the hill.

She was out of breath when they reached Sully's door. Like Jewel's, it stood open and she rolled him inside.

Whereupon he thanked her nicely and got out of the chair to offer her a seat on his couch.

Rachel regarded him with stupefaction. "You can walk!"

"Of course I can. It was only a little stroke;

I'll be as good as ever soon." He sat down in a comfortable armchair. "I'm still using the wheelchair because it's easier for me, but I'm coming back just fine! Legs are a little weak, but everything else works just like before! Sit down. You're a pretty woman, nice figure, where do you live?"

"Houston," said Rachel and perched on the arm of the couch. "Having the chair gets you a certain amount of sympathy, I'll bet, and lunches. Does Jewel know you can walk?"

"Sure! Well, I suppose she does. All the ladies know that old Sully's as good a man as he ever was. Too bad you don't live around here; we could get together. We've got a great little community here. You wouldn't believe the action."

"Action? Are you talking about sex?"

"Sure! You didn't know? Around here the loving never stops. We're all old enough to be realists; we all know there isn't much time left and the next screwing might be the last one. Take me, for instance, I got no time to waste. The next stroke might not be little. Get it while you're still here, that's the motto in this town! I never had this much action, not even back in school. I don't suppose you . . ."

Rachel held up a hand. "Thank you, no. I really must be going back to Houston." She hastened to get to her feet and start out the door.

"That's okay!" he yelled after her. "The next one will be along any minute. I've found out how to beat out all the other guys; all you've got to do is outlive them!"

Jewel had hauled the little stacks that were her sandwiches out of the freezer. She and Rachel each took a serrated knife and a cutting board and sliced the rigid bread stacks across, creating dainty "finger" sandwiches, strips divided by strata of cream cheese in various flavors.

"I don't think I've seen one of these since the Eisenhower administration," Rachel remarked.

"Isn't it nice?" said Jewel. "I love having time to do all these fun little things we used to do back in the fifties!"

"You're re-creating the times here, are you?"

"Not really, just some of the nicer things. No, we're not in a time warp. You'd be surprised how active the people are here."

"Oh, I'm already astonished," said Rachel.

"We've got all kinds of things we do; it's

not just crafts and games. We've got sports and educational courses and all kinds of community service. A lot of it is just taking care of each other; but folks are volunteering in town, too, or even holding down real jobs. Like crossing guards for schoolchildren or working in the thrift shop. Of course the musicians are all still active. They play for dances and stuff and if there's nothing else to do, they just get together and jam. They say old musicians never die, they just blow away."

"I'm glad you are content here, Jewel. I don't think this life would suit me."

"Sure it would! You ought to get rid of your big house and get out of town somewhere. Get a little place that doesn't cost much and you'll have some money to be comfortable on. I've made lots of new friends here, but it would be nice to have somebody around who's an old friend, like you . . ."

"Actually, I seem to be planning rather a large house, in Houston. I might get married."

"Oh, I didn't know you were planning that! Tell me about it."

Rachel made an attempt, but it was like trying to explain snow to an audience of

Samoan schoolchildren. How could she make Jewel understand about the flying, Coe, and how he was changing her life? She couldn't make her own children understand.

Twenty-five

Rachel hung little tags on everything in the house, labeling the items to be kept for her apartment in Houston, to be sold, given away, thrown away. She pulled things out of closets, sorted, packed, and generally made the place uninhabitable. Then she hated the mess, and it made her sad to sit in it, alone in the evening. It made her remember that she had often been lonely in this house.

She phoned Coe, just to hear his voice, and he asked at once, "You need some help? Do you want me to come?"

"No, Coe, we've already kicked this around and decided you didn't need to make the trip. You'd only have to go back to Houston on Wednesday."

"That's okay. I don't mind. I miss you."

"Well, if you're determined to come, I know better than to try to stop you! Let me know when your flight will get in and

I'll pick you up at the airport." She said it in a businesslike voice, but life was suddenly brighter. Gladness flowed through her like an intoxicating drink. Coe was coming!

He mumbled something about calling her when he had the flight number, but he didn't mean it. The very next morning, so early and dark even birds were not awake, he was banging on her front door, ringing the bell. She toiled downstairs in her robe to let him in.

Laughing, he tossed his flight bag on the floor and grabbed her in a massive hug. "Yeah, it's me! I'm back!"

"Why are you banging on the door? I know I gave you a key."

"I didn't want to scare you by walking around your place in the night when you didn't expect me."

"That's right. I didn't expect you until tomorrow. Why do you fly the redeye when you don't have to?"

" 'Cause I miss you," he said between kisses. "And this way I catch you already in bed. And wearing that nightie I like." His hand explored her curves under the satin fabric of her new, Neiman-Marcus nightgown.

"Let's not play another one of those scenes in front of that window in the door," she warned.

"Nobody's around this early," he promised. "I don't know which feels nicer, the satin or your skin."

"Coe!"

He turned a sour look on the dark square of the window. "When I build our house, I'm going to make sure it has a solid front door."

"How is your ankle now?" she asked.

"I don't feel it any more."

"Then why are you limping?"

"I'm not limping. I'm just a little tired, that's all."

"Are you hungry? Would you like something to eat? Or maybe just a warm drink, a cocoa, to help you sleep?"

"Woman, I didn't come here to sleep. What I'm planning to do in your bed requires us both to be wide awake."

"Oh, my bed," said Rachel.

She had, as usual, been sleeping in the small room where she kept her things, but the bed in there was only a single. So, when they went upstairs, she turned right and went into the guest bedroom.

As Coe put down his bag and jacket, Rachel began folding back the spread on the big bed. Coe watched her, slightly puzzled. "Why aren't we going in your room?"

"The bed in there's only a single. It used to be Barbara's room."

"This is the master bedroom, then? It's your house, why don't you sleep in the master bedroom?"

Rachel piled the folded spread on a chair. "Oh, just . . . because."

Just because, in spite of redecoration, this room was still full of memories of Pete. The tall dresser where he had once kept his clothes remained, as did the antique blanket chest at the end of the bed. The windows still looked out in the same directions they always had. Thousands upon thousands of nights Pete had undressed in this room, had slung his clothes onto that chair, only now the chair was upholstered in a different color and the clothes were Coe's.

The bed was different and the linens were the latest thing dreamed up by decorators and there was no problem, of course there wasn't. All she had to do was lie down on those expensive new sheets and accept being loved by Coe. He was coming toward her, undressed, big, hearty, male, and ready. He reached for her.

Rachel said, "Oh, no, not now, Peter," and jumped up, pulling away from his hands. She bolted out of the room, down the stairs. She ran into the living room, but that didn't feel right either and she veered into the kitchen.

In her accustomed place before the sink she stopped. What was she doing there? Why was she running? What was she running away from? She put her hands on the familiar porcelain edge and began to cry. She bent over, her tears dripping into the kitchen sink.

It seemed like she had been there a long time before Coe came in. He had put his pants back on, but he was barefooted and bare-chested. He padded over the vinyl and asked, "What's wrong, Rachel?"

"I don't know."

"It's something to do with Pete, isn't it?"

She was still bending over the sink. There were no pockets in her nightgown and the tissues were out of reach, over by the refrigerator. She said, "Thirty-five years! Thirty-five years we were married, and we spent most of them in this house. It seems like a betrayal—no, that isn't what it is. It's more a belittling the marriage and our life together. As if it weren't anything or were just a kind of machine. When something wears out in a machine, you get a replacement for the worn part and it's as good as new."

"Aw, come on, Rachel, you're just upset. I shouldn't have wakened you up in the middle of the night."

"It's not your fault, Coe. I'm sorry." She turned and slipped into his arms and buried her wet face against his chest. "I'm just being silly."

"Well, you are, kinda, but thirty-five years of your life counts for something, too. I know you loved him. He loved you, too; and if he could talk to you right now, he'd tell you to get on with your life. You're alive, you're here, your life is in this world."

"Hand me a couple of tissues, will you?"

He gave her a handful and used a few to mop his chest. "Tell you what. If you feel better in Barbara's room, we'll sleep in there. No ghosts in that room."

"There are ghosts in every corner of this house, but maybe you're right. I'm more relaxed around Barbara's."

They crowded together into the little bed

and did not find it too narrow at all. He kissed her very tenderly and said good night, and they slept nestled together the remainder of the shattered night.

In the morning Rachel hung a "to be sold" tag on Barbara's bed and moved her clothes into the closet of the master bedroom. Coe helped her shift things. He asked, "You're sure about this?"

"We're too old to crowd together in that little bed. We'll get cricks."

"Fighting the memories in here, you could get a different kind of crick."

"I was pretty silly last night. Maybe you're right, it was just getting awakened unexpectedly."

He stacked shoeboxes neatly on a shelf. "Have you ever noticed that you do that? You belittle your own feelings. Why do you do that? They're just as important as anybody else's."

"I'm a grown woman, not a baby having tantrums."

He came out of the closet to face her, his expression serious. "You've got a door to close, too, Rachel. You've got a right to feel sad about doing it; it was more than half your life."

She smiled at him. "And what did I say

when you were closing your door? Something about pigs flying? I think I am not going to get the high marks for sensitivity around here."

Later she called Barbara. The sale tag on the bed had made her think, and she said to her daughter, "I'm making up a box of your things to send to you. Is there any of the furniture you want?"

Barbara said, "What?"

"Since I'm going to be selling out, I got to thinking that perhaps there is something here you children might want or could use."

"You're selling out? You mean everything? You're selling the house?"

"I told you that, dear, last time we talked. I told you I'm moving to Houston."

"Yes, you told me—but you're going to sell the house?"

"Barbara, stop saying that. Of course I'm selling the house. I'm not going visiting; I'm moving."

"I thought you'd keep it anyway. It's worth a lot of money."

"Another excellent reason to sell it. How

are the children? What does Nancy weigh now?"

Nancy was thriving, all the children were fine, and crews were gathering at the ranch for the summer roundup. When the conversation was finished, Rachel phoned her son Dan in New York, but he was as vague as Barbara had been.

Then she called Kenny. She didn't do that often; it was expensive and Kenny was often away doing field work and therefore out of reach. But this time she got Kenny and he was definite. He did not want her to ship anything to him in Australia, but he requested she keep his athletic trophies for him.

It was something definite at last, but Rachel grumbled anyway. Not to Kenny, of course, but she said to Coe, "The apartment I get in Houston is going to have to be bigger than I was planning on. There's a lot of those trophies, all of them ugly. And some of them are big and ugly."

"What did he do to get all those trophies?"

"Everything. I think he played every game known to man, and he usually won."

"You could box 'em up and put them in storage."

"It's a thought. I'll have to crate them to ship them anyway, and if they stay in boxes, at least I won't have to look at them."

"I'll go down to the storage place and get you some more boxes," he offered.

Rachel was sweeping the front porch late on Wednesday afternoon, when Marc's car turned into the drive. Of course it was Marc's car; she had driven it often enough in Arizona to recognize it at once, and besides, there were the Arizona plates and a coat of road-dust. She rushed to the car as Barbara got out.

"Barbara!" she cried, taking her daughter in her arms. "What's this? You drove here all the way from Arizona?"

Barbara was pointing at the sign the realtor had sunk into the lawn that very morning. "It's true! You're going to sell our house! Oh, Mother, how can you?"

"Well, it's easy. You get a realtor and. . . . Is that the baby in the car? Let's get her inside." She regarded her weeping daughter and added starchily, "There's nothing to cry about, Barbara. It's only a house."

"How can you say that? It's our home! This is where our family was, where I spent my whole life; doesn't that mean anything to you anymore?"

"Your whole life? Really, Barbara. Your life is in Arizona with Marc now. This was the family's house, but it isn't anymore. It isn't the family and it isn't a monument either."

"I thought it would always be here. I thought someday we'd all come here at Christmas, the whole family, and have Christmas like when I was a little girl . . ."

Rachel reminded her, "You've been married seven years, and so far we've spent every Christmas at the ranch."

"That's because I was always pregnant or there was too much snow . . ."

"It was because your family is with Marc now, and this family broke up when you children left home. I'm not going to stay here and pretend it's all going to come back. I've got other things to do."

Barbara looked at her accusingly. "You've got a whole new life that doesn't have anything to do with us!"

"Let's take the baby in the house, dear, and I'll make you a little something to eat. You must be exhausted. Such a long drive!"

The baby was sleeping, and Rachel lifted

her out in her car bed and carried her into the house. Barbara followed with bags.

The car bed was heavy and Rachel did not feel like carrying it upstairs, so she put Nancy down in the living room and they went to the kitchen. Coe was there, searching the refrigerator for a beer. Barbara regarded him with hostility.

"This is all your fault! Why are you breaking up my home? Why are you boinking my mother when you're not married?"

"Really, Barbara, what a shocking thing to say!" Rachel reproved. To Coe she added, "She's had a long trip and she's hungry. I'll fix her some eggs."

Coe held up his hand like a traffic cop. "It's okay. The kid's asking a legitimate question. Hello, Barbara, it's nice to see you again. I want you to know that your mother and I are planning to marry, and I figure it's going to happen just as soon as my divorce comes through."

"And then you'll go to Houston to live? Oh, Mother, it's so far away!"

"Your brother Kenny's in Australia, Dan went to New York, and you're in Arizona. What is there for me here?"

Barbara flopped down in a kitchen chair.

"I knew it. I just knew it was going to be like this!"

"Well, it's not exactly ESP, darling; I told you all about it on the phone."

Her daughter looked up with large, angry brown eyes. "Well, what are you going to do with all the things? Some of them are mine, you know!"

Rachel sat down across from her. "Barbara, you've had a long, hard trip and I know you're tired and upset, but I've had about enough of this temper tantrum of yours. Please calm down, and let's discuss our plans like the adults we both are."

Barbara burst into tears. "Oh, I know, I know you have a right to do . . . whatever it is you have to do, but it's so hard! I've been homesick on the ranch, homesick for you, for Dad, for this house; and now none of it's going to be there any more! I can never go back!"

Rachel gave her a tissue and a shoulder. "You can never go back anyway, Barbara. Life goes on, and if you're a balanced person, you move with it."

Barbara used the tissue. "It's so hard."

"Yes, sometimes it's very hard. Is the baby okay? Does she need a bottle or anything?"

"She's all right. Every time she cried, I pulled over to the side of the road and nursed her. She'll probably sleep another hour or so."

"You need liquids. I'll get you some fruit juice."

Barbara wiped her eyes and looked at Coe, who sat across from her, arms folded belligerently. "I'm sorry, Coe. I shouldn't have said that. I guess it's none of my business."

"Well, it ain't," he replied, grouch lines strong on his face. "But I think I can understand about your worrying about your mother."

She managed a smile, all the sweeter for being a bit tremulous, and said, "Scramble some eggs for me please, Coe, the way you make them."

She knew exactly how to please him. He sprang to his feet and took the eggs Rachel had been about to prepare. Then he was bustling about the kitchen, chopping, mixing, cooking. Barbara went to check her sleeping baby, and by the time she returned, he was putting a steaming dish on the table for her.

"Oh, thank you, that smells good! I didn't realize how hungry I was."

"You're nursing; you must keep your strength up," said Rachel and even as she said it reflected that Barbara probably knew that.

She asked, "How are Marc and the children?"

"Oh, just fine," said Barbara around a mouthful of eggs. "Some of the hands are already on the place getting ready for roundup, and as soon as they come, so does Celestina."

"Oh, yes, she's the cook, isn't she?"

Barbara grinned. "She weighs a couple hundred pounds and she can punch cows and bale hay, too; but mostly she cooks and generally helps out. She follows the crews around; but they stay in the bunkhouse and she's in the house, so she'll be there to help Marc with the kids and I can stay here a couple of days."

"You had better get some rest before you go back. Such a long way!"

"Maybe four hundred fifty miles; that isn't so much. We put that in every couple of days, driving around the ranch and into town and visiting. Did you mean what you said, you're not going to take anything with you to Houston?"

"Well, maybe a few things, but I'm starting a new life and I'm going to start it with all new things. So whatever you children want or need from this house, it's yours."

"Really? I want the Chinese rug and Grandma's tea set."

Unerringly, the child had selected two items that Rachel had planned to keep for herself, but she had promised. It was better that way. The fewer things she took to Houston with her, the less she would have to remind her of the past. She said, "Of course you may have them."

That evening Coe left for Houston and Rachel almost didn't miss him; it was so good to be alone with Barbara for a little space. They worked together, sorting and allocating, packing up the things that would be shipped to Dan in New York.

Whenever they came upon anything that had belonged to Pete, Barbara wanted it. She appropriated his cuff links, his books, even his power saw. When she nursed her baby, she sat in the chair that had been Pete's favorite, a big, comfortable chair. It was among the pieces of furniture she chose to have shipped to her home in Arizona.

Well, Barbara didn't have to forget her father. In a way, Rachel envied her that.

Friday night—no, Saturday morning early—there was the same thing all over again, Coe back from Houston, banging and ringing as he let himself in the front door. The only trouble was, this time he woke Nancy, who howled.

Rachel hurried downstairs, scolding. "Can't you come in quietly? We knew you were coming; we wouldn't have been frightened."

He picked her up and whirled around the entry with her. "I couldn't wait to tell you. I'm divorced! She went ahead and did it! Not only that, she did it fast and clean, no contest, no challenges to the property agreement. I had hardly gotten back to Houston when they served me with the papers. I don't know what scared her so bad."

"Maybe she just wanted to get her own life in order."

"We can get married!"

"That's wonderful!"

"We'll have the wedding right away."

"Oh, yes, very soon."

Barbara had succeeded in quieting her baby and she came downstairs to ask, "What's going on?"

"We're going to get married," said Coe.

"Wonderful! I'm glad for you both." Barbara gave her mother a kiss and then had one for Coe. Rachel watched with approval. Her daughter was growing up. She did it unevenly, but she was getting there.

"So, when is it going to be?" asked Barbara.

"Let's do it right away, while Barbara's here," Coe suggested. "She can stand up for you."

"Oh, that would be great!" said Rachel. "Will you, Barbara?"

"I'd love to."

"This calls for a toast," said Coe. "Let's open a bottle of champagne."

"Barbara can't do that. She's nursing."

Coe headed for the kitchen anyway. "Oh, well, I'll open a bottle of tomato-juice cocktail, then."

Rachel followed him. "We'll have to do something about this house. It's a mess; we've been turning out all the closets . . ."

"It doesn't matter. We can fix it when we get back from Houston."

"Houston? But of course we're going to have the wedding here. All my friends are here."

Coe paused, hand on the refrigerator door. "All mine are in Houston."

Barbara said, "The bride gets to choose."

He ignored her and asked Rachel, "Well,

what are we going to do? Pick a city in the middle? How about Las Vegas?"

"Certainly not!" snapped Rachel. "The town where you can get a drive-in marriage? Never!"

"Well, there isn't much else but desert out there. I guess we could tell all our friends to bring their RV's and a covered dish and just have a big tailgate party out in the desert."

Rachel had to laugh. "Oh, Coe, cut it out! We don't need to fight about this. It's not as if it were a first marriage, with the white veil and the orange blossoms."

"But you have to do something special!" protested Barbara.

He scratched his chin. "It's really just a party."

"A party!" said Rachel. "Of course, you're right; the party is the thing. All we have to do is have two parties, one here and one there."

"Okay. The first one here, then we have the ceremony in Houston and a party there."

"No, we have to have the ceremony here and then the party," said Barbara.

"There's this place in Houston . . ." Coe

began and stopped himself. "Oh, gee, I don't know."

Rachel suggested, "How about Las Vegas?"

"Mother!" said Barbara.

"But you don't like it," Coe reminded her.

"I like it better than fighting over where the wedding will be."

Coe brought out the tomato juice. "That settles it, then. After the party here, we'll fly to Vegas and take Barbara with us. We can use my 340. Then we'll fly to Houston, and that party will be waiting for us. We'll hold it in one of the hotels at the airport."

"Oh, I like that idea," said Rachel. "They have hotels at the airport here, too. I'll have my party there and I won't have to do anything to the house."

The juice was poured. Coe raised his glass. "Okay, here's to us and our wedding. I'll tell you what, next week when I get back from Mexico, I'll bring the 340 here. It will be available and we can have the wedding on Saturday. That'll give us a week to make arrangements and stuff."

"Okay," said Rachel.

"A week!" Barbara gasped. "We have to get the clothes and arrange the parties and. . . . Mother, how are we going to do it?

Don't you remember my wedding? It took a month just to get the announcements printed!"

"The telephone, my dear. We're going to do it all by telephone, and you're going to help!"

Twenty-six

Rachel made a list of friends and relatives. Then she reserved a bucolic little restaurant on the airfield for her party and ordered a lunch to be served on their spacious patio. She was ready to begin phoning her friends.

But of course, Coe had a list, too, and there was only one phone. While they sat trying to figure out the best way to share the phone, it rang.

It was the realtor. She was going to show the house and wanted them to leave while she did it.

The realtor was a lovely woman and came highly recommended by friends who had recently sold a house in this same neighborhood. Her name was Muriel and Rachel liked her, not the least because she was well into middle age. Muriel's experience was extensive, and you could talk to her.

Rachel protested, "I have guests, can we

put this off? I'm going to get married in a week, and after that you can show it all you want."

"Congratulations!" Muriel cried heartily. "I can hold the showings for a while, only let me do this one. I've already set up the appointment, told them about the house . . ."

"All right, but after that, please hold off."

Coe thought up an errand to run, and Rachel took Barbara and the baby over to Deena's. When they told Deena what was going on, she volunteered the use of her phone. Rachel began the phone calls to her friends right there, skipping over people who lived in other area codes. She would call them later on her own phone.

Muriel and her group took forever. Every time Rachel thought they surely would be gone, she would look out the window and Muriel's Mercedes still stood at the curb.

At last they left and Rachel rushed home to call Dan. She got Angelìque, his wife. "Dan's out jogging," she explained.

"How are the children? How did Eric's recital go?" Rachel asked.

"Everybody's fine. He did very well. It wasn't such a big deal, just a piano-class recital, but we were proud of him. Dan says you're planning a big move."

"I am! Angelique, I'm going to get married!"

"Oh, Rachel, I'm so glad for you! Congratulations! Is it somebody we know?"

"No, he's from Houston; that's why I'm moving there. We will have a reception before the ceremony; it's a week from today. It would be wonderful if you and Dan could come."

"A week? Of course, Dan should be there; but a week from today? Is Barbara going to be there?"

"Yes, she's already here. That's why we're in such a hurry, so she can be at the wedding. Even a week's a long time to be away when your children are so little."

Angelique thought a moment. "Well, school's still out and Dan has some vacation days coming. . . . I know he's going to want to be there. I'll talk to him."

"You'll stay with me, of course."

"Yes, of course."

Rachel hung up feeling elated. Dan called his wife "Angel" and truly she was one, the perfect daughter-in-law. If she got on Dan's case, he would come for the wedding. Rachel would get to see her son; she would get to see the little boys.

She checked the next number on the list and dialed.

When Coe returned from his errand, she relinquished the phone to him and went to the kitchen to prepare lunch. When the sandwiches were ready, she called Coe.

"How's your phoning going?" he asked.

"So far, not one person has turned me down. I hope that restaurant is going to be big enough."

"Yeah, my party is looking more sizable all the time, too. Chief's going to help me out. He'll be best man."

Rachel almost dropped a coffee cup. "Chief is coming? Chief is coming *here?*"

"He's my best friend," said Coe defensively.

"But Deena's mine, and you want to put them together in the same room? You want to put him and *Ethan* in the same room?"

"We'll just have to keep them apart."

"How? Are you going to call out the National Guard?"

"Aw, come on, Rachel. We're all adults. Nothing's going to happen."

"First there was the L.A. riots," she grumbled. "Then there was the Moreland-Flaherty wedding."

He laughed. "Not to mention the Moreland-Flaherty marriage." He ducked and scuttled out of the room as she made as if to throw the coffeepot at him.

While the baby was napping, Barbara made phone calls for her mother. Well, she made a few calls from the list. Most of her time was spent talking to Marc in Arizona.

She was able to report, "Marc's coming! The roundup's almost finished and he can take a couple of days off when it's over."

"Wonderful!" cried Rachel. "It will be so good to see the children! Dan's coming, too, with his family. Where will we put everybody?"

"Let's put cots in Kenny's room and it'll be a dormitory for all the kids. Dan and Angel can sleep in his old room, Nancy and Marc and I in my room."

"It's rather a narrow bed in your room."

"We won't mind."

Rachel almost mentioned that she and Coe had tried it and found it not entirely satisfactory, but she decided not to. You don't tell your children things like that.

So she asked, "When does Marc get here?"

"He can't get away until Wednesday. He's going to drive his pickup truck to Phoenix and then fly."

"Coe leaves for his Mexico trip Wednesday night and won't be back until Friday. Suppose we put you and Marc and Nancy in the master bedroom. Perhaps you should have Susie with you, too. She's the littlest and the only girl, and the boys might tease her if we put her in Kenny's room with them."

"I love it," said Barbara. "Marc and I will have the big double bed, and Dan and Angelique will have to use the bunkbeds in Dan's old room!"

"I think I'll have a roast at dinner and peach pie. It's peach season. I have to go shopping!"

"Maybe we better just send out for pizza."

"Oh, no! It's going to be so wonderful, the family around my dinner table again—almost all of it; of course Kenny can't come, and I can cook all the things everybody likes best."

She turned the phoning over to Barbara and Coe and went out for a week's groceries. As she was going out the door, she paused to yell back, "Don't forget to tell them no gifts!"

The shopping was tedious and, as always, took longer than she had expected. When at last she arrived back home, the afternoon was fading into evening.

Coe came to help her carry in the sacks. "What do you say we all knock off for a while?" he asked. "We can get to phoning again after supper and catch all the people who are only home in the evening."

"Don't stop me now, I'm on a roll," said Barbara. I've had three people in a row who were people, not answering machines."

"I've some things to put away," said Rachel. "Take your drink, and I'll join you on the patio in a few minutes."

She decided to make the salad, as long as she was washing lettuce anyway. As she worked, she saw a shadow cross the window of the kitchen door and glanced out, but it was only Lonnie. She wondered briefly what he wanted on her side of the hedge, but quickly forgot about it and went on chopping celery.

When she had finished the salad she looked out into the patio, and there was Lonnie, deep in conversation with Coe. An odd pairing.

Or was it so odd? She looked again. Coe was doing the talking, gesturing, explaining. The young student at the feet of an old, wise teacher? Well, it could be.

Rachel hauled a couple of cans out of the refrigerator and went out to the patio. She held up the cans and twinkled sweetly at the two guys. "Another beer, Coe? Hi, Lonnie. Soft drink?"

They took their drinks and mumbled thanks but had not another word to say, either of them, until she had left the patio. Guy conversation, obviously. Rachel went back to the kitchen.

By the time she had laid everything out, ready to be cooked for dinner, Lonnie was gone. She poured a beer for herself and went out to the patio.

He asked, "What are you doing in there, anyway?"

"Getting the meal ready to cook. What did Lonnie want?"

"Oh, just to talk. A little advice. Teen-ager stuff."

"Really? What did you tell him?"

"Just to keep cool. And use a condom." He gave her his defiant-grouch look. "Then I told him how to use it."

Rachel was so startled she nearly dropped her beer. "You told the neighbor's kid . . . the very first time you ever even talked to him. . . . How did he even know who you are? Why didn't you tell him to go ask his dad?"

"If he felt like he could talk to his dad about it, would he have been over here asking me?"

Rachel shook her head helplessly. "I don't know what it is about you, Coe. You just sit there, grouchy as a bear, and people rush to tell you all their secrets. What causes it?"

"I don't know. Maybe it's because I don't go spreading things around."

Rachel's mouth pinched with thought. "I wonder if I ought to tell Deena that her son is asking around about condoms."

"Don't you even think about it."

"Well, maybe he . . ."

"Asking about it doesn't necessarily mean he needs a condom; it could be he only wants the information."

"Could be," said Rachel.

They devoted Sunday to phone calls and had excellent results. Most people seemed to be at home on Sunday afternoon. Rachel had only a few names left of friends she had not been able to reach. Coe turned the balance of his list over to Chief, who would make the calls from his own home in Houston. As soon as they stopped making serial calls, the phone rang constantly with call-backs, congratulations, and excited friends who wanted to talk.

And Muriel, the realtor. She said, "I have an offer. When can we bring it over?"

"Muriel, what are you doing working on Sunday? Go home to your family," Rachel advised.

"In my business, weekends are when we work," Muriel explained. "And this is hot. They won't show the offer to me, of course; you get to see it first, but I think it's close to the asking price."

They arranged the meeting for the following morning. When she mentioned it to Coe, he agreed with her that it would probably be nothing but a waste of everybody's time.

"The real estate market isn't that good right now," he said. Uselessly; she already knew that. "You've only been on the market a couple of days. Nobody sells that fast now. You'll be looking at a lowball offer or some flake who can't get a loan."

"We'll see," said Rachel.

It was business, so she put on a business

suit and pulled chairs up to the dining table in readiness for the meeting.

Coe also put on his suit, explaining that he had some business to do later. Barbara was wearing shorts and one of her loose tunics, so she disappeared upstairs as soon as the doorbell rang.

Really, Rachel thought, when she had so much to do, it was a bore to have to put up with a whole squad of strangers, all of them armed with briefcases. In came the other broker and the buyer and another guy whose function Rachel never quite got straight—and Muriel, of course, and they all crowded around her dining table. Rachel offered coffee, introduced Coe. She was glad to have him on her side of the table, for she suddenly felt alone, as if even Muriel were against her. Well, in a way she was, for she was with this group and they were all intent on separating Rachel from the home that had been hers for thirty years.

The other broker ceremoniously removed his papers from the briefcase and passed a copy each to Muriel and Rachel. Her eye went straight to the figures.

Asking price. Rachel muttered, almost to

herself, "There's a catch in here someplace."

"Of course there is," said the broker. "We want to arrange a fifteen-day escrow."

"Nobody can get a loan in fifteen days," said Rachel.

"My client is here on a corporate transfer, and the company is putting up the money to buy his house. He doesn't need to get a loan. They're handling the finances because they need him here right now, and he needs a place for his family."

"But I'm having a wedding!" said Rachel. "My whole family is going to be here."

Coe said softly, "Rachel, may I talk to you a minute?" He glanced at the others. "You'll excuse us?"

"Take all the time you want," invited the broker.

Coe and Rachel stepped into the hallway. He said, "You've got to take this offer."

"Coe, don't tell me what to do."

"I'm not going to; but if you blow this, you're crazy. The asking price! You'll never get that again. The way the market is right now, you could wait a year for another offer; and when you get it, it will be lower than this one—that's a sure bet. Maybe way lower. In the meantime, you'll be in Houston; the house will be standing empty—do you know what that's going to cost you?"

"But I need the house! The children are coming!"

"It's no problem! Everybody's going to leave right after the wedding. The movers come in and it's done."

"Of course you're right, Coe. It's too good an offer to turn down, but I feel like I'm having my wedding in the back of a moving van."

Even as she signed the papers she was making desperate little glances around. All that furniture! What was she to do with all that furniture?

She managed to smile and shake hands and put her visitors graciously out the front door. Instantly, Barbara scampered down the stairs to find out what happened.

"I've sold it," Rachel told her. "The house is sold and I have two weeks to get out of it!"

"Oh, Mother, what are we going to do?"

"We are going to do exactly as we planned," said Rachel briskly. "Right now we are going to put the house in order and get ready for our guests. Next week we ship out the things you children want and what

I want in Houston, and the balance will be sold."

Barbara looked down at her toes. "I'll help you, Mom."

"Thank you, dear. Let's sort out the things you want, box them for shipping, and put them out of the way in the garage."

"I've got an appointment," said Coe, looking at his watch.

"You're too well-dressed for this job, anyway. We'll put you to work when you get back," Rachel promised.

"You're pretty well-dressed yourself, Mother," Barbara reminded her, and Rachel went upstairs to change. Donations, she was thinking. There were a lot of things that would be useful to charitable organizations.

Rachel and Barbara stacked cartons in the garage, put the house in order. Rachel ordered cots from a rental agency, got out the toys and games she kept for the grandchildren, put fresh linens on the beds.

Barbara wanted to explore the attic storeroom since some of her belongings were there. They got the stepladder and climbed through the opening in the ceiling. Soon both were sweating in the hot dusty space right under the roof.

She heard Coe calling and looked down to see him peering up at her through the crawl hole. "Come down," he said. "I've got something for you."

Rachel wiped her dusty hands on the seat of her jeans and stuck out a foot. "Hold the ladder for me."

He did and Barbara handed her a carton to carry down. Rachel relayed the carton to Coe and came down the ladder.

She gave Coe a quick kiss but no hug; after all, he was wearing a suit. "Hi, what's up?"

"Well, I went to the jewelry mart," he explained and took a velvet box from his pocket.

Velvet? Rachel didn't know much about jewelry, but she did know that your average mall jewelry store these days issued plastic boxes. Velvet must surely be reserved for some extra-special outlets. She took the box and opened it.

It was a wedding ring set of white gold and diamonds, so many diamonds she could not immediately get a count. The one in the center gleamed like a headlight and looked about as big. Rachel said, "Uh." It was about all she could manage with her mouth open.

Coe took the box from her, pulled out the ring with the big diamond. "Here." He took her dusty hand and slipped the ring on. "Now we're engaged."

Rachel stared at her hand. "Coe, you are so extravagant!"

"Hey, I finally found something you'll let me buy for you."

"Even a lady never turns down diamonds."

Barbara was on the ladder. "What are you doing?" She caught sight of the ring. "Holy, mackerel, I've got ice cubes in my freezer that are smaller than that! Coe, it's gorgeous!"

"Gorgeous," repeated Rachel feebly. Still staring at her hand, she wandered toward the staircase.

Barbara said, "Where are you going?"

"Sorry, dear. You're going to have to finish that job by yourself. I'm going to go put on something silk!"

Marc arrived Wednesday morning, and Barbara went to LAX to pick up her family. Rachel was already busy with the pies. She made peach and apple and black bottom for the kiddies. She had three kinds of sandwiches ready for lunch, even though she knew the children would go straight for the peanut butter.

Susie and Peter were wild with the confinement of travel and had to have a run in the back yard before they could be interested in lunch. It was good to see them again, to hear their shrieks as they tore through her flower beds. It had been barely a month since she had seen Peter, and he had grown. She could see the difference in his legs.

In the afternoon Rachel went to pick up Dan and his family. The two little boys were seven and nine now, so much bigger than they had been the last time she had seen them, and dressed alike in long pants and white shirts. She wondered if she ought to worry about them; they had just flown clear across the country and their shirts were still clean.

Well, Angel was an angel and probably angels can always cope. Rachel hugged her and Dan. Dear Dan, her middle child. He had always been middle Dan, quiet and agreeable, middle height, medium-brown hair. More like his father all the time. She let him drive them home so she could catch up on all the news with Angel and the children.

Then they had to get through the meeting with Coe. He was dressed in his suit again for the dinner and for his flight to Houston later that evening. He and Dan sized each other up while the three little boys and Susie edged nervously around each other. It was explained to them that they were cousins; but only Jason, who was nine, had any memory of Barbara's children.

"I'm seven," Eric bragged. "How old are you?"

"I'm five," Peter admitted.

"That's just a baby." Eric's tone was scornful for he was scrambling for his position in the pecking order. Peter was nearly as tall as he and probably weighed more. Muscular, tanned Peter was a contrast to his pale, slender cousins.

Coe and Dan had gotten as far as ascertaining that the flight from New York had been pleasant when Marc came in and hurried to the rescue. "Hi, Dan!" he yelled, slapping his brother-in-law on the back. " 'Bout time you got here. Mother Moreland and Barbara are making us a real feast. How about something to wet your whistle before the feed?"

It all came together for Rachel at the dinner table. Her children around her, her grandchildren, and Coe. Surely, this was what they meant by having it all.

Barbara and Angel insisted on cleaning up the kitchen and shooed Rachel outside to sit with the men on the patio. The children were sprawled in front of the television set, Peter in charge of the flicker. He was being surprisingly good about it, sticking with the same show sometimes for minutes at a time; and Dan's two little boys were remarkably subdued and quiet. Jet-lagged, probably.

Marc asked Coe, "Are you leaving tonight as usual? Do you need a ride to the airport?"

"Thanks, I've got a rental car. I have to take it there and turn it in."

"As usual?" Dan questioned. "Do you go every Wednesday?"

"I told you about that, Dan," Rachel reminded him. "He's flying medical assistance to a remote area of Mexico."

Dan was not warned by the slight sharpness in his mother's voice. "It's sort of a job? I thought you were retired."

Rachel opened her mouth, but Coe silenced her with a little wave. "I am. It's just a thing I do."

"You've got to understand this is a whole new idea for me," said Dan. "How long have you two known each other?"

Rachel and Coe exchanged glances, figuring. Rachel said, "Since the air show, that was July . . ."

"A little better than two months," Coe supplied.

"You've been married before?"

"Yup. My divorce was final last week."

"Oh. Do you have children?"

"Nope."

Angel and Barbara came chattering from the kitchen.

"All put away," said Barbara.

"Does anybody want anything before I sit down?" asked Angel. "Can I get anybody a drink? Coe?"

"No, thanks, I'm going to be driving to the airport soon."

Dan was saying, "Mother, don't you think it would be a good idea to put the wedding off for a while? You two could get to know each other better, and it would look better. This soon after his divorce, it looks as if you were going together while he was still married."

"We were," said Coe.

Barbara said, "Dan, get off his back. We know Coe really well. He helped us all so much when I was sick. The kids are crazy about him."

"Well, Barbara," Dan kept right on going. "She does have assets to protect. Mother, have you considered a pre-nuptial agreement?"

Considering the size of her assets compared to Coe's, Rachel started to laugh, but Coe said, "You know, that's not a bad idea. We ought to have something in writing. The way it is, if I kicked off tomorrow, my will says my nephews get everything."

"Don't you have one of those trusts?" Marc asked.

"Not on your life. A trust assumes the beneficiaries all can agree. My nieces and my nephews fight like animals with each other." He thought about it briefly. "They fight like animals with everybody. Most of 'em are lawyers. It won't hurt 'em to pay inheritance taxes."

"I'll see to it that my children's interests are protected," Rachel promised. "And now, Dan, will you please change the subject? I'm going to swat the next person who mentions money."

"The boy's only concerned about you, Rachel," said Coe. "He's got a right to ask what you're getting into."

"He's questioning my judgment," said Rachel. "I'm not senile yet, son, and I know what I am doing." She reached out and took Coe's hand. "Oh, yes, I know what I am doing."

Twenty-seven

All three boys woke early and made so much racket in Kenny's old room that they woke the baby. Nancy began to cry, and then everybody in the house had to get up.

Rachel hurried to the kitchen to mix up batter for pancakes, and soon the family was at the table eating them as fast as she could turn them out.

The boys were getting used to one another and they grew noisier and more competitive all the time.

"Bet you can't ride a horse," Peter challenged.

"Bet you can't play soccer," Jason countered. "You're too little."

"I have my own horse; his name is Papoose."

"Tunder," said Susie. "Tunder my pony!"

"I'll bet you can't play the piano," Eric told her. "You're too little."

Marc broke in. "Do you play soccer at school, Jason?"

"Yeah! We got a team! We win all our games!"

"Well, not entirely all, but they are very good," said Angelique with a smile.

"I go to music school," insisted Eric. "You don't get to go to music school unless you can play the piano."

"He is very talented," said his proud mother. "And it's an excellent school. They're very strong in the basics; and he gets two hours of music every day, too. That's why I love living in New York, for the cultural opportunities."

"We were hoping you might be able to bring the boys out to our ranch sometime this summer," said Barbara. "It would give them a chance to get outdoors in the sun, get some color in their faces."

"Lovely invitation, Babbs," laughed Dan. He was her brother and knew she didn't like being called Babbs. "Let me know when you're going to visit us, and I'll get some concert tickets."

"Maybe after breakfast Eric will play something for us," Angel suggested.

"That would be nice," said Rachel. "Let's find something special for all the boys to do together today. Would they like to go swimming?"

"Not swimming," said Marc. "Peter hasn't learned yet."

"My boys don't swim either," said Angel, "but surely we can find a constructive activity for them. There must be some cultural opportunities here."

"Disneyland!" said Jason.

His mother gave him a reproving glance. "I was thinking of the museum."

"The Natural History Museum!" said Barbara. "I loved that place when I was a kid. They've got great dinosaurs."

"The Air and Space Museum is right next to it," Rachel pointed out. "That's the one Dan always liked the best."

"I was thinking of the art museum," Angel admitted. "Jason and Eric are very fond of art."

"How about just taking them to a park somewhere and letting them run off some steam?" was Marc's contribution.

"I haven't seen that Air and Space museum in years," said Dan. How about that, Marc? Let's take our boys to Expo. Besides having museums, it's a park, too."

Marc said, "Okay. I guess Susie's too little to go."

"Susie had better stay home with me," said Barbara.

"Is she musical at all?" Angel asked her. "Sometimes when there's talent in a family, it's the girls who get it."

"She's pretty little," Barbara pointed out.

"She's three. We knew when Eric was three that he was musically gifted. It just seemed to burst right out of him!"

"If he keeps working, maybe he'll get good enough to play rhythm in a rock band," Marc suggested mischievously.

"Who wants some more pancakes?" asked Rachel.

After he had eaten, Eric was coaxed into washing his hands and going to the piano. He was wearing shorts and a T-shirt this morning, and his little legs looked skinny and white as he climbed onto the bench and struck a cord.

Lifting his hands as if he had been stung, he cried, "My God, this is *so* out of tune!"

"I already sold it," Rachel apologized. "We're only waiting for the men to come and move it, and it always has to be tuned again after that."

"Play something anyway," Angel suggested softly. "Play the piece you played at your recital."

He played, quite creditably, a fragment of Chopin, while Peter squirmed. Peter knew he had triggered this whole performance and therefore he had to listen all the way through, but he was obviously jealous when Susie toddled out of the room to go and play with toys.

Eric was duly applauded, and then Marc and Dan gathered up the boys and went off to Exposition Park.

After the dishes were cleaned up, Barbara was looking after her girls, and Rachel and Angelique were in the kitchen, getting ready for the next meal. Angelique asked, "What will you wear for your wedding?"

Rachel paused in the middle of shaking up a marinade. "Well, I. . . . I've been so busy, I haven't given it a thought."

Angelique smiled. "Let's go shopping."

"We don't need to do that. I have a nice new silk suit."

"Of course you have to have something new for the wedding! Come on, forget the cooking for now and let's go find a mall."

"Mall," said Rachel, a glazed look coming into her eyes. "Which one should I choose? Northridge? Topanga? Fashion Square? Promenade! You're right, Angelique, I need something new. I need something smashing, something good enough to go with this diamond ring! I need to get my fingernails done, too, and my hair! And a new nightgown. Maybe I can find another one in charmeuse. The one I've got really turns him on."

Angelique said, "Rachel!"

She was shocked. Rachel thought how strange it was; she had turned into the kind of old lady who shocks young people.

They shopped most of the afternoon, for Rachel had a hard time finding that exact outfit that would be right for Saturday's events. She was going to attend a party, fly a plane to Vegas for the wedding, get married, then fly to Houston and another party. It seemed to demand something special in the way of clothes.

But it had to be somewhere, and Rachel found it. It was a jumpsuit, but only a distant relative of the yellow one. This one was white silk, with a plunging neckline and a flare to the pant legs. Not a big one, she was too short for that, but a definite flare.

She and Angelique went to the salon and had their hair and nails done. Rachel's hair ended up pretty much the way it always looked—it was too short for any changes—but it was nicely fluffed up, and something in the salon's magic potions made it a pearly gray that went well with the white suit.

Then she looked at the diamonds glittering on that hand with the perfect fingernails and she knew what to do next. She bought Coe a ring. A big flashy gold one, a highly noticeable wedding ring.

They were ready to leave the mall, on their way to the parking lot, when Rachel spotted the picture. It was a painting, neatly framed and not too big, the subject an old fruit tree in the spring. The trunk was thick, gnarled and black, the branches sparse; but all of it was covered with blossoms, pale pink blossoms spouting exuberantly from every inch of the old veteran tree.

Rachel said, "I need a new picture for my new house," and turned into the shop.

"This isn't a real art gallery," Angel pointed out. "It's just a store in a mall. If you're going to buy pictures you ought to go to a gallery."

"I want that one," said Rachel.

The shopkeeper took the picture from the window and put it reverently on a stand for Rachel to admire. It took some pressure to make her admit the price—she was trained to deliver her sales pitch first—and when she finally did, Angel began to whisper.

"Mother Rachel," she hissed. "I don't want to pry, but you've already spent a lot of money today. You can't afford to pay so much for a picture. It's terribly overpriced, anyway. It's just a landscape, a representational landscape, and nobody ever heard of the artist."

"I want that picture for my new house," Rachel repeated. "I like the feeling it gives me. It seems to me that I know exactly how that tree feels. I'm going to have it crated and shipped to Houston."

She was making Angel worry; she could tell. The poor child probably thought she had gone senile overnight, so she added, "It's okay. Coe is quite well-off, and anyway, I've already sold my house."

But she was pretty sure Angel didn't believe her.

By the time they got home, the boys were back from the museums and Barbara had prepared the evening meal. Marc and Dan had even thought to stop off at the video store and rent a stack of movies for the children. That kept them occupied while the adults had a pleasant evening together.

Somehow, during the night, Jason found

a soccer ball in Kenny's room. He carried the limp thing to breakfast and nagged until Dan searched out the pump and blew it up for him. Then he bounced it against the garage door for an hour or so and when he tired of that, spent the next hour putting it through the basketball hoop.

Eric and Peter wrestled in the living room until Rachel threw them out into the back yard, where they resumed their contest. They seemed pretty evenly matched, as nearly as she could tell, and probably not capable of hurting one another, so Rachel left them alone. At various times, whichever boy was on the bottom would yell for his mother, but Barbara was nursing the baby and Angel was getting dressed, so there was no response.

After the baby was put down to sleep, Marc and Barbara came downstairs. Marc observed the boys in the back yard and Susie, whining while Rachel tried to interest her in a toy, and he said, "I think we need to take the kids someplace where they can run off a little steam. Again."

"How about Balboa Park?" suggested Barbara. "It's nearby. We'll pack some sandwiches and give them lunch over there. That way, the crumbs will fall into the grass."

A scream from the back yard caught Marc's attention. "Let's just get going now. Forget the picnic. We'll come back here to eat."

"Tell you what," said Rachel. "I'll make some sandwiches and bring them over there about noon. Meet me . . . Oh, on this side of the lake."

"What lake?" asked Barbara.

"Oh, I guess you wouldn't know. There's a new, man-made lake in the park."

Barbara scooped up her elder daughter. "Thanks, Mom. If Nancy cries, give her some water. We'll see you over there."

They gathered up the boys, loaded everybody into the car, and were gone. Rachel went to the kitchen and began assembling sandwiches. In due time, Angelique appeared. She took longer to get ready than anybody Rachel had ever known, but it was always well worth the effort and she was always exquisitely dressed. Slender and fine-boned, she had glossy black hair, a white, heart-shaped face, and she favored very red lipsticks. She looked like the princess in the fairy tale.

Rachel explained the lunch plan and Angel said, "So there will be only adults for lunch? Let's have something special. I'll make a vichyssoise; would you like that?"

"Sounds great," said Rachel. "I'll be back as soon as I've delivered the sandwiches. Don't forget to look after Barbara's baby; she's asleep in their room."

She assembled the picnic in a cooler, loaded it in her car, and took off for Balboa Park.

She found the family with no trouble. Actually, all she had to do was go where she saw that soccer ball rising up, as Jason endlessly kicked it straight up in the air and then caught it as it came down.

Susie was sitting contentedly on the blanket with her parents; Eric was poking the water of the lake with a stick. Peter was watching Jason, waiting for him to miss so he could grab the ball. But Jason was good at this trick; and on the rare occasions that he did miss, he always recovered the ball before Peter could get his hands on it

Rachel put down the cooler, and they began to unpack the lunch. Eric saw that his grandmother was there and came up to give her a hug and get first choice of the sandwiches.

Marc called cheerily, "Come on, boys! The food's here!" and Jason glanced at him. Only a glance, but enough to spoil his kick and the ball arced into the lake.

It was Peter's chance. He was closer to the water than Jason; he jumped in instantly and waded after the ball.

Marc jumped up, yelling, "Hey! Come back here!" and ran toward the lake.

"Peter can't swim!" shrieked Barbara.

"It's okay," Rachel tried to tell her. "The water's only a couple of feet deep."

But Marc was already at the edge of the lake. He took a great leap, belly-flopped into the water, and scooped up his son, who already had captured the errant ball.

Somebody yelled, "Hey, you're not supposed to swim in there!" as Marc trudged out of the lake, carrying Peter. Peter was muddy only to his knees, but Marc might as well have flopped into a mudhole. His whole front was plastered with mud, slimy stuff, slightly green and smelly.

He put down his son and flapped his muddy hands uselessly. "I'm going to have to go home and change. Oh, damn! I had my wallet in my pocket!"

Rachel couldn't help laughing. "Well, now you have cool cash."

Barbara rocked with laughter. "The creature from the black lagoon—and son!"

"They're both too dirty to be allowed to eat," Rachel decreed. Let's pack this picnic back up, and the boys can eat it in the back yard. I'll take Eric and Jason and Susie in my car. You can have the creatures from the black lagoon in yours."

Barbara was still laughing and ignoring black, muddy looks from her husband. "Thanks, Ma! I'll return the favor sometime, and that's a threat!"

When they got home, Barbara turned the garden hose on her husband and son and sent them upstairs to shower wearing only towels. Marc was taking the whole experience with bad grace and regarded being forced to trek through the house in a towel as the ultimate affront. Rachel could hear them upstairs, sniping at each other over the sound of the hair dryer that Barbara was using to dry out the wallet.

Rachel had confiscated the soccer ball, and she sat with the children while they ate their picnic in the back yard. Who had taught these precious innocents to be so competitive? She wondered, then she remembered Dan and Kenny at similar ages. Maybe they don't have to be taught.

Fortunately there were a couple of videos left, and the boys plunked themselves down in front of the TV set for the balance of the afternoon.

Coe arrived earlier than usual; it was not quite nine o'clock when he and Chief came through the door. Rachel flew to kiss Coe and greet Chief. "How nice to see you again, Chief. I was hoping you would bring Tricia with you."

"She couldn't get away, had some things to do." Chief's smile was as sunny as ever; he looked handsome in his suit. He kissed her on the forehead and said, "Good to see you, Rachel. You don't surprise me a bit. All brides are beautiful."

"Same old Chief," she chided. "I'm so glad you got home early, Coe."

"That's because I came in my own ship. I didn't have to wait for the commercial flight. And I landed it over at Van Nuys, so I didn't have to make the drive from LAX, either."

She took Chief's arm. "Come and meet the family. My children are here, well, most of them.

Chief gave the men his firm handshake, called Angelique an angel, and flipped over Barbara, who happened to be sitting with the baby in her lap.

"A madonna!" he exclaimed. "There is

nothing more beautiful than a mother with a baby. A beautiful mother and a beautiful child." He then kissed the baby, who did not object. Chief even had a way with infant females.

"We're going to have a party tomorrow?" he asked as he sat down.

"Yes, I'm afraid Coe is going to be subjected to all my friends," said Rachel. "Nobody's had a look at him yet, so they're coming in droves."

"And then we're going to Vegas for the wedding? How many are going with us? The 340 only holds six."

Rachel explained the plan. "There will be just the four of us, and the baby, of course. After the wedding we will take Barbara to Phoenix and we go on to Houston for Coe's party."

"We don't live in Phoenix," Barbara explained, "but we have friends there. I'll stay with them until Marc gets there. He'll be driving with the other two children. I'll even have transportation; Marc left his pickup at the airport in Phoenix when he came here."

Dan asked, "What's a 340?"

"Just a little two-engine Cessna," Coe answered. "Mine's kind of an old ship; it was built in the seventies."

"I wouldn't call that really old," Chief put in. "Now, if you want to talk about *old* . . ."

Coe exchanged that glance with him that Rachel had come to dread, and his voice took on a country whine. "Old? Yeah, they's some of us so old we flew airplanes that you only see in museums nowadays."

Of course, Chief encouraged him. "Didn't have much on them, did they?"

"Well, they didn't have no SCUD-killers on them, if that's what you mean, but that was okay. We didn't have no SCUDs, then, neither."

"You told me about it, a couple hundred times, I guess. You didn't have a weatherman; there was just an old guy with arthritis."

"Didn't have no radio. When we wanted to communicate with the ground, we threw out a note wrapped around a rock. Why, that first airplane they gave me didn't have no armament on it at all. Sometimes they'd give us a pocketful of rocks."

"Or a frying pan to sit on, in case somebody fired at you from the ground?"

"Frying pan? I think it was a stove lid."

"And when you were going to take off,

some guy had to stand out there in front and spin the propeller . . ."

"Switch on! Contact!" recited Coe gleefully. "I chewed up more crew chiefs that way!"

Rachel said, "All right, that's enough of your silly routines. Everybody's a comedian. While I've got you all together, I want to remind you that I'm selling the house and I need all the keys back. Anybody who has a key, please remember to leave it on the table in the entry when you leave."

Coe asked Dan, "What are you going to do after the party?"

"The kids want to go to Disneyland."

Angel rolled her eyes. "I suppose we must. They are insisting!"

"We might as well," said Dan. "We don't get out this way often; let's do it while we have the chance."

"You'll have fun, Angelique," Rachel assured her.

Coe squinted at her. "You might have to let your hair down a little."

Rachel offered, "If you like, Dan, use my car. I'll be in Houston for the next couple of days, and I won't be needing it."

"Thanks, Mom. Don't forget to give me the keys."

"Don't forget to give them back! I'm going to put a basket on the table by the front door; and when I get back, it had better be full of keys!"

It took her a while to explain to Coe why he had to sleep in the single bed in Barbara's room. He threatened to evict Barbara and her family from "his" bed until Rachel whispered in his ear, "It's not such a bad deal, Coe. Dan and his wife are in bunkbeds; Barbara and Marc have the children in with them. We're the only couple in the house with privacy."

He made grump lines. "Well, okay, but only if you promise we'll make use of our privacy. This has got to be worth my while."

She made cow eyes. "Oh, but sir, we're not married yet!"

"The hell with that! If you want me to sleep with you in a single bed, you've got to put out!"

"What's in it for me?"

He considered briefly. "Some pretty fancy kissing."

"You talked me into it."

"Say good night to the kids; we're going to bed."

"They've already gone, you silly man. There's nobody down here but Chief. He has to sleep on the couch." She poked her head around the corner and asked, "Do you have everything you need, Chief? Enough blankets?"

"Just fine, Rachel," came the reply.

They walked sedately up the stairs, closed the bedroom door quietly behind them.

In the morning he woke her with kisses. "Wake up, Rachel. Come on, open your eyes. It's our wedding day!"

They both were still naked, piled together in the narrow bed. Rachel rubbed her leg against his. "This is the way to begin a wedding day. Why didn't anybody else ever think of it?"

"Oh, I reckon they have, now and then. Wait a minute, I've got something." He reached onto the night stand and handed her another velvet box, this one as big as her hand. Inside was a necklace of diamonds and pearls.

"Oh, Coe, you shouldn't have!"

"Why do people say that? Of course I should have!"

"Well, I bought you something, too. You can have it later on today."

His smile was broad, pleased. "Yeah? What is it?"

"I got you a wedding ring so everybody will know that you're taken."

"Aah! She's putting the manacles on me!" he cried with mock terror. "Here, gimme the beads."

He took the strand and fastened it around her bare neck, then shoved down the blanket to admire the effect. "I think that's about the prettiest thing I ever saw." He kissed her, fondling her neck and breasts. She opened to him, readily.

It had to be the best way to start a wedding day.

Afterward, Rachel slipped into jeans and went downstairs to start breakfast. Angel was already there and had the meal nearly ready. The boys were arguing; Susie was howling over some infant frustration, and it was just like the last few days. Probably everybody was glad it was the last one.

Barbara volunteered to clean up, and Rachel went upstairs to dress.

She took an extra-long shower, then combed her hair out the way the salon had done it. She fastened on her pearls and wrapped herself in a robe for the trip back to the bedroom.

Coe was in the room and, somewhat to her surprise, Chief was with him. She paused just outside the door, which stood ajar. For some reason, she didn't want to go in there, even if it was her own room, and show herself to Chief wearing nothing but a robe and jewelry.

She could see Chief through the crack in the door and, like any good best man, he was knotting Coe's tie for him.

Coe's voice, whining. "What am I doing, Chief? Why did I think I wanted to get married again? Look what a dog's mess it was last time!"

"This is different," Chief said soothingly.

"It's marriage, and I couldn't hack it last time."

"No offense, Coe, but I don't think that was something anybody was going to be able to hack. I never in my whole life met but one woman who couldn't warm me up, and that woman was Addie."

"Rachel's different." There was a question mark in his voice. "Rachel's different?"

"Rachel is very different."

"Here, carry the ring for me. And don't give it away to the first pretty face you see."

"Well, I'll try."

Rachel thumped the door to make a noise as she entered. "If you don't mind, Chief, I need to dress now. We want to be at the restaurant and check things out before the party starts."

Chief left, and Rachel went to the closet and began pulling the plastic off her white jumpsuit.

Coe remained standing in the middle of the floor, stricken. "You heard what I said to Chief, didn't you?"

"Yes, I did. You know, you can still back out of this. It's not too late."

"Not too late? With two parties laid on? Our friends about to charge us like an army of wild Comanches?"

"Well, we can't stop the parties. But we could tell people they are engagement parties. Then, if the wedding never happens, well . . ."

"I didn't mean it, what I said, Rachel! I was just having cold feet. It's because I have such a rotten track record."

"Just jitters? You're sure? You'd better be sure!"

He reached for her, fumbled her into his arms. "Rachel, I love you. Don't leave me. Don't ever leave me."

"I love you, too, Coe, and that's just why I don't want you to be pressured into doing anything you don't want to do."

"Hush, hush." He kissed her silent. "We've got this. Nothing's ever going to spoil it."

Twenty-eight

The restaurant Rachel had picked for her reception was an arty little place full of antiques, including a couple of vintage airplanes. There was a broad patio with a view of the airport and a roof deliberately tattered to provide partial shade.

Deena stood by the railing, watching Rachel. There her old friend was, resplendent in white silk, glittering with new diamonds, beaming with happiness as she greeted her friends. Deena felt glad for her. How wonderful it was to be in love.

To be in love and about to marry.

To be in love and about to marry when you are old enough to appreciate your own happiness. And Rachel had it all.

In Coe's eye there was something of the panic of a man overwhelmed by strangers he was supposed to be cordial to, but he was bearing up about as well as might be expected.

Or maybe Deena wasn't exactly concentrating on Coe. Her eye kept drifting to Chief, who obediently stood next to Coe and got himself introduced to Rachel's friends. He was doing his thing, charming everybody. It was obvious how he did it; he was delighted with every single person he met.

How handsome he looked, smiling, cocking his head to catch some inanity from an old woman. He could wear a suit. Well, Coe could, too, but Chief did it better.

Deena turned away and looked out over the airfield. Something was landing out there. Most likely it was an airplane.

She had been watching for only a short time when a well-remembered voice said, "You're looking particularly beautiful, Deena."

She turned. "Hello, Chief. You're looking well. You didn't bring Tricia with you?"

"She remembered something else she had to do. I don't think she feels really welcome here."

"Things are all right between you two, then? I've been worried that I might have caused you trouble."

He smiled, and her joints went watery, just like old times. He said, "No, no problem. I worried, too, about you. I know I made trouble for you."

Deena stood straight and let her voice rise to a normal level. "Actually, you did me a big, fat favor. You shook me loose from thinking that I couldn't change anything, that I couldn't make things happen to improve my marriage. Until you came along, I didn't even realize it needed changing."

"I'm sorry things came out the way they did."

"I'm sorry to have to tell you this, but I'm not sorry at all."

Ethan said, "Come on, Deena, there're some people who want to meet you." She had not even noticed him coming up behind her.

Chief stuck out his hand. "Hey, Ethan, what do you say we shake and let the bygones be bygones?"

Ethan made no response, and Chief turned his smile up a notch. "I made an ass out of myself, everybody here knows it, but I'm not the first guy who ever did. I should feel bad; the old Greeks fought a whole war over a beautiful woman. Compared to that, I'm pretty mild."

Even Ethan couldn't help returning that smile. He shook and said, "Okay, bygones."

It was wonderful seeing all her friends at once, Rachel thought, although her feet were aching and she was glad they were almost through with the receiving line. Some of these people she had not seen for months. Some of them, she realized a little queasily, she had not seen since before Pete died.

Hey, what the heck, they were her friends, and they were here now. She stood with Coe and Chief and Barbara and Dan; and the friends and relatives filed by her, squealing with proper delight about her marriage, gasping with proper awe at her diamonds.

Chief had wandered around for a while and then returned. Marc had been with them for a space, but he had gone off to help Angel organize a table for the children, who were hungry and beginning to whine. Intelligently, the restaurant had provided a special table for them, and they were served first.

Dan was complaining that everybody knew who he was and he was having trouble placing some of them. Silly boy, didn't he realize that the people who recognized him were also recognizing his strong resemblance to his father?

Coe was doing his best to catch the names and say something gracious to everybody, but Barbara and Chief were goofing off. Somehow they had gotten to swapping lawyer jokes, and they were paying no attention to anybody but only guffawing away together.

Angel drifted up to Rachel, looking ethereal in a floaty gown that somehow was white with blue edges. It set off her exotic looks, her sweet expression. She said, "They want to serve the lunch now. If you two will come and sit down, maybe everybody else will, too. Come, Barbara, Chief. We need you at the head table."

Rachel sat down with Coe on one side of her and Barbara on the other. Chief was next to her and then Angel and Dan. Marc was fussing with the children's plates, and he came up later to take a place next to Coe.

He reported, "Eric won't eat the prime rib because he says he doesn't eat beef."

"He ate it at my house," said Rachel.

"That was different," Dan explained. "At your house it was just dinner. Somebody here must have said the word beef. All the kids are into animal rights these days."

"I don't think mine are," said Marc.

"Well, it wouldn't be very practical on a ranch," Barbara said, giggling. "What's he going to do? Let his horse ride him?"

She and Chief both laughed heartily, and Chief suggested, "Maybe they could take turns."

Angel said, "Both my boys are very sensitive to current issues."

Chief leaned a little her way. "Really into the important stuff, huh?"

"Oh, yes. I feel children should be exposed to ideas even when they are very young, don't you?"

Barbara laughed. "Right! Catch them young enough and it's like vaccination; they'll be immune the rest of their lives."

Chief laughed and Angel said, "She is witty, isn't she?"

He leaned again toward Angel, saying something about ideas. With no outlet but to talk to her mother, Barbara smiled and said, "Are you having a good time, Mother?"

Rachel was glaring at Chief, who sat between two women young enough to be his daughters, playing them off, one against the other. "What's wrong with Angel?" she demanded. "I didn't think she liked Chief. She doesn't even approve of him."

"Of course she doesn't," agreed Barbara. "She just can't stand for anybody else to get the attention."

"Maybe I could ask the management to set up another table. Obviously we've got more children than can be accommodated at one table."

Chief stood up and clanged a silver knife against his water glass. "Has everybody got their champagne? Come on, pass the bottle around, get poured down there. Look lively! We're going to drink a toast to the bride and groom. Well, they're almost a bride and groom. They're going to make it legal a little later on today. I guess they're going to. If he doesn't get away first."

That got him a laugh and the attention of his audience, and he went on cheerfully. "Now in case some of you are wondering how these two met, I'm going to tell you right now. It was right over there on the north runway." He pointed. "At the air show last July. They tell me there were a hundred thousand people at that show, but these two found each other! Well, maybe she found him; because Coe Flaherty, I'll tell you about him, he's pretty slippery. Well, how many guys do you know as old as he is and still not caught? I think he's been netted this time, though. He's been caught by this lovely lady, and he's lucky to get her. He's really lucky. Now everybody raise a glass to Rachel and Coe!"

The guests managed a respectable cheer, sipped, and then turned their attention to the food. Coe and Rachel touched their glasses to their lips but did not drink for they would be flying shortly. They smiled into each other's eyes. Rachel hoped it wasn't illegal to pilot a plane when you were in love. Maybe it should be, it was more intoxicating than champagne.

She ate a little of the lunch. Everybody said it was excellent, but she could not tell. There was so much demanding her attention, she couldn't concentrate enough to taste anything.

All too soon Chief, playing his part as the best man, was pointing meaningfully at his watch. "We've got a time reserved at the wedding chapel in Las Vegas," he reminded them. "We've gotta go."

Helpful friends drove them onto the airfield, and the wedding party climbed into Coe's 340 for the trip. Most of the guests lined up along the edge of the patio of the restaurant to watch them take off and to wave goodbye.

Some of them may have tired and gone away, waiting for Rachel and Coe to get through the checklist, but Rachel never saw any of them anyway. She was far too busy watching the runway when they took off even to give a glance to her friends.

Takeoff made the baby cry, and Barbara took her from her car bed and nursed her. Chief made a point of leaning over the back of the pilot's chair and checking the instruments, like a crew chief, until he judged that Barbara had finished.

They were over the desert, the Tehachapis below them, the ship on automatic pilot. Rachel and Coe both kept scanning, watching for traffic in this busy corridor, but frequently they scanned one another and exchanged a smile. Or a kiss or two.

Rachel said, "Really, Coe, do you often neck with your copilot in flight?"

"Of course I wouldn't do a thing like that!" he roared. "What do you think stewardesses are for?"

Rachel laughed and scanned. "Oh, my male chauvinist hero! You'll never change."

"Don't reckon I will," he reported with

satisfaction. "By the time a guy gets to my age, he's had a lot of the hell beat out of him. Also the arrogance and the need to control people. He's over sulking and pouting to get his own way. Makes him a rotten hero. Who needs a hero like that?"

"Oh, I guess you're hero enough for me," said Rachel and gave him another kiss.

From the rear of the plane came an angry exclamation from Barbara and the sound of a slap.

Chief was never going to change, either.

The wind was favorable. They landed at Las Vegas in plenty of time and took a taxi to the wedding chapel.

The taxi pulled up in front of a low stucco house, decorated with trellises and plastic flowers. Rachel groaned. "I knew I shouldn't have agreed to be married in a place that was picked out by a travel agent."

"Maybe it's nicer inside," Chief suggested helpfully. "There's supposed to be organ music and a lady that sings."

"I want to go home," said Rachel. "I don't think I want to get married today."

"Quiet down, Mother," said Barbara. "This is no time for an attack of nerves."

"When's a good time?" asked Rachel.

"In you go, Mother. Keep those feet moving."

The room they entered was tastefully decorated, if a little too strong on the white lattice. There were real flowers in a big vase and a wizened little old woman playing on a small, spinet-type organ. She played soft chords as they signed the magistrate's book.

The flowers Coe had ordered by phone were ready, a bouquet each for Barbara and Rachel, boutonnieres for the guys. Nancy was cooperatively asleep, and Barbara put her portable car bed down on a bench.

The magistrate stationed Barbara and Rachel at one end of the room, Coe and Chief at the other, standing between the organ and the flower vase. He opened the book and nodded to the organist and she hit the first stirring chords of the wedding march.

Rachel and Barbara moved obediently to stand with Coe and Chief. It wasn't until she was standing near it that Rachel noticed the lid on the organ was loose. Any note in the lower register, and the musician was fond of low chords, made the lid vibrate noticeably. Rachel watched it with apprehension, fearing it might shake itself off, but it was apparently fastened somewhere.

A sidewise glance at Coe told her that he had seen it, too; and they gave each other warning looks, as if to say, "Don't smile!"

The singer stepped through a curtain, took a stance, and began to sing. "Oh, Promise Me . . ."

She was no exception to the rule that sopranos must be fat, and she sang flat most of the time. She had been trained to "drop" her jaw . . . wide open, let the sound out! So she sang loud and flat and dropped her jaw with every long note.

She was only a few bars into the song when Rachel noticed that she was in sync with the organ lid. Every time she dropped her jaw, the organ lid opened and did its little dance in rhythm.

"Oh pro-o-o-mise meee . . ."

Rachel raised her bouquet to her mouth to suppress her giggles. She sneaked a glance at Coe, and his scowl was growing heavier with every note. His eyebrows covered his eyes and his mouth turned down, but the corners of it were twitching. It made her almost convulse with suppressed laughter and she stopped looking at him.

The poor woman, what a way to make

her living! Probably every day she sang for unappreciative, impatient, itchy audiences at cut-rate weddings. Probably she knew she was flat, but even flat sopranos have to eat.

No, she was not going to laugh.

The song ended at last. The magistrate stretched the ceremony with a carefully ecumenical speech and then began the vows. Rachel looked into Coe's eyes and promised to love him.

She didn't need to promise; she was going to anyway.

Chief handed over her ring and it was slipped onto her finger. Barbara produced Coe's ring and Rachel put it on him. They kissed and it was over.

The organ crashed and vibrated; they marched outside into the blazing desert sun, and the soprano followed to toss a dutiful handful of birdseed at them. Just one, and then she went back inside, where it was air-conditioned.

The four of them stood there and laughed until they had to hold their sides. Barbara and Chief were hugging each other with hilarity; Rachel and Coe needed only to look at one another to guffaw again.

Then Chief hoisted the baby in her car bed and carried her back to the plane, and they all got aboard. Time for the flight to Phoenix.

Nancy was asleep, Barbara fussing with the bouquets in the back of the ship.

Chief stretched himself out across two of the seats. He decreed, "You two are married now, so you can do your own darn checklist. You may take off at your discretion, pilots! Let's go! We're flying high!"

Twenty-nine

They had a wedding cake at the hotel in Houston, decorated with white-icing birds in pairs. It looked as big as a high-rise to Rachel, and like a high-rise, it seemed to attract pigeons.

Big as it was, Coe had enough friends to eat it. His CAF buddies turned out in force and clustered together, swapping tall tales. There were people from his factory, all of the docs, of course, and some people from charitable committees he had never mentioned serving on. Rincon turned up and so did all the nieces and nephews. The nieces and nephews were young and handsome, and every one of them wore black. Everybody knew that black was the fashionable color of the year, but it did seem they were expressing a certain amount of grief.

Rachel was still shaking hands and accepting congratulations when a man with a concierge button in his lapel pushed his way through the line and murmured, "Mrs. Flaherty, I have an emergency telephone call for you."

Rachel said, "What?" Mrs. Flaherty, that was her, now. Emergency? Her children were all traveling. Almost everyone, maybe everyone, was on the road or in a plane somewhere. She dropped the hand she had been shaking and, without another word, rushed off after the concierge.

He led her to a bank of phones, picked one up, and asked for the connection. Then he politely handed her the receiver.

A tinny, faraway voice said, "Rachel? It's Muriel."

Muriel? Who the hell was Muriel? Oh, yes, the realtor. "Muriel? Muriel, why are you calling me in the middle of my wedding reception?"

"I had to," explained Muriel. "You've got termites."

Rachel's voice was rising so dangerously that the concierge stepped back and quietly disappeared. "Termites? You're calling me to tell me I have termites in my house? Every house in Southern California has termites!"

"But we have to have it tented right away!

Escrow closes in a week, and your son won't let the termite inspector inside the house!"

What had gotten into Dan? No matter. Rachel said icily, "I'll deal with my son. You will please leave him alone, and I will discuss this on Monday. On Monday during business hours!" She hung up before Muriel could say another word, and then she returned to the party.

She met Coe in the hallway, looking for her. "What's going on?" he demanded.

Still angry, Rachel tried to keep her voice down. "That wretched Muriel! Imagine her calling me here! I chose her over the other brokers because she had gray hair; maybe that isn't always the best criteria."

"It worked for me," he said, smiling at her. "What did she want?"

"Some nonsense about tenting for the termites. I'm not even going to think about it until Monday."

"Maybe you ought to. You don't want to queer the deal on your house . . ."

She took his arm. "If I do, I don't care. This is more important. It's our wedding party!"

He was still smiling as they returned to the ballroom.

They spent the night at Coe's apartment,

not a very exciting choice, but a necessary one. Rachel had not once thought to pack a bag for the trip, so she had to go to Coe's place for some clothes.

When the phone rang at what she considered a ridiculously early hour the next morning, Rachel tried to ignore it; but it kept ringing until she picked it up.

Her son's voice said, "Mother! G'day!"

"Kenny! How nice of you to call! I tried to call you, but you were out in the field. Are you at home now?"

His laugh was easy and slightly condescending. "That's what I'm trying to tell you, Mother. I'm at your house."

Stunned, Rachel repeated, "You're at my house? In Encino?"

"I tried to get here for the wedding, but my plane was delayed."

"Oh, Kenny, that's awful! Is your family with you?"

"No, it's too far to bring them for such a short visit. They'll come another time."

"How long can you stay?"

"I go back in a couple of days."

"A couple of days! This is getting worse and worse! Is Dan there?"

"No. Is he supposed to be?"

"It depends. Look in the garage. If my

car isn't in there, he hasn't come back from Disneyland yet."

"Dan went to Disneyland?" Kenny repeated, unbelieving. "Dan and *Angelique* went to Disneyland? I have been in the garage and there's no car. Great! I was hoping to see Dan. And you and Barbara and everybody, of course. Fair cow about me missing that airplane."

"Well, stay right where you are. I have to come back and move the furniture out of the house anyway, so I'll get a plane right away. Did somebody come by about the termites?"

"Yes, I'm afraid I booted him out. I didn't know you were in such a hurry to do all that, and I thought a bloke wanting to look through the house for termites on a Saturday evening would be a grifter. Somebody named Muriel has been screaming at me ever since. She's just a bit of a bot, wot?"

"I'm not exactly sure what you said, but I'll deal with Muriel. We'll be there the next plane I can get. Do you have a car? Want to pick us up?"

"Sure."

"Okay, I'll call you when I get a flight number."

Coe had tired of waiting for her call to be finished and had gone into the kitchen to make coffee. He said, "What was that all about?"

"It was my son Kenny. He came all the way from Australia to be at our wedding, and missed it! He's in Encino now, and I have to be there this week to take care of the things about the house, so I want to leave right away. That's okay with you, isn't it?"

Coe said, "Well, no. I've got a couple of appointments tomorrow. Doc Sam's found two guys for us to interview. They're brand new doctors who say they wouldn't mind putting in a couple of years in remote places if it will help them pay off their student loans."

"You're going to find a permanent doctor for the town down there? That's wonderful, but why do you have to interview him tomorrow? What happened to our honeymoon?"

His frown was firmly in place. "I don't know. I wasn't figuring on spending it killing termites at your place in Encino either. What did you have in mind?"

"Oh, dear, I don't know what I had in mind. I thought if we could just get this wedding out of the way, things would be peaceful; but it's worse than before!"

"I think the coffee's ready. Want a cup?"

"Please. I'll fix some breakfast in a minute."

He poured the coffee. "Let's talk about this first. Sit down with me. I know I pushed the wedding too fast. I wanted to get it over with, too. I was afraid if I stalled around and gave you a chance to think about it, you might change your mind."

She smiled at him. "No, I'm not going to change my mind about you."

"The trouble is, we haven't got anything arranged. If it'd been a normal vacation, we would have been planning it for months and have tickets, all that stuff. Now we want to go someplace and we can't; we've both got things to take care of."

"I guess we can't just buy a plane ticket for Tahiti and let everything go, but I wish we could."

"It does sound good, but we're adults. We take care of the obligations first. That house of yours has to be taken care of. I'm the one told you to take that stupid fifteen-day escrow, so about all I can do now is back you up."

"Thank you, Coe. Kenny has to go back

to Australia in a couple of days. I want so much to see him! But you can't leave today."

"Sure I can. I'll tell Doc Sam either to reschedule those interviews or do them himself. He probably knows more about medicine than I do, anyhow."

She laughed. "I wouldn't be surprised if he does."

"As soon as your escrow closes, I'll come back here and check up on what Sam's been doing. If I approve of the guy he's picked, I'll probably take him to Mexico for orientation to see if he thinks he's going to be able to hack it there."

"Then you're coming back here to Houston Wednesday? The escrow won't be closed."

He cracked a small, rueful smile. "You were right. Long-distance romances are for the birds. They're cheaper for birds, too. Tell you how let's do this. I'll get Sam to reschedule those interviews for Wednesday. Then, if the guy's willing, I can take him to Mexico with me the next day. I might take both of them, call it part of the interview. Then I can go with you today."

"Oh, thank you, Coe! Thank you again!

I'll get breakfast started; you get on the phone and get us a plane for L.A."

Ken met them at the airport. He had never been a fancy dresser, and his version of a proper outfit for meeting a plane was baggy trousers and a sleeveless T-shirt with a kangaroo painted on the front. His hair was so long he had pulled it back with a rubber band. His muscular arms were red with sunburn, and he had apparently mastered the currently-fashionable trick of always needing a shave. Rachel was glad to see him anyway.

Coe wore his suit. Rachel was still dressing to her pearl and diamond necklace, and she had on a silk dress with a blazer over it. She hugged and kissed her son, hoping that if she were effusive enough, people would not think he was there to carry their luggage.

"Oh, Kenny, it was too terrific of you to come! I wish you had let us know; we might have been able to wait for you."

"My fault," he admitted. "I wanted to surprise you, but I was the one got surprised."

She introduced him to Coe, who said, "I'm glad you're here. Your mother's been missing you."

"Congratulations and all that. You got any luggage?"

"Just this," said Coe, waving his flight bag. Rachel carried only a purse.

"We can nick off, then," said Kenny, and they trudged down the long tile tunnels to the outside.

As soon as Rachel got to the house, she started cooking. Coe asked her, "What are you doing that for? We could go out someplace."

"Tomorrow we will, because tomorrow I am boxing up every scrap of food and taking it to a charity. But tonight we will have one last family dinner in this house. I want to see my family, and you, at the table one more time; and besides, we've got to use up as much of this food as we can."

"Don't get carried away making a lot of stuff. There's only the three of us."

"Oh, Dan and his family will be here, too."

"What makes you so sure?"

Rachel looked at her watch. "About three this afternoon, Angel had been at Disneyland for twenty-four hours. What do you want to bet they're on their way back right now?"

Coe looked only half-convinced, but Dan

and Angel arrived in plenty of time for dinner. The boys were still hyper with excitement, and the whole family had obviously ridden all the water rides in the park. Even Angel's clothes were crumpled and grubby.

She took her children upstairs to be washed, and Dan came into the kitchen to chat with Rachel while he waited for his turn at the shower. He asked, "Where's Coe?"

"For that matter, where's your brother?" Rachel had been so busy she had not noticed that the two men were not around.

"Kenny's here? Why didn't you tell me? Where is he?"

Rachel flapped her arms. "Well, I'm sorry, but I don't know. They were here a few minutes ago. Maybe they went to the market. They've been kicking back together ever since we got here, and they've probably gone through all the beer in the house."

She was almost ready to serve the meal when Coe and Kenny returned. They brought beer, but it was all inside them and they were silly and laughing at everything. They explained they had been to the local sports bar, where there was a new, state-of-the-art big-screen TV that Kenny wanted to see. They had enthusiastic greetings for

Dan and his family; Kenny, in fact, was boisterous. He intimidated the little boys; and Angel turned away, gently, from the smell of beer on her brother-in-law's breath.

Rachel began serving the meal at once to get something into everybody's stomach.

Kenny said, "Well, Jason, how was Disneyland?"

"It was swell," said Jason.

"I rode Space Mountain!" bragged Eric.

"That really is an achievement," his father affirmed. "If you can stand in that line, you can do anything."

Angel said, "Really, it seems like all that time and money could be better spent on something not quite so trivial. Something creative and cultural."

"I guess that's how you spend all your time in New York?" asked Kenny.

Coe didn't give her a chance to answer. "We don't do that much in Houston," he drawled. "It takes all our time just trying to walk on cement in our cowboy boots."

"Well now, in Australia, we're real cultural," Kenny assured him. "Around my place we got the best dingo choruses in all the southern territories. When the moon's full and they start up, we got these bleachers so folks can sit around and listen to the music. They're way over the hill, of course, but you can hear them."

"Dingoes, huh?" Coe wiped at his mouth and looked serious. "We got coyotes. That's almost as good; but for real music, did you ever hear wild asses?"

"Never heard any, but I'm acquainted with some," Kenny allowed. "We got some really important graphic artists, too. This one painter, he puts his canvas down in the road and drives the sheep over it—calls it ovine art."

"That's nothing. We got a guy does the same thing, only with brahma bulls. Puts the canvas down right there when the rodeo's on, and then he tries to take it away from the bull. That's the interesting part."

"You two will please eat your dinner," Rachel instructed, "and stop setting a bad example for the little pitchers around here."

First thing Monday, she called the realty office and complained about Muriel. The manager didn't seem to think there was a problem.

"Muriel was only looking after your interests," he insisted. "I'm sure she'll apologize, if that's what you want."

"It wouldn't help," said Rachel. "I gave

her a direct order not to bother my son anymore, and she phoned him several times after that. I will not be pestered by people I am paying to serve me. I'm so angry with her, I never want to talk with her again. However, I don't want to lose the deal she is making for me either. It suits my purposes almost as well as it does the buyer's. Can you suggest a solution?"

"Not unless I handle the rest of the business myself. I guess I could do that. Would that be okay with you?"

"That would be fine. What happens to her commission?"

"Well, of course, we'll have to work something out . . ."

"When you say we, you mean that you and she will work something out. I'm not interested in the arrangements you make, but I want it well understood that I won't pay any additional commission."

He mumbled assent.

"All right. I want you to let me know the results of the buyer's inspection. I will be engaging a service for the termite work myself, so please tell your man not to trouble himself further. And please see to it that Muriel does not contact me again, about anything."

Rachel phoned a termite service and arranged for the preliminary inspection. Then she phoned around until she found some secondhand dealers who would buy a whole household at once. While she waited for them to come and make an offer, she worked on emptying drawers and cupboards, packing up the contents.

When it came to it, Rachel could not part with her pots and pans. She could give the china, the silver, the linens and crystal to the children, but her tools for cooking she was going to need. She was starting a new life, but not without her sauté pans, her saucepans, her favorite stockpot. There would always be cooking to be done.

There was so much to do, she sent Dan and his family to the airport in a taxi. The little boys each carried a couple of books their father had enjoyed as a boy so they would have something to read on the plane.

In spite of all his protests, Kenny had found a great pile of things he wanted to keep. Most of it he cozened his mother into storing for him, but he made up several large packages to carry on the plane. He referred to them as "swag" which seemed to describe the bundles perfectly.

"This is terrible," Rachel complained.

"You've come so far and we've seen so little of each other, and now you have to go back."

He smiled through his stubble. "I'm glad I did it anyway. I was worried before I came, afraid you were shook on some take-down. Now that I know Coe and he's fair dinkum and well in besides, it's too right. He's financial; why don't you get him to take you to Australia and visit me?"

"It would be very nice, Kenny, but I was planning to spend my honeymoon some place where they speak English."

Kenny laughed. "Oh, you're full up of my yabber, are you? That's jake; it sounds like my taxi's out there honking anyway."

Rachel called, "Coe! Kenny's leaving!" and he came running to make his good-byes.

They were still loading Kenny and his swag into the cab when the first of the furniture dealers arrived, and she was so busy after that, she forgot to cry.

She felt like it, though.

She struck a deal with one of the dealers, and he began at once to take furniture out of the house. The shippers came and carried off the cartons that had been packed for Houston, for New York, for Arizona.

The charities came and took away the donated items.

The furniture man had promised to leave the beds for the very last thing, but Rachel moved to a hotel anyway. The sight of her destroyed household was beginning to depress her. What could be worse than camping out in your own home? In the place that had always been your own, always comfortable and homey, and now was stripped? Even to brush your teeth, you had to go get the brush and the paste out of a suitcase. No, it was time to leave.

They spent the night in a comfortable hotel room and the next day finished all the details at the old house. As the last of the furniture was carried out the door, the termite men were already unloading their equipment out in front.

It would be tented for twenty-four hours, then aired for twelve. Nobody could enter until then, and her job was done. Rachel and Coe got into her car and left.

"What a letdown!" she complained as they pulled away from the house. All that work and now I have nothing, absolutely nothing more to do for two days!"

"Well, you've got me to cope with," Coe reminded her.

"Oh, I wish I were going with you tomorrow! I wish this were all over and we didn't have to be apart!"

"It's only two days. I'll be back Saturday. As soon as the escrow is closed for sure, we'll get in the car and head for Houston."

"It will be fun making the drive together."

He begged, "Just don't put anything else into this car; you've got it so stuffed, the axle's dragging."

"It is not! It's only my clothes. And stuff."

"It's a good thing I'm building a house. We're going to need it for your clothes."

"All I need is a closet somewhere. Let's worry about it when we get to Houston," said Rachel.

"Okay." He grinned at her in the seat beside him. "Right now we've got a whole evening together, and I've got big plans."

"Yeah? Tell me about them."

"We're going to go someplace fancy. The Music Center or something. You're going to get dressed up and forget about business, and we're going to remember it's our honeymoon."

"I love your plan, but we don't have tickets for the Music Center and sometimes it's a drag standing in their lines before a show. Have you noticed that the hotel we're staying in has two restaurants and a nightclub? We can have dinner in a restaurant, then go upstairs and see a show; and when we get mellow, we're already in the same building as our bed."

"Uh-huh. You may be a little gray, but you've got a good head on your shoulders," said her husband.